The Amen Trail

*Also by Sharon Sala
in Large Print:*

Annie and the Outlaw
Snowfall
A Place to Call Home
Butterfly
Dark Water
Deep in the Heart
Mission: Irresistible
Out of the Dark
When You Call My Name
Whippoorwill

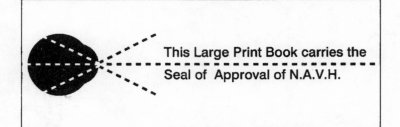

The Amen Trail

Sharon Sala

Thorndike Press • Waterville, Maine

Published in 2006 by arrangement with Loveland Press, LLC.

Thorndike Press® Large Print Romance.

The tree indicium is a trademark of Thorndike Press.

The text of this Large Print edition is unabridged.
Other aspects of the book may vary from the original edition.

Set in 16 pt. Plantin.

Printed in the United States on permanent paper.

Library of Congress Cataloging-in-Publication Data

Sala, Sharon.
    The Amen trail / by Sharon Sala.
        p. cm. — (Thorndike Press large print romance)
    Sequel to: Whippoorwill.
    ISBN 0-7862-8675-X (lg. print : hc : alk. paper)
    1. Prostitutes — Fiction.   2. Kansas — Fiction.
3. Colorado — Fiction.   4. Clergy — Fiction.   5. Large
type books.   I. Title.   II. Thorndike Press large print
romance series.
PS3569.A4565A78 2006
    813'.54—dc22   2006006538

Dedication
The Amen Trail

I'm dedicating this book to my Auntie, Lorraine Stone, who, like the heroine in my book, didn't accept the word, no.

As I write this dedication, she has just finished chemotherapy for her third bout with cancer. At the age of 79, and with nothing but faith and persistence to guide her, she refused to quit on herself.

The cancer that was supposed to be fatal, is at this point, undetectable, and we celebrate her strength and her news while accepting the fact that none of us is promised a tomorrow.

I feel blessed knowing that we share the same blood, and I face each day of my future hoping that I will live with as much honor and fortitude as she's exhibited to us, her family.

To Alice Lorraine Shero Stone.

Good friend.
Christian woman.
Loving daughter.
Faithful sister.
Devoted wife.
Beloved mother.
Honored grandmother.
Blessed great-grandmother.

You are, and always will be, an example to us all.

National Association for Visually Handicapped
------------------------------ *serving the partially seeing*

As the Founder/CEO of NAVH, the only national health agency solely devoted to those who, although not totally blind, have an eye disease which could lead to serious visual impairment, I am pleased to recognize Thorndike Press* as one of the leading publishers in the large print field.

Founded in 1954 in San Francisco to prepare large print textbooks for partially seeing children, NAVH became the pioneer and standard setting agency in the preparation of large type.

Today, those publishers who meet our standards carry the prestigious "Seal of Approval" indicating high quality large print. We are delighted that Thorndike Press is one of the publishers whose titles meet these standards. We are also pleased to recognize the significant contribution Thorndike Press is making in this important and growing field.

Lorraine H. Marchi, L.H.D.
Founder/CEO
NAVH

* Thorndike Press encompasses the following imprints: Thorndike, Wheeler, Walker and Large Print Press.

AUTHOR'S NOTES

In research taken from MILE HIGH CITY, by Thomas J. Noel, we know that during the 1840s and 1850s, the Arapaho had been camping along Cherry Creek near its junction with the South Platte. A chief named Little Raven really did exist, and did what he could to maintain a cordial relationship with the white man, whom the Arapaho called "spider people", which was a reference to the white man's web of roads, survey lines, and fences. Too late, they realized the significance of this practice.

From time to time, it was the practice of the Arapaho to share their women with others and was not considered immoral.

Mexicans had gold diggings before in the area around Cherry Creek, but it was dismissed as inconsequential by the big strike of 1858 and the huge influx of whites to the area.

To my knowledge, there was no smallpox epidemic during this time, although history has shown us time and time again, how devastating it was to the Indians when it did occur.

In creating my story, I took license with

some of the historical time lines, as well as historical facts, i.e., the smallpox epidemic.

This story is purely fictional.

In no way is it intended as a book of historical fact.

Enjoy the story of Letty and Eulis's triumph, but without judgment, as it was meant to be read.

Hark! Thy Name Is Brother

For Eulis Potter, stepping into the shoes of a dead preacher had not been his idea. He'd been persuaded to play the role partly because of his weakness for liquor and partly because of Letty Murphy, the whore at the White Dove Saloon, who'd promised him free pokes for life if he'd help her hide the dead preacher's body. Poor Letty had been in the act of servicing the real Reverend Randall Ward Howe when he had literally, up and died on her. At the time, creating the deception had seemed imperative, but going through with it had almost been the end of them both.

Who could have known that Eulis, the town drunk/local gravedigger, would actually relish the role into which he'd been thrust? Even more unbelievable was the fact that during the ensuing events of that day, Letty had gotten religion and given up the role of Lizard Flats' only whore. Those free pokes that she'd promised him were definitely now out of the question, but Eulis didn't really mind. They were both caught up in their new lives and the new names under which they were living. The difficulties now lie in forgetting who they'd been and concentrating on who they'd become.

It had been months since Letty and Eulis had left Dodge City. Months of preaching in places so small they didn't even have a name, traveling by stagecoach when possible and sleeping in way stations, eating the same menu of beef and beans at every stop, and pretending they did not hear or smell the constant waft of bodily gasses that were expelled from the bloated travelers every time the stagecoach hit a pothole, or swayed from the dusty trail.

Letty, who now went by the moniker of Sister Leticia, continued to hold a handkerchief to her nose and glare at the offending travelers on the seat opposite where she and Eulis were sitting. One was a traveling salesman named Morris Field, who carried a reticule full of fine laces, the other a gambler by the name of Boston Jones, who kept flipping through a deck of cards with monotonous regularity. Letty had seen right off that the cards were marked, but since she wasn't going to be risking their money at a game with him, she chose to ignore the fact.

Tired of looking at their grumpy faces, Letty pushed aside the thin panel of green homespun that was passing for a window curtain for a peek outside at the passing scenery. All she got for her efforts was a face full of dust and a sneezing fit.

"You all right?" Eulis asked.

Letty dropped the curtain back in place and hopelessly brushed at the dust that was settling on the front of her bosom.

"Yes, Brother Howe, but thank you for asking."

About that time, the coach lurched again. Everyone went up, then everyone came down — rumps first. It had to be said that the jolt caused another round of farts to erupt that threatened their existence. Letty glared at all three men and then clasped her handkerchief to her face as if her nose was about to fall off. Eulis had the grace to blush while Boston Jones, the gambler, added a burp to the mix.

Personally, Eulis couldn't understand how Letty could be so pissed off about a fart and a burp when less than a year ago, she would have taken any one of them to bed for the price of a dollar. Just in time,

Eulis resisted the urge to snort. Her high-falutin ways were still new enough to him to render some amusement, but he didn't have the guts to laugh.

The coach swayed again, this time sending a fresh cloud of dust boiling in beneath the window curtains, which only added to the heat and misery of the ride. Eulis licked his lips and thought how tasty a shot of whiskey would be about now, but not to get drunk — just a sip to settle his nerves. Then he caught Letty staring at him and reached for his Bible. Sometimes she was just plain scary. If he hadn't known better, he would have sworn she'd just read his mind. Then he thought again, if she was such a damned good mind reader, she would know that he'd just been thinking about a drink. He wouldn't really take one — not even if it was offered to him free. After all, he had a reputation to uphold and preaching and drinking didn't mix. He'd already decided he liked the high he got from preaching more than he did the hangover on the morning after, so Letty could just wipe that frown off her face right now before it stuck there.

He nodded at the two men facing them, manly ignoring the state of the air, and opened his Bible, although with the dip and sway of the coach, he couldn't focus good enough on the words to make many of them out. And so they continued to roll west, hoping to outrun nightfall to the next way station.

Forney Calder had been working for Gibson Stage Lines for almost two years. Most of the time he was satisfied with his lot in life. Only now and then did he start wondering what it would be like if a few things were different. For one, he needed a new pair of shoes, but he hadn't been paid in two months and didn't figure he'd be buying anything anytime soon. And, he could hardly saddle up and ride to Fort Mays, even if he had the price of a new pair of shoes, because it was a two day ride and there would be no one left here to tend to the horses or meet the arriving stagecoaches. So, until something changed, he was stuck at the way station.

He stabbed the pitchfork into the hay and tossed a forkful over the fence into the corral. The horses crowded toward the feed, pushing and nipping at each other in an effort to be the first to the evening feeding.

"Hey, there! Get back you miserable hay burners. There's plenty for ever'one," Forney yelled.

He tossed a little more hay over the corral fence then went to draw water to fill the water trough. The only thing Forney really minded was lack of female companionship. In fact, he'd been suffering the lack for some months now and had toyed with the idea of giving notice. But if he did that, he would most likely forfeit his back pay. Come October, he would be forty-five years old — or forty-six. He never could remember for sure because his mother hadn't been sure of the year he was born. Either way, he'd come to like the comfort of a roof and a bed too much to go back to a bedroll on the hard ground.

Once his chores were done, he went inside the station to give the stew a quick stir. It had been cooking all afternoon because there was a stage due before night. At least he'd have some human conversation to look forward to.

A few hours later, the stew was in the warming oven and Forney was humped over the table near the lamplight, trying to cut a piece of old saddle leather to fit inside his right shoe. When he heard the familiar creak and groan of the approaching stagecoach and the thunder of horses' hooves, he tossed the leather aside and got up.

It was about time they got here, he

thought, and moved the stew from the warming oven to the front of the cook stove, lit a lantern and headed for the door.

As always, dust boiled up into the air as the weary horses came to a stop.

Shorty, the stagecoach driver, tossed the reins to Forney as Big Will, the man riding shotgun, began climbing down. Once on the ground, Big Will dropped a stepstool in front of the door and opened it wide.

Letty leaned out and whispered something near his ear. Big Will nodded politely, then turned around and yelled at Forney.

"Hey, Forney, you better have some grub and a lot of it. I'm hungry as a bear and not particular of what I eat . . . and Sister Leticia needs the facilities."

"Yeah, yeah, Big Will, I've heard it all before. Stew's inside and you know damn good and well the facilities are behind the station."

"We need a lantern," Big Will said.

Forney handed him the one he was holding and started to unhitch the team when a flash of color caught his eye. He stopped, then his mouth went slack as he saw a small foot, a hint of slender ankle, then the blue fabric of the female passenger's dress. A few moments later he got a good look at the woman Big Will referred to as Sister Leticia. A drop of spittle slid out the corner of his mouth as he watched her brushing dust from her skirt.

Lord have mercy. Sister Leticia was a looker.

He dropped the reins and yanked the lantern out of Big Will's hands.

"Ma'am . . . you might best take my arm so's you don't stumble. I'll be happy to show you the way."

Letty hesitated, then glanced toward Eulis, who was completely oblivious to the improprieties of her being escorted to an outhouse by a total stranger.

"Um . . . I don't think . . . uh, Brother Howe will. . . ."

At that point, Eulis looked up, noticed that a rather grimy, bearded man had hold of Letty's arm with no signs of letting go.

"I say here . . . what's going on?"

Forney frowned. He hadn't noticed the dandy in the bowler hat.

"Ain't nothin' goin' on, mister, 'cept that I'm gonna take this lady here to the out-house."

"It's Reverend . . . not Mister," Letty said, and then frowned. She wasn't sure, but proper ladies wouldn't be having any of this. Just to be on the safe side, she decided to get pissed and removed herself from Forney's grasp.

"The lantern please," she said, took it from Forney before he could argue, then glared at Eulis, as if it was his fault she'd been put in this position. "Brother Howe . . . if you would see to my bag, I'll be inside shortly."

Eulis scrambled to get her bag as Forney reluctantly retrieved the reins to the horses, unhooked them from the coach and led them to the corral. His only consolation was that the dandy with the bowler hat was a preacher and Leticia had called him brother, which meant they were kin. The arrival of a pretty female led Forney to meander through all kinds of fantasies as he fed and watered the weary team of horses. And while Forney was tending to his business, Letty was tending to some business of her own.

The lantern shed a pitiful beam of light through the dark as Letty rounded the side of the way station. She held it above her head in hopes of lighting a broader area and followed her nose to the outhouse. The door was hanging on one hinge, and she thought she caught a flash of something furry scurrying out the door as she went in, but she couldn't be bothered. She needed to pee and there wasn't any kind of creeping denizen that could be worse than some of the men she'd bedded. What did slow her down was the realization that if she took the lantern into the outhouse, her every action would be backlit for the world to see. Reluctantly, she set the lantern down a few feet from the door, gritted her teeth, and stepped inside into the darkness.

Between the stench, the heat, and the pressure on her bladder, she was about to pass out. Reminding herself that the smell emanating from the dark hole was only a degree or so worse than the inside of that stagecoach had been, and that she'd only been a proper lady less than a year, this was no time to become delicate. So she hitched her skirts up around her waist, pulled down her drawers, and aimed toward what she hoped was the hole in the seat.

About the time that the water started to flow, she heard a snort, then a snuffle, then horror of horrors, the little shed started to sway. She squeezed her eyes shut and tried to stop what she'd started, but there are certain things that, once started, are almost impossible to stop — one being the emptying of a very full bladder.

In the middle of her panic, the snorting stopped and the outhouse settled. She shifted her position just enough to peer out, but all she could see was darkness. Relaxing, she continued her business with an easier mind until the hole over which she was bending suddenly shifted out from under her. She heard pee hit the floor at the same time the walls started to lean.

Instinctively, she dropped her skirt and slapped her hands against the opposite wall, putting all her weight against the rough, hand-hewn wood in an effort to settle it back and tried to ignore the fact that she'd peed in her shoe. As she did, the tilt of the outhouse stopped, rocked a bit, then started to sway back onto an uneven foundation.

"Lord have mercy," Letty muttered, and was reaching for the door when something hit the back wall with a thud. Even as she was falling, she started to scream. She'd heard of being shit-faced, but never thought she'd be experiencing it.

Eulis was dipping into the stew when he heard the first scream, and when he did his blood ran cold. He'd heard women scream

19

before, but the only woman around here was Letty, and he didn't want to think about what it would take to make that happen. He also knew there were all levels of female screams. There was the high-pitched squeal that signaled anything from the sighting of a mouse to something that creeped or crawled. And there was the scream of joy upon being presented with an unexpected gift. But neither of these fit what he was hearing. It was a gut-wrenching, spine-chilling scream of mortal fear, coupled with a rage he didn't want to consider. He dropped the ladle back into the stew and bolted for the door, horrified to even consider what might have elicited such a frenzy from the reformed whore.

Eulis bolted out the door as Forney and Big Will were running from the corral. Boston Jones and Morris Field came out of the dark where they'd been relieving themselves, as well.

"What in hell?" Big Will yelled.

"What's happenin'? Where's your sister?" Forney asked.

"Sister? I don't have a sister," Eulis said, and pushed past him as he ran.

While Forney was trying to assess the confusion of facts, Shorty appeared out of the dark with a rifle in his hand.

"What's happenin'?" he shouted. "Is it Injuns?"

"It's the woman," Big Will said.

Eulis ran behind the station, following the glow of the lantern light and the sound of Letty's screams.

The others followed, but it was Eulis who grabbed the lantern from the weeds and held it high, expecting to see Letty in the throes of death. Instead, all he saw was a pile of lumber and Letty nowhere in sight.

"Letty! Letty! Where are you?"

She screamed again and he jumped and looked down, certain she was lying at his feet, only there was no one there.

"Oh hell," Forney muttered, and shoved his way past the others and began fumbling about in the wood.

"Leave the goddamned woodpile alone and help me find Letty!" Eulis shouted.

"That ain't a woodpile. It's the privy, and I reckon your sister's in there," he said.

"Holy Moses," Eulis muttered, and started pulling frantically at the shamble of boards. "Letty! Letty! Can you hear me? Are you all right?"

Letty moaned. She could hear him just fine. She just wasn't sure she was ready to face the humiliation.

"Yes, I can hear you, and no, I'm not all right! Get me out of here!"

"I'm tryin'," Eulis said. "Grab some boards . . . all of you!" Then he pointed at Forney. "If you value your hide, you'd better start heatin' up some water. Sister Leticia is right fond of baths, and I'm thinkin' she's gonna be in need of one real soon."

Forney looked wild-eyed toward the shifting pile of boards and the stifled sound of something that sounded suspiciously like curses, then made a run for the well, leaving Shorty, and the rest to fish the woman out. His hopes of making any headway with her had been dashed, and all he could hope for now was a glimpse of bare flesh when she peeled down to wash off the shit.

"I've got a foot!" Boston yelled, and tugged at Letty's foot.

"I see an arm!" Morris shouted, and thrust his hand between some boards and started to pull.

"Damn it to hell! I am not a wishbone! Quit pulling at me and get me out of this woodpile!"

Eulis pulled away a large portion of one wall while Big Will hefted away what was left of the roof.

"Here you go, little lady," Big Will said, then reached down, grabbed Letty beneath her arms and pulled her out.

She staggered backward, then yanked at the hem of her dress and swiped it across her face.

"Nasty . . . filthy . . . stupid . . . ramshackle . . . pitiful excuse for a . . . idiot who built . . . head up his ass."

Big Will whistled between his teeth and then grinned. Boston took a second step back out of the range of her anger while Morris took a handkerchief from his pocket and offered it to Letty.

"Um . . . ma'am. . . ."

She slapped it out of his hands and then pointed at Eulis.

"Water . . . hot . . . out of my sight . . . never again."

Eulis wasn't sure what she was leaving out, but what she'd managed to utter was enough to jar him out of his shock. He pointed toward the station.

"Take a breath, Sister Leticia. It'll be all right. Forney is fixin' you a bath as we speak. All you need is —"

"Don't talk to me!" she muttered, then turned and pointed a finger at every man staring. "Don't any of you dare talk to me."

"Yes, ma'am," they uttered in unison.

She stomped toward the way station, dragging her wet skirt tail in the dust and tearing at her clothes with each step. By the time she hit the porch she was half-naked and in full stride.

Forney heard the door hit the wall as it flew open. He got a momentary glimpse of her bare neck and arms before she screamed.

"Get out!"

Shocked, he dropped the water bucket onto the floor, soaking his pant legs and his shoes. He felt water soaking into his socks through the hole in his shoe just before he bolted for the door.

Letty slammed the door shut behind him then tore off the rest of her clothes and stepped naked into the hip bath Forney had been filling. The water was tepid and there was no soap in sight, but it didn't slow her down from going headfirst into the water. She came out spitting, then sat down in the bath and started to cry.

An hour later, the men were lined up on the porch, staring blindly out into the dark and pretending they didn't know that there was a naked woman in the house behind them.

Boston's belly growled. He sighed deeply, absently shuffled the cards he was holding, then spit for lack of anything else to do.

"I shore am gettin' hungry," he said.

Morris, Shorty, and Big Will were talking quietly among themselves.

"Food's in the house," Forney said, woefully eying Eulis for inspiration as to how to get it outside.

Eulis shrugged. He'd been hungry before and was perfectly willing to sleep hungry tonight rather than mess with Letty. He knew her well enough to know that the worst was yet to come. He'd seen her in action. She screwed a man to death and hid his body beneath a rotting trapper without turning a hair, then resurrected Eulis from town drunk to reputable preacher in less than twenty-four hours. Someone, most likely Forney, was going to pay for what had happened to her. He was just almighty glad it wasn't him.

Shorty sighed and then stood.

"I reckon I'll go check on the horses."

"I'll go with you," Big Will said.

But before they could move, the door behind them opened. Letty was standing in the doorway.

"Gentlemen, I believe supper is getting cold."

They stumbled up the steps en masse and then pushed and shoved their way through the door, anxious to get some food before she changed her mind. The dress and undergarments Letty had been wearing were as wet as the hair hanging down her back, and still dripping from the hook where she'd hung them. She was wearing a modest nightgown and robe and her feet were bare. But the pot of stew was on the table as were bowls enough for herself and the hungry men.

Forney ventured a quick glance at the woman before he moved closer. She seemed stable. Nothing like the screaming maniac she'd been after they'd fished her out from under the outhouse. It appeared that she'd not only cleaned herself and her clothes, but the table looked way cleaner than he could remember it being, so he suspected that she'd scrubbed it down, too. Anxious to regain some control of his own way station, he waved a hand toward the table, indicating that the passengers should take a seat.

"Ya'll sit. I'll get coffee."

"Already made," Letty said, and lifted it from the stove and set it on the table, too.

"Well then," Forney said.

Letty sat down, pulling her robe a little

closer around her neck and then put her hands primly in her lap and waited for them to join her. They did so, each casting a nervous glance toward her before taking a seat at the table.

"Smells real good, Forney," Shorty said.

Still put out by her bossy ways, Forney sniffed briefly then nodded.

"Just stew," he said, then took a proprietary step toward the stew pot, grabbed the ladle and began serving it up. Then he took a pan of cornbread from the warming oven, cut it into hunks and set it on the table. Several sets of hands reached for the pan at once as Letty cleared her throat. They all froze, their hands still in midair as Letty glanced at Eulis.

"Brother Howe . . . maybe you would like to say grace."

It wasn't a question and Eulis knew it. He took off his hat and bowed his head. Praying still didn't come easy but he was some better at it than he'd been months earlier. He cleared his throat.

"Dearly beloved, we are gathered —"

Letty sighed loudly. Eulis winced. He'd done something wrong. He just wasn't sure what. He glanced at Letty who rolled her eyes then frowned. He decided to give it one more try.

"Uh, thank you for the food and the hands that have prepared it?"

He hadn't meant to end the brief prayer on a question, but it didn't seem to matter to the hungry men. They all echoed an 'Amen', then fell to eating like starving pigs at a trough while Eulis looked at Letty for confirmation. She nodded primly and picked up her spoon. Eulis sighed and reached for a piece of cornbread. The stew looked a bit thin and the cornbread would be good for soppin' up the juice.

They were nearly done with the meal when something hit the front door with a thud. Letty flinched and then jumped to her feet. She recognized the sound and wasn't going to be caught sitting down again, no matter where she was.

"What is that?" she asked.

Forney frowned. He was hoping the evening would pass without having to explain what had happened at the outhouse, but it looked as if he wasn't going to be so lucky after all.

"What was what?" he asked.

Another thud sounded and the door rattled on its hinges.

"That!" Letty said, and pointed toward the door. "That's what I kept hearing right before the outhouse tipped."

Forney's face turned red. "Well now . . . I reckon that might be ole Billy."

Letty reached for the fireplace poker leaning against the wall and approached the door with trepidation.

"Here now, lady, what do you think you're doin'?" Shorty asked.

Forney jumped to his feet. "You can't!"

Letty opened the door.

"Baa . . . baa."

Eulis's eyes popped.

"Ole Billy is a goat?"

Forney grinned. "Yeah, he's right stubborn, but —"

Letty swung the poker and hit the goat on the large hump of bone between its horns. The goat reeled as if it had been poleaxed, then sat down with a thump.

"Buuu."

"Same to you," Letty said, then slammed the door in its face.

She set the poker back against the wall, poured herself a cup of coffee, and then sat down as if nothing untoward had happened.

The men stared at each other, then at Forney, waiting to see what he was going to do. Both Shorty and Big Will knew that Forney was right fond of that goat.

Forney glared at the woman, then cleared his throat.

Letty looked up, letting her glance slide over him as if he mattered not at all, then let it settle on Eulis.

"Brother Howe, I think I will retire to my bed and leave you men to your visit." Then she stared at Forney, daring him to speak against what she'd done. "It's been a very tiring and disappointing end to a long, dusty ride. I certainly hope my sleep will not be disturbed as our meal has been."

A red flush spread from Forney's neck up his face and disappeared in the thick brush of hair on his head. He kept thinking of Billy sitting out there on the porch and wanted to tell her what she could do with herself, but he didn't dare. Gibson Stage Line had hired him to take care of the passengers and letting an outhouse collapse on one, and a female at that, wasn't what they'd had in mind.

"I'll be back in a few minutes," Forney said, and got up from the table.

"Where you goin'?" Shorty asked.

"Reckon I'll tie ole Billy up for the night."

Letty blew on her coffee and then took a small, dainty sip, grimaced from the strength of it, and then downed it like a field hand before disappearing behind the curtained off corner of the room where the sleeping cots were set up. She chose the one against the wall, crawled beneath the cover, and lay down. The bedclothes smelled like wood smoke and didn't feel all that clean, but she was too weary to care. She was almost asleep when a thought occurred. She got out of bed, dug through her bag for her pistol, then put it underneath her pillow before getting back into bed.

A short while later the others began to retire. Eulis took the cot next to Letty while Boston and Morris chose cots closer to the door. Shorty and Big Will took the ones that were left while Forney climbed the ladder to the single bed in the loft.

A few minutes ensued of boots hitting the floor and belts and buckles coming undone. Then Letty heard Shorty and Big Will converse briefly about tomorrow's journey. After that, someone hiccupped then burped. Someone else cursed softly about the length of the cot versus the length of his body and then all went silent.

Letty waited until she could hear their breathing begin to slow and they were on the verge of sleep. Then she took the gun out from under her pillow and sat up in bed.

"Gentlemen, I have endured the stench of men's bad digestion and even ruder behavior in sharing it since seven o'clock this morning. As if that wasn't enough, I was buried beneath an outhouse full of crap. So I want you to know that my point of endurance has come and gone. Sleep well, but know that I will shoot dead the first man who passes gas within my vicinity tonight."

Boston Jones sat up with a jerk. Morris fell off the cot, hitting the floor with a thump.

Shorty muttered under his breath while Big Will just wadded up his bedclothes and headed for the door.

"Where you goin'?" Shorty asked.

"To the barn," Big Will said.

"Wait a minute," Boston called. "I'll go with you."

"And me," Morris added.

Shorty sighed, then sat up in bed and looked at Letty.

"Lady, you wouldn't really —"

She cocked the gun.

He grabbed his covers and his boots and lit for the door.

"What's goin' on down there?" Forney called.

"We're sleepin' in the barn," Shorty said,

and shut the door behind him as he went.

Letty pointed the gun at Eulis.

"What about you?"

"What about me?" Eulis mumbled.

"Aren't you afraid I'll shoot you in your sleep?"

Eulis snorted softly in his pillow. "No, ma'am."

"Why not?" Letty asked.

"If I'm dead, then you're without a preacher, which means Sister Leticia is dead, too."

Letty thought about it a minute and then stuffed the gun back beneath her pillow and lay down. A few seconds later, she rose up again and whispered.

"Eulis."

He frowned. "Brother Howe, if you please."

Letty rolled her eyes and then tugged at the neck of her nightgown.

"Sorry. Brother . . . where do you reckon we'll wind up next?"

Eulis sighed. "I suppose wherever the Good Lord leads us."

Letty thought about that a moment, then nodded. Satisfied by the godly answer, she lay back down. An owl hooted outside the station. She caught herself waiting to hear if there was an answering hoot from somewhere else, then thought of how she used to listen for the call of the whippoorwill, waiting endlessly in hopes of hearing the mate's answering call.

She snorted softly, disgusted with herself for still being a dreamer after all the wasted years, and poked the thin, lumpy pillow into a different shape in hopes of making it more comfortable. She was a reformed whore and well past the marrying age. Even so, there had been one man, a gambler, who'd seemed to care for her despite her disreputable past. After he'd died in a gunfight, she figured it was her punishment for even imagining she could deserve such happiness. She considered it her penance to follow a man who'd dedicated his life to bringing the word of God to the Territories. Even if Eulis wasn't a real preacher, and even if he hadn't made the decision on his own, she was in a better place now than she had been last year.

Something banged beyond the curtain, then lamplight suddenly glowed.

"Something wrong?" Eulis called.

The bail on a bucket rattled as Forney pulled it out from underneath a bench. It had a hammer and what he hoped were enough nails to do the job he had planned.

"Seein' as how we got ourselves a

woman on the property, I reckoned I'd go put the walls of my outhouse back together before someone had the need to use it again."

Letty snorted.

Forney jiggled the bucket, taking satisfaction in the clank and clatter of the nails to punctuate what he'd left unsaid, then slammed the door behind him as he left.

Eulis wasn't quite sure what to say, although he knew a remark was needed to settle the air.

"That was right thoughty of him, don't you think?"

Letty snorted again.

"I don't think that Forney man has the capacity to have two thoughts in his head at the same time, that's what I think."

"Well then," Eulis said.

The sound of hammering shattered the silence of the night. Letty wondered what the men trying to sleep in the barn thought about all that noise, then decided she didn't care.

"Good night, Brother Howe," Letty said.

"Good night, Sister. Sleep well."

"I intend to," she said curtly, and blanked out the sound of the hammering just as she was learning to bury the memories of sleeping with men for money.

Shutting the Barn Door After the Horse Is Out

Mary Farmer was the oldest of six children and her daddy's favorite, plus being the only one who'd taken her looks after her mother, Lillian, whom her father adored. She was sixteen, book smart and common sense smart, both traits that her father took credit for, although it was her mother who'd taught all six of her children their learning. Mary worked behind the counter at the family dry goods store in Plum Creek and was a big draw in getting all the business from the local cowboys on payday. She'd been named the Harvest Queen during the town's annual fall festival two years in a row, only Mary was certain it wasn't going to happen a third time. She was pretty sure that pregnant, unmarried girls weren't named anything but loose, which meant that Harvest Queen was out.

She didn't really mind about not being Harvest Queen. She'd had her two years in the limelight. What she did mind was that her daddy had forbidden her to even speak to Joseph Carver, the wild young cowboy who worked on the Double R Ranch. She'd minded so much that she'd done the unthinkable. Not only had she slipped around to see him, but she'd fallen in love with the dark-eyed wrangler and made love with him every time they got the chance. Now she was about to pay the ultimate price for her indiscretions. Last Saturday night, Joseph Carver had gone and gotten himself arrested for horse thieving and cattle rustling. Caught hands down with the branding iron in his hand, he'd been tried and found guilty. It was bad enough that she'd gotten herself pregnant, but tomorrow morning, her baby's daddy was going to be hanged. She was not only up a flooded creek and drowning, but going down for the last time. Too heartsick and afraid to admit to her situation, she'd decided to do herself in. It was just the how and where of it that she had yet to figure out.

She fainted at the sight of blood, so using a knife was not an option, and she didn't know how to shoot a gun, so that was out, too. Each night when she went to bed she tried to stop breathing, but so far that hadn't been successful because she kept falling asleep and waking up each morning to a new day. The way she figured it, she just needed to wait for the arrival of the next stagecoach and throw herself beneath its wheels. It would probably hurt real bad before she died, but maybe that was her penance for committing her mortal sins. She didn't think about the fact that she would be ending her baby's life too before it had a chance to begin, mostly because the baby didn't seem real. She'd felt nothing but panic since the day she'd learned of its existence, and it was far easier to be a coward than to face the consequences of her actions.

Dooley Pilchard walked with a limp and had to squint a bit to see clear out of his right eye, but he was a good hand with a fire and bellows and satisfied the residents of Plum Creek's needs for a blacksmith just fine. His shoulders were broad and his hands knotted from long hours hammering iron and shoeing horses. He looked older than his twenty-seven years and stood seven inches over six feet tall. He wore a beard to hide a scar that ran the length of his chin and neck and wore the beard short and his hair long, tied back from his face with a thin piece of leather. His eyes, his best feature, were robin's egg blue, but hard to see beneath dark, shaggy eyebrows.

He was a lonely man who witnessed life in Plum Creek without any participation beyond the casual hello and goodbye to his customers. Because of his size and his limp, few single women ever noticed him, and none gave him a second glance. By his habits alone, he'd become anonymous, almost invisible, and because of that, he knew way more of the goings on in Plum Creek than most people could have imagined.

He knew that the mayor downed a flask of whiskey every afternoon in the alley behind the saloon and that Mary Farmer had been sneaking out to see Joseph Carver for several months. He knew that Joseph Carver bragged about his prowess among the other cowboys with whom he worked, and he knew that Joseph Carver's laughing days were almost over. What he didn't know was that when Joseph Carver died, he was leaving a piece of himself behind. Ironically, Joseph Carver didn't know it either, but that was of no comfort to Mary and immaterial to Dooley. What he did know was that when Joseph Carver had been sentenced to hang, Mary Farmer had changed.

Her pretty face was no longer wreathed in constant smiles and her demeanor had turned into one resembling a whipped dog. She walked with her head down and her shoulders slumped, and he wanted more than anything in this world to put his arms around her and protect her forever from hurt or harm.

However, Dooley Pilchard was a realist and knew his dream was about as far-fetched as a dream could be. So he admired her from afar, watched her when she didn't see him looking, and wished Joseph Carver to hell for making Mary Farmer sad.

Adam Farmer knocked sharply on Mary's door. When his daughter didn't answer, he shouted out.

"Mary! Mary! You need to come down and help out at the counter. Seems like everyone has come to town to see the hangin' and your mother can't help because Maybelle is sick."

"Yes. All right," she said. "I'll be down shortly."

"Well, hurry up and get dressed. Customers are thick as flies."

"Yes, Father," Mary said, and listened to his footsteps disappearing as she stared blindly out the window to the gallows in the town square below.

She couldn't believe she was in such a terrible fix. The more she thought about it, the more she realized what a fool she'd been. Her mother had told her that wild cowboys weren't to be trusted, but she'd been so certain her mother had been wrong. She put a hand on her belly, testing it to see if she could feel a difference, but it still felt as firm and flat as always. If only she could change the past, she would not give those cowboys a second glance.

She looked back down at the street, saw the sheriff climbing up the steps to the gallows and quickly turned away. She was ashamed she'd ever believed herself in love with Joseph Carver and even more ashamed she'd let him have his way with her.

"Mary!"

She jumped at the sound of her father's voice.

"Coming," she said, and hurried out of her room and down the stairs to the store below.

The room was packed, mostly with people who were waiting inside out of the sun for the hanging. She scooted behind the counter and tied an apron around her

41

waist before moving to her first customer, a woman she recognized as the wife of a settler named Mordacai Reed. The harried woman had a baby in her arms and three young children playing at her feet.

"May I help you?" Mary asked.

"I need this order filled," the woman said, and slid a grocery list across the counter to Mary.

"It will only take a few minutes," she said.

"Take your time, dearie," the woman said, then whacked her oldest child on the back of the head. "Stop puttin' your finger up your nose."

The child let out a bellow of dismay that only added to the underlying rumble of voices all talking about the same thing — the man who was about to be hanged.

Mary blinked back tears and hurried to fill the order, took the woman's money, and moved to the next, then the next, and suddenly someone yelled.

"They're coming! They're coming!"

The store quickly emptied out as if the building had caught on fire. Mary's heart hurt and her hands began to shake. She moved to the window in time to catch a glimpse of Joseph's face. The laughter was missing. He looked scared.

"Mary! Come away from there!" her father ordered.

Mary turned around. There was no one in the store but her and her father. She opened her mouth, wanting to tell him what she'd done.

Then the crowd roared and she flinched. She could hear the sheriff talking and thought he asked Joseph if he had any last words.

There was a long moment of silence. She wanted to turn around — needed to see the horror of what was happening yet afraid she would break down. Her father wouldn't understand why she was so upset over some thieving cowboy she shouldn't even know.

Then she heard a solid thump, followed by the faint wail of an infant and wondered if the settler's baby was the only one who would cry for Joseph Carver this day.

A few moments later, the crowd in the street began to disperse. A few came back into the store to finish their shopping while others loaded up their wagons and buckboards and started the trip home. They'd seen what they had come to see — hard justice in a sparse land.

Mary lifted her chin and found herself staring blindly at the merchandise lining the front of the shelves, then at her father, memorizing the studious expression on his face as he posted a line of figures into his account book. Upstairs, she could hear the sounds of her little brothers and sisters playing and the intermittent creak of a floorboard above her head as her mother rocked her little sister to sleep. It was so familiar and so dear. But the innocence of her life was gone, and if she told her parents what she'd done, then all this would be gone, too. She glanced at the clock. It was almost time for the stage to arrive. She took off her apron and hung it on a nail by the staircase, smoothed her hands down the front of her dress, and slipped out the back door unobserved.

When Shorty topped the hill above Plum Creek, he breathed a huge sigh of relief. The preacher and his female companion would be getting off in town, and it was none too soon for him. Sister Leticia was a fine looking woman, but in his opinion, not worth the trouble she had caused. He hadn't slept in a barn since the night his wife had kicked him out of the house and went back to Indiana to live with her folks. He still had the itch from the damn fleas he'd gotten out of his impromptu bed of hay. He could appreciate Sister Leticia's feelings, but she wasn't looking realistically at the ways of men. She shouldn't expect a man to mind his manners so close when it took everything he had just to survive from day to day.

Unfortunately, Shorty didn't come by his name for no reason. Not only was he small in stature, but he was shortsighted as well. Being the man that he was, he completely ignored Leticia's feelings and expectations as important. That was why he was no longer married and why he had to pay for female favors if he had any at all.

"Plum Creek, comin' up!" he yelled, and whipped the horses into a faster gait because he liked to arrive at his destinations with a flourish.

Big Will knew Shorty's predilection for speed and held his rifle a bit closer to his chest as the stagecoach started down the hill at a steadily increasing pace.

Inside the coach, Boston Jones pocketed the cards he'd been flipping while Morris Field began a mental recital of the sales pitch he used to peddle his laces and ribbons.

Eulis dusted off the front of his frock coat as he clutched his Bible close to his chest.

Letty felt a twinge of anxiety as they came closer and closer to Plum Creek. She'd never been here before, but she knew cowboys who had. Her worst fear was that in the middle of their new life, a ghost from her past would appear and blow it all to hell. It would be hard to maintain a pious appearance if there were men out in the Reverend's congregation who'd seen her bare-assed and bouncing all over the place. A few minutes later, the first buildings of Plum Creek came into view. Letty lifted her chin and steeled herself for whatever awaited.

Mary Farmer was wearing her favorite dress, a pale yellow cotton with tatting around the collar and the edges of her sleeves. The skirt belled around her legs, giving anyone who cared to look quick glimpses of her shiny brown shoes and trim ankles. She'd tied her long blonde hair at the back of her neck with a wide yellow ribbon and pinched her cheeks until they stung. She wanted to appear in good health and color when she "fell" beneath the stagecoach wheels; that way her folks would believe that her death was a horrible accident, rather than a coward's way out of a willful mistake.

The gallows were empty now, but its very presence was a bitter reminder of why she was here. A hot gust of wind caught her skirt as she moved past the alley between the saloon and the barbershop. She lifted her hand to shield her eyes from the dust and missed seeing Dooley Pilchard fall into step behind her.

Dooley had been momentarily blinded too, but from Mary Farmer's beauty, not the hot wind and blowing dust. He'd watched Joseph Carver hang and at the same time, took note of Mary Farmer's absence. Now here she was, walking the streets as if nothing out of the ordinary had happened. He was still trying to figure her out when he caught a glimpse of her face in the window glass of the barbershop. The pain on her face was so vivid he almost stumbled and fell.

He was still trying to right himself when he heard the stage approaching. He turned around just in time to see Shorty cracking his whip over the horses' heads and whooping and yelling as they rolled into town. Dust boiled out from under the rolling wheels and he could smell the horses' sweat and hear their wild, labored breathing as they neared the hotel. He turned his head sideways to shield himself from the worst of the dust and as he did, caught another glimpse of Mary Farmer. Then his blood ran cold.

Mary Farmer was still walking down the sidewalk, but with every step, she was moving closer and closer to the edge. One misstep and she'd be under the horses' hooves before Shorty could stop.

"Miss Farmer! Miss Farmer!" he called.

To his dismay, she neither slowed down nor looked back.

He started to move, lengthening his stride as he hurried to catch up.

"Miss Farmer!"

He could feel the sidewalk shaking as the horses thundered even closer. She had to know they were there, yet again, she neither slowed down nor moved back. Suddenly, he thought of the pain on her face and the man who'd been hanged, and his blood ran cold.

Before he could speak out again, the stagecoach was upon them. He could see the lead pair of horses from the corner of his eye and knew that she saw them, too, because without hesitation, she just took a short step to the right and let herself fall.

Dooley saw her arms go up and the skirt of her yellow dress billow outward. Her hair, the color of corn silk, lifted up from the back of her neck and then fanned outward. The long yellow ribbon flew up and then out like the tail of a kite and before he could rethink the motion, he lunged forward, stretching his height to its fullest and using the weight and power of his body as a shield between her and the team and coach.

She was in midair when their bodies connected. Dooley grabbed her with his left arm and the lead horse's harness with his right as they continued to fall. They hit fast and they hit hard, before they were dragged along the ground, only a heartbeat away from the thundering hooves.

Now it was no longer a matter of saving Mary. It became a matter of saving himself, too. He could hear the frantic shouts of both Shorty and Big Will trying to get the horses stopped, and the scream of some female bystander who must be witnessing it all. Dirt from the horses' hooves flew into his face and his arm felt as if it were being ripped from his shoulder. Still, he held on to Mary and the harness with all of his might.

Through it all, in a small corner of his mind he was horribly aware of Mary's silence. She hadn't screamed, she hadn't fought; she hadn't moved at all. It was as if she was just waiting for it all to be over.

And suddenly it was.

The absence of motion was as startling as the fact that they were still alive. Once he realized that the team had been halted, he quickly turned loose of the harness and rolled out of the way of the restless horses and their stomping hooves, taking Mary with him. For a few priceless seconds, he felt the softness of her body against him and the thunder of his own heartbeat pounding in his ears. He looked down at the woman beneath him as she slowly opened her eyes and looked up.

They stared, each into the other's eyes.

His widened.

Hers filled with tears.

Time stopped.

Covered in dust and aching in every muscle, Dooley Pilchard knew that he'd just fallen in love. Then he saw the dust and abrasions on her face and neck and thought to ask.

"Miss Farmer . . . Mary . . . are you all right?"

A single tear slipped from the corner of her eye, leaving traces of its passing through the dust on her face. Her chin quivered. Her lips started to shake. She took a deep breath and then shuddered.

"Oh Dooley, what have you done?"

Then everyone descended upon them.

Big Will began pulling at Dooley, as Shorty and the sheriff yanked Mary out of his arms.

"Miss Farmer! Miss Farmer! Are you all right?" the sheriff asked.

Shorty was pale and shaking as he helped the sheriff stand her up.

"Missy . . . I'm right sorry . . . I saw you falling and tried to stop the horses, but it wouldn't have been in time. If it hadn't been for Dooley, here, we would have run clean over ya' and that's a fact."

Dooley dragged himself up and brushed himself off as Big Will thumped him on the back.

"Boy . . . I didn't think you was goin' to make it!" Big Will said.

Dooley straightened. He wouldn't look at Mary. Couldn't look at her and know that she would rather be dead than live in a world without Joseph Carver.

"I didn't think I was goin' to either," Dooley muttered, and walked away as the stagecoach door opened.

Boston Jones got out, eyed the businesses, focused in on the saloon, and started across the street as Morris stepped out. He was looking for Shorty to register his indignation about the abruptness of their arrival.

"I say, Shorty, that could have been a much smoother approach."

"Had to stop sudden-like," Shorty said. "This little lady here fell right in front of the stage. Didn't think I was gonna be able to miss her!"

Eulis and Letty got out in time to hear Shorty's comment and both looked at the young girl in question. Grabbing onto the opportunity to insinuate themselves into the goodwill of the residents of Plum Creek, Eulis quickly stepped forward.

"Dear girl . . . won't you let Sister Leticia assist you to your home?"

Mary shuddered. Home? It was the last place she wanted to be.

Letty saw the empty expression in the girl's eyes and read it as more than shock. She slipped an arm beneath the young girl's elbow.

"Mary is it? My name is Let . . . uh, Sister Leticia. Will you allow me to walk with you?"

Mary could see the woman's lips moving, but she couldn't hear her voice. Then she started to shake.

Without waiting for an answer, Letty slipped an arm around her shoulders and pulled her close, then looked to the sheriff.

"Where does she live?"

He pointed down the street. "Her parents run the dry goods store. They live above it."

Letty nodded, and then patted Mary's arm. "Lean on me," she said softly.

Mary was halfway home before she realized her feet were moving. She stopped, looked down at herself and saw a rip in her bodice and dirt all over herself. She'd lost the heel on one shoe and her face was starting to burn where her face had been skinned. She touched her face, then helplessly tugged at the tear, trying to pull the torn sides together.

"It will be okay," Letty said softly.

Mary swayed on her feet, then looked up. She didn't know the woman, but she saw kindness in her face, and it was enough to break the wall of her defenses.

"No, it will never be okay," Mary said. "I am with child and this morning, they hanged the man who got me this way."

Letty sighed. She'd heard plenty of similar stories from girls who'd worked in her position, but never from a girl of a proper family.

"Do your parents know?"

"No."

"You need to tell them. They'll know soon enough, as it is."

The girl swayed where she stood then looked away.

"No. I'd rather die than see the disappointment on their faces."

Suddenly, for Letty, the near-fatal accident took on a whole other connotation.

"Look at me," Letty said.

"I can't," Mary said. "I'm so ashamed."

Letty took her by the arms and shook her.

"So ashamed that you'd kill yourself instead of face the truth?"

Mary just covered her face with her hands.

Before Letty could speak, someone put a hand on her shoulder and turned her completely around. She found herself staring at the middle of a big man's chest. From that point, she looked up, then took a studied step back.

"Are you makin' Miss Mary cry?"

Letty wasn't in the habit of being intimidated by any man, no matter the size.

"No. She's doing a fine job of it all on her own," Letty snapped. "And who are you?"

"Dooley Pilchard. Pleased to make your acquaintance," Dooley said, and then frowned at himself. He wasn't sure that was true, but the manners that had been drilled into him as a boy had popped out without thought.

Dooley didn't know that his heart was in his eyes as he looked at Mary Farmer, but Letty recognized the look. She'd seen it on a miner's face as he'd promised to love and honor Letty's friend, Truly Fine, until death did them part. Letty stared long and hard at the man, then back at the girl.

"Does he know?" Letty asked.

Mary gasped and looked up.

"Know what?" Dooley asked.

"Don't!" Mary cried, and then covered her face again.

Dooley pulled himself up to his full height of six feet, seven inches, and gently moved Mary's hands away from her face.

"Miss Mary, we need to get you home and those scratches tended to on your face."

"I can't," she whispered.

He frowned. "What do you mean, you can't? Are you hurtin' in your limbs? I can carry you easy. Just let me —"

"Tell him!" Letty said.

Mary turned on Letty.

"Shut up! Shut up! I shouldn't have told you. I don't know what I was thinking."

"Told her what?" Dooley asked.

"She's with child."

Mary groaned and started to wilt.

Dooley grabbed her before she could fall and then scooped her up in his arms.

"I reckon I'll carry you the rest of the way," he said softly.

"I don't want to go home. I want to die."

Dooley felt like dying himself, but he didn't have time to let the feeling fester.

"Yeah, I already figured that out," Dooley said. "Might near took me with you."

Letty's eyes widened. "Are you the man who saved her?"

"I reckon I am," Dooley said.

Suddenly, it was as if the good Lord himself leaned down from heaven and whispered the answer in her ear.

"I know how to fix this," she said shortly.

Dooley pulled Mary away from Letty as if she'd just tried to attack her.

"You ain't doin' nothin' to this girl or her baby. You hear me?"

Letty hid a smile. It might just work after all.

"I wasn't going to suggest anything of the kind," Letty said, then looked at Mary. "You got a baby that's gonna be missing a daddy and you got yourself a man, here, who treasures the ground you walk on."

Dooley's face turned a dark, angry red as Mary gasped. She looked up at Dooley, and for the second time today, found herself unable to look away from those big blue eyes.

"I didn't know," Mary said.

Dooley frowned. "Didn't matter then. Still don't matter. I ain't anyone you'd ever care for and I know that."

"She needs a husband," Letty said.

Mary's eyes widened further as she began to understand where the woman's conversation was leading.

"Put me down," she begged Dooley.

"Don't reckon I will," he said. "Least not until I'm sure you're under the watchful eye of your folks."

"I said . . . she needs a husband," Letty muttered, unwilling to turn loose of her idea. "You got a problem raising another man's child?"

Dooley looked down at Mary, then slowly shook his head.

"I reckon it would be real easy to love any part of Mary Farmer, be it her or her child."

Mary started to cry.

Dooley glared at Letty. "Now see what you went and done. I told you not to make Mary cry."

Letty hadn't survived all these years without persistence, and she wasn't about to give up on what she considered was her first mission of goodwill.

"She's not crying because she's mad. Ask her and see what happens."

"Ask her what?" Dooley said.

Letty rolled her eyes. "Save me from the stupidity of men. I reckon the Good Lord took more than a rib from man to make his mate. I'm thinking He took the smart half of his brain as well."

"Are you insultin' me?" Dooley muttered.

"I rest my case," Letty muttered, and rolled her eyes. "Mr. Pilchard, ask her to marry you and see what happens."

Dooley looked down at Mary, who had again, covered her face with her hands.

"There ain't no way a girl this pretty would ever want anything to do with me. Besides, she gave her heart to another."

"He's dead," Letty countered. "You're not. I said ask."

Dooley felt himself coming undone. This morning he'd gotten out of bed with nothing more serious than a good bait of ham and biscuits for breakfast. Now this. He didn't know what to think. But he did know that he didn't want to let Mary

Farmer out of his sight for fear she'd try to do herself in again.

He cleared his throat.

Mary flinched, then looked up at him. He was as dusty as she was and skinned up even more. Suddenly, she realized she hadn't even thanked the man for what he'd done. Without knowing her intent, he'd put himself in harm's way to save her. She at least owed him a thanks.

"Dooley."

"Yes, ma'am?"

"You put yourself in harm's way for me. I thank you for that."

He felt himself blushing.

Letty rolled her eyes and started muttering beneath her breath, which made Dooley nervous all over again.

"You're welcome, Miss Mary."

Letty made a sound between gritted teeth that sounded somewhat like a growl.

Being sandwiched between these two women was more female companionship than Dooley had encountered in some years. He didn't know whether to run, or state his case. Then Mary Farmer touched his arm.

"Dooley, please don't. My shame is not your concern."

He frowned. "Well now . . . it could be,

if you was to let me take up your care."

"I'm sorry?" Letty asked.

The embittered whore in Letty shoved its way past Sister Leticia's act as Letty punched Dooley's shoulder.

"For God's sake, mister, say it or get the hell out of my sight."

Dooley was too startled by the rough words coming out of Letty's mouth to argue. Instead, he took Mary by the hand and tried not to think about how tiny it felt against his palm.

"Miss Mary . . . I'm not presuming to think that you care anything for me, and that's all right. I reckon if you was to do me the honor of being my wife, I could care enough for the both of us."

Mary's breath caught in her throat. She kept looking at this mountain of a man and remembering the strength in his arms and that he'd chanced his life to save hers.

"I can't," Mary said.

Both Dooley and Letty exhaled as if they'd been gut-punched.

"At least not until I confess my whole sin," Mary added.

Both of them drew a new breath, taking fresh heart.

"That's not necessary," Dooley said. "I know about you and Joe Carver."

Mary paled. "But how?"

Dooley shrugged. "Mostly people don't pay me no mind, which usually means they say stuff around me that they might not say around others."

"You knew and you'd still consider me for —"

Dooley put one huge finger across her lips, silencing her before she could finish.

"Miss Mary, I would consider you just about the prettiest, sweetest thing this side of heaven. I reckon that cowboy took advantage of your innocence and lied to you to have his way."

Mary sighed. She could stand there and let him believe that and then have to live with the lie. She couldn't bring herself to do it.

"No, Dooley. It wasn't quite like that. I suppose he lied to me, all right. But he didn't force himself upon me. I fancied myself in love with him and, and. . . ." She shrugged.

"Do you love him, still?"

Mary frowned. "No."

"Do you reckon you'll be able to love that babe you're carryin'?"

"I don't know," she said truthfully.

Dooley nodded. "Fair enough. Well, if after it gets here and you find that you can't, I reckon I'll pick up the slack."

Again, Letty was struck by the strength of true love and wondered why she had been cursed to spend her life alone. Of course, technically she wasn't really alone. There was Eulis. But they would surely never be able to share anything but the lie that bound them to each other.

"So?" Letty urged.

Mary's eyes teared again, only this time with shy, growing joy. This morning she'd planned her death. Tonight she would be planning her wedding. Sometimes life was just too confusing to explain. She looked at Dooley, and then nodded and managed a weak smile.

"Yes, Dooley Pilchard, I would be most honored to be your wife, and I will spend the rest of my life making sure that you never want for companionship or comfort for as long as you live."

Dooley felt like shouting the news to the whole town. Instead, he tucked Mary's hand into the crook of his elbow.

"Then I reckon we'd better go have a talk with your Pa."

"Thank goodness," Letty muttered, then thought to add. "My, uh . . . traveling companion, Reverend Howe, is a minister. He'll be happy to perform the wedding.

We'll be staying at the hotel for the next two days. Just let us know."

"Yes, ma'am," Dooley said, as Letty strode away, confident that she'd completed her mission in true godly fashion.

"Don't tell Father that I'm with child," Mary begged.

"I won't tell him anything but the truth," Dooley said.

Mary paled. "And the truth is?"

"That I've been in love with his oldest daughter ever since she quit wearing pigtails."

"Truly?" Mary asked.

"Yes, truly," Dooley answered.

The horrible weight in her heart began to shift and lessen. By the time they reached the dry goods store, she was smiling.

In Sickness
and in Health

Harvey Ditsworth, the barber, dashed into
Farmer's Dry Goods, yelling as he ran.
"Adam! Adam! Come quick. Mary has
been in an accident!"

Adam Farmer dropped the bolt of cloth
he was holding and ran out from behind
the counter.

"What happened?" he asked as he followed Harvey out the door.

"The stage. Someone said she fell under
the stage."

Adam stopped. It felt as if all the
bones in his legs had just turned to
mush. But how could this happen? Only
minutes before she'd been in the store
waiting on customers. When she'd disappeared so suddenly, he'd assumed she
had gone to use the facilities. This just
couldn't be! He couldn't bear to think of
his beautiful daughter all mangled and
bloody.

"Dear Lord . . . no!" Then he thought of

his wife. "Mama. Mary will be wanting her Mama."

"Wait!" Harvey said, and grabbed Adam by the arm. "Look there! Dooley Pilchard is bringing Mary home."

Adam gasped. Seeing her alive and walking when only moments before he'd been preparing himself for the worst was such a relief that he burst into tears and ran toward her.

Mary was still in shock, both from surviving the accident and accepting Dooley's proposal when she saw her father and Harvey in the street. She stumbled.

Dooley caught her before she could fall and picked her up in his arms.

"I'm sorry," she said, conscious of her weight and his limp.

"I'm not," he said softly, which made her blush.

"My father. Someone must have told him about the stage."

"Accidents happen."

Mary studied on what Dooley just said and decided there were no underlying meanings. Dooley Pilchard was too straightforward to be referring to her pregnancy.

"Yes. That's right. Accidents happen."

It was all they had time to say before Adam Farmer's arrival.

Adam took one look at the abrasions on Mary's face and the condition of her clothing and knew what he'd just been told must be true.

"Is it true? Did you fall beneath the stage?"

She hesitated just a moment too long for Dooley.

"Well sir, Mr. Farmer, I saw it all. She misstepped and fell right off the sidewalk into the path of the oncoming stage. But she's fine now as you can see."

Mary gently patted Dooley's chest.

"Because of you," she said softly. "And you can put me down. I can walk the rest of the way."

"No. I reckon I'll be carrying you . . . just to make sure," Dooley said.

Mary blushed.

Adam frowned as he looked from Mary's clothes to Dooley's clothes, then from the abrasions on her face to the same sort of wounds on his face and hands.

"I say, Dooley! Was it you? Did you save our Mary?"

Mary nodded. "Yes, Father. It all happened so fast I hardly remember it well, but I know he caught me and held me tight with one hand and caught the team's harness with his other until the stagecoach driver could stop."

Adam threw up his hands and began crying anew, which embarrassed Dooley to no end. He wasn't accustomed to crying people, especially men.

"I just happened to be there," Dooley said. "And I reckon we better get Miss Mary home and see to her face."

"Yes, yes, of course," Adam said. "Follow me."

Dooley did, still carrying the woman who was going to be his wife. He hadn't completely absorbed the impact of all that had happened in the last thirty minutes, but he knew his life would never be the same. Then he looked down at Mary, remembered the loneliness of his life and decided that would be just fine.

Adam hurried into the store to find his wife waiting on a customer.

"Mother! Mary has had an accident."

Lillian Farmer gasped as she saw the huge blacksmith carrying Mary into the store.

"Oh dear!" she cried, and ran to Mary. "What happened?"

"She fell off the sidewalk in front of the oncoming stage," Dooley said, feeling more and more comfortable with his part in the lie.

"Dooley saved me," Mary added, thankful that her part in the story was still the truth.

"Thank God and thank you," Lillian said, and hugged them both. "Can you bring her upstairs?"

"Yes, ma'am. I reckon I'd be happy to."

Then Lillian remembered her customer. "I'm sorry, Mrs. Dewar. I'll get your order right now."

The banker's wife shook her head. "No, no. I can come back later. You tend to your child." She patted Mary's arm. "You are a very lucky young woman, and you sir, are a brave young man to do what you've done. You should be honored."

"That's not necessary, Mrs. Dewar. I just happened to be there," Dooley said, then carried Mary up the stairs with both parents trailing closely behind.

Dooley carried her to her room and laid her down on her bed. Mary felt bereft when he put her down and realized how safe she'd felt in his arms. She watched him trying to get out of the way as her parents hovered around her and suddenly realized how big he really was. His shoulders were almost as wide as her door, and he had to bend his head slightly so as not to bump the ceiling. Thanks to the persistence of the recently departed Joseph Carver, she knew what went on between a man and a woman and wondered what it would be like being married to this giant of a man. Would he hurt her? Would he demand things of her that she couldn't fulfill? Then she caught him looking at her with those gentle blue eyes and knew he could do none of those things. In that moment, her heart felt full.

"Mother. Father. I have something to tell you."

They stilled. Dooley looked nervous.

"Dooley Pilchard has asked for my hand in marriage and I have given him my consent."

Lillian and Adam gasped in unison, then turned and stared at the hairy giant in their daughter's room and instinctively moved between him and Mary's bed.

"No," Adam said. "I'm sorry, but you must understand that is out of the question. You're too young and he's . . . he's. . . ."

Dooley had been expecting this. After all, it had to appear to Mary's parents as if he and Mary had both lost their minds.

"I'm sorry," Lillian said. "We so appreciate what you did for our Mary, but under the circumstances, you must see that —"

Anger surged. They were dismissing Dooley as of no consequence and solely because of his rough appearance.

"No, Mother! Father! It's you who don't understand."

Dooley reached forward, intent on saving her from admitting her shame.

"Mary, you don't have to."

Mary winced as she got out of bed, but she was intent on standing her ground.

"Yes, Dooley, I do have to. I won't have them saying anything against you when it's I who have a reason for shame."

Dooley sighed.

"Mary, what are you trying to say?" Adam asked.

Mary faced her parents. "I will marry Dooley. I will because I must. I am with child and the father is dead. Dooley has learned of my plight and offered to marry me . . . to care for me and my child."

Lillian covered her face and turned away while Adam sat down on Mary's bed with a thump.

"Dead? Who could it be?"

"It doesn't matter," Mary said.

Adam's face turned a dark angry red.

"It does to me. No one has died around here in months except —"

Mary flinched.

Adam stood. "No. Not him."

Lillian turned. "What are you . . . ?" Then it hit her. "That cowboy?"

Mary slumped. Dooley put his arm around her.

"I can't believe you have brought such shame upon us," Adam muttered.

Dooley frowned. "Well sir, that's just it. If you and your wife keep your mouth shut, no one has ever a need to know. And I won't have Mary's name bandied about. I care for her, sir, and in time, maybe she will come to care for me."

Adam pointed at Dooley. "I say, Dooley. We're her parents and you have no right to —"

Mary pushed his hand away. "No, Father, he has all the right he needs to speak for me. I have said I will marry him, and I do so with pride. It's more than I deserve, but I will spend my life in thanksgiving for what he's doing."

Dooley hugged her briefly as he pulled her close.

"I don't want your thanks, Mary girl."

Lillian was in tears as she looked at her eldest child.

"What's done is done," she said. "But there's no preacher to perform the ceremony."

"Actually, one came in on the stage that nearly ran Mary down," Dooley said.

Mary looked up at him.

"Will you speak to him . . . see if he can perform the ceremony tonight?"

Dooley's heart surged all the way to his throat. Tonight he would sleep with Mary Farmer in his arms. It seemed too good to be true.

"Yes, Mary. I'll speak to him." Then he tipped his hat to Mary's parents. "I'll be back, but before I go, I must ask you not to berate your daughter any more. She's already suffered far more than you can imagine, and it's only by the grace of God that you still have her with you. Be thankful for the arrival of your first grandchild instead of grieving for the loss of Mary's innocence."

He looked at Mary one last time. When she smiled at him, he nodded then left.

Mary's heart surged as she watched him go and knew that she'd just been given a second chance. Then she turned to her mother.

"Mother, will you help me clean my wounds? I want to look as decent as possible for the ceremony tonight."

Lillian sighed. "Yes, of course, Mary dear. Adam, go downstairs and bring up some of that witch hazel and some clean rags from the back room. I'm going to my room to get my wedding dress out of the trunk. I don't have much time if it's going to need any alterations."

Mary sat down on the bed with a thump as her parents left in two different directions. The silence was startling, even lonely, but she knew that because of Dooley's big heart, she would be able to keep her good name and after today, she would never be lonely again.

Letty was still wearing a smug expression as she settled into her hotel room. This business of doing God's work seemed simple. All she had to do was discover the problem and fix it. It didn't occur to her that while she was meddling in other people's business that she was ignoring the mess in her own.

She had taken her good dress out of her carpetbag and was in the act of hanging it in the armoire when there was a knock at her door. Assuming it would be Eulis, she opened it wide.

It wasn't Eulis, and it wasn't good news. In fact, it was her worst fear that had come knocking.

The man had at least a four-day growth of beard and was six months past needing a haircut. His hat was sweat-stained and crumpled — the kind that served as a shade or a bucket, whichever was necessary at the time. He was wearing a dusty shirt and even dustier pants. His boots were scuffed and run down at the heels, but the guns strapped to his hips hung loose and low and the smile on his face was a go-to-hell grin that she'd seen many times before. She wasn't sure, but she thought his name was Willy or Billy or something like that.

"Letty . . . it is you!"

She frowned and pretended indignation, which was difficult because she distinctly remembered he had a mole on his dinkus that he called Spot.

"I'm sorry, sir, but you have mistaken me for someone else."

The smile slid sideways. "But you look just like —"

"I have that kind of face," Letty said, and closed the door in his face.

"Oh Lord," Letty muttered, and sat down on her bed with a thump. What was she to do? They couldn't leave every time they ran into someone from their past or they'd be running for life.

A knock sounded on the door again. She frowned.

"Who is it, please?"

"It's me," Eulis said.

"Are you alone?"

"Yes."

Letty opened the door, grabbed him by the wrist and yanked him inside before slamming the door behind him.

Eulis glared. "What the hell's wrong with you?"

"Nothing," Letty said, and then threw up her hands and started pacing the floor. "That's not exactly true. Someone who knew me from Lizard Flats just knocked on my door."

Eulis groaned. "We're found out. It was bound to happen."

"No, no, that's not so," Letty said. "I told him he was mistaken. I think he bought it. I mean . . . I don't look exactly like I used to, you know."

Eulis looked at her and squinted, as if trying to assess her now against the way she'd been at the White Dove Saloon. She was minus the red feathers she used to wear in her hair, and her dress didn't exactly bare all her charms. And her face was scrubbed clean as opposed to that lip rouge and black stuff she used to put on her eyes.

"Yeah, I reckon you're right."

Letty nodded. "Of course I'm right. I'm always right."

Eulis frowned. "That ain't exactly so. Remember the time you —"

Letty slapped him on the shoulder.

"I do not wish to be reminded of the dark deeds of my past. I have been saved, remember?"

Eulis thought of the baptism he'd performed on her in a moss-covered watering trough down at the Lizard Flats livery stable and sighed.

"Yeah, I remember."

"Then what should we do about the cowboy?"

"Nothing."

"Nothing?"

"What do you want me to do?" Eulis asked. "And before you ask, I ain't diggin' you no grave to hide another body in."

Letty gasped, then grabbed Eulis by the collar and shoved him up against the wall.

"Dang it, Eulis, didn't we just agree not to discuss my past?"

Eulis batted at her hands, trying to dislodge them from around his throat.

"Dad blame it, Letty. You're shuttin' off the air to my gizzard. Let go. I say, let go."

"Not 'til you promise you'll never talk about Lizard Flats again."

"I promise. I swear to God, I promise."

Letty frowned. "You bein' a preacher and all, I don't think you oughta be swearin' anything to God."

"Oh yeah . . . right. I'm sorry. It was just a figure of speech, you know. I'll watch it better from now on."

"So, what did you want?" Letty asked.

Eulis frowned. "When?"

Letty rolled her eyes. "You knocked on my door. You had to have a reason."

Eulis slapped himself up beside his head and then laughed.

"Oh yeah, right. I was comin' to see if you wanted to go get some dinner downstairs in the dining room."

Letty patted her hair and then pinched her cheeks.

"Well yes, that would be fine. Thank you for asking Brother Howe."

Eulis sighed. So all of a sudden he was Brother Howe again. "Do you want me to wait outside for a bit or —"

"No, I'm ready," Letty said. "And now that I think of it, I am hungry."

"So, fine. Let's go eat."

Letty walked to the door and then stopped. Eulis was right behind her and had to do a fancy side step to keep from running into her. When she didn't move, he walked around in front of her and stared.

"What's wrong?"

Letty arched her eyebrows so high they disappeared beneath the bangs she'd taken to wearing.

"Why, nothing is wrong, I'm sure, except that your manners are sadly lacking, Brother Howe."

Eulis's shoulders slumped. "Dang it, Letty. . . ."

She frowned.

He stifled a curse. "Excuse me . . . dang it, Sister Leticia, how am I ever gonna learn the right way to do things if you keep making me guess what they are? Just spit it out. You'll feel better to get it off your chest, and I'll do whatever it is you want me to do that much faster."

Letty was debating with herself whether or not to chastise him for mentioning her "chest" when Eulis got in her face.

"Sister Leticia, are we going to eat or not?"

Letty pointed to the door.

"A gentleman always opens a door for a lady."

"Yeah, so?"

Letty grabbed the door and yanked it open, then let it shut in Eulis's face.

Eulis groaned. He'd done it again. Dang it, she was just going to have to give him a little more time to get used to their new identities. After all, she'd been a whore a whole lot longer than she'd been Sister Leticia.

He opened the door and hurried out, running to keep up with the pissed off woman who was stomping down the stairs.

It was nearing sundown when Mary Farmer walked out of the dry goods store and out onto the sidewalk. Since Plum Creek had no church, they'd decided to hold the wedding at the dogtrot between the hotel and the telegraph office. There was a roof over the alley, which would serve as a fine shelter in case of rain, and there was all kinds of room out in the street where the ceremony could be viewed.

And viewed it was bound to be. The news of the burly blacksmith getting wed to the Farmers' oldest daughter was something of a shock. No one had any notion that they'd been seeing each other, and gossip had been rampant until they'd learned of Dooley's heroism earlier in the day. By the time the traveling preacher arrived to perform the ceremony, the gossip had turned into fact and Mary Farmer had fallen immediately in love with the man who'd saved her life. Women thought it a fine and romantic reason for the wedding while the men were somewhat doubtful that it had happened that way. However, it was hard to deny the lovesick look on Dooley's face, or the smile on Mary Farmer's as she and her family came hurrying down the sidewalk.

Her mother's wedding dress was a tiny bit too long, but Mary held it up as she walked, and she had reason to want to hasten this wedding along. She wasn't certain, until she saw Dooley waiting beneath the dogtrot, that it was really going to happen. Then she saw that Sister Leticia woman, and a man in a dark frock coat and pants that she took to be the preacher, and knew it was going to be all right.

Dooley didn't know until he saw Mary's face that he'd been inclined to hold his breath. He exhaled slowly and then stepped forward and took Mary's hand.

He wanted to tell her she was beautiful. He wanted to say how blessed a man he believed himself to be. But he couldn't speak past the lump in his throat.

Mary's eyes widened with appreciation. Well, well, Dooley Pilchard was a man who cleaned up just fine. His hair and beard had been trimmed neatly since she'd seen him last, and the new clothes he was wearing, while tight across his shoulders, fit the rest of him just fine. She decided he was a prime figure of a man.

Eulis patted his pocket to make sure he still had the ring Dooley had given him.

"Are we ready?" he asked.

Mary nodded.

Dooley looked at Mary. "Yes, preacher, we're ready."

Eulis gazed out at the large crowd assembled in the street behind the young couple and was considering tossing in a little sermon for free when Letty started hissing. Hearing that always meant he was messing something up, so he quickly took out his book of sermons and turned to the page marked weddings.

"We are gathered here today to join these two people in holy bliss."

More hissing meant he'd said something wrong.

"Uh . . . wedded matrimony."

The hissing got louder. He turned abruptly and gave Letty a silencing stare that sucked her next hiss back down her throat. She hacked a bit and then delicately lifted a handkerchief to her lips and coughed once more before silencing.

Eulis turned back to the couple and took out a note on which he'd written their proper names and tucked it between the open pages of his book.

"Now then . . . Mary Faith Farmer, do you take this man, whether he's sick or well, to be your husband until you die?"

Mary's heart fluttered once and then she remembered the man who'd been hanged and took a deep breath.

"I do."

Eulis nodded with satisfaction. Halfway through the ceremony and he was still doing fine. He turned to Dooley.

"And do you, Dooley John Pilchard —"

Letty interrupted the recital with a hack that startled everyone. He turned, afraid she was choking only to hear her muttering something about a ring.

"Oh. Oh yes, I almost forgot." He took the ring from his pocket and handed it to Dooley.

"Here you go, young man. Now put this on her finger and listen."

Letty sighed. She didn't think Eulis was ever going to get this stuff right.

Eulis continued. "Do you, Dooley Pilchard, take this woman to be your wife even in the hard times and the sick times, to be your wife until she dies?"

Dooley's throat tightened with emotion as he felt his Mary's fingers clutching his hand. Poor little lamb. She was still afraid he'd change his mind and she'd be found out.

"I sure do," Dooley said, and put the ring on her finger. It had been his mother's, who'd been a sight bigger woman than Mary and it was a bit large on her finger, but Mary kept it in place, which seemed to him, a good sign.

Eulis knew the rest of this ceremony by heart.

"Then by my powers and God's blessings, I announce you man and wife. Give her a kiss Dooley. She's yours."

It wasn't exactly the words they'd expected, but the citizens of Plum Creek knew that it took when Dooley Pilchard lifted Mary into his arms and kissed her soundly.

"Well now," Dooley said softly, as he put Mary back on her feet.

Mary's lips were still tingling, partly from his dark wiry beard, and partly from shock. There was a lot more fire in this man than she'd expected.

"Thank you, husband," she said softly.

He smiled and squeezed her fingers. "I'm the one who should be thankful."

Then he turned to the crowd. "Cake and punch in the hotel dining room."

A cheer went up. It was done.

Letty was breathing a small sigh of relief as the crowd began to disperse. Most of them drifted toward the hotel, while a few sidled off to their buggies and buckboards to go home.

Eulis was shaking hands with people who'd made up the congregation while Letty gathered up Eulis's Bible and sermon book.

"Ma'am?"

She looked up and then stifled a groan. It was that damned cowboy Willy, or Billy, or whatever his name.

She clutched the books close to her breast and stepped backward as if his mere presence was a personal affront.

"Sir?"

He frowned and moved forward. "It's sure something," he muttered.

Letty frowned.

"You shore do look like this woman I knew."

"Indeed?" Letty said.

He nodded and moved another step forward.

"Sir, you are getting far too close for good manners. I must ask you to step back."

The cowboy frowned. "But you shore don't talk like her."

"Then that must mean I'm someone else, don't you agree?"

He thought about it for a minute and then nodded.

"Yes, ma'am, I reckon that's so."

"Then if you'll excuse me?"

It took him a bit to realize he'd just been dismissed.

"Oh. Yeah. Uh . . . nice wedding and all."

Letty sniffed what she hoped was a disapproving sniff and sailed past him with her head high and her lips clamped tightly in a small, angry pucker. She grabbed Eulis's arm and none too gently pulled him away from the crowd.

"That cowboy is back. We need to go."

Eulis sighed. "You're gonna have to quit botherin' me when I'm workin'."

"I don't know what you mean," Letty snapped.

"When you weren't hissing like a pissed-off snake, you sounded like you was comin' down with the ague. I can't keep my mind on my business with you doin' all that."

85

"I was just trying to warn you that you were saying it wrong . . . again," she added, and gave his wrist a yank. "Hurry up. I can feel that cowboy's eyes on the back of my head."

"It ain't my fault that most of your acquaintances knew you better without your clothes."

Letty frowned. She wouldn't let Eulis know that his words had hurt.

"Shut up, Eulis. Just for once, why don't you shut up?"

"I'm sorry, but you must have me confused with someone else. The name is Reverend — Reverend Randall Ward Howe."

Letty shoved the books in his arms and stomped off to the hotel.

Eulis grinned.

It wasn't often that he got in the last word with Sister Leticia, but it always felt good when he did.

Get Thee Behind Me, Satan

Thanks to Orville Smithson's rigid, strait-laced beliefs, his daughter Fannie was withering on the vine. Fannie was nearing twenty-five years old and people were beginning to label her an old maid. Never a woman to lay claim to great beauty, her bargaining power as a marriage candidate for Harley Charles, the last decent single man Dripping Springs, was waning by the day. Her attraction for him had been her strong back and wide hips, the same physical attributes he looked for in his breeding mares. Fannie wasn't kidding herself that Harley was smitten by whatever charms she could lay claim to. She was all too aware that he'd been willing to overlook her rather homely features because of the fine dowry her father was offering.

Harley had finally proposed almost a year ago and the wedding had been set. Four weeks before the ceremony, the preacher suffered a heart attack during a rather virulent tirade from the pulpit and died in front of the entire congregation. And while Fannie was sorry for the preacher's demise, she was even sorrier for herself. No preacher meant she was not going to become Mrs. Harley Charles anytime soon. What was even worse, she'd heard rumors that Harley was seeing one of those women down at Griggs' Saloon. Even though she didn't really hold him accountable for succumbing to his manly needs, she feared that the longer he had to wait for her, the less likely he might want to become her husband. The pressure of it all had finally boiled over last night and during a fit of pique she'd told her father that if he didn't find a preacher to marry them before the month was out, that she wasn't going to marry anyone at all. Ever.

The ultimatum had been a low blow and she knew it. Her father, Orville, had been courting Henrietta Lewis, a local widow, for several months and Fannie suspected he'd been counting on her moving out to clear the way for a new wife. Since her mother's death, Fannie had been the "lady of the house" and Orville was wily enough in the ways of women to know that he couldn't bring a second wife into his house and unseat his daughter's place without a whole lot of friction.

Now, Fannie sat silently at the breakfast table, watching her father sop up the remaining sorghum molasses on his plate with the last of the biscuits. He had a way of eating that she absolutely abhorred, yet as the daughter of the house, knew it was not her place to correct her father's table manners. Still, as she watched him push two halves of a biscuit through a well of dark cane sorghum then slap them together before stuffing them in his mouth, she couldn't help but wonder if Mrs. Lewis had ever seen him eat.

His silence regarding her complaints was getting on her nerves. She wanted answers. She wanted action. She wanted out of this house before what was left of her dried up and blew away.

"Father."

"Whttt?"

Fannie sighed and ignored the fact that he was speaking with his mouth full.

"I am going to do some shopping this morning. Is there anything you need that I should add to the list?"

"Shvvvvng ssop."

Fannie frowned. "I'll add shaving soap

to the list. Should I expect you home for the noon meal?"

"Hmm ummp."

"Dining with Mrs. Lewis, then, are you?"

Orville blushed and then nodded. It didn't seem right that his daughter should be discussing his relationship with Henrietta, especially since Henrietta had started letting him feel her breasts. Of course, Fannie didn't know he was feeling up the widow's breasts, but it still seemed awkward.

He pushed his chair back from the table and stood abruptly, taking one last swallow of his coffee to wash down the biscuit and sorghum.

"Father."

Still bothered by Henrietta's breasts and Fannie's curiosity in the same thought, he was more abrupt than usual.

"What?"

"Are you going to the shop now?"

As barber and sometimes dentist, Orville was never at a loss for customers and hated to keep them waiting. Besides that, he was still peeved at her for giving him an ultimatum about finding a preacher. He glanced at his pocket watch before dropping it back in his pocket.

"Yes. What did you want? It's almost seven o'clock and if I don't hurry, I'll be late."

"Aren't you forgetting something?"

He frowned. "If you're bringing up the issue of finding a preacher again, then I simply don't have the time."

"No, I wasn't talking about me."

"Then what?" Orville muttered.

She pointed. "You have molasses in your mustache."

Fannie stifled a grin as her father yanked out his handkerchief, then hurried to a mirror. Good. He was not only bothered, but also embarrassed, as it should be. That hanging judge who'd come through Dripping Springs in March had been willing to marry them then, but Orville had deemed it unseemly that the ceremony be performed by a man who's job it was to sentence criminals to hang. So, it was all his fault that she and Harley were still living apart.

Even though Harley was still holding up his end of the bargain by coming to Sunday dinner every week like clockwork and called on Fannie every Wednesday night to play whist, she didn't feel as if his heart was in it. Personally, Fannie didn't like whist. She thought it a bit boring and much preferred poker, but was not allowed to play a game of chance.

"I'll see you tonight," Orville mumbled, and started out the door.

"Father, wait," Fannie called.

Now Orville was thoroughly pissed.

"What it is now?"

Fannie held out her hand. "I'll be needing some money."

Orville muttered under his breath as he dug into his pocket, pulled out a handful of coins and dropped them onto the table, ignoring Fannie's outstretched hand.

"If you need more, just charge it," he said, and slammed the door behind him as he left.

His rudeness was, for Fannie, the last straw. If she had been born a son instead of a daughter, he wouldn't be treating her this way. Even Harley Charles was casual about her feelings, assuming that her opinion, if she even dared to have one, was not worth consideration. Orville wanted her out of the house but wasn't willing to go out of his way to make it happen, and Harley cared so little about her that he was making no attempt to hide his indiscretions with the women at the saloon. These were supposed to be the two most important men in her life and neither one of them cared a flip about her feelings.

She got up from the table and carried the dirty dishes to the dishpan when she stopped suddenly. She looked down at the cups in her hand, then back at the table with the sorghum smears and biscuit crumbs and put them back where they'd been. Her father didn't seem to think what she wanted was important. She wondered what he'd think when he came home for supper and found breakfast dishes still on the table and nothing cooking for the evening meal.

"That's what's wrong," she muttered, as she tucked the wayward strands of her hair back into the tidy bun at the back of her neck, and scooped the coins her father had given her from the table and dropped them into her pocket.

She might not be pretty, but she wasn't dumb. She had a skill that she was willing to match against any man in Dripping Springs, but putting it into action was going to take a lot of nerve — maybe more than she had. However, if she didn't try something, she was going to hate herself for the rest of her miserable, lonely life.

Her heart was pounding as she headed for town. Mrs. Patton, the gunsmith's wife, waved at her from the back yard where she was hanging a load of laundry on the clothesline.

"Good morning, Fannie," Mrs. Patton called. "Going shopping?"

"No, ma'am," she answered, and kept walking forward, even though her heart was starting to pound and her hands had begun to sweat.

She turned the corner and stepped up onto the sidewalk with purpose, then hesitated briefly as she glanced across the street to Griggs' Saloon. There were half-dozen horses tied to the hitching rail in front and a couple of teams pulling wagons in front of Mercer's Mercantile. She recognized Muriel Foster's husband, Richard, who was carrying a fifty-pound sack of flour on his shoulder to load in the wagon. Two of the Foster children were playing with a puppy in the back of the wagon. Their laughter and the puppy's playful yips drifted across the distance, warming Fannie's heart. That's what she wanted — a family of her own, including the pups. She looked back at the saloon. If she followed through on this impulsive stunt, she might be putting every dream she ever had in jeopardy. Then she sighed. Therein was the problem. If something didn't change, they would forever be dreams and not the reality she so desperately desired. So she took a deep breath, patted the handful of coins she'd dropped into her pocket and stepped off the sidewalk and headed toward Griggs' Saloon.

Myron Griggs had been born in Philadelphia. The fourth son of a well-to-do cotton broker, he'd been expected to go into the family business as his three older brothers had done. But Myron had looked into the future, saw himself as a middle-aged man still living under his father's thumb, and rebelled. That very day he'd packed a suitcase, taken all of his money out of the bank and headed West. He'd had no definite destination in mind, and he'd even considered going all the way across country to California until the stagecoach had stopped at a way station on the western edge of the Kansas Territories. The sun was just about to set and the sky a vivid palette of orange, red and yellows. He had taken one look at the sky then at the vast, seemingly endless horizon and knew he was home. He'd talked the station manager into letting him stay on until he could get a place of his own built. It was somewhat ironic that a way station and a saloon were the first two businesses, but not nearly as ironic as the fact that they'd named the place Dripping Springs when there was nothing but a dry creek bed to be seen for miles. The only time there was any standing water to be had was when it rained, at which time the dry creek bed would flood and take whoever, or whatever, was in or around it to glory. To date, a pair of Stanfield Smith's pigs, an old mule, and one stranger, had gotten caught in the flash floods and drowned.

Josiah Merriwether, the town blacksmith, had suffered a close call when he'd fallen into the creek bed one night while chasing a runaway horse during an approaching storm. The fall had knocked him out, and it was only because the stupid horse came back to see what had happened to Josiah and wakened him by nibbling on his ear, that he hadn't suffered the same fate as Stanfield Smith's pigs. Still, despite the intermittent rain and water, Dripping Springs survived and flourished.

Only now and then did Myron wonder what his life might have been like had he stayed in his father's business. Most of the time he considered himself a fortunate man, if a bit lonely. Peace of mind and being his own boss usually overruled any regrets he might have had and today was no exception.

He was standing behind the bar pouring a drink for a cowboy who'd stopped in asking about work in the area. Three men were playing cards at the back table while Dewey, his hired help, was sweeping up the floor. The sun was shining. The wind was brisk. It was promising to be a fine day. He heard the squeak of the swinging doors, which indicated a new customer.

He looked up then momentarily froze. Fannie Smithson was standing in the doorway. The first thought in his head was that she was looking for her fiancé, Harley Charles. Thank goodness Harley wasn't in here yet. It would have been insulting to Miss Smithson if she were to see her intended with another woman on his lap. It wasn't until she took a step inside that he came to himself and bolted around the bar.

Fannie's heart was pounding so hard she thought she might faint. It was the first time she'd seen the inside of a men's sporting establishment. She didn't know what she'd expected, but it wasn't this.

The room was large and rather dim. It smelled of stale air and smoke, although it had to be said that the place appeared cleaner than she'd imagined. The large mirror at the back of the bar was cracked from one side to the other in three places, the obvious victim of its locale. There was a steep and narrow stairway at the back of the room, the only way up or down to the rooms above. She knew for a fact that at least three women worked in this place and slept above it during the day. She knew because she'd seen them near sundown, out on the balcony in their scanty garments calling down to the men in the streets below. There was a scraping of boots against flooring. Startled, she suddenly realized she was the center of attention. The cowboy at the bar and the three men at the table in the back of the room were all staring at her. Not only that, but Myron Griggs was coming toward her with a startled expression on his face. At that point, she realized that what she'd been considering was not only foolish, but impossible. She clutched her hands against her middle and willed herself not to cry as the bartender spoke.

"Miss Smithson . . . please . . . you shouldn't be, I mean . . . is there someone you . . . uh, are you looking for your father? Is something wrong?"

Fannie cleared her throat. Even though she'd gotten herself in here, it appeared it was going to be more difficult to get out. Her fingers were trembling and her voice was two octaves too high and thready, as if someone was choking off her airway even as she spoke.

"I, uh . . . I mean, I was going to. . . ."

She shrugged. No need embarrassing herself any further by admitting the truth. The least she could do was lie and save what was left of her reputation.

"My, father . . . I was trying to find —"

Immediately assuming that something dire had transpired to force Fannie Smithson into his bar, Myron took her by the elbow and escorted her outside to the bench beneath the windows. Once he'd settled her onto the seat, he sat down beside her.

"Has something happened? Your father is not here, but I'd be happy to go look for him."

It was the sympathy in his voice that was Fannie's undoing.

"I lied. I wasn't really looking for my father," she said, and then tears started to roll.

For lack of anything else to do, Myron took a handkerchief from his pocket and handed it to her.

"Please don't cry, Miss Smithson."

She swiped at her tears with his handkerchief then delicately blew her nose before crumpling it into a wad between her fingers.

"I'm not crying," she muttered.

Myron looked at the tears in her eyes and sighed. It had been years since he'd kept company with a decent woman and wasn't sure what to do next. However, he was convinced that arguing with Fannie Smithson wasn't smart, even if he could still see the tears.

"Yes, ma'am," he said.

She took a deep breath and then sighed. There was no use taking her hurt feelings out on Myron Griggs.

"I'm sorry," she said softly and began fussing with the front of her dress, smoothing down the bodice as if it was the most important thing on her mind. "I wasn't looking for my father. I was coming in to talk to you about a job."

Myron's mouth dropped. "A job? Oh no, Miss Smithson. A saloon is no place for a lady like you." Then he added. "As for that, why on earth would you feel the need to work? Surely your fiancé would not want —"

Fannie slapped the flat of her hand on her knee.

"My fiancé . . . my father . . . everyone seems to know what's best for me without consulting my feelings." She drew a shuddering breath, unaware that it revealed her vulnerability even more. "You see, Mr. Griggs, I'm a realist. I know I'm not pretty but —"

Before he thought, Myron took her hand.

"But Miss Smithson, that's just not true."

Fannie frowned. "I'm sorry?"

Myron let go of her hand. "No, it's me who is sorry. I didn't mean to be forward. Please forgive me. Will you let me escort you to your father's barbershop?"

Fannie stood abruptly. "No, but thank you for your concern. He's already dismissed me for the day, so I hardly think my arrival at his place of business would endear me to him even further. As for my fiancé, he could care less about my feelings. He doesn't care for anything but my dowry." Then she laughed, but it was not a happy sound. "It's called a dowry, you know, but it's really pay-off money."

Myron frowned. "Miss Fannie, you really shouldn't —"

"Shouldn't what? Care that I will grow old without ever being loved? Care that

I'm nothing but a thorn in my father's side?" She shrugged as tears welled. "Maybe you're right." She stuffed the handkerchief back in Myron's hand. "I'll just be going now."

Myron felt as if he'd just failed a huge test, although for the life of him he couldn't imagine what he could have done or said differently.

"Miss Fannie?"

She paused, then turned around.

"You are a very handsome woman."

Fannie frowned. "I do not like to be made fun of."

Now it was Myron's turn to frown. "What are you talking about?"

"I am not blind nor am I fanciful. I am not a handsome woman and I don't appreciate your facetiousness on my behalf."

Myron's frown deepened. "I don't know what you've been told, but I can assure you I was not making jest of you. I think you're a fine, upstanding woman, as well as a handsome one. And just for the record, I think Harley Charles is an ass and your father, a fool. Now, if you're certain I cannot help you further, I will be getting back to my work."

Fannie's mouth was open. She knew because there was just the faintest taste of grit on her tongue from the dust in the air. However, she couldn't find the good sense to respond to what he'd just said.

Frustrated and embarrassed by what he'd just said, Myron headed back to the saloon. His hands were on the swinging doors when he suddenly stopped and turned around.

"Miss Fannie?"

"Hmm?"

"Exactly what kind of a job did you expect to get here?"

Unconsciously, she straightened her shoulders and lifted her chin.

"I'm quite adept at cards. I was hoping you would allow me to play poker in your saloon."

"Poker?"

She nodded. "I am proficient in several styles of the game."

"Poker."

A slight frown creased Fannie's brow. "Yes, Mr. Griggs. Poker. Are you hard of hearing?"

He grinned. Not only was Fannie Smithson a handsome woman, but it would seem she had her fair share of grit.

"No, ma'am, my hearing is just fine."

"Well then," she said, and started to walk

away, only this time it was Myron who spoke up.

"Miss Smithson . . . Fannie?"

"Yes?"

"How would you feel if I was to call on you this evening?"

Now it was Fannie's turn to be stunned.

"Excuse me?"

"I said, may I call upon you this evening?"

"Call on me."

He nodded.

"This evening."

He nodded again.

Fannie blushed. "I'm spoken for."

"I don't see a ring on your finger."

Unconsciously, Fannie touched the third finger on her left hand. It wasn't the first time that the thought had occurred to her, either. Harley had asked for her hand in marriage, but he'd never given her an engagement ring, and after the preacher's demise, he'd quit speaking of their impending marriage at all.

"I don't have one," she muttered.

"Then what do you say?" he asked.

"About what?"

He sighed. "Now whose hearing is defective?"

She glanced toward the upper floor of

the saloon, imagining the sleeping trollops in their beds of sin and tried to imagine what he expected of her.

Myron could tell she'd been taken aback, but she couldn't be more surprised than he'd been when he'd asked to come calling.

"So, Fannie Smithson, what do you say?"

She pointed to the second story of the saloon.

"I am not as those women are," she stated.

He frowned. "Of course, you're not. I would never have assumed you to be so."

"Then sir, I must ask, what are your intentions?"

Myron looked at her dark eyes and the sturdy cut of her chin and shoulders and grinned.

"It's like this Miss Fannie, it's just occurred to me that I have been wasting a lot of years by not seeing your charms before this and . . . well . . . I reckon I intend to send Harley Charles begging."

Her eyes widened and then she stifled a smile.

"Is that so?" she said, and hoped that the heat she was feeling did not show on her face. "So, if you would care to have supper with us, I expect it will be done around six."

He tried to imagine who he would get to tend bar and then knew it didn't matter.

"Yes, ma'am, you can count on me."

Fannie smiled.

"Until six," she said, and started backtracking toward home as fast as her feet would take her. She had a kitchen to clean and a house to put to rights. She didn't know what her father was going to say about the owner of the saloon eating a meal in their home, but for once, she didn't care. Myron Griggs had shown her more interest and kindness in the last thirty minutes than her father or Harley had ever done. She paused once as she reached the corner of the sidewalk and looked back. To her surprise, Myron Griggs was standing in the doorway to the saloon, still watching her go.

He waved.

She hesitated briefly, then lifted her hand and waved back. Then stunned by what she'd just done, she turned around and ran the rest of the way home.

Hours later, Orville Smithson came home, found Fannie in the kitchen taking a dried apple cobbler out of the oven and chicken frying on the stove and rubbed his hands together in anticipation of the meal.

"This looks like a fine meal, daughter. What's the occasion?"

"Company is coming to supper," Fannie said, and turned the chicken in the frying pan before adding a small stick of wood to the stove. "Would you mind opening the window a bit, Father? It's getting hot in here."

"Certainly," Orville said, and opened the windows beside their dining table. A tired breeze stirred the curtains just enough to let them know it was there. "What time is Harley coming?"

Fannie stopped. "Oh, it isn't Harley. I haven't seen him in days. Have you?"

Orville was so taken aback by the news that it wasn't Harley they would be entertaining that, for a moment, he forgot to ask who was coming.

"No, I haven't seen Harley, but I'm sure he —"

"He's been keeping regular company with the whores at Myron Griggs' saloon."

Orville gasped. Not only was he shocked that she'd used the word whores, but that she knew of Harley's indiscretions.

"I'm sure he didn't mean to —"

Fannie turned and faced her father, then pointed at him with the carving knife she was holding.

"Harley Charles doesn't care for my feelings because he doesn't care for me. He asked to marry me because he wants your money."

Orville didn't know what stunned him most — the fact that Fannie was pointing a knife at him, or that she'd figured Harley out. What she didn't know, and what he hoped to God she never knew, was that Orville was the one who'd promised Harley money if he'd take Fannie off his hands.

"Even so, you have to —"

Fannie's chin jutted as she pointed the knife in Orville's face.

"I don't *have* to do anything," Fannie said.

Orville suddenly remembered his place in this house and raised his voice into a stern shout.

"You will put down that knife and remember your place," he said. "You are my daughter and as long as you stay under this roof, you will do as I say."

Fannie blinked back tears, determined not to let her father's anger stop her.

"That's just it, Father. I am doing what you say. If it wasn't for you, Harley and I would have already married. You're the one who called off the wedding. You're the one who wouldn't let that judge marry us. So if you don't like what's happening, you're the one to blame. Now stop shouting at me. I have to finish cooking this chicken and then change into fresh garments before my company arrives."

Orville's frown deepened. "Your company? Exactly who is it who's coming to supper?"

"Myron Griggs. Shall I set a place at the table for you or are you going back to Henrietta's again?"

Orville stared. "Griggs? Myron Griggs who owns the saloon?"

Fannie pretended to study the question, when she already knew the answer.

"Why yes . . . I believe he does own his own business which makes him quite the entrepreneur. I do so admire a man who shows initiative in this respect, don't you, Father?"

"Yes . . . no . . . I won't have it," Orville sputtered.

Fannie stared at the chicken, pretending to misunderstand his remarks.

"I'm sorry, Father. Did Henrietta fix you chicken for dinner at noon? If I'd known, I would have chosen another course for us. As it is, it's too late to fix another meat."

In frustration, Orville grabbed a pot-holder and threw it across the kitchen.

"I was not referring to the chicken. It looks fine."

Fannie beamed. "Good. It's almost done. You might want to wash up. Mr. Griggs will be here at six."

"No. I won't have it."

Fannie shrugged. "Sorry. It's chicken or nothing. Of course, you could revisit Henrietta again. Maybe she's serving up something besides what you had at noon."

Orville blushed before he thought. Henrietta had served something different up at noon all right, but it had nothing to do with food. Then he remembered the point he'd been trying to make.

"I was not talking about chicken," he shouted.

"Good," Fannie said, and then gasped when there was a knock at the door. "That must be Mr. Griggs now."

She handed Orville the knife and dashed out of the room before he could stop her. She knew her father well enough to know that he was basically a coward and once Myron Griggs was inside their house, his manners would forbid any sort of bad behavior.

Fannie was smiling when she opened the door.

Myron took one look at her and found

himself dumbstruck. He still couldn't believe he'd never noticed her in this way before. He took off his hat and combed his fingers through his hair.

"Miss Fannie, something sure does smell good," he said.

Fannie beamed. "Come in, come in," she said. "It's just fried chicken and apple cobbler."

Myron groaned. He hadn't had anything but steak, eggs or beans in so long he'd almost forgotten there was any other kind of foods.

"I'm at your mercy," he said, as he entered the house and let Fannie hang his hat on the coat rack in the hall. Then he saw Orville walk into the hallway and knew that they'd been arguing. Probably about him. He nodded.

"Orville . . . haven't seen you in a while. Heard you're keeping company with the Widow Lewis."

Fannie turned and looked at her father as if he were a stranger. She hadn't known he'd frequented the saloon but she did now.

"Well then," she said. "Since you two are old friends, I'll go dish up the food. Supper will be ready in about five minutes." Then she pinned her father with a look that left him both nervous and startled. "Father . . . perhaps Mr. Griggs would like a sherry before dinner?"

"Yes, of course," Orville muttered, then waved Myron into the sitting room as Fannie disappeared.

"Nice house," Myron said, and then pointed toward a gilded mantle clock. "My mother had one of these back in Philadelphia."

Orville's complaint died on his lips as he turned around.

"You are from Philadelphia?"

Myron nodded. "Born and raised. Youngest of four sons. Father expected me to go into the business with him, but frankly, there were already too many Griggs' in the company as it was."

Orville eyed Myron curiously, wondering what else he hadn't known about the man who sold liquor and women on a daily basis.

"What business was your father in?" Orville asked.

"Not *was* in. He's still in business," Myron said. "Cotton, actually. The family owns and operates a dozen cotton mills along the coast as well as the cotton exchange in Philadelphia."

Orville's mouth dropped. "Your family is well-to-do?"

Myron grinned. "I suppose so, but then one never really thinks of one's family in that way, you know. After all, your mother and father are just that. Nothing less. Nothing more. Don't you agree?"

Orville nodded. Not because he necessarily agreed with the man, but for the life of him, he couldn't find the good sense to form a sentence of complaint.

"About that sherry?" Myron asked.

Orville frowned. "To hell with sherry," he muttered, and took a bottle of whiskey from the sideboard and poured two generous shots into two glasses. He handed one to Myron then took the other for himself.

Myron lifted his glass in a toast. "To Fannie," he said.

Orville stared a moment, then shrugged. "What the hell," he muttered, and the glasses clinked. "To Fannie."

They didn't know she was standing in the doorway, or that her heart skipped a beat when she heard them toast her name.

"Supper is ready," she said.

Myron downed his whiskey neat and then headed for her with a smile. He offered her his elbow.

"Miss Fannie, may I escort you to the table?"

Fannie smiled primly. "Yes, thank you." She looked back at Orville, who had yet to taste his drink. "Father, are you coming?"

"Yes," he said, and once they were gone, not only drank his whiskey, but refilled the glass and emptied it again.

Hard Luck and Honeymoons

Harley Charles ran a comb through his mustache, grooming it carefully until it curled just right at the ends. Satisfied that he looked every inch the handsome gentleman he perceived himself to be, he still turned from one side to the other, admiring his reflection in the mirror. Judging himself fit, he settled his hat at just the right angle and headed for the door.

He'd put in a hard day out on the range with his two hired hands, separating bull calves that were to be castrated from the rest of the herd. The summer had been hot and drier than normal and the dust, mingled with the scent of blood and the bawling calves had been wearing. Even so, he'd spent the day looking forward to riding into Dripping Springs. There was a woman named Lola at Griggs' Saloon who set his teeth on edge in a very nice way.

Just thinking about what awaited him in town made him lengthen his stride as he hurried out the door. It occurred to him only after he was mounted up and riding away that it was Wednesday night — the night he normally spent with Fannie Smithson. Now he was torn between duty and desire. He didn't want Fannie but he wanted Fannie's dowry, and to get it, he'd sold his soul to Orville Smithson, the devil in disguise. Orville had paid him a thousand dollars to propose with a promise of ten more when they were wed. He figured any woman, no matter how homely, was worth that much money. And once he had the money in hand, he was going to sweet-talk Widow Taggert into selling her land to him, which would double the size of his ranch and make him the rich man he intended to be. But since he needed Fannie to make this all happen, he reluctantly gave up the idea of Lola and set his mind to endure the evening of whist that lay ahead.

Fannie got up to refill Myron's coffee cup while eyeing the plate of rapidly disappearing chicken as her father and Myron ate in relative silence.

Orville was still in shock that this man was eating at his table and didn't know what to make of it all. He kept eyeing Fannie, uncomfortable with the constant smile on her face and the warm, almost familiar tone in Myron Griggs' voice as he praised Fannie's cooking.

Fannie basked under the compliments while trying to appear as stunned as she felt that Myron Griggs had told her she was a handsome woman and, in his words, "a damned fine cook". It did her good to see people enjoy her food, but even though she enjoyed them, she wasn't accustomed to compliments. Even so, Myron Griggs had done nothing but compliment her tonight — from the attractiveness of her hair, to her way with biscuits, and she knew her father was seething. That, in itself was a satisfaction she hadn't expected. Seeing her father furious, but helpless to act upon it, was oddly satisfying. As the meal progressed, she began to relax more and more. By the time they got to the apple cobbler, she was heady with the power of being somewhat in control.

"Father . . . Mr. Griggs, would either of you care for some clotted cream on your serving of apple cobbler?"

"Yes, please," Orville said, while Myron only shook his head and shook his finger at her in a scolding but playful manner.

"I've told you twice already to call me

Myron, and I would love clotted cream on my cobbler. I haven't had anything this wonderful since I left Philadelphia."

Orville wanted to be pissed about the unwanted guest, but he couldn't rid himself of his curiosity. Who would have ever guessed that the owner of the saloon was a Philadelphia blue blood?

Fannie picked up the cream pitcher then, instead of pouring, dipped the thick, sweet cream onto the servings of warm cobbler.

Still curious, Orville leaned forward, ostensibly to put a spoonful of sugar in his coffee, but it was to give himself something to do while he thought about how to form his next question. He dropped the sugar into the cup and then began to stir.

"So, Myron . . . you say your family is still in cotton."

Myron nodded. "Yes. I get letters regularly from Mother and occasionally from Father. My two oldest brothers run the cotton mills we own in Boston and New York City, and the brother just older than me works with Father in Philadelphia."

"So you're not estranged from the family or anything like that?" Orville asked.

Myron laughed, which made Fannie stop what she was doing and stare. She couldn't remember thinking a man's laugh a sensual thing, but Myron's exuberance was so delightful she couldn't help but smile with him.

"Lord no," Myron said. "Oh, initially they weren't pleased when I wanted to do something besides work in the family business, but they understood my desire to strike out on my own. In fact, I've been having Father invest some of my money over the years. He thinks my business of choice quite ironic."

"Why is that?" Orville asked.

Myron laughed again. "Because it's whispered in our family that great-great-grandfather Dupree, on my paternal grandmother's side, was a privateer."

Fannie chuckled. "Don't you mean a pirate?"

Myron's eyes twinkled in appreciation of her forthright manner.

"Why yes, Fannie, I suppose that I do."

Then he laughed again, and this time Fannie felt it all the way to her toes, while Orville frowned.

"I see nothing humorous about thievery," he muttered.

"Of course you don't," Fannie stated, and set the bowl of cobbler at her father's place. "Enjoy," she added, and handed him a spoon.

Then she gave Myron his cobbler, set the spoon neatly beside the bowl and stifled a giggle when he winked.

Myron quickly scooped up the first bite and then moaned in ecstasy as the flavors exploded on his tongue.

"Absolutely delicious," he said, chewing and talking at the same time.

Fannie ignored the faux pas in manners to bask in her moment of glory.

"Thank you, Mr. . . ." She stopped, blushed, then corrected herself. "Thank you, Myron. I'm pleased you enjoy it."

Orville was decidedly uncomfortable with their constant byplay of flirtatious remarks and tapped his spoon against his cup to infer his displeasure.

Fannie glared at her father, yet maintained a cordial tone to her voice. "Is there something you need?" she asked.

"I would like some more cream on my cobbler," Orville said.

"Here, man, serve yourself," Myron said, and shoved the cream pitcher toward Orville's bowl. Then he waved his spoon at Fannie. "Aren't you having any? It's quite good, you know."

"Why yes, thank you, I believe I will,"

Fannie said, secretly enjoying being the center of attention, and left her father to add his own cream.

Orville sputtered and snuffed about, muttering beneath his breath, and shoved the cream pitcher away without adding any to his dessert.

Fannie had just seated herself and was chewing her first bite when a knock sounded on the door. Almost instantly, she realized it was probably Harley, and suffered first a moment of panic, before reality set in. The meal that she'd just shared with Myron had been more fun than she'd ever had with Harley in their two years of courtship.

When the knock sounded again, she arched an eyebrow at Orville.

"Father? Are you going to answer the door . . . or shall I?"

Orville shoved his bowl aside and stood up. "You know who it is," he said cryptically.

"Was that a question or a statement?" Fannie asked.

Orville tossed down his napkin and stomped out of the room.

Myron swallowed the bite he was chewing, then laid his spoon down.

"Is something wrong?"

Fannie shrugged. "Not from my perspective."

"Then who's at the door?"

"Well, since it's Wednesday, it's most likely Harley. It's the only day other than church on Sunday that I ever see him. The rest of the time I believe he is frequenting your place . . . and your women."

Myron's face reddened. He wasn't aware that Fannie knew of Harley's rather public indiscretions.

"They're not actually *my women*. They consider themselves self-employed and I'm sorry," he said, and laid his hand over Fannie's clenched fist.

"Why?" she said. "It's certainly not your fault he doesn't really care for me."

Myron frowned. "That's not the first time you've implied that."

"It wasn't an implication, it was the truth," Fannie said.

Myron leaned back, fixing Fannie with a curious look.

"Do you care for him?" he asked.

Fannie didn't answer.

Myron persisted.

"You're promised to him, aren't you?"

"My father introduced us. My father is the one who brought up Harley's intentions. My father is the one who set a date.

If the preacher hadn't died, I would already be a married woman."

"That doesn't answer my question," Myron said.

"I don't know what I feel, but I know what I want," she snapped, and then stood up and walked away from the table.

Myron followed her to the back door, and when she would have gone outside, he stopped her with a hand on her shoulder. Fannie froze. It was the first time she'd ever been touched so intimately by any man other than her father. She should have been reminding him of his boldness, but instead she was surprised to discover how much she liked it.

"Fannie . . . ."

"What?"

"What do you want? Tell me."

She turned, and the words spilled out before she thought.

"I want what every woman wants. I want a husband who loves me. I want children and in the years to come, grandchildren." Then her voice softened until it was barely a whisper. "I don't want to grow old and die alone."

Myron knew just how she felt. It was an echo of his own sentiments.

"Fannie, dear . . . I —"

"What the hell is going on here?"

They both turned. The anger in the question was impossible to ignore, as was the indignation on Harley Charles's face.

"Fannie! I would like to know why you think this behavior is acceptable."

"What behavior?" Fannie asked. "We just finished a meal. Everyone eats. Would you care for some food? There's plenty of leftovers."

Harley doubled up his fists.

"I don't want to eat. I want to know why my fiancée is keeping company with another man."

Fannie put her hands on her hips and lifted her chin.

"Now we're getting somewhere," she said. "I'll tell you after you tell me."

Harley frowned. "Tell you what?"

"Well, I'll tell you why Myron was having supper with us, if you'll explain your behavior with a certain woman at Mr. Griggs' saloon."

Harley's face turned three shades of red before he went pale. He stared first at Myron, then at Orville, who'd just entered the room before meeting Fannie's gaze.

"I don't know what you're talking about," he sputtered.

Fannie frowned. "You mean you don't

know that you've been paying money to a woman for her favors? Somehow, I find that ridiculous. Now you're going to try and tell me that you've been doing it all in your sleep . . . that you're sleepwalking when you visit Griggs' saloon?"

"No, that's not what I was saying at all," Harley shouted, and then doubled up his fists and started for Myron. "It's all your fault. You've been talking out of turn and —"

Fannie threw the pitcher of clotted cream in Harley's face, which succeeded in stopping him dead in his tracks.

"You have ignored my feelings, and because I was raised to be a lady, I let it slide. You treat your horse better than you treat me, but because I was raised not to question men's decisions, I let it slide, but you, Sir, do not insult my intelligence. No one had to tell me what you're doing. I have eyes, and despite what you obviously believe, I also have feelings. I do not wish to be your fiancée anymore and since you never bothered to give me a ring, then I have nothing to fling back in your face but my words. So get out, Harley. I don't want to see you again."

Orville's heart fluttered. He also had visions of dying dreams. If there was no marriage, then his plans for Henrietta Lewis were over.

"Fannie! You can't be serious!" Orville cried.

Harley blanched. Visions of owning Widow Taggert's land began to fade.

"No, Fannie, you can't," Harley muttered, and reached for Fannie's arm.

"Get out," she said.

Harley grabbed her.

Myron grabbed Harley.

"Turn her loose," Myron said.

Harley sneered. "What is this? Surely you're not trying to pretend that you care for her, too?"

Fannie's face flushed with embarrassment. Pretend? Dear God, how much more humiliated could she be?

"I don't have to pretend," Myron said. "She's a fine figure of a woman and any man would be proud to call her his wife."

"Wife?" Harley said, and then laughed as he looked at Orville. "How much did you pay him? More than me, I'd say for him to be so vehement."

Fannie gasped. Paid? No, it could not be.

"Father! Please say this isn't so."

Orville couldn't meet her gaze.

Fannie would have turned and fled the

room had Myron not stopped her intent.

"No," he said, and then softened his voice. "Please. Stay."

Fannie sat down with a thump and covered her face with her hands.

Harley turned his anger and disappointment into rage as he struck out at Myron.

Myron took a step back, ducked the swing and then hit Harley square in the nose with his fist. Blood spurted. Harley grabbed his nose.

"Oh! Oh! You boke by dose."

"Yes, I expect I did," Myron said. "Now apologize to Miss Smithson."

Harley glared at Fannie. "Frr whud?"

Myron hit him again, this time in the mouth.

Harley screeched and then spit two teeth out in his hand.

"Oh! Oh! You boke by teed."

"And I shall next break your balls if you do not apologize to Miss Smithson at once."

Harley moaned and clutched his private parts.

"Bannie . . . I'b zorry," he mumbled, then spit out another tooth before turning on Orville. "Id's ober, bud ju dodn't get jur bunny back."

Orville frowned. "Bunny? What bunny?"

Harley started backing out of the room, still holding his balls.

"Bunny, ju owd coot. Bunny. Wun towsend dowwers. Webember?"

Myron stared at Orville as if he'd suddenly grown horns.

"You paid this slimy bastard money to humiliate your daughter?"

Orville moaned. "It wasn't like that," he mumbled. "I only wanted what was best for —"

Suddenly a shot rang out, then bits of plaster from the ceiling began falling down upon their faces.

Harley dropped to his knees and began praying for mercy while Orville stared at Fannie as if she'd just lost her mind.

"Daughter! Put that shotgun down before —"

She aimed it in Harley's face. "Get out."

He started to get to his feet when she shoved the gunbarrel up against his nose.

"No," she muttered. "Crawl."

Harley couldn't believe this was happening. Only an hour ago he'd been thinking about bedding sweet Lola and now he might never be able to get it up again. Not only that, but his looks had definitely been damaged. He didn't want to think about what that might mean.

"Now!" Fannie suddenly screamed, and cocked the hammer back on the shotgun.

"Doh, pease," Harley begged and began crawling out of the kitchen on all fours.

Fannie turned the gun on Orville.

"Daughter! Put that down this —"

She shot, missing his head by mere inches. The buckshot hit the wall to Orville's right, blasting a hole clear through into the next room.

Orville watched in horror as Fannie reached into the cupboard for more ammunition, at which time, he bolted and ran.

Fannie was so angry she was shaking. There was plaster in her chicken and a piece of wood in what was left of her cobbler. The hole in the wall was about the same size as the one she'd put in the ceiling and she wondered who she could hire to fix it, then wondered why she cared. She'd just alienated her father, kicked her fiancé out of her life, and humiliated herself in front of the only man who'd shown true interest in her life.

"Have mercy," she said.

"Fannie . . . give me the gun."

Fannie jumped. She'd forgotten that Myron was still here.

"Are you still here?"

"Yes."

"Aren't you going to run away, too?"

Myron grinned. "Not unless you shoot at me, too."

She sighed. "I don't know what came over me."

Myron took a slow step toward her and when she didn't turn the shotgun on him, he carefully removed it from her hands.

"Well now, Miss Fannie, I have to say that this was probably the most memorable evening I've ever spent in my life."

She moaned and covered her face.

"I'm so ashamed."

"Yeah, I don't blame you," Myron said. "You have one hell of a father. But you know, you're going to have to learn to forgive him one of these days."

"Why?" Fannie said.

Myron set the gun aside and then took her by the shoulders.

"Because we can't have our children's grandfather barred from the door just because he is an ass."

Fannie gasped. "What?"

Myron felt his apple cobbler churning low in his gut. He knew this was fast, but something told him that Fannie Smithson was too precious to let go.

"I know this is hasty, but I truly admire you, Fannie, and I would be honored if you would consider being my wife."

Fannie gawked. "Have you lost your mind? Today was the first time we've ever spoken to each other and you think I'm so desperate that I'll agree to something so outrageous?"

Myron sighed. "I suppose I have lost my mind, but it's all your fault for being so audacious. I think it was right about the time you mentioned wanting to work in my saloon playing poker, that I fell for you."

Fannie blushed. "I am a fool."

Myron touched her cheek, then cupped it.

"No. The fools are Harley Charles and your father for not seeing what a handsome woman you really are. And just for the record, I don't want your damned dowry. I don't need your father's money. I have plenty of my own. What I don't have is you. I'll wait for as long as you wish, but please, Fannie dear, please consider being my wife."

"You're serious."

"As a man can be."

"You truly consider me handsome?"

"Truly."

"I swear if you're making jest of me in any way and I find out about it later, I will shoot you dead."

He started to grin. "I believe you and I swear that I'm true."

Fannie put her fingers against her lips, trying to stifle the urge to cry.

Myron lifted her hands away from her mouth, then clutched them against his chest.

"So . . . Fannie . . . what do you say?"

"I say we're both crazy," she whispered.

He nodded. "Two of a kind. Perfect match, wouldn't you say?"

She sighed. "Yes. I say, yes."

His fingers tightened as his heart leaped. "Are you saying that you'll be mine?"

"Yes, but just remember —"

He swooped her up into his arms and swung her off her feet.

"I know, I know," he said, as he started to laugh. "If I'm lying, you'll shoot me dead."

"Where you stand," she added.

"Right," Myron said. "Now all we need to do is find a preacher."

Fannie frowned. "I've heard that before."

"I'll find one before the week is out," Myron promised. "So you'd better start sewing your wedding dress. I don't want to wait any longer than necessary."

"Truly?" Fannie asked.

"Yes, Fannie, dear. Truly. And if I can't

find a preacher, I'll scare the hell out of your father and have him marry us himself."

Fannie started to grin. She would never have imagined when she woke up this morning that by night she would have ended her betrothal to Harley, pointed a gun at her father, and promised to marry the man who ran the saloon.

All in all, it had been a very good day.

The Fragility of Woman

They'd been riding in the stagecoach for hours and the dust sifting into the coach beneath the limp green curtains was thick in the air. Every breath Letty took smelled of dirt, and when she gritted her teeth, which was often, she could feel the fine grit of it between her teeth. Added to that, she needed to pee worse than she'd ever needed to go in her life — even worse than she'd needed to go at Forney's way station. Being the only female on board made it difficult to ask for consideration. Determined to bear up and not call attention to herself, her intentions were changed when the front and back wheel on the right side of the coach abruptly rolled in and out of a hub-deep rut. It threw her up into the air and then back down so hard that she physically moaned from the pain. It was all she could do not to wet her bloomers so she knew she had to speak up. Desperate, she grabbed Eulis by the arm.

"Tell the driver to stop."

Eulis had been dozing when the stagecoach rolled in and out of the rut and he was still rubbing the side of his head from the impact of hitting it against the door when Letty grabbed him.

Boston Jones was riding atop with Shorty and Big Will and Morris Field, the salesman, had been asleep on the opposite seat when they'd hit the big rut, at which point, he had fallen onto the floor. Disoriented by waking up face down with a bloody nose, he reacted instinctively and grabbed onto the first thing he could feel. Unfortunately, it was Letty's leg — midway between her ankle and knee — and with a grip that was both unexpected and painful.

Startled, Letty screeched and kicked out in reflex. It was unfortunate that the first thing she connected with was the salesman's already bloody nose.

His scream overpowered her weak shriek as he rolled over onto his back with both hands clasped to his face.

"God . . . Goddab it woban!"

To her credit, Letty felt awful. She hadn't meant to hurt him. Lord knew it wasn't as if she'd never had a man's hand on her leg before. She pulled a handkerchief out of her bosom and stuffed it up against the salesman's nose.

"Here," she said. "I'm sorry. I didn't

mean to hurt you, but you startled me."

"Bercy," he moaned, and stuffed two ends of the handkerchief up his nostrils in an effort to staunch the flow of blood.

Eulis was still focused on what Letty had asked, and without knowing why she needed to stop, he sensed her anxiety. He side-stepped the bloody salesman as he stood, then grabbed onto the side of the door, bracing himself as he leaned out the window. Before he could yell at Shorty, the coach lurched again. To everyone's horror, including Eulis's, the door swung open, taking him with it.

Letty couldn't believe it. The horses were still running at full speed. Shorty showed no signs of slowing down and Eulis was gone. Horrified by what might have happened to him, Letty ripped back the curtains and leaned out the window, for the moment, her need to relieve her bladder forgotten.

"Stop! Stop!" she screamed. "Please! Please! You have to stop!"

Almost instantly, Shorty could be heard shouting to the horses. To Letty's relief, the coach began to slow down. The dust they'd been trying to outrun suddenly rolled inside the coach, adding insult to the multitude of injuries.

"Whud's habbening?" Morris mumbled.

Ignoring his question, Letty climbed over him and jumped out before the coach stopped moving.

She staggered as she hit the ground, then stood for a moment, looking back to where they'd been. In the distance, she could see a dust-covered pile of what looked like discarded clothing more than a hundred yards back. Terrified for Eulis, she yanked up her skirt and started to run.

"What the hell's happening?" Shorty hollered.

Boston Jones had been riding backward and had seen it all.

"Someone fell out of the coach," he said, and started climbing down from the top just as Morris started to crawl out. Inadvertently, Boston's foot stomped directly on top of Morris's head causing Morris to lose his balance. Instead of stepping out of the coach, he fell face first into the dirt.

His scream was a high-pitched wail of unbelievable pain, and then fearful his travail was not yet over, he scrambled to his knees and crawled under the stagecoach. With the horses still stomping and the coach rocking slightly from the weight of their movements, the chance of being run over seemed far less painful than facing the people with whom he'd been traveling.

"You said someone fell out? How the hell did that happen?" Shorty asked.

When no one answered, he tied off the reins and got down to see for himself. The woman who'd been a plague to them all was running hell bent for leather away and he wished her a fine trip. However, Boston seemed to be following her exit and Morris was now underneath the coach.

He frowned. Someone was missing. He looked again, and then realized it was Reverend Howe who was gone.

"Where's the preacher?" he asked.

Big Will pointed behind them.

"I reckon that's him laying back yonder in the dirt."

"The hell you say!" Shorty muttered, then reached up into the seat where he'd been sitting and came away with a gun.

"What you reckon to do with that?" Big Will asked, as Shorty started down the road after the rest of his passengers.

"Might have broke his leg," Shorty said.

Big Will frowned. "Hell, Shorty, he ain't no horse. You cain't just shoot him cause he's crippled up some."

Shorty stopped, looked down at the rifle then shrugged.

"Reckon you're right," he said, and kept walking.

"So what you gonna do with that gun?" Big Will asked, as he fell into step beside Shorty.

Shorty glared, then spit. "If that woman pitches herself another fit, I might just shoot myself so's I don't have to listen."

Big Will laughed. "She is a pistol, ain't she?"

"It's women like her that makes me glad I'm a single man," Shorty muttered.

"I wonder how come the preacher fell outta' the stage?"

"Who the hell knows," Shorty said, then pointed at Letty, who was now crouching over the downed man. "For all we know, she pushed him out and beat us all there to finish him off."

"Why would you go and say that?" Big Will asked. "They act like they like each other just fine."

Shorty shrugged, then spit again. "Maybe he went and farted."

Eulis came to with a finger up his nose. Startled, he gasped and sat up just as Letty rocked back on her heels.

"What the hell was you doin?" Eulis asked.

Letty frowned. "Your nose was all full of dirt. I thought you couldn't breathe."

Eulis groaned and then sneezed. Something that looked like mud flew out of his nose and landed on Letty's skirt.

"Oh that's just fine!" she said, and got to her feet.

The shift in her posture also shifted her bladder and she suddenly remembered her urge. Without a word to Eulis, she turned and dashed off toward a grove of trees at the side of the road.

"Where you goin'?" Eulis called.

Letty stopped, then turned and glared at him while lowering her voice to a hiss.

"I need to pee," she said, and then headed for the trees.

Eulis's eyes widened. "Is that why you wanted me to stop the stage?"

She kept running without looking back.

Eulis staggered to his feet. The horizon was floating about a foot off plumb and he could only see from one eye, but it didn't stop his indignation.

"Damn it to hell, Letty! Did I just fall out of that coach on my head because you needed to pee?"

Letty's face was flaming. If she had had a gun, she would have shot Eulis where he stood. As it was, she didn't have time to commit murder because pee was running down her leg. She was pulling up her skirts even before she reached the trees.

Boston Jones got a real good view of her bare legs and backside before she disappeared into the brush.

"Where's she going?" Boston asked, and then wondered why the preacher was picking his nose.

Eulis snorted as a tiny pebble fell out in his hand, after which he started to sneeze.

"You okay, Preacher?" Boston asked.

Eulis wiped his nose on the back of his sleeve then looked up. He forgot about being gentle and turning the other cheek. It never occurred to him that a preacher probably wouldn't be cursing, no matter what pain he'd be in.

"Hell no, I'm not okay. I can't see outta' one eye. I mighta' busted my head. I got rocks up my nose, I can't feel my lips, and all because she needed to pee."

He started limping toward the stage when he saw Shorty and Big Will coming toward him.

"What happened?" Shorty yelled.

Still pissed at what happened, Eulis opened his mouth and shouted, even though the sound made his head feel like it was splitting in two.

"She had to pee!" He pointed toward the trees. "Sister Leticia had to pee!"

In the trees, Letty was still squatting to relieve herself when she heard Eulis shouting. Then she heard what he was saying and cursed beneath her breath. Traveling was hell on women and that was a fact. A goat had tipped her over in Forney's outhouse and all because she needed to go. Now she was forced to endure more public humiliation because of a perfectly natural bodily function. It just wasn't fair. Men didn't have to hitch up a bundle of clothes, or find a place to hide their bare butts while squatting to relieve themselves. For just a moment, she almost wished she was still back in Lizard Flats at the White Dove Saloon. At least there she'd had her own clean bed and a bath every night. Then she reminded herself that she'd gotten salvation and left the sinful part of her life behind. However, she couldn't help but wonder what her decision might have been if she'd known how difficult it was to be a moral woman.

As soon as she was finished, she stomped out of the trees and strode toward the road. The men were straggling back to the stage, every now and then giving an assist to Eulis, who seemed unsteady on his feet.

142

She knew that he was hurt and she was real sorry, but it wasn't her fault Shorty hadn't missed even one hole in the road all day.

By the time she got back to the stage, Shorty and Big Will were up top. Eulis and Morris were inside and Boston Jones was standing by the door, holding it ajar for her. His lanky build and his greasy black hair made her think of a snake. Still, she'd seen worse and was inclined to withhold judgment until someone proved himself false. After that, God help them, because she would not.

She had one foot on the step when Boston suddenly leaned down near her ear.

"Feeling better now, are you?"

Letty stopped. Her gaze landed on Eulis, who was already regretting his rash behavior. He'd heard Boston's question and he knew Letty in a way that the rest of the men did not. To begin with, she was no fragile shade of femininity and right now, she looked like she was coming out of hell with her tail on fire.

Letty glanced toward Morris, who was cowering in the corner with his hands splayed across his face, then she took a deep breath and backed down off the step. Once she and Boston were on firm ground, she looked at him and smiled.

"Why yes, I am. How about you?" she asked, then grabbed the gambler by his dingus and gave it a hard yank. To add insult to injury, she added a short twist before turning loose and climbing up into the coach.

Stifled by both shock and pain, the blood immediately rushed to Boston's face and then flowed out as quickly as he grabbed his crotch and dropped to his knees.

"Ever'body inside?" Shorty hollered.

"Aagghh," Boston said, and threw up.

Shorty leaned over and looked down.

"What in hell is wrong now?"

Boston rolled over onto his side, drew his knees up to his chin and started talking in a tongue Shorty didn't understand.

"Hey, Will, somethin's wrong with the gambler. Throw him in the coach and let's get movin'. I got me some time to make up."

Big Will climbed down off the seat, thrust his hands beneath Boston's arms and lifted. Despite the gambler's best intentions, gravity prevailed and his legs dropped, which only increased his pain.

"Oooommmmyyyygggoooddd."

"What's wrong with you, man?" Big Will asked, and pushed him toward the open door of the coach.

Tears were streaming down Boston's face. He visibly shuddered as he reached for the coach to steady himself.

"Come on, man," Big Will said. "Shorty's on a tear and ready to go, so you need to get on inside."

Boston nodded as Big Will gave him another push. Boston tried to step up, but it felt as if someone had tied one end of a rope to his guts, tied the other end to his testicles, and tied it too short. He couldn't get his foot off the ground without feeling as if someone had clamped his dingus in a vice, so he crawled in instead. He was still on his knees when he glanced up. Letty was staring down at him in silence.

He whimpered. "Don't hurt me."

She leaned down until they were eye to eye.

"Were you speaking to me?" she whispered.

He whimpered again. "No, ma'am."

"I didn't think so," she said, while tucking stray bits of her hair back into the bun at the top of her head.

Eulis eyed Letty nervously out of his good eye and then ran his finger along the swelling on his lower lip. He'd shot his wad of rebellion and was now willing to suffer in silence, if only she'd let him live.

"I'm sorry," he muttered.

She didn't bother to acknowledge his presence.

Morris chanced angering her further by helping Boston into the seat at the same moment that Shorty started the team.

The horses leaped forward.

The coach lurched.

Later, the injured men would swear it was the look Sister Leticia gave them that kept them pinned in their seats. But at any rate, their journey resumed and four hours later, they arrived at Fort Mays.

It was then Letty and Eulis learned the bad news. The stage didn't go any farther. It was the end of the line.

Now if they intended to stay on the "Amen Trail" and play preacher and assistant, they were going to have to do it on horseback. And as if that wasn't enough grief, the past caught up with Eulis.

Eulis's eye was swollen shut, his lower lip was twice its normal size, and an upper tooth was loose where he'd hit the ground. His clothes were filthy, dust was matted in his hair, and there was a large purple bruise on his chin. So when they rolled through the stockade gates and Big Will jumped down and opened the door for the passengers, Eulis found his muscles had seized up so badly that he couldn't move.

"You firss," he mumbled, and pointed to Letty.

She eyed Boston and Morris, who were making pointed efforts to get their feet out of her way so that she could pass. Nodding politely at their thoughtfulness, she grabbed her purse and made her way to the door. Big Will offered her a hand down, which she gratefully took, and missed seeing the sighs of relief from the three men left inside.

Boston was nearest the door and got out next, wincing visibly as he stepped down. He picked up his bag from the pile of luggage Shorty had unloaded and started across the parade grounds to the sutler's store.

Both of Morris's eyes had turned black, his nose was swollen to twice its size, and he was now forced to breathe through his mouth. Once out of the coach, he picked up his bag and looked for the commander's office to see if there was a military physician at the fort.

That left Eulis still inside the coach. Big Will leaned forward and looked in.

"You all right, Preacher?"

"No," Eulis mumbled.

"Can you get up?"

"I don' know," Eulis said, and then proceeded to scoot across the seat toward the door, but when he went to lean forward, every muscle in his back protested. "Don't think I can," he said.

"I'll help," Big Will said, grabbed Eulis's hand and yanked.

Eulis came up before he was ready and went headfirst out the door in the same manner that he'd fallen out earlier. Certain that he was going to fall, he cried out in anticipation of the pain he would feel.

"Easy there, Preacher," Big Will said, as he steadied Eulis on his feet and then gave him a sturdy whack on the back. "Nice meetin' you, Reverend. You have a safe trip west and watch out for Injuns."

Eulis blanched. He'd been so set on getting out of Lizard Flats without being found out that he hadn't given that possibility any thought. Only now, he and Letty were at the last outpost of civilization. Beyond the western edge of the fort lay a lot of unsettled territory, the occasional wagon train trekking across the Rocky Mountains for California, and a whole lot of unruly Indians in between. This set up a whole new set of problems, which meant he and Sister Leticia needed to have a talk before bedtime tonight. They could always backtrack and head for the southern states, although he thought he remembered hearing some rumblings from travelers regarding the state of their politics. There were rumors of secession and going to war, and if this was so, the last place he wanted to be was in the middle of a fight. He'd had all of that he ever wanted to see in this lifetime.

He looked around, wondering where Sister Leticia had gotten to, then snorted, figuring that wherever the privy was, she'd found her way there. In all his years, he'd never seen a woman make so much trouble over taking a piss.

"Brother Howe!"

He flinched. Letty's strident tone covered the distance between them as surely as if she'd just whispered in his ear. He turned and then squinted his good eye against the evening sun. She was waving at him from across the way. Eulis waved back, then picked up his suitcase and limped to her.

"They have an empty barracks. It is dormitory in style, but we will each have a bed."

Eulis nodded.

Letty frowned. "You don't look so good."

It was impossible to roll one's eyes when

there was only one functioning, and it hurt too much to blink, but he managed a small snort.

"You don't say," he muttered. "Where's that barrack? I need to clean up and then we have to talk."

Letty's frown deepened. "I would think you'd be wanting to practice up some on a sermon."

"Sister Leticia, it might have escaped your notice, but I cannot breathe easily through my nose, and my lip is too swollen to speak comfortably. I intend to take a bath and sleep until sunrise tomorrow. After that, we need to decide where we're going next. We haven't a lot of money and —"

"Are you saying you want to quit preaching?" Letty asked.

Eulis heard panic in her voice and knew that if he said yes, her only alternative to starving was to go back to sleeping with men for money. He sighed. Being responsible for someone else's life was a new thing for him. He wasn't sure if he was up to it, but he wasn't ready to quit yet.

"No, that's not what I'm saying. I'm saying we might need to go somewhere besides West, what with the Injuns and all."

Letty paled. She had her own demons to deal with when it came to Indians. She'd been orphaned because of them, then taken to a sinful way of life because of that. Meeting up with them again was the last thing she wanted to face.

"We could try south," she suggested.

Eulis shrugged. "I heard tell there might be a war."

"Over what?" Letty asked.

"There's some that don't hold with keeping slaves and others that do."

Letty frowned. "And they want to fight a war over that? Surely we won't be fighting among ourselves."

"I don't know," Eulis said. "Southerners have their ways just like the Yankees have theirs."

"Yeah, well we're neither of those," Letty said. "We live out west. We mind our own business and encourage others to do the same."

"I still don't think we oughta go south."

"Maybe so," Letty said. "We'll talk about it later. Now come with me. I'll show you where we're gonna sleep."

They were walking across the parade ground past the sutler's store when a uniformed officer strode out of the doorway directly in their path.

Letty gasped and stepped back as the soldier paused and tipped his hat.

"Pardon me, madam. I didn't see you there."

Letty nodded and wished she still had her handkerchief so that she could dab the sweat off her face and neck, but the last time she'd seen it, it had been stuffed up Morris Field's nose.

"That's quite all right, uh . . . Major?"

The officer nodded. "That's correct. Major Lawrence Canfield at your service."

Letty extended her hand. "Sister Leticia Murphy, assistant to Reverend Randall Ward Howe."

Canfield eyed Eulis. "Sir, you appear to be in need of medical attention. I've already authorized the post physician to see to another passenger who also was on the stage. What happened to you people? Was there an accident?"

Eulis's mouth was open, but no words were coming out. Letty could tell something was wrong, but didn't know what. Still, she could tell she needed to intervene.

"In a matter of speaking," she said, and then took Eulis by the arm. "Once he gets cleaned up, I think he'll be fine, but we thank you just the same."

Canfield bowed briefly and then nodded. "Let me know if there is anything we can do for you while you are at Fort Mays."

"Yes, sir. Thank you, sir," Letty said, and then stepped aside as the major moved on. As soon as he was gone, Letty grabbed Eulis by the elbow. "What's wrong with you?"

"Get me to the barracks," Eulis muttered.

Letty shrugged. "Fine then. Follow me."

Eulis did, but not without looking over his shoulder every other step.

Old Sins and New Hope

The empty barracks building set aside for travelers was at the far end of the compound. There were bed linens on a half-dozen of the narrow cots and a washbasin and ewer on an old sideboard. A cracked mirror was hanging above the basin and a shaving mug with a shriveled cake of shaving soap stuck to the bottom of the brush lying beside it. There was a rusty straight razor on top of a piece of old linen that probably served as a towel. All in all, it was blood poisoning-in-waiting but Eulis glanced at it in only in passing. He was too busy worrying about the Major to give a rat's ass about shaving or sleeping. As soon as Letty was inside, Eulis shut the door and then peered through a dusty window to see if they'd been followed.

Letty frowned. "Eulis!"

He flinched. "Don't be yellin' at me. My head's hurtin'."

"I didn't yell. I just said your name."

Eulis shifted nervously and then took off his jacket.

"I'm gonna clean up some. You tell me if you see anyone coming."

Letty's frown deepened. "What does it matter if —"

Eulis threw up his hands and shouted.

"Damn it all to hell and back, woman, can't you just, for once, do what you're told without asking questions?"

Letty bristled. "You don't yell at me, you old sot."

"I'm a sot and you're a whore and we're gonna both be in trouble if anyone finds out I'm not the preacher I'm pretendin' to be."

Letty was pissed. Being reminded of her past didn't fit in keeping with her new persona.

"You want to say that again, only maybe yell a little louder? I don't think they heard you at the sutler's store."

Eulis grabbed a bucket on the floor by the sideboard and headed for the door.

"Where are you going?" Letty asked.

Eulis swung the bucket at her. "Well, Sister Leticia, I'm gonna go get me some water and then I'm gonna pour it in that basin over there. Then I'm gonna strip nekked and wash the goddamned dust off my achin' body . . . if that's all right with you."

Letty snatched the bucket out of his hand.

"I'll get the water."

"Why?"

"Because I'm not hiding from anyone and you are."

Eulis flinched. "How did you know?"

Letty sighed. "I didn't for sure until you just admitted it."

Eulis's mouth dropped. "You're sneaky."

"And you're lying."

"It's none of your business," Eulis muttered.

"You are my business," Letty countered. "I'm going to get the water. When I come back, we're gonna talk."

Eulis frowned. "We can't 'cause I'm gonna take me a bath."

Letty shrugged. "I've seen you naked before."

"That's 'cause I was drunk and you was desperate," Eulis muttered.

"Now you're the one who seems to be desperate, so figure out what you're gonna say because by the time I get back you're gonna tell me what's wrong, and if you're lying I'll know, which will pretty much piss me off and we both know that's not good."

Letty walked out, leaving Eulis to strip or run, and he strongly feared there was nowhere left to run. By the time she came back, he was sitting on a cot in his underwear and feeling more miserable by the moment. Every muscle and joint was aching from his fall out of the coach, and he feared the clothes he'd been wearing were ruined. It wasn't his best suit, but he only had one other one and unless they ran across another dead preacher who no longer needed his clothes, he might be back in buckskins, whether he liked it or not.

Letty poured some of the water in the basin, a bit more in the ewer, and then dug through her bag until she found a piece of lye soap and laid it by the basin.

"You can use some of my soap, but don't go wasting it," Letty said.

"I appreciate that," he said, but when he tried to get up, staggered briefly before dropping back onto the cot.

Letty frowned. "Are you all right?"

"No. I fell out of a moving stagecoach, remember?"

"Don't be a smart mouth, Eulis Potter."

"My name is Randall Howe and I'm going to get nekked now."

This time when he got up, he managed to stay upright. He stepped out of his drawers and walked stiff-legged to the basin.

157

"Want me to help?" Letty asked.

Eulis shrugged. "I don't mind if you pour that water over my head."

Letty nodded and picked up the bucket. "Bend over a mite," she ordered.

"What about the floor?" Eulis asked.

"Look at it," Letty muttered. "There's space enough between these planks to grow 'taters."

"Yeah, I reckon so," Eulis said, and bent down.

Letty poured some of the water over his head as he scrubbed at his scalp. When his hair was completely wet, she stopped.

"Wait a minute," she said, and rubbed the bar of lye soap through his hair.

"What's that?" he asked.

"It's my soap."

"Reckon that's okay to use in your hair?" Eulis mumbled.

"I don't see why not," Letty said. "Be still now. I'm gonna pour the rest of this water on your head so you scrub up that soap and let it rinse out while I pour."

"Yeah, all right." Then he added. "I 'preciate this, Sister Leticia."

Letty stifled a grin. "Sister Leticia would not be caught dead in a room with a naked man. It's Letty who's helping scrub down your miserable self and you know it."

Eulis chuckled a bit. It had been a while since Letty had let herself go and he realized he missed the old Letty.

Letty emptied the bucket, then gave Eulis a thump on the back to signal she was done.

"It's empty," she said. "I'm gonna go fill it up again. When you're done, I think I'll take myself a bath, too."

"I'll be done when you get back," Eulis said, and picked up the rag beside the shaving mug, sloshed it through the basin and began to wash the dust from his face as Letty went out the door.

She met Morris on the step. He took one look at her and clasped his hands over his newly bandaged nose. She ignored the implication that she was dangerous and kept on walking.

Morris eyed her carefully until he was sure they were going in different directions and then hurried inside, only to come up short when he saw the preacher, naked as the day he'd been born.

"Oh! I apologize for the intrusion," he said, and started back out the door when Eulis realized he was no longer alone.

"What's that you say?" he asked, then frowned. "Dang, Morris, you don't look so good."

Morris gently fingered the bandage on his nose.

"Neither do you," he countered.

Eulis paused, then nodded. "I reckon you're right."

Morris pointed toward the door. "Sister Leticia. . . ."

"Yeah?" Eulis asked, as he soaped the underside of his chin.

"Well . . . wasn't she just in here and —"

Eulis nodded. "Yes, what about it?"

Morris eyed Eulis's skinny shanks and potbelly, then pointed at his dingus.

"You're naked."

"Yeah, well, it's hard to take a bath without takin' off your clothes," Eulis added.

"But Sister Leticia . . . didn't she —"

"She went to get some more water so's she can clean up when I'm done. She's right partial to her baths."

Morris thought about it a moment and remembered how she'd been at Forney Calder's way station.

"Yes, she did insist upon a bath, didn't she?"

"Yeah, but there was the shit and all. Couldn't blame her for wantin' to clean up then, you know."

Morris nodded, then dropped onto the

side of a cot. If they weren't going to be bothered by the situation, he was too tired to care. He glanced down at the dust on his clothes and then eyed the basin of water.

"Do you think I might use some of that soap when you're done?"

"It's Sister Leticia's, but I figure once she's done she might let you use it, too."

"What is it I'm going to do?" Letty asked, as she carried in the second bucket of water and set it down on the floor near the door.

Her rapid reappearance startled the men as Eulis automatically cupped his hands over his manly parts and Morris reached for his nose. When she made no move on either of them, they both relaxed.

However, Morris was embarrassed to be in the same room with a naked man, even if he was a preacher, and the woman who was not his wife. He wasn't even sure they were brother and sister as they claimed, then decided it was to his benefit not to dwell too deeply on these people's business. Sister Leticia would be a formidable enemy.

"Nothing," Morris said quickly. "Just nothing."

Eulis was not so standoffish. "Morris

161

was wonderin' if he could borrow your soap once you're done with it," he said.

Letty frowned. It was one thing to wash up after Eulis, who she'd known for years, but she didn't know what she thought about letting a total stranger have at it, too.

Morris could tell by the look on her face that she wasn't liking the idea.

"It's all right," he said. "I didn't realize it belonged to you and I would never presume to —"

"You can use it," Letty said. "Just make sure you don't leave any hair on it when you're done."

"Oh, thank you, Sister Leticia. I promise I'll —"

"Save it," Letty said. "It's the least I can do after hurting your poor nose."

Morris patted the bandage. "Yes, well, it was an accident, right?"

"Of course it was an accident," Eulis said. "She's a little clumsy, but she's not outright mean."

Letty resisted the urge to roll her eyes.

"Thank you for the kind words, Brother Howe, and you're dripping all over the floor."

Eulis frowned. "So? We poured water all over it while ago when we were washin' my hair. A little more can't hurt."

Letty chose to complain instead of admitting he was right.

"Aren't you about done there?" she said.

Eulis dipped the rag back into the basin. "I haven't washed my dingus yet."

Morris froze. He wanted to look at Sister Leticia but was afraid to.

"Do it and be quick about it," she said, then added, "there's not much of it to wash so it shouldn't take all that long."

"You don't have need to malign my manly parts," Eulis muttered.

"I simply stated the truth," Letty countered.

Morris stood abruptly, looking frantically from the preacher to the sister and back again. Neither one of them seemed the least bit bothered by what they were doing, but he couldn't believe he was hearing this conversation, let alone standing in the room with them.

"I believe I'd best wait outside," Morris said.

"Good idea," Letty said. "Brother Howe will be joining you once he's done."

"Dang it, Sister, I was planning on taking me a rest. I'm still right sore," Eulis said.

"I like to do my washing alone," Letty said.

Eulis slapped the rag back into the water and then began sloshing it up and down his spindly legs.

"I might say the same, but I reckon it wouldn't do me any good."

"All you had to do was say so," Letty said, picked up her skirts and sauntered out of the barracks as if she was trying to sidestep a pile of shit.

Morris shifted nervously. The preacher had as good as asked them all to leave, but if he did, that meant he would be on the porch alone with Sister Leticia. He wasn't sure his body could take any more abuse.

"I suppose I should give you some privacy, too," Morris said.

Eulis nodded.

Morris sighed.

"Uh . . . I'll just uh . . . be right outside."

He nodded again as he dug the wet rag into one ear and then the other.

"Let me know if you need anything," Morris added.

Eulis didn't answer and Morris was left with nowhere to go but out.

Letty was sitting on a bench to the right of the door with her arms folded across her chest and her eyes squinted slightly against the glare of the setting sun.

Morris closed the door quietly behind

him and chose a seat on the bench to the left of the door. He fidgeted some with his collar and his coat while keeping a wary eye on the Sister.

Letty knew he was there, but for the time being she chose to ignore him. Besides, it was hard to look at the man and not laugh. What with his black eyes and the bandage on his nose, he looked a whole lot like a raccoon. She leaned against the outer wall of the barracks and closed her eyes, listening to the sounds of the fort and wondering why Eulis was so spooked and wondering where they would go from here. Even though it was a bit unsettling not to know where their next meals were coming from or if they would find a place to set up a preaching session, it was still better than dancing with drunks and sleeping with men for money.

Morris, on the other hand, couldn't relax. All he wanted to do was hawk his wares at the sutler's store and catch the next stage heading east. Being self-employed had seemed like a fine thing when he'd started on this trip, but that was two months ago. He wanted to go back to civilization where women still fainted at the sight of a mouse and tended to their men with unswerving devotion. The women out here were far too hardy and independent to suit him.

Then he glanced at Sister Leticia. In his estimation, she was a prime example of what a woman should not be. Outwardly, she seemed feminine enough, but there was something else. He frowned. He couldn't put his finger on exactly what it was, but she was different. He didn't know a woman who would have knowingly gone into a room where a man was bathing, but she had. What was that all about? Even more confusing, who were they? They weren't like any religious people he'd ever known. But then he looked out onto the parade grounds to the mounted soldiers coming and going and the unseen dangers of the land beyond and decided that nothing was normal out here, including the people. At that point, the door between him and Sister Leticia opened. The preacher came out.

"I'm done, Sister Leticia."

Letty got up. "Thank you, Brother Howe." She glanced at Morris on her way into the barracks. "I won't be long."

"Yes, ma'am."

Eulis sat down on the bench that Letty had vacated and then glanced nervously around.

166

"How's your eye feeling?" Morris asked.

Eulis touched the one swollen shut and then ran a finger along his busted bottom lip.

"It's some sore, but I reckon it'll heal up all right. How about your nose?"

"Broken."

They both thought about their injuries then glanced toward the door. It as all that stood between them and the Sister. Even if Eulis was somewhat pissed at her for what he'd endured, he felt obligated to say something in her defense.

"She's usually a real gentle soul."

Morris's eyebrows arched perceptibly, at which point he winced.

"I'm sure," Morris said, then folded his hands and leaned back. "It's right hot, isn't it?"

Eulis shrugged. "It's August."

"Since this is my first trip out West, I'm assuming your answer means this is normal temperature for this time of year."

"Yep."

"When does it usually start to cool down?"

"First frost or first snow, whichever comes first."

Morris frowned. This just reinforced his decision to go home. He could always work in Boston. At least there, you had warning when the seasons were going to change.

"I'm going to catch the next stage east," Morris said. "What are your plans?"

Eulis glanced toward the officer's quarters. "Not sure. Might head up north."

"Well, when the doctor was fixing my nose, I heard that someone in Dripping Springs was looking for a preacher."

Eulis sat up a little straighter. "Dripping Springs? Where is Dripping Springs?"

"I don't know. You might ask the Major."

That was the last thing Eulis intended to do, but he wasn't going to talk to Morris about it. Still, the news that he was needed made him feel a bit better. Now all he had to do was get out of Fort Mays without being hanged.

He was still trying to come up with a plan when Letty opened the door and came out. She was wearing a modest wrapper and the same slippers he'd seen her wear in her room back at the White Dove Saloon. It wasn't exactly proper ladylike clothing, but she was all covered up, which was really what mattered if they were to continue their charade.

"Mr. Morris, I am finished with my bathing. I left enough water in the bucket for you and the soap is on the table. I trust it will be enough."

Morris was so pleased by the normalcy of their conversation that he actually bowed when he stood.

"I thank you again for sharing your soap. I won't be long. Then maybe after we've bathed, we can go to the mess hall and eat with the soldiers. The doctor said that stage passengers are always invited."

"Good," Letty said. "I'm hungry."

Morris slipped past her and in his haste to get inside, he stubbed his toe on the threshold and started to fall. On instinct, Letty grabbed him by the back of the coat near the collar and yanked. Morris flew backward, landing on his backside unusually hard, which jolted loose a rather large fart. He groaned.

"Sister Leticia, I am so —"

Letty interrupted. "Didn't mean to grab you so hard, but I was afraid you'd fall and hurt your nose again."

Morris was so happy she wasn't going for her gun that he rolled to his feet. If she was willing to pretend the fart had never happened, Lord only knew he was willing to do the same.

"Yes. Thank you," he said, then straightened his coat, raised his chin and walked

169

into the barracks and closed the door.

Letty looked at Eulis, then grinned.

"I got them all buffaloed, don't I?"

Eulis frowned. "You don't need to be so proud about it."

Letty shrugged. "If I'd known being proper had this much power, I might have tried it years ago."

She sat down beside Eulis, then lowered her voice.

"Talk to me."

Eulis pretended ignorance. "Morris says that a preacher is needed in Dripping Springs."

"That's good," Letty said. "But that's not what I'm talking about and you know it."

Eulis glanced around, then hunched his shoulders.

"I can't talk about it."

Letty punched his arm.

"Ow. What's the matter with you? I fell outta moving coach, remember?"

"What's wrong?"

Eulis sighed. In all the years he'd known Letty Murphy, he had yet to win an argument from her. But this wasn't just about an argument. It was about his life.

"Dang it, Letty, why can't you let sleepin' dogs lie?"

"Who is the sleeping dog? Is it that

Major? What's his name, Banfield?"

"Canfield," Eulis said, and then realized that he'd fallen into her trap.

"You know him, don't you?" Letty asked.

"Sssh," Eulis hissed.

"Then talk," Letty whispered.

"We gotta get out of here," Eulis said.

Letty's heart started to pound. She'd never seen Eulis this upset — not even when Will the Bartender back at the White Dove Saloon had cut him off the whiskey.

"Tell me why," she asked.

"If he recognizes me, I'll hang."

It was the last thing Letty expected Eulis to say.

"Why? What on earth can he —"

"I used to ride with Canfield, only he wasn't a major then. He was a lowly soldier, just like me."

"You were a soldier?" Letty asked.

Eulis slapped a hand over Letty's mouth.

"For God's sake, Letty, not so loud."

She leaned forward until their foreheads were almost touching and whispered.

"Sorry. So why would he want to hang you?"

Eulis swiped a shaky hand across his face.

" 'Cause I'm a deserter. I rode off my post and I didn't look back."

Letty straightened, and then stared at Eulis as if she'd never seen him before. She couldn't believe that the no-account drunk who'd barely sobered up enough to sweep floors for drinks had any kind of a past like this.

"You're kidding."

"I wish," Eulis said.

"Lord have mercy," Letty muttered.

"I hope He has more than that for me," Eulis said. "If not, I'm a goner."

Letty frowned, then got up and started to pace. "Shut up, Eulis. That's loser talk."

Eulis snorted, then groaned when the act caused him pain.

"That's because I am a loser," he mumbled.

Letty grabbed him by the shirtsleeve and pushed him against the wall.

"You are not a loser! You are a preacher. You have married people and buried people and baptized a kid with no name. You said words over a killer in Dodge City before they hanged him for murder. Losers don't do good. They do nothing at all."

"Fine then," Eulis argued. "I'm not a loser, just a liar."

Letty drew back her hand and slapped him square on the face.

He grabbed his face and then groaned.

"Damn it, Letty, you don't have call to do that. I'm already hurt."

"Do you want to be dead?"

Eulis gawked. "Well, hell no."

"Then shut up whining and help me figure out what we're gonna do."

Eulis drew back, looking at Letty with new respect.

"You aren't pissed off?"

She sat down with a thump, then put her hand on Eulis's knee.

"Isn't there some story in that Bible of yours that says something about having to be all pure and everything before throwing rocks?"

"Let he who is without sin cast the first stone."

Letty's eyes widened. She eyed Eulis with new respect.

"That's good, Eulis! Real good."

Eulis grinned. "I been practicin' up on my scriptures."

"Then there might be hope for us yet," she said.

"What are we gonna do?" he asked.

"Go to supper."

"But what about —"

"Are you hungry?"

"Well, yes, but —"

"Eulis, how long ago was it when you were a soldier?"

"I don't know . . . maybe seventeen . . . eighteen years ago."

"And what did you look like?"

He almost laughed. "I was the skinniest fella you ever saw. And I had hair . . . lots of —" All of a sudden, he started to grin. "I get it. So maybe it's a good thing I tried to drown myself in drink."

"It sure did a job on your face," Letty said, then rubbed a hand through his short, shaggy gray hair. "And your hair's a different color and some thinner. Somewhere down the road, you solved the problem of losing your pants with that pot-belly you've got now. Add to that the fact that your face is all red and skinned up and your eye is swelled shut. Your own mother wouldn't recognize you and we both know it."

"You're right," Eulis muttered, then slapped his hands on his knees. "And you're right about something else."

"What's that?" Letty asked.

"I'm hungry, real hungry."

She grinned. "Then as soon as old Morris gets himself cleaned up, I'll get dressed and we'll all go have us some supper."

"Then find out how to get to Dripping Springs."

"Right," Letty said. "Dripping Springs, here we come."

If Eulis hadn't been so stiff and sore, he would have done a little jig. As it was, he settled for rubbing his hands together in a gleeful manner.

"But first we eat."

Lead a Horse to Water but Can't Make It Drink

It wasn't until their third day at Fort Mays that Letty and Eulis were able to leave, and when the time came, they readily packed their things, mounted up, and rode out of the fort. Eulis was happy to put the fort, his past, and Major Canfield behind him, even though their mounts left something to be desired.

It was a hot, windy day as they paused on a hill overlooking the fort and looked back. The stagecoach on which Morris Field had been waiting was just pulling out of the fort for a return trip east. Boston Jones, the gambler with whom they'd been traveling had bought a horse and moved on after their first night at the fort. Letty had heard rumors that Boston had gotten into a card game with some of the soldiers and won big. There were also rumors that the game hadn't been fair, which figured since he carried a marked deck. She figured it had been in Boston's best interests to get out while the getting was good. Personally, she was glad to be rid of the lot.

Her horse nickered. Eulis's mount answered back with a bray, which was a large part of their problem. They hadn't had the money to buy good mounts and had to settle for a horse and a mule. The horse was old and mostly blind. The mule was big and broad and stayed in a pissed off mood, but the pair were oddly compatible, somewhat like Eulis and Letty.

The hostler who'd sold them the mounts had given them only one instruction. Aim the mule where you wanted to go and the horse would follow. Therefore, Eulis was on the mule. Letty was on the horse. It wasn't the most ideal of arrangements, but Letty and the mule had struck sparks off one another from the start. The mule didn't like her any more than she liked it, which left Eulis no choice as to what he would ride. If they wanted to get to Dripping Springs, he would be riding point with Letty following along behind — in the dust — on a blind horse that was being led by the smell of a mule's ass.

To Eulis, their situation was somewhat comical and he would have enjoyed a good laugh, but judging from the expression on Letty's face, it would not have been a good move. This momentary setback might be uncomfortable, but it wouldn't kill either one of them. The town of Dripping Springs was supposedly only a day and night's ride away. Without misfortune, they should arrive at their destination before noon tomorrow. Surely they could endure their discomforts for one night.

"Well, let's get moving," Eulis said, and turned the mule away from the fort toward Dripping Springs.

"Do you know where you're going?" Letty asked.

Eulis frowned. "You heard the directions the same as I did. If you have a different opinion as to where I should aim, then let me know now."

"I suppose we're going in the right direction," Letty said.

"All right then," Eulis muttered. "Giddyup mule," he said, and kicked the mule lightly in the flanks.

It responded with a buck and a kick and something that sounded suspiciously like a fart. Letty rolled her eyes. Someday she was going to live in a fine house and surround herself with people who talked pretty and smelled the same way. However, it did occur to her that if it got dark and she could no longer see where they were going, all she had to do was follow the smell, which her old mare was already doing.

A faraway mountain range broke the contour of the horizon, strung out along the edge of the world like a length of discarded blue ribbon. Something about the scene accentuated the emptiness with which Letty lived. She took a deep breath around what felt like a sob, then focused on the man and the mule in front of her. She couldn't afford sentimentality. That was for women who still had hopes and dreams.

And so they rode — across the unending prairie and toward the ribbon of blue mountains — bringing them ever closer to Dripping Springs. Beyond that, only the Good Lord knew what might happen and Letty was hoping and praying that He understood they meant no disrespect for their pretense.

They made camp in a grove of cottonwoods on the bank of what Eulis called a fair-to-middlin' size creek, which he explained was one too wide to jump over, but not deep enough to drown in.

Letty didn't care where they stopped, only that they had. She'd ridden cowboys

179

for the better part of her life and had never been as sore as she was now after only one day on the back of that mare. And as if that wasn't misery enough, she'd hoped to bathe in the creek. That dream had been dashed by the stupid mule who not only waded into the creek to drink, but had then proceeded to get down and roll until it was wet all over and the water was the consistency of thick soup.

Her mare had smelled the water and stumbled down the creek bank and into the water with such thirsty desperation that Letty couldn't bring herself to care that her plans for a bath had been thwarted. She unpacked their meager store of supplies, walked up the creek a short distance to try and find some water that hadn't been muddied, filled their canteens as well as a small bucket, and started back to camp.

Even though she couldn't see him, she could hear Eulis talking to himself as he gathered up deadfall for firewood. It sounded to her like he was practicing a sermon. She had to give him credit for perseverance. Never in a million years would she have believed that her moment of desperation when the real Randall Ward Howe had up and died on her — and in her — that their lives would have taken such a drastic turn. Sobering up Eulis, the town drunk, and passing him off as the preacher from back East had been the gutsiest and the craziest thing she'd ever done. That it had worked still amazed her. And here they were, following Randall Howe's itinerary down the "Amen Trail", preaching and marrying and burying wherever the need arose. She didn't know what awaited them in Dripping Springs, but after what they'd endured, it was bound to be a snap.

Still following the meandering creek back to their campsite, Letty paused to re-settle the canteen straps on her shoulder and get a better grip on the bucket. As she did, something rustled in the bushes behind her. She turned abruptly, and as she did, accidentally spilled the water in the bucket she was carrying. Disgusted that she was going to have to make another trip back for water, she stared into the darkness, trying to see what was there. Nothing moved. She stared for a moment more, then bent down, picked up her bucket and started backing up.

The sound came again, only off to her right.

Her heart started to thump erratically.

Whatever or whoever it was, there had to be more than one.

Letty never had felt comfortable being outnumbered and decided it was time to call for help. She raised her voice. Not loud, but enough that she hoped to be heard a short distance.

"Eulis!"

He didn't answer her, although she could still hear him preaching somewhere off in the distance.

She took another step back. The sound followed her — now from behind. She spun, the bail of the empty bucket held tight in her hand and ready to swing.

"Eeuulliiss!"

She was moving away now at a swifter pace, and because she wasn't looking where she was going, she fell. Head over heels — bucket up — canteens down — and into a tangle of scrub brush and vines. The vines came loose as she fell and once loose, automatically curled around the first thing in which they came in contact, which happened to be Letty's arms and neck.

Certain that she'd been captured by heathens and wasn't long for this world, she began to scream in earnest.

"HELP! HELP! EEEEUUULLLIIISSS!!! THEY'VE GOT ME!!"

Something rustled near her left ear — scratching closer and closer in the dead leaves and dirt as she struggled helplessly to get up. Now it was around her ankle, then her wrist. She whimpered.

"Don't hurt me," she begged, then took a deep breath and started to gag.

Eulis was right in the middle of his third recitation of the Ten Commandments and had gotten to *Thou shall not kill* when he thought he heard Letty call. He paused, tilting his head to one side as he listened. He heard crickets, some birds, and a coyote somewhere off in the distance on an early evening hunt, but no Letty. Shrugging off the notion, he bent down to pick up another stick of firewood and resumed his recitation.

"Thou shall not commit —"
"HELP! HELP! EEEEUUULLLIIISSS! THEY GOT ME!"

The hair on the back of his neck stood on end. Letty! Something was happening to Letty! He dropped the armload of firewood and started to run, calling out her name as he went.

Letty heard Eulis calling, but was too busy dying to answer. Every breath she took was followed by a retch that turned her guts inside out. She tried once more to call Eulis's name but couldn't stop puking long enough to say the word. She was caught in a snare of vines, lying in her own puke and as scared as she'd ever been, except for that one other time.

She was twelve years old all over again — listening to her father's dying screams and smelling the fire as their home burned to the ground with her father in it and praying that the badger hole she was hiding in would be deep enough to keep the Indians from finding her.

Her muse quickly ended as someone began pulling at her, freeing her arms and her neck, then dragging her out of her own mess. She wanted to see — needed to know who it was that had come for her — but she was still gagging too hard to ask.

All of a sudden, she was in the water and being dragged farther and farther from the bank. She gasped as the water washed over her face and up her nose. Dear Lord. Just when she thought she'd been saved, they were trying to drown her instead. With one last surge, she came up from the water, windmilling her arms as she tried to break free.

Eulis ducked to miss her fist, then let her go. Satisfied that she was coming to herself, he ran out of the creek and up onto the bank, putting as much distance between them as he could. There were some things that were stronger than friendship and being skunked and all that came with it topped the list.

"Letty! Letty! Take yourself a breath now, but just a little one. Easy now, girl. You can do it. Splash some of that water on your face and then breathe."

Letty shuddered then splashed, following the advice. It was Eulis. He'd saved her after all. She tried to get up, then tried to look up, but was beginning to realize her troubles were far from over. She couldn't see, and it was all she could do to keep breathing. Her throat was tight and swollen from the inside, and her eyes burned something fierce. Still, she did as he said, splashing water and then inhaling, splashing again on an exhale until slowly, slowly, the gagging reflex began to slow down.

"Oh God, oh God," she mumbled, then rolled from a sitting position in the water to her hands and knees. Her dress was plastered to her limbs and she could feel the long wet locks of her hair swinging back and forth against her face and neck as she rocked.

"I'm gonna die," she said, and then gagged.

Eulis sighed. Poor Letty. Once when he was a kid, he'd suffered a similar fate and he knew from experience that nothing but time was going to cure what ailed her.

"No. You ain't gonna die," he said. "You might want to, but it ain't gonna happen tonight."

She bent down and sloshed her face through the water, then raised up again.

"I am. I am going to die. Something got me. Something bad. I'm blind and my guts are coming out my mouth and nose."

Eulis shifted nervously and took a couple more steps back. He was upwind from her and it was still not far enough away to escape that putrid stench.

"You ain't blind, Letty."

"I am so," she said, and started to cry.

Eulis sighed. "Don't cry. Please, Letty, don't cry. You know how I hate to see a woman cry."

"Just shoot me now and put me out of my misery," she begged, then dipped her face in the water again to relieve some of the pain.

"I can't," Eulis said.

Letty slapped the water with a fist and then pushed herself upright. Her hair was plastered to her scalp. Her dress was saturated clear to her skin and near to weighing her down as she swayed where she stood.

"Damn it to hell, Eulis Potter. I'm begging you to shoot me to put me out of my misery. After all I've done for you, you're too big of a coward to grant the only thing I've ever asked of you."

Eulis frowned. "You're a fine one to call a man a coward, and it's damn sure not the first thing you ever asked me to do and you know it. I'm not the one who went and killed the preacher, but I am the man who helped hide his body and kept you from gettin' hanged. I've waited on you hand and foot at the White Dove Saloon every night for the past twelve years and you've still got the guts to stand there all stinkin' to high heaven and accuse me of not helpin' you?"

Letty's shoulders slumped. He was right.

"I'm sorry," she said, and shed tears anew. "You're right. I'm wrong. So please let me die."

Die? Why did she keep wanting to die? Eulis could tell that she wasn't going to get off that pity horse unless he dragged her. As badly as he hated to get close to her again, he held his breath and waded back into the water.

Letty staggered when he grabbed her by the wrist and started pulling at her. She kept rubbing her eyes with her other hand and bending over to puke, only there was nothing left to come up.

When she could catch her breath, she begged for him to stop.

"Eulis, wait. I can't walk in these clothes."

He frowned, then took a knife out of his pocket and started cutting at the cloth.

Letty screamed and started grabbing at herself. "What do you think you are doing?"

"Taking off your clothes so you can walk."

"You can't do that! They'll be ruined."

"Hells fire, Sister Leticia, they're already ruined."

She ignored the sarcasm as she swatted at his hand. "What are you talking about!"

Eulis paused. "The smell. It ain't never gonna come off the clothes, and it'll be a while before it comes off of you."

"Smell? What smell?" Letty asked.

Eulis gawked. She had to be kidding. Then he realized that if her eyes were swelled shut, she'd probably gotten it square in the face, which meant that the smell had so overpowered her senses that they were most likely damaged. On the one hand, that was unfortunate, but on the other, she wouldn't be likely to be complaining about farts anymore.

"You got skunked," he said. "Real good, or I guess I should say, real bad. It swelled up your eyes some and that's what's makin' you sick. That will pass, but you're gonna stink for a while."

Having diagnosed her situation, he ripped off the last of her dress, leaving her standing in her bloomers and a short shift that covered most of her top parts.

Letty, on the other hand, was so shocked by what he'd said that she didn't even object when he ripped away the last of her clothes.

"It was a skunk? That's what I heard in the bushes? That's what did me in?"

"I reckon so," Eulis said, and tossed her clothes into the brush. They were too wet to burn and their camp was across the creek so the smell shouldn't bother them much. Letty's presence, on the other hand, was going to be a hindrance to a good night's sleep.

Letty groaned and then gagged. "I still wish you'd just shoot me."

"I can't," Eulis said.

"I know, I know. You don't have the guts."

189

Eulis glared, although the emotion was wasted on Letty since she couldn't see his face.

"No, ma'am that's not it at all. It ain't from lack of guts; I just don't have a gun."

His answer was as rude as a slap to the face. Just as she was about to give him a piece of her mind for making light of her plight, her stomach turned on itself and she began gagging all over again.

Eulis cursed beneath his breath, tightened his grip on her wrist, and pulled.

"Follow me, and for once, don't argue. We're goin' back across the creek. You're gonna lay down and be quiet while I cook us some supper. Then —"

It was the word supper that did her in. She bent all the way over until her forehead was nearly touching her knees and puked until she finally passed out.

Eulis thought about leaving her where she'd dropped, and then realized he couldn't do that again. Like it or not, he was responsible for her welfare.

He bent down and tried to pick her up, but he'd spent too many years lifting nothing heavier than a bottle of whiskey. Not even his intermittent jobs of grave digging had prepared him to be able to lift Sister Leticia's dead weight. So he grabbed her by the wrists and began dragging her off the bank, back into the creek and then out the other side. By the time he got her to the campsite, she was covered with a thin layer of dirt, which was rapidly turning to mud and peppered with a second layer of grass and leaves.

He retrieved the firewood and quickly built a fire so that she wouldn't catch cold, then covered her up with one of their blankets. It was a shame to use it because the smell would stick to it, too, but he could hardly leave her there to catch pneumonia and die. Like it or not, they were in this together.

Later, after the fire had burned down some, Eulis cooked up a piece of fatback and made a pan of johnnycake. When he'd asked Letty if she wanted to eat, he'd gotten a moan and a gag for an answer and took it for a no. He would have liked some coffee but that would have meant a trip back up the creek. He didn't want to leave Letty alone, so he settled for a swig from one of the canteens and called it a night.

Letty had come awake only once in the night. She'd lain there for a moment trying to figure out what was wrong, but couldn't focus her thoughts. At that moment, she heard a whippoorwill call and wanted to cry. All her life, the whippoorwill had meant home and family — sitting with her mother out on the front porch as darkness fell and listening for the call of that small brown bird, then waiting to hear if there was an answering call from its mate.

She'd spent her entire adult life listening for the first call of the evening and wishing for a mate of her own. But it had never happened. Once she'd come close, but death snatched him away and she was too hardened by failures to care to look again. Only now and then, the call of a whippoorwill would remind her of what she'd lost, and she would suffer a moment of pain. But it never lasted long. Living was difficult enough without wishing for things that would never be.

And so she ignored the small bird and let her misery take her under as she slept the rest of the night away.

Letty came awake in increments, hearing first the shuffle and snorts of their animals, then the scolding chatter of a squirrel in a tree somewhere overhead. The early morning sun had found a pathway through the leaves and was shining on her face. She knew because she could feel the warmth against her cheek.

Eulis was reciting the Twenty-third Psalm and she could smell wood smoke, which meant breakfast was probably cooking. She started to roll over and sit up and then realized her eyes were swelled shut. She gasped, then moaned as she remembered last night. Frantic, she quickly sat up and began running her hands all over her face and her hair. At that point, the overpowering smell of skunk began to resonate all around her.

"Oh my God," she moaned.

Eulis looked up. "Oh. You're awake."

"That smell," Letty cried.

"It's you," Eulis said.

"I'm going to puke," Letty moaned, and rolled over on her hands and knees.

Eulis rolled his eyes. "Not again, and not here. I'm a'cookin' our breakfast."

"Christ All Mighty," Letty said, and then retched one for good measure. "Stop talkin' about food."

"Oh. Sorry," Eulis said.

Letty stumbled to her feet, then grabbed at her hair.

"What in hell happened to my hair?" She touched her breasts. "And my clothes . . . where are my clothes?"

Eulis frowned. Since her eyes were swelled shut, he should have felt safe enough to confess, but he still found himself taking a couple of steps back.

"I reckon there's some dirt and a little grass in your hair. Course it will wash right out. I can't say the same for the smell."

Letty gritted her teeth to keep from screaming. "I can feel the dirt and grass. What I'm asking you is how did it get there?"

"Uh . . . what do you remember about last night?" Eulis asked.

Letty threw her hands up in the air and would have stomped away, but she couldn't see where she was going.

"Going to get water. I was going to get water."

"You did. I used some of it to cook su—" Eulis stopped. "Sorry. I forgot. We ain't talkin' about cooking, right?"

Letty's stomach lurched, but to her relief, it was only a small spasm.

"Eulis. I swear to God when I can see again I will kill you with my bare hands if you don't stop beating around the bush. What happened to me? Why am I covered in filth?"

"After you got skunked, I dragged you into the creek to help you stop pukin' then you went and passed out on me and so I dragged you out of the creek and back to camp. I put you to bed all cozy like and there you stayed 'til now."

Letty moaned. No wonder the backs of her legs and heels hurt.

"I need to pee," she said.

"Okay," Eulis said, then bent down and took the frying pan off the campfire and set it aside. Wouldn't do to let their last piece of fatback burn.

Letty stood for a moment, then heard Eulis puttering about. She exhaled on a sigh and told herself to remain calm.

"Eulis."

He put the coffee pot down and looked up.

"Yeah?"

"I said I need to pee."

"Well, go on ahead," Eulis said.

"I would if I could see where I was going."

"Oh. Yeah. Sorry," he said, then hurried toward her. He took her by the arm and started leading her toward the trees.

"Here's good," he said.

Letty reached out, feeling the shelter of being surrounded by bushes, then she frowned.

"Can you see me?"

Eulis sighed. "Well, hell yes, Letty. I'm a'standin' right here."

She took a deep breath, smelled too much of herself and gagged again, and then hit him on the arm.

"That's not what I mean. If I squat down here, are you gonna be able to see me?"

"Not if I walk away," Eulis said.

"Then git."

"Oh. Yeah. All right. When you're done, just holler."

"I was hollering my head off last night and you didn't hear me."

"I'll be right over there," Eulis said, pointing to indicate his location, then grinned sheepishly. "I forgot. You can't see."

"Go away, Eulis. Walk away and turn your back, please. I am humiliated enough as it is."

"All right."

Letty stood, listening until she could no longer hear Eulis's footsteps.

"Are you looking?"

"No, Sister Leticia, I am not looking at your bare ass, although I am probably the only man within a hundred mile range that hasn't seen it."

Letty would have liked to give him what for, but the truth was a hard thing to ignore. Instead, she pulled down her bloomers and squatted, taking no small

196

amount of comfort from the relief of emptying her bladder. Now if she could only see and rid herself of the smell on her body, she might never complain about anything again.

A few moments later, she walked out of the bushes.

"Eulis."

Eulis turned around. Letty was out of the trees, but she was looking toward the creek.

"I'm here," he said.

"Oh," she said, and turned to face him.

"Do you mind taking me down to the creek? I know I won't be able to wash off the skunk, but I would sure like to get rid of the dirt and weeds."

"Yeah, sure," Eulis said. "Want me to go get your soap?"

Letty smiled. "That would be wonderful."

"Okay," he said. "Don't move. I'll be right back."

Standing on the Promises

Once Letty had given up trying to maintain any sense of modesty, she stripped down to her skin then eased into the creek. Eulis handed her the soap and then patted her on the head as she sat down.

"I'll wait for you up here on the bank," he said.

Letty hesitated. It would be comforting to know he was nearby, but she remembered the breakfast meat he'd been cooking.

"I'll be fine," she said. "You go on back and have your breakfast. I'll yell at you when I'm ready to get out."

Eulis eyed the buxom sway of her breasts and the soft curves on her body and then sighed. She was a fine looking woman, but that was as far as it went.

"You sure?"

"You don't see any snakes or such?" Letty asked.

Eulis looked carefully around. "Nope. All clear."

"Then run along."

Eulis waded out of the water and up the

side of the creek bank. He looked back once to make sure Letty was okay, and then hurried back to camp.

The water was spring-fed, so it was cold on Letty's skin, but she didn't care. She'd never felt so disgusting in her life. She scrubbed at her undergarments with some of the soap and then rinsed them in the water. Bracing herself against the swift flow, she then lowered herself backward until her hair was completely submerged and let the current have its way with the filth. Once the worst of it was gone, she sat up, scrubbed the soap through her hair and then rinsed again and again.

When she was satisfied with the feel of her hair, she began working on her skin. Time passed until only a small sliver of soap was left. She'd rubbed her skin raw and her swollen eyes were seeping tears. Her hair had been scrubbed clean and shiny, but she still smelled to high heaven.

She lifted her arm to her nose and inhaled, then coughed and choked. The worst of the nausea she'd experienced last night was beginning to pass. If it weren't for the smell and her eyes, she'd feel close to normal.

She combed her fingers through her hair several times to get out the tangles, then turned so that it caught the sun to let it dry. She thought about getting out and calling for Eulis, but he was probably packing up camp. He'd bring her clean clothes when he came back, but for now she would enjoy the quiet.

She sat still for a bit, feeling the current of the water pushing against her flesh as well as the layer of sand and pebbles on the bottom of the creek. There was a slight breeze in the air, but not enough to carry away the smell stuck to her skin. She wondered if she would ever smell decent again.

The birds calling to each other from the treetops, mingling with the circling air, and the sounds of running water filled Letty with a rare sense of peace. She couldn't remember when she'd been this miserable physically, and still calm within her soul.

As she was sitting in the water and feeling sorry for herself, she suddenly realized she was singling out a particular bird call from the multitude of sounds, and it was something she'd never before heard in the bright light of day.

It was a whippoorwill's call.

She turned toward the sound, hoping to catch sight of the small brown bird and then realized she couldn't see. The irony of it all made her laugh, but when she opened her mouth, the sound wouldn't come. To her horror, she started to cry. At first, it was nothing but the hot wash of tears seeping out from beneath her swollen lids, but soon the sobs caught up with her pain.

She'd been a willful and prideful woman who'd lived a life of sin. Just because she'd gotten religion and left the life of a whore, didn't prove anything. She remembered her impatience with the men on the stage, then the rage she'd laid at their feet when it was Forney Calder's goat that should have garnered the blame.

She was convinced that her latest travail was a warning directly from God's hands. He'd judged her and found her wanting, then handed out this punishment. Because she'd been hateful, even vengeful toward her traveling companions just because of their lowly behaviors, God had smitten her with a vile scent of her own — one that would linger long enough to remind her that only those who were without sin should cast the first stones. Afraid that she'd lost her religion before it had a good chance to stick, she laid her head on her knees and started to bawl.

Raven's Call had been watching the white woman from the opposite side of the creek bank for almost an hour. The smell of the small skunk was still strong about her, although she looked cleaner than when she had stumbled into the creek. The dirt and grass that had been stuck to her body was gone, revealing heavy breasts, strong legs and a flat, muscular belly. But her eyes did not open and she had rubbed her white skin until it looked like the inside of a gutted deer. He understood her misery. He knew of the fire behind her eyes. He remembered well the lingering stench and the laughter of his brothers when it had happened to him. They had made him sleep alone outside their wikiup. Even the camp dogs had refused to come near him.

He glanced back over his shoulder, checking to make sure his pony was still in sight, then turned back toward the woman. He had been gone from his camp two sleeps gathering plants and roots for healing. The gathering had been successful, and as healer for the Turtle clan, it was his duty to make sure he had what might be needed to get his people through the winter. Even though he felt sorry for the young white woman, she was not his problem. He stood up, intent on leaving before the white man came back, but then she started to cry.

He stared at the woman for a few moments more, then looked past her to the other side of the creek. The white man was nowhere in sight. He stared at her again and then sighed. If he followed his instincts, he should get on his pony and ride away. But the woman's misery was strong, and while he couldn't take away the smell from her body, he could ease the pain in her eyes.

Before he talked himself out of it, he stepped out of the trees and down into the water, ignoring the soaking to his moccasins and leggings.

Letty heard the footsteps on the creek bank and then the splash as they came through the water. She felt around and grabbed onto the undergarments she'd been washing and quickly wrung them out. It didn't occur to her that the footsteps had come from the wrong side of the creek or that Eulis hadn't called out. She was too busy trying to hide the fact that she'd been crying.

Before she could think of what to say, a hand encircled her wrist and pulled her upright. Clutching the wet clothing against her breasts, she let herself be led, then stumbled once when she stepped on a sharp rock. Immediately, she felt him catch her and set her back on her feet.

"Thanks," she said, and had yet to wonder about his silence. When she began to feel the brush of leaves and vines against her skin, she knew they were back in the trees.

"I still smell awful," she said, stating the obvious.

All she got for her truth was a grunt. She shrugged it off, figuring Eulis was taking the high road by no comment at all.

A few moments more and she heard the snort of a horse. When the hand on her wrist moved from her arm to her shoulder and pushed, she took it as a sign to stop.

"Eulis, I need my clothes," she said.

He didn't answer, but she heard him walking through the brush, then heard a low, steady murmur as he steadied the horse with a sound that resembled a low hum.

She frowned. That didn't sound like something Eulis might do. Still, being sightless made everything seem frightening and strange, so she didn't question her confusion.

"Come on, Eulis. I'm not claiming any large amount of modesty, but be fair. Please hand me some clothes."

She stretched out her hand, expecting to feel fabric. Instead, she felt something like grass or leaves in her palm. She fingered it, then decided it was leaves and lifted them to her nose. They had a sharp, medicinal smell and when she crushed one, it left an odd, oily substance on her skin.

"What's this?" she said.

He touched her eyes then put her hand on the leaves then touched her eyes again.

"You want me to put this on my eyes?" she asked, and took a leaf and held it near her face.

He moved her hand to her eyes then gently pushed until the crushed leaves were lying next to her skin.

Almost immediately, her burning eyelids felt a measure of relief.

"Oooh, that feels good," she said, and reached back into her palm, took another pinch of the leaves, crushed them between her fingers and rubbed it on her other eye.

She felt him put more leaves in her hand, then he touched her on the shoulder in what felt like a gesture of goodbye, which she found strange. Moments later, she heard the shuffle of feet and then the horse nicker as it accepted the man's weight.

"Eulis?"

He didn't answer. She curled her fingers

around the precious stash of leaves and then reached out with her other hand, searching for his location while thinking, surely to God he isn't going to run off and leave me.

She lunged forward, felt the familiar warmth of the horse's shoulder and realized there was no saddle and that made no sense. On a good day, Eulis was not much of a rider. Bareback, he would have been laughable, and yet someone had mounted this horse.

She moved her hand again. Instead of Eulis's long, bony leg, she felt a strong, muscular calf encased in wet buckskin. This wasn't Eulis.

"Oh. Oh, God," she said softly and instinctively crossed her arms across her breasts, although to be honest it was way past the time for modesty. "Who are you?"

She heard what sounded like a sigh. When she frowned, she heard a soft chuckle. The sound was foreign to anything Eulis had ever done, but at the same time, it was still very male. It frightened her and intrigued her. Whoever it was obviously meant her no harm or he would have already taken advantage of her state of undress.

Frustrated by her inability to see, she

scrubbed angrily at her eyelids, rubbing even more of the medicinal properties of the oil into her skin and as she did, realized she was beginning to see daylight. It wasn't much of an improvement, but it was the first sign she'd had that this too shall pass. Then she heard the horse moving and knew whoever was on it was backing away.

"Wait!"

She heard the horse stop. She stepped forward, holding her hand out before her as she felt her way.

Suddenly her hand was enveloped in one much larger and stronger. She felt the brush of hair against her arm and knew it was not her own. She opened her mouth, then immediately shut it when his hand touched her face. She felt a fingertip tracing the path that her tears had made earlier and knew that he'd seen her cry.

"I don't ever do that," she said.

He took her fingers, put them back onto the leaves and then touched her eyes once more.

"You want me to put some more on my eyes? Is that it?" Quickly, she grabbed some leaves and began scrubbing them against her eyes. Each time that she did, the felt relief from the swelling until the misery was almost gone. She looked up

again, and this time saw more than daylight.

His expression was blank, his eyes
hooded and dark. His shoulders were
broad — his belly flat. He sat the paint
horse as if they were one and the same,
while wearing nothing but a feather in his
hair, a breechclout, buckskin leggings and
moccasins to cover a lot of brown skin. She
should have been scared out of her mind.
Instead, she felt an odd sort of empathy.

He touched his eyes once, then pointed
at hers and suddenly she understood. He
knew how she felt.

She held out her hand, showing him the
leaves.

"Thank you," she said, and touched her
eyes, then her heart.

He stared at her for a moment, letting
his gaze wander over her nudity without
lust or shame, then nodded.

Suddenly, his gaze slid from her to the
creek behind her.

Letty turned. Eulis must be coming.

He grabbed the reins and turned his
pony to the east.

There was a moment when their gazes
met again, this time in a silent acknowledg-
ment of what had transpired and then he
kicked his horse in the flanks and was gone.

It wasn't until he disappeared that Letty started to shake.

"Lord, Lord, this is twice in my life that you've saved me from murdering Indians."

Then she scrambled through the brush and into the creek just in time to see Eulis coming through the trees.

She turned once, looking behind her to make sure the Indian was gone and then shivered. It dawned on her that, until she'd seen him, she'd not been afraid. She wondered what God was trying to tell her with that encounter, and then said a mute prayer of thanksgiving that the Indian had left her with her hair on her head and — she silently added — the ability to see.

"Hey, Letty, your eyes opened up some, didn't they?" Eulis said, as he helped her out of the creek and up the bank.

"Yeah, probably the cold water," Letty said, and then wondered why she didn't tell Eulis the truth.

There could be a whole band of Indians just over the hill waiting to swoop down on them and do them in, just like the ones who'd killed her father. But that didn't fit the gentleness of the man as he'd led her out of the creek, or the leaves he had given her that led to the blessed relief to her swollen and burning eyes. She touched her face where he'd traced the paths of her tears and shuddered, too miserable and confused to figure everything out.

Eulis walked just a bit in front of her so as not to be staring rudely at her nudity, which would have been impossible to ignore.

"I didn't plan on you bein' able to see, so I already laid out some dry clothes for you. If I picked the wrong stuff, you just trade for what you need."

"Whatever you laid out will be fine," Letty said, still holding her wet bloomers against her breasts.

Eulis scratched at his whiskered cheeks as he nodded. When they got to Dripping Springs, he was going to need a good bath and shave, too. A few moments later they reached the campsite. Letty grabbed her clothes and slipped behind a bush then began to dress.

Eulis politely kept his back turned as she put on her clothes, although he couldn't, for the life of him, figure out why it now mattered to be modest. Before, when she hadn't been able to see, she hadn't cared a bit. Now, because she could see again, she was hiding in the bushes. If he lived to be a hundred, he would never be able to figure out women.

"Hey, Letty. I saved you some meat and johnnycake. Reckon you're up to eatin' a bite before we set out?"

Letty's stomach rumbled. She was hungry and she thought the worst of her nausea had passed.

"I wouldn't mind," she said.

He set aside the leftover meat and johnnycake and then began packing up the bits and pieces of their camping gear. A few minutes later, Letty came out from behind the bushes wearing a wrinkled but clean skirt and shirtwaist. Her hair was still wet, so she'd left it down to dry, but had put some hair combs in her pocket for later.

"Where are my shoes?" she asked.

Eulis pointed toward her saddlebag. "In there."

She took them out and then held her breath as she put them on. They smelled to high heaven and so did she. Still, she couldn't go all day on an empty stomach or she'd be puking again before night. She picked up the sandwich he'd made of the meat and corn cake and took a big bite. It had a faint taste of skunk, but she figured that was a lingering taste in her mouth, not on the food.

"It's good, Eulis. Thank you for fixing it."

He nodded.

"I'm sorry I still smell," she added.

"Ain't your fault."

"I know, but still —"

"You're gonna be downwind of me today anyway, so I reckon it won't matter."

Letty nodded as she took another bite, although that came close to being an insult. However, the lingering stench of skunk was a brutal reminder of how she'd been humbled. She wasn't in any mood to chastise Eulis for the remark for fear of what might happen to her next.

A few minutes later, they mounted up, set their direction by the position of the sun and rode out of camp toward Dripping Springs.

It was midafternoon when Eulis and Letty got their first glimpse of their destination. It was out in the middle of a wide, flat valley, which, if they hadn't been so travel-weary, would have made them wonder where the isolated little town had gotten its name.

There was a mountain range far, far to the west and a large herd of cattle barely visible in the south. The obligatory saloon sat squarely in the middle of town. Letty could read the sign from here.

Griggs' Saloon.

It crossed her mind that there might be women working in there that she knew, then discarded the notion. There was no reason to assume they would even cross paths. Letty's recent conversion to the Lord had automatically moved her to socially acceptable, especially if no one knew her from before.

She looked at Eulis. There was a strange, faraway expression on his face.

"Eulis?"

"What?"

"What are you thinking?" Letty asked.

Eulis looked at her and then sighed. "I reckon I was wonderin' who it was I was gonna lie to this time."

Letty frowned. She didn't know how to deal with Eulis's conscience.

"There's no call to look at it like that," she said.

Eulis shrugged. "Then how do you look at it? I'm gonna go down into that town and pretend I have the legal right to marry two perfectly decent people. Those people will then live the rest of their lives believing they are legally wed and their children and grandchildren and all that come after them will legally be bastards. That's how I look at it and it's startin' to bother me some."

Letty's frown deepened. She'd had no

idea that Eulis was capable of such deep thinking.

"So, what are you saying? Are you blaming me for getting you into this?"

"No . . . I don't know . . . maybe."

Suddenly, Letty felt the weight of the world settling on her shoulders. Through sheer terror and no small amount of determination, she'd kept the people in Lizard Flats from finding out that the real preacher they'd been expecting from back East had died in her bed. She'd dragged Eulis out of his normal drunken stupor, cleaned him up and passed him off as the preacher because it had suited her purposes, not his. She'd pushed and prodded him every step of the way and not once had she thought about what they were doing. It had been all about what she wanted. She'd had a change of heart and quit a life of sin, and she wondered now whether it had been a real change of heart, or from fear and guilt. She couldn't say she was sorry she was no longer letting men have their way with her body, but she was sorry she'd used Eulis.

"What do you want to do?" she asked.

He glanced at her then looked away.

"I don't know."

"Are you sorry you're not still in Lizard Flats?"

He shook his head vehemently. "No. No, not that. I won't ever be sorry about that, and I got you to thank for helpin' get me outta' that. I reckon I woulda' just drunk myself to death if you hadn't . . . if we didn't, uh . . . well, you know."

"Look, Eulis, don't think I need you to take care of me," she said. "If you want to strike out on your own then don't let me stop you." She pointed to the little town nestled down in the wide valley. "There's a saloon down there and I've still got a few good years left in me. I might not like it, but it won't kill me and I won't starve to death."

Eulis saw the bravado on her face, but he also heard the desperation in her voice. Even though he wasn't sure about pretending to be someone he was not, he knew he couldn't let Letty slide back into her life of sin. Not when he'd preached her right out of that life and baptized her into redemption. It might have been in a horse trough, but it was a sincere baptism just the same.

"That ain't gonna happen," he said. "And I don't want to stop preachin' either. I reckon I was just a little bit nervous, but

I'm feelin' fine now. Besides, I'm sure ready for a bath of my own."

The mule he was riding suddenly lifted its head and brayed. He grinned.

"See. Even this old mule is ready for a little rest, so let's go see what there is to see."

The relief Letty felt was so startling that she had to look away to keep from letting him see her tears. She swiped a hand beneath her nose in lieu of a handkerchief and got a strong whiff of herself all over again.

"Lead the way," she said. "Me and this old hay burner won't be far behind. Oh, and Eulis —"

"What?"

"Maybe it would be best if, when we get into town, you go on ahead into the hotel and get us some rooms. They might not let me in if they smelled me beforehand."

Eulis grinned. "Good thinkin', Sister Leticia."

"Yep, that's me. Always thinking ahead," Letty muttered, then urged her blind mare forward as they began their descent into Dripping Springs.

Vinegar, Vanity, and Visions

It was Orville Smithson who first saw the strangers riding into town. One man on a mule. A woman on a blind mare. He knew the mare was blind because he could see the white film over the mare's eyes from inside his shop. He frowned, wondering how that worked — riding into a strange place on a horse that couldn't see.

The man was dusty and trail-weary, but the cut of his suit was fine and the hat on his head was a bowler, a style men out West didn't much cotton to. His hair was a mixture of brown and gray and hung a few inches past the collar of his shirt. His face was ordinary, with less than a week's worth of whiskers waiting to be shorn. The woman was some younger than the man. Her clothes were nothing to write home about, but she had a nice face, a voluptuous body, and a fine head of brown hair.

He put down the straight razor he'd been sharpening and walked out onto the sidewalk. He caught the scent of polecat as the couple passed by and wrinkled his nose. He continued to watch as they rode all the way down the street to the rooming house. A cowboy ambled out of Griggs' Saloon, mounted his horse, and rode out of town as Henrietta Lewis stepped out of the mercantile.

Orville waited for her to look his way so that he could wave, but she, too, had seen the strangers and was curiously watching as the man dismounted.

"Hey, Orville, I need a haircut."

Orville turned around to see who had hailed him, then frowned. Harley Charles was coming up the sidewalk. It was the first time he'd seen him since Fannie had run him out of their house on all fours. He wasn't certain how to behave toward a man who'd been humiliated in this respect, especially since it was his daughter who'd done the deed. But Harley didn't seem all that bothered about their face-to-face, so Orville took his cue from Harley and waved him into the shop and set him down in the barber chair.

"Want a shave with that, too?" Orville asked, as he fastened the barber cape around Harley's neck and tried not to look at the man's swollen nose and black eyes.

Harley rubbed a hand on his jaw, testing it for soreness, then nodded an okay.

"Yeah, sure. My face isn't as tender as it had been."

"That's good," Orville said, tilted the chair back enough to get a good angle for a shave, and then poured some hot water into a basin.

He dipped a clean towel in the water, wrung it loosely, then wrapped it around Harley's face, making sure to leave his nose free to breathe.

"Damn, Orville, that's hot," Harley said.

Orville knew it, but pretended innocence as he worked up a lather in the shaving mug.

"Sorry," Orville said. "Softens up the whiskers good, don't you know."

Harley grunted, crossed his hands across his belly and relaxed, unaware that Orville had walked back to the door.

"Got a couple of strangers in town," Orville said.

Harley could have cared less and let it be known.

"So what? Hurry up with my shave and haircut. I got business later."

Orville figured Harley's business was monkey business and took his own sweet time getting back to the job at hand.

Finally, he removed the towel, slathered on a good dose of lather and began shaving Harley.

He had finished the shave and was working on the haircut when, to his surprise, the stranger appeared in the doorway.

"Sir, I am Reverend Randall Howe. I understand that you've been needing the services of a preacher."

Orville's mouth dropped. It was the same man who'd ridden in on the mule. He knew because he recognized the clothes and the hat, but he would never have guessed the man to be a preacher.

Harley froze, gave Orville a nervous glance, as if he feared Orville was going to try to hold him to his original promise, then started to undo the cape.

"Sit still, damn it," Orville said. "I only cut one side of your hair."

"Then hurry up," Harley said. "Lola's waiting on me."

Orville frowned. None of this mess would have happened if Harley had been able to keep his prick in his pants. Then Fannie wouldn't have gone all crazy and gotten herself engaged to Myron Griggs. How was it going to look to decent folks with his daughter married to the man who sold women and booze on a daily basis?

"Orville? Did you hear me? I got business."

Orville glared at the back of Harley's head and then started to snip.

At first it was just one angry snip, but then another followed, and then another, and the first thing Orville knew, he had one side of Harley's hair at a good two inches shorter than the other. He turned the chair toward the windows so Harley couldn't see himself in the mirror and started working on the long side, trying to even it up. He was doing all right until he saw that woman who'd ridden in on the mare walking past his shop. She walked like a warrior, with her chin up and her shoulders straight and proud. Her stride was long and purposeful and that long, brown hair was still flying out behind her like a sail. He got another whiff of polecat and frowned. It was strange that every time he saw the woman he smelled skunk, then discarded the notion.

"Are you done?" Harley asked.

Orville looked down at Harley's hair. There was a big hunk out of the crown that shouldn't be there and what had been the short side of Harley's hair was now the long side again, which also meant that he'd royally messed up this haircut.

"Pretty much," Orville said, whipped off the cape and gave Harley a push. "This one's on me."

Harley stood up and grinned, revealing a three-tooth gap in his once perfect smile as he set his hat back on his head without bothering to look.

"Well, thanks, Orville."

"Don't mention it," Orville muttered, then stepped out onto the sidewalk again, looking for the strange woman, but she was nowhere to be seen.

Fannie was hanging laundry out on the clothesline in back of the house when she heard someone calling her name. She dropped the piece of wet clothing back into the basket and then moved toward the fence.

"I'm out here," she called.

Moments later, Myron came running around the corner of the house. He vaulted the fence and swooped her up into his arms.

"He's come, Fannie Mae! He's come. It's a sign from God himself that this marriage is right!"

Fannie was laughing before she even knew what Myron was talking about. She was laughing because someone loved her.

She was laughing to keep from crying because someone cared.

"Myron! Myron! You have to put me down," she finally said, and thumped him on the arm. "What will people think?"

Myron laughed, but he stole a kiss on her cheek as he set her back on her feet.

"I suppose they'll think I'm in love with my girl," he said.

Fannie blushed, but her heart was singing.

"What brought on all this fuss?"

Myron clapped his hands. "The preacher. He's here."

Fannie's eyes widened. Even when Myron had said he'd find one, she hadn't really believed it would happen.

"Are you sure, I mean, are you sure he's a preacher?"

"Sure as anyone can be. He showed up about an hour ago riding a mule. Said someone at Fort Mays told him they were needing a preacher in Dripping Springs. That had to be Tanner. He was in the saloon the night I proposed to you. I told all the customers that night to spread the word that a preacher was needed and Tanner was on his way to Fort Mays."

"Oh my!" Fannie murmured. It was going to take a bit of getting used to, to accept that her husband sold liquor and women, but then she laughed. So what. He'd kept his word, which was more than her father or Harley had even pretended to do.

"I've already talked to him," Myron said. "He's not going to be in town for long, so I thought maybe tomorrow. . . ."

Fannie smiled, then laid her palm against the side of his face. His skin was smooth and he smelled of witch hazel. She could feel the pulse of his lifeblood beneath her skin, and it was the closest she'd ever been to a man in her life. And if she married him as she'd promised to do, she was going to give herself to this man in the most intimate of ways. Could she do it? Myron smiled at her then and her heart fluttered. She put her hands over her heart to still the nervousness and nodded.

"Tomorrow would be fine."

He whooped again and kissed her soundly.

"I'll be back tonight. We can finish making plans together, okay?"

Fannie's heart skipped a beat.

"Mrs. Bartlett brought us some fresh pork this morning. I was going to fry it up tonight. How does that sound?"

"Like heaven," Myron said, kissed her

once more for good measure, and then vaulted back over the fence and took off down the street.

Fannie turned back to the clothesline and began hanging up the rest of the laundry. Nothing seemed any different than it had been five minutes earlier. The laundry was still wet. The sun was still shining. She hung her father's shirt on the line and then bent down to pick up another article of clothing. Instead, she stopped, ran her fingers along the surface of her lips and smiled. Her lips were still tingling. Her heart was threatening to leap out of her chest. Tomorrow night she would be a married woman and all that implied. At the thought, she felt a moment of panic, then remembered the gentleness in Myron's touch. She might not know much of what was expected of her, but she wasn't going to deny herself the opportunity to learn.

She could sew and cook and clean house better than most. She knew how to take good care of a man in every way but one. If only her mother were still alive. She very badly needed a woman to talk to, but there was no one in Dripping Springs with whom she was close enough to get so familiar.

Never one to dwell on what was missing in her life, Fannie threw the rest of the wet clothes across the line without care for how they were hanging and headed for the house. If she was going to get married tomorrow, there were some things she needed to buy.

Mercer's Mercantile was empty except for one woman at the back of the room as Fannie entered the store. Lucy Mercer stepped out of the storage room long enough to see who'd come in, and called out.

"Fannie, dear, I'm in the back," Lucy said. "I'll be with you in a few minutes if that's all right."

"Take your time," Fannie said.

Lucy waved merrily and went back to counting out the eggs she was buying from a local farmer, leaving Fannie to stew in her pre-marital woes a little longer.

Fannie moved toward a table where several bolts of fabric were stacked and fingered the textures, wishing she had time to send off for something suitable for a veil. There were a couple of bolts of something sheer near the bottom of the stack and she started shifting them to get a better look. As she was struggling with a rather large bolt of calico, she smelled skunk. Before she had time to consider the oddity of the scent with where she was standing, the woman who'd been in the back of the store spoke to her.

"Need some help?"

Fannie turned, then wrinkled her nose as the skunk scent grew even stronger.

Letty sighed. She could tell by the look on the woman's face that she'd gotten a whiff.

"Sorry," she said. "I had an unfortunate encounter with a skunk."

Despite the woman's objectionable smell, Fannie grinned.

"Bless your heart," Fannie said. "I can't say I know how you feel, but I can honestly say I know how you smell."

It was the forthrightness of the remark that both startled Letty, then made her laugh.

"At last. An honest woman," Letty said, and then reached in front of Fannie and lifted the top bolts away, giving Fannie access to the cloth she'd been eyeing.

"Thank you," Fannie said, as she pulled it out from beneath the pile. "My name is Fannie Smithson."

"I'm Leticia Murphy, traveling associate of Reverend Randall Ward Howe. He's come to Dripping Springs to marry a couple."

Fannie gasped. "Oh! How fortuitous! I'm the one who's going to get married."

Letty smiled, although it must be said she felt a moment of pure envy. Why couldn't she find someone with whom to spend the rest of her life? This little woman was somewhat homely and even she had found true love.

"Well, now," Letty said. "It seems congratulations are in order. I'll bet you're as nervous as a cat, aren't you?"

"Not so much nervous as just uncertain," she said, then fearing she'd said too much, began fiddling with the fabric, unwinding some and then holding it up to the light to see if it was sheer enough to pass as a veil.

Letty glanced toward the back of the store where the owner was still deep in conversation with the farmer who'd brought in the eggs. After her success with the young woman in the other town who'd tried to do herself in, she felt it was her duty to caution new brides. Not that she knew what the hell there was to caution them about, but it seemed like a duty that a traveling associate of a preacher should do.

"You say you're uncertain. Are you referring to your feelings, because if you are, you should not marry a man you don't trust."

Unconsciously, Fannie clutched the fabric against her breasts as if it were a shield. She started to speak and then stopped. It seemed ridiculous to confide in a total stranger. But then the more she thought about it, the less ridiculous it seemed. Who better than a stranger? She would never see the woman again. What did it matter if she embarrassed herself once if it got her the answers she so desperately desired.

"It's not that I don't trust him," Fannie said. "Because I do. He's a wonderful man."

"Then what's the problem?" Letty asked.

Fannie glanced over her shoulder, making sure they were still alone, then lowered her voice.

"He doesn't have a problem. I fear it is I who is lacking."

Letty frowned. "Lacking how?"

Fannie glanced at Letty, then quickly looked away.

Suddenly, it dawned on Letty that the girl was embarrassed, and if that was the case, it had to be about sex.

"Have you spoken to your mother about your fears?" Letty whispered.

Fannie quickly shook her head. "My mother is deceased and I can't speak to Father about such things."

Letty stifled a smirk. Being skunked hadn't dulled her instincts. It was about sex and the Good Lord only knew she was an expert at such.

"What things are you talking about?" Letty asked.

Fannie blushed.

Letty put a hand on the young woman's back and pushed her toward the door.

"Let's take a little walk, shall we? I know I smell bad but it's not so disgusting in the fresh air."

Fannie didn't realize how desperate she looked as she put the fabric down.

"I shouldn't bother you with such things," Fannie said.

Letty grinned. "Trust me, dear, it's not a bother."

Fannie beat her to the door.

"Ask away," Letty said. "I'll tell you anything you want to know."

Fannie clasped her hands beneath her chin and swallowed nervously.

"Truly?"

"Truly."

"Are you a married woman?" Fannie asked.

"Not now," Letty said, letting the young woman assume that she had been but was now widowed.

"Oh. I'm so sorry for your loss," Fannie said. "Maybe I shouldn't. My asking you about such personal things could only bring back sad memories for you."

Letty slipped her hand beneath Fannie's elbow and started walking her down the street.

"Memories are nothing but parts of the past that I haven't had time to forget," she said. "Now tell me, what do you know?"

Fannie flushed. "I know what happens, but not how or what my part in it has to be."

Letty stifled a grin. She reckoned there was going to be one really happy bridegroom when she got through with Fannie Smithson.

"Okay," Letty said. "Are you interested in enjoying your wedding night, or are you the kind of woman who just intends to do her duty?"

"Up to now, I haven't had much in my life to enjoy, but I would certainly like to enjoy my husband."

Letty smiled primly as she aimed them for a bench on the shady side of the street. "I totally approve, now sit with me. We can see who's coming and going without being overheard."

They sat.

Letty leaned forward until she and Fannie's foreheads were almost touching, then she started to talk.

Any passerby that might have noticed them would have seen nothing untoward except the intermittent flush of color on Fannie Smithson's cheeks. Every now and then Fannie would interrupt to ask a question, which Letty promptly answered in depth. There was no need for the woman to go into a marriage blind. Besides, she wasn't the prettiest bride Letty had ever seen, but she intended for her to be the wisest. Tomorrow night, Fannie's new husband was going to think he'd died and gone to heaven.

A short while later, Letty straightened up and mentally dusted her hands for the job she'd just done.

"And that's about the best advice I can give," Letty said.

Fannie's mouth was gaping and her cheeks were flushed, but there was a glimmer in her eyes that hadn't been there before. She eyed Letty closely.

"And you're sure Myron won't think I'm too forward?"

It was all Letty could do not to laugh.

"Honey, I'm sure and then some. I promise you, if you do exactly what I suggested, your husband is never going to have a roving eye, and you're going to be one happy bride."

Fannie nodded briskly. "Then that's that. I need to be sure, you know."

"Why?" Letty asked.

"Well, because he owns the saloon. The women who work for him sell their bodies to men for money, you know."

The smile died on Letty's face.

"Yes, I know all about that kind of woman."

Fannie frowned. "I don't think we should judge them, you know."

It was the last thing Letty expected to hear from a so-called decent woman.

"Why not?" Letty asked.

"I've thought about it some," Fannie said. "And the way I see it, if it had been my father who'd died and not my mother, there's no telling what would have happened to either one of us. Women don't have it easy out here, you know, and we rarely have choices as to how our lives will be lived."

Letty eyed Fannie with new respect.

"You're entirely correct, Fannie dear. And you know what? I think you're going to be, not only a wonderful wife, but an absolutely marvelous mother."

Fannie beamed. "You do?"

Impulsively, Letty hugged her. "Yes, I do." Then she remembered she stunk. "Sorry for the smell. I forgot," she said briskly, and stood up. "So, you better get back to Mercer's Mercantile and buy that piece of fabric you were looking at. It would make a fine veil."

"Are you sure?" Fannie asked.

"As sure as I am about what I just told you," Letty drawled.

Fannie pivoted sharply and started to walk away when she suddenly stopped and turned.

"Sister Murphy."

"Yes?"

"Your husband must have been the happiest man on earth before he died."

Letty's heart did a funny little jerk as she thought about all the men who'd lain between her legs.

"Why do you say that?" she asked.

"You not only know the way to a man's lustful natures, but I venture to guess you knew the way to your own man's heart, as well. I'm so sorry that he'd passed, but he was a fortunate man during his time on earth."

Letty couldn't speak. There was no way she could acknowledge the blessing without lying, and she'd already been faced with Eulis's fading faith in himself. It didn't seem prudent to test God's patience any further by adding pride to the lie.

"It's always sad when a good man dies," she muttered.

"Yes, ma'am, that it is," Fannie said, then added, "I can't thank you enough for what you've done."

Letty shrugged. "Trust me, honey. It was nothing."

"I wish there was something I could do for you in return," Fannie added.

"The only thing I need is to get this smell off my skin," Letty said.

Fannie frowned, then offered some advice. It was the least she could do, considering the advice Sister Murphy had given her. "I don't know how much faith to put in the remedy, but there's an old trapper who used to come into my father's barbershop a couple of times a year. I remember him talking about taking a vinegar bath once to get rid of such a smell." Then Fannie blew her a kiss and hurried away.

Letty sat back down on the bench with a plop, refusing to look up toward the heavens for fear she'd see God frowning down on her.

"Vinegar, huh? Do you reckon it would work?" When God didn't send her a sign, she quickly added. "I didn't lie to the girl," she said under her breath. "It is always sad when a good man dies. I just didn't bother to say the good man wasn't mine now, did I?"

She sat for a moment, waiting for a clap of thunder or possibly a lightning bolt to come shooting out of the sky and strike her dead.

A cat trotted by, paused to sniff at her feet then hissed and ran away.

She frowned.

"Everyone is a critic," she said, and made her way across town to the boarding house.

Maybe she'd send Eulis to the mercantile for some vinegar. It certainly wouldn't hurt to give the remedy a try.

Eulis knocked briskly on Letty's door and then entered without waiting for her to answer. She was lying flat on her back on the bed with a wet cloth draped over her face. Eulis frowned.

"Are you ill?"

"I didn't say you could come in," Letty

muttered, without removing the cloth.

Eulis looked crestfallen. He'd been so excited about his news that he had forgotten about her extenuating circumstances.

"Sorry. I'll come back later."

Letty flung the cloth onto the floor and sat up.

"You're already here, so talk," she said.

Eulis frowned. Danged if he would ever understand women. "The wedding will be tomorrow. I'm marryin' the owner of the saloon to the barber's daughter. It's the talk of the town."

"I can only imagine," Letty said. "They're hardly the perfect couple."

"Oh, that's not all," Eulis said. "Up until a few days ago, she had been engaged for some time to a local rancher. Story goes that her old man paid off the rancher to propose, then promised him a big dowry to boot. Only the fiancé wasn't being true to his woman. While he was waiting for her father to announce the proper time, he was messing around with one of the whore's . . . uh, women . . . at the saloon. The bride-to-be got wind of it and had herself a fit. Broke the rancher's nose, blacked his eyes and ran him out of her house. Then they say she shot at her father and ran him out, too."

By now, Letty was open-mouthed and in shock. The meek and somewhat homely little woman who'd been asking advice about sex hardly seemed the type who would have pulled such a stunt. Suddenly, she was smiling.

"Way to go, lady," Letty muttered.

"What?" Eulis said.

"Nothing," Letty said. "What else?"

"Not much, I reckon," Eulis said. "Somehow, between that incident and today, she got herself engaged to the saloon owner and now I'm gonna marry them tomorrow before noon."

"Two? She had two fiancés?"

"Almost," Eulis said.

I would be happy with just one.

"That's hysterical."

"I guess," Eulis said, then pointed to the wet cloth she'd flung on the floor. "Are you sick?"

At heart? Yes. "No, just sick of smelling myself, which reminds me," Letty said. "Someone told me that a vinegar bath would help take away this smell. I want you to —" Then she caught herself. The demanding tone in her voice wasn't right. "I'm sorry. I meant to say, would you mind going down to Mercer's Mercantile and see if they have a jug of vinegar?

I'm willing to give anything a try."

"Yeah, sure," Eulis said, and patted his pocket, feeling the coins jingle as he did. "Which reminds me. Myron Griggs, the future bridegroom, was so happy to see us that he's sort of gone overboard on payment."

Letty's eyes narrowed. "How so?"

"Well, someone told him about the mule and the blind mare, so he's giving us a wagon and team and a grubstake to get us going."

"You're not serious?" Letty said.

"Dead serious," Eulis said. "And there's more."

Letty leaned against the bedpost. "I'm afraid to ask."

"There's talk in town of a gold strike in the Rockies."

Letty's heart skipped a beat. "Gold?"

"For the taking. Anyone can stake a claim."

"Are you giving up preaching?" Letty asked.

"Not totally," Eulis said. "If the need arises, I reckon I could always, well, you know."

Letty was frozen with fear. After all they'd been through, was it coming down to this? She would rather be dead than go back to being a whore.

"So, what do you think?" Eulis asked. "Would you like to give this a try?"

"You mean I'd go with you?"

Eulis frowned. "Well, yes. We're in this together, remember?"

For a moment, Letty was too moved to speak, then she cleared her throat and got up from the bed, retrieved the wet rag from the floor and dropped it into the basin.

"Of course, I remember," she said. "Now go see if they've got that vinegar. I don't want to be smelling so bad I can't go see that wedding tomorrow." Then she grinned. "If it's your last one, I don't want to miss it."

Eulis slapped his leg and laughed as he ran out of the room.

Letty sat down on the side of the bed.

"Gold. He wants to find gold." Then she started to laugh. "Well, why the hell not? We've already found religion, and for two sinners like us, that was near to impossible. After what we've been through, finding gold oughta' be easy."

Blessed Assurances and the High Road

There was a glint in Fannie Smithson's eyes as she fastened her makeshift veil to her hair. Her father had already yelled at her once to hurry or they were going to be late, but she wasn't worried. Myron knew she was coming and he would wait.

With a last look in the mirror, she pinched her cheeks to give them more color, tucked a stray lock of hair beneath her veil and tugged at the neckline of her dress. It was her newest dress, only a year or so old, and it was yellow, which was her favorite color. For the first time in her life, she actually felt beautiful, and she knew it was because Myron loved her.

Before this day was out, she would be a married woman in her own house. It was with no small amount of relief that she knew she wouldn't be living in rooms above the saloon. Myron had a house on the south side of town. She couldn't help but wonder what it would be like and then accepted the fact that she didn't care. It would be hers — and she wasn't being married to a man who'd had to be bribed to propose.

She felt a moment of sadness; longing for her mother's arms around her while assuring her everything will be all right. But her mother had been dead all these many years and she'd been doing just fine on her own, so she lifted her chin and walked out the door without once looking back, willingly leaving the only sanctuary she'd ever known to be Myron Griggs' wife.

Letty poured the last of the vinegar into the basin. It was her third bath since last night when Eulis had brought her the jug. Truthfully, she couldn't tell if it was helping or not. The scent of skunk was so strong in her nostrils that she feared she'd never smell anything else again.

Last night, when she'd tried without success to fall asleep, she'd even snorted some vinegar up her nose in hopes that it would clear out the scent, but all she succeeded in doing was choking herself with vinegar. She'd coughed, then puked, and this morning, her tongue was sore and a tiny bit numb, as if she'd eaten something too hot.

Lesson learned. Do not inhale vinegar, no matter what the need.

Now, in less than an hour Eulis was going to marry Fannie Smithson to Myron Griggs. As the traveling associate of Preacher Howe, it was her duty to be in attendance. But unless this last vinegar bath did more good than the other two, she was going to be standing a good ways downwind.

She was scrubbing at her arms when a knock sounded at the door.

"Sister Leticia, it is I. May I enter?"

Letty rolled her eyes. Eulis was obviously already walking in preacher shoes, so she gave him back an equally flowery response.

"If your feet will get you in here, you've got my okay," she said.

Eulis was all the way into the room before he realized Letty was naked from the waist up.

"Oh! Uh . . . I . . . you said to —"

"I know what I said," Letty said, then doused the rag back into the basin of vinegar and then swiped it across her breasts. "And don't act like you've never seen these before. You floated 'em in the horse trough when you baptized the devil outta' me, and you saw 'em night before last when I got skunked in the woods."

Eulis flushed. "Maybe so, but it wasn't like I was tryin' to sneak a peek. They was swingin' free before I baptized you and they was swingin' free when you stripped off and crawled in the creek, both of which you did on your own. So don't go gettin' all prissy with me about them things. I sure as hell have seen better."

Letty chose to ignore the slight to her physical appendages and pointed the vinegar rag in his face. "You said, hell."

Eulis flushed. "It's your fault," he said. "You made me forget myself."

She thought about it for a minute as she finished up her bath, then knew it was time for them to face a few facts.

"No, Eulis, you didn't forget anything. You were just being yourself. Maybe the other day you were right about the preacher thing. I don't think it's working for either one of us."

Eulis slumped against the wall as Letty tossed the rag back into the basin and reached for her shirtwaist.

"And don't feel bad about cursing. I backslid a time or two myself lately. Maybe the gold fields are the place for us after all."

Eulis looked up. "You think so?"

She shrugged. "I don't know, but if we

go there, we'll find out, won't we?"

Eulis smiled. "Yeah. You're right, we'll find out."

Letty followed Eulis out the door, taking care to stay a distance behind, just in case the vinegar wore off before the service was over.

Fannie Smithson was a blushing bride. She clung to Myron's arm as if it were a lifeline while accepting the good wishes of the citizens of Dripping Springs. They'd come out in good numbers to see this wedding and whatever fireworks came with it. Griggs had let it be known that he was enamored of his bride-to-be, even going so far as to defend her honor by punching out her ex-fiancé, Harley Charles. But it was nothing to what Fannie, herself, had done to Harley. More than one resident of Dripping Springs had seen Harley crawling out of the Smithson house on all fours. It was the talk of the town, and nobody wanted to miss the wedding in case there were some more fireworks to be seen.

Just as the preacher was asking if there was anybody who knew why this ceremony should not take place, all eyes turned to Harley Charles, who was standing at the back of the crowd with

Lola from the saloon on his arm.

He'd looked startled to be singled out, and responded angrily.

"What are you all looking at?" he yelled. "Griggs can have her. I damn sure don't want her."

There was a long uncomfortable silence. Fannie went pale and shrank back against Myron in humiliation. In turn, Myron took the affront to his intended personally. He doubled up his fists and his face turned red from anger.

Eulis realized if he didn't do something quick, there would be a fight before anyone could say, 'I Do'. He shook his head at Myron, as if discouraging him from following through on what he was thinking and then stepped forward to address Harley, himself.

"Amen, sir, and from what I hear, the feeling was mutual. The Good Lord loves honesty. How astute of you to realize that the best man won."

Laughter rippled through the audience. Fannie lifted her chin once more and cast a nervous glance in Myron's eyes. When she saw him wink, she breathed a sigh of relief. Once more, the preacher resumed his duties. Harley was old news and all eyes were on the bride and groom.

★ ★ ★

Due to the direction of the wind and the heat that had revived the skunk scent on Letty, she was standing at the back of the crowd. But she had seen the pain on Fannie's face and knew first hand the shame of being second best. And, since she and Eulis were giving up the preaching life and heading for the gold fields, she felt safe in giving Harley a little something to remember them by.

She sauntered up to where he was standing, eyed the woman on his arm as well as the henna rinse on her hair, and recognized her for what she was.

"Nice dress," Letty said.

Lola gave Letty a hard look. Even though the preacher's woman was wearing regular clothes, there was a tilt to her chin and a glint in her eyes that was more suited to Lola's way of life.

Letty smiled, but it was a cool, calculating smirk that matched the jab of her words. "I had a dress just like it about three years ago. Course it's a long ways from nowhere out here. Stands to reason that the fashions would be out of date."

While Lola was still smarting from the slight, Letty turned to Harley.

"Too bad about your face," she said.

"You must have been a nice enough looking fellow once."

Harley's face turned a dark, angry shade of red. "Lady, how dare you insinuate that —"

Letty shoved a finger against Harley's chest.

"Heard about your last visit to the Smithsons. It's a damn shame Fannie didn't shoot you while she had the chance," Letty said, eyed Lola once more, then grinned at Harley as she shook her head. "Man, oh man, you are the prince of losers. You gave up a woman who cooks food fit for a king, keeps a spotless house, and who knows ten ways to bring a man to the point of ecstasy, four of which are without using her hands."

Harley's mouth went slack, revealing the space where his three front teeth used to be.

"Uh —"

Letty leaned forward until her mouth was against his ear.

"I know this, because I told her how. In fact, I taught her everything I know." Then she put her hands on her hips and thrust her breasts outward in a sexual taunt, to assure him she knew of what she spoke.

Harley looked sick.

Letty grinned. It was time to finish him off.

"It must make you crazy to know that for the rest of your life, the only women who'll ever have anything to do with you again are the ones that you have to pay."

Harley gave Lola a wild-eyed look, and when she flushed and looked away, he gasped. Cursing beneath his breath, he shoved Lola out of his way and headed for his horse. Dust from his hasty departure was still thick in the air when Eulis finally pronounced Myron and Fannie husband and wife.

A cheer erupted.

Letty eyed Lola with disdain. Lola glared back.

"You smell like a skunk," Lola said.

"Mine will wear off," Letty said. "What's your excuse?"

Lola doubled up her fists.

Letty leaned forward. "Honey, trust me when I tell you that you don't want to mess with me."

There was something in the tone of Letty's voice that got Lola's attention. Instead of punching Sister Leticia in the nose as she'd intended to do, she stomped her feet in frustration and took off in a huff.

Letty sighed. Not one bit of that had

been proper godly behavior. Her redemption must be wearing out. She was going to have to get Eulis to say a prayer for her soul. Then she glanced back toward the happy couple, eyed the preacher dressed in black, and headed for the rooming house. If they were going to go panning for gold, she was likely going to need a different kind of wardrobe.

Emory James was forty-seven years old and just under five feet, six inches tall. His elongated face was partially hidden beneath a long, red beard and even longer hair. He was a trapper by trade and a scoundrel by nature. He'd gotten away with thievery and fraud so many times that he'd come to believe he was impervious to the rules and laws that others lived by. He'd made a pretty good living at it for a good number of years and then he'd run afoul of an Apache half-breed who called himself Black Dog.

If he'd known the Kiowa woman sitting on the Appaloosa pony outside the sutler's store at Fort Mays had belonged to a man who didn't like to share, he would have left her alone. But it had been almost a year since he'd seen any sort of female who didn't walk on four legs. He'd manfully ignored the long scar down the right side of her face and neck and offered her some beaded necklaces for a roll in the hay. The upshot of their meeting was that she'd taken the necklaces and giggled all the way to the livery stable where their rendezvous was about to take place. The downside of it was that Black Dog found his woman down on her knees with her face in Emory's crotch. He'd managed to get away, only because the Kiowa woman had thrown herself at Black Dog's legs, begging forgiveness. Black Dog promptly pulled out his knife and cut off her braids, alerting Emory to look anew at her scar and accept the possibility that this had happened before. When Black Dog started beating on the woman instead of taking the knife to Emory, he took that as a sign that he would not die today. He managed to escape by riding out of Fort Mays just as the sun was setting, ensuring himself at least an eight-hour lead before Black Dog could see where he'd gone.

What he hadn't counted on was the half-breed's dogged persistence. It was two weeks and counting since he'd traded beads for some booger and the son-of-a-bitch was still on his trail.

Emory stood on the edge of a dry land plateau looking into the setting sun and knowing that the tiny trail of dust about a half day's ride behind him meant death, probably his. He wasn't in the mood to die for something as inconsequential as getting some feminine attention, even though the female hadn't been his. But his moods were of no consequence to Black Dog, who seemed determined to make Emory pay. Emory was out of options and had to make a decision.

He knew if he kept going southwest, he would ride straight into Apache territory and Black Dog's people. He couldn't go back without running into the man, himself, and he was in no mood to face a man out for nothing more serious than using his woman. This left him with only one option.

Cursing the weakness that had gotten him into this trouble, he turned, squinting slightly as he looked toward the jagged skyline of the Rockies and knew the distance was deceiving. It would take days to even reach the foothills. He had no supplies for such a long trek and little hope for surviving, even if he managed to lose Black Dog in the process. Yet it was this way or no way.

With a long sigh and a short curse, he mounted his horse and took the short trail down off the plateau, aiming for the far, blue mountains.

Letty didn't know exactly when it had happened, but sometime during the past eight days she and Eulis had spent on the trail, she'd lost her fear of everything, including dying. It all started as they were making camp the first night out of Dripping Springs.

After taking the team of mules down to the creek bank to drink, Eulis brought them back up to the campsite, hobbled them so they could graze for a bit, and began loading his rifle as Letty dug through the wagon for their cook pot.

"There's a good number of elms and willows along this creek. I reckon I might be able to shoot us a squirrel or a rabbit for supper."

"I'll get wood," Letty said.

"Watch out for skunks," Eulis said, and then grinned and dodged when Letty chunked a small rock at his head.

He shouldered his rifle and headed into the woods as Letty began picking up deadwood. She gathered an armful and dumped it near the wagon, took a drink from her canteen, then went back for more. It would be a long night and a fire kept all manner of less than desirable critters at bay. She wiped the sweat from her forehead with the hem of her skirt and then paused a moment to survey the area before going back to gather more wood.

The lay of the land was deceiving. The hills were hardly more than intermittent mounds and the valleys between were shallow, giving a viewer the impression that the land was nearly flat. But in truth, there was plenty of room for a man on horseback to be hidden from the human eye until he topped one of those small hills. Even though the knowledge made her nervous, she saw nothing to be concerned about. With a heartfelt sigh and the thought of hot stew later, she resumed foraging for firewood.

On her third trip back to camp, the largest mule, a big black that Eulis called Rosy, followed Letty back to the wagon, knowing that there was a bag of oats to be had. Letty could feel the heat of the mule's breath as it hobbled along behind her, and even though she felt no threat, she couldn't help but walk a little faster.

She got to camp and quickly built the

fire, taking time twice to stop and shoo Rosy away from the wagon. About that time, Eulis walked into camp with a skinned squirrel on a stick.

"Lookee here! It's squirrel stew tonight."

"Good, I'm starving," Letty said. "I've got the water already on boil."

Eulis squatted down beside the pot. Without wasted motion, he hacked the squirrel into chunks, tossed a little salt into the pot, then pulled a handful of wild onions from his pocket, and added them to the water.

"Wild onions," he said, pointing to the small greens. "It'll give it a little extra flavor, I reckon."

Letty gave the stew a quick stir and then laid the spoon on a nearby rock as she stood. When she did, she noticed the mule was back at the wagon.

"Dang it, Eulis. You fed that mule some oats the other day and it's turned into one big pest." Then she waved her hands at the mule. "Shoo! Shoo! Get on with you!" she yelled.

Before she knew what was happening, the mule let out a squeal and began stomping in the dirt. Letty let out a squeal of her own and ran backward just as Eulis grabbed the mule's ear.

"Here, now," he said, trying to gentle it, then happened to look down. "Whoa!" he yelled, grabbed the mule and moved them both back. "Letty! Look at that! No wonder Rosy was doin' all that stompin'. You nearly stepped on a rattler."

Letty gasped. Eulis was right. There between the front and back wheels of the wagon was what was left of a fat brown diamondback. She could see at least ten or twelve rattles on it and knew, if the mule hadn't reacted, the rattler would have struck her dead.

"Oh Lord, oh Lord," Letty said, and without thinking, walked backward then stumbled. She felt the heat even as she was falling and knew she was falling into the fire. In a panic, she twisted as she fell and hit the ground hard, numbing her elbow on a rock. For a moment, she couldn't move, and by the time she did, her skirt was on fire.

"Oh! Oh Lord, have mercy, I'm burning up!" Letty screamed and started scrambling, trying to get up.

Eulis rose up from beneath the wagon where he'd been removing the snake, and for a moment, was too startled to move. Then he saw the flames running up the hem of her skirt and bolted.

It was pure panic that made him grab for the stew pot hanging over the fire. It was full of hot water, skinned squirrel and wild onions, and he tossed it at her backside as she was trying to get up. It dampened the flames, but the fabric was still smoldering. At that point, Eulis began kicking dirt on Letty, most of which landed in her face instead of on her skirt.

"Eulis! No . . . don't . . . wait . . . let me . . . am I still —"

"Smokin'? Not much. Just hold still though while I make sure your bloomers ain't burnin'."

Letty gasped, then choked as more dust went up her nose. Eulis bent down, swiped another handful of dirt onto what was left of her skirt, then began beating at it with the palm of his hand.

Nervousness added more power to his swat than he meant and his third thump brought tears to Letty's eyes.

"Oow," she yelped. "That hurt."

"Sorry," Eulis said. "I think the fire is out, but you still got yourself a problem."

Letty stood up and started unbuttoning her skirt.

"No need to do that," Eulis said.

"Why not?" Letty asked.

"Cause there ain't nothin' left of your skirt but what's in front."

Letty grabbed at her backside, felt nothing but bloomers and groaned.

"Oh no! Oh, Lord! It's gone! My last dress! Skunked up the first one. Burned up the last."

She stared at Eulis, waiting for him to say it was a mistake, but he was already abdicating the job of savior and vacating the premises.

"Eulis! Damn it! Where do you think you're going?"

"Huntin'," he muttered.

"Hunting? I nearly died and you're going hunting?"

"Yes. For some more supper. I throwed that first squirrel on your butt." He pointed to the graying lumps of meat that lay scattered in the dirt and ashes. "Reckon I'll go shoot us another one before it gets too dark to see."

"But, Eulis, I —"

"Look, Letty! You didn't even know there was a rattlesnake at your feet till the durn thing was dead. Yes, you set yourself on fire, but it's out. You didn't die. You didn't even get burned much. The world didn't stop. I'm still hungry and all you're missing is a skirt, so I'm gonna go get us another squirrel."

He stomped off, leaving Letty to think about what he'd just said. It was after she'd taken off her skirt and given it a good look that she had to admit he was right. So she wasn't the best at roughing it anymore. Somewhere between the age of twelve, when she'd had to learn to survive without parents and now, she'd lost her edge. She'd gotten soft, accustomed to having nightly baths and someone cooking her food — wearing soft clothes and sleeping in a clean bed. Then she looked up at the darkening sky and sighed. If anyone had asked, she would have said she preferred sleeping with a roof over her head.

Then she gave herself a mental kick in the butt, tossed what was left of her skirt into the back of the wagon and started digging through their meager belongings. It didn't take her long to realize that the only person left with extra clothing was Eulis. She dug through his pack until she found the smallest pair of pants he owned and held them up to her waist. They were inches too long and even more inches too big in the waist, but they would cover her bare backside, which was all that mattered. She cut a piece of rope to use for a belt and adjusted it around the waist of the pants until it was tight enough to keep them up, then rolled up the pant legs until she could walk without tripping. She frowned at the thin kid shoes she was wearing and told herself the next time she got a chance, she was going to get herself a pair of men's boots, too.

Later, as she strode around the campsite, rebuilding the fire and washing up the stew pot to ready it for fresh meat, she slowly realized how convenient it was not having a whole swath of skirt tail swishing between her legs and dragging on the ground. A few minutes later, she heard a single gunshot.

"That better be supper, 'cause I can't take any more surprises," she muttered, and tossed another stick on the fire to bring the fresh water in the stew pot back up from a simmer to a boil.

When Eulis stomped back into camp, he was grinning and holding up a freshly skinned squirrel.

"Got it with one shot!" he crowed, then did a double take when he saw Letty in pants — his pants. "What's that you're trying to wear on your legs?"

"I'm not trying, I'm doing it," she said, took the squirrel, hacked it up into a few large pieces and tossed it into the stew pot.

"Them's my pants," Eulis said.

"Not anymore," Letty said.

Eulis frowned. "It ain't seemly for a lady to —"

"Oh, shut up, Eulis. I might be redeemed and got myself some religion, but that only means my sins were forgiven. It still doesn't make a lady out of me. I'm out of dresses and you've got pants to spare. I can't cross the Rockies butt naked."

Eulis sighed. She had a point, but he still hated to give up those pants. Since he couldn't complain about her mode of dress, he figured he'd take a shot at her cooking skills since they both knew they were nonexistent.

"Don't forget to toss in a little salt," he said, as he pointed to the pot.

Letty nodded and reached behind Eulis's bedroll for the salt bag. She got a big pinch, tossed it in the pot and gave it a quick stir.

"I'm going to the bushes," she said. "Be right back."

"Watch out for —"

"Yeah, yeah, I know. Watch out for the skunks."

Eulis frowned. "Just watch out, all right?"

Letty wiggled her fingers beneath Eulis's nose and made a face at him.

"I'm watching, you do the same."

Eulis was watching all right — watching her shapely hips swaying hither and yon as she walked into the trees. It occurred to him to be glad that the only emotions he ever felt towards her were either empathy or fear, because she looked a whole lot better in those pants than he did.

And so the squirrel cooked, the meal was consumed, and the night passed. The next morning they broke their fast, hitched up the team and resumed their journey. The days and nights became a collage of heat, hunger, thirst and misery, interspersed with an occasional moment of realization that they might not live to see the Colorado gold fields.

Letty couldn't remember a time when they hadn't been on the trail. Her years of screwing drunken cowboys seemed like it had happened to someone else. She'd lost weight, but was stronger, and browner and she wouldn't let herself think about the times when she'd had plenty to eat and a bath every night.

At the same time, Eulis had sweated away the last of his yearnings for whiskey, become a better shot, and learned to appreciate Letty's tenacity and her refusal to quit.

The trail they'd been following was vague at best, and most of the time nonexistent. They gauged their direction by sunrise and sunset and the stars at night and knew they were doing it right because the thin blue line of the mountains on the horizon was gradually growing larger and darker. Danger was with them every mile of the way, sometimes they knew it, sometimes they did not.

On a dark, moonless night when they'd been without water for almost twenty-four hours, they were forced to stop and make dry camp. Their water barrel was empty and the canteens had been empty even longer.

"We need water bad," Eulis said.

Letty sighed. "Well, don't look at me. I haven't had a bath since Sunday, and then it wasn't a real bath. I just rolled around in that muddy creek and pretended I was clean."

Eulis frowned. "What day is it now?"

"It's Thursday, I think."

"So, what do you think we oughta do?" Eulis asked.

Letty turned and stared toward the mountains. Her gut knotted as she thought about how many days they had yet to go before they even reached the foothills.

"I'd say, first off, we better say our prayers real good tonight before we go to sleep, because if we don't get ourselves a miracle, we won't ever have to worry about anything again."

Eulis sighed. "I'm sorry."

"What for?" Letty asked.

"I'm the one who suggested tryin' out the gold fields."

"Yeah, well you didn't hear me begging you not to go, did you?"

"No, I reckon not," Eulis said.

"Look at it this way. We're closer than we were the day before, and that's called progress. So if we're still making progress, then what more could we ask?"

"Beats me," Eulis said, and took their bedrolls out of the back of the wagon.

"What are you gonna do?" Letty asked.

"I thought you might want a little privacy while I shake out the bedrolls."

Letty did a three hundred and sixty degree turn and then gestured wildly around them, to the treeless land and the horizon that went on forever.

"Privacy? Where do you suppose I might find me some of that?"

Eulis frowned. He hated it when she caught him saying something dumb, and this was one of those times. There wasn't a bush to be had for forty miles in any direction, nor a hill to climb, or a ditch in which to squat.

"I suppose you'll have to use your imagination," he said.

Letty thumped him up beside his ear.

"Then close your eyes while I go over there and pee and imagine I have a gun up your ass, because one look from you and constipation will be a thing of the past.

Eulis frowned. "All you had to do was say so. I don't need to be threatened to do the gentlemanly thing, you know."

Letty stomped off a short distance away, untied the rope around her waist, then glanced over her shoulder to where Eulis was standing. Even though they'd seen each other naked more than once, their relationship was still one that needed boundaries. Satisfied that Eulis was looking in the other direction, she dropped her pants and squatted. Then to be on the safe side, she closed her eyes, reasoning that if she couldn't see him, then he couldn't see her.

Night came. They chewed on a piece of jerky, hobbled the mules and then to be on the safe side, tied them to the opposite side of the wagon.

"You gonna build a fire?" Letty asked, as Eulis shook out their bedrolls.

"Nothing to burn," Eulis said.

Letty looked up. The sky was peppered with stars, but she could barely make out Eulis's shape.

"Sure is dark."

"Yeah."

"I think I'll sleep in the wagon," Letty said, then crawled up into the wagon and shoved some boxes around to make room for her to stretch out.

"I'll bunk under it," Eulis added.

A few minutes later, except for the occasional snort from the mules, the prairie was quiet. Letty fell asleep looking up at the sky and listening to Eulis snore. She was dreaming that she was back in Lizard Flats at the White Dove Saloon and some drunken cowboy was breathing hard against her ear.

"Go 'way," she mumbled, and swatted at the cowboy, but his persistent kisses and snuffles against her ear didn't stop.

Letty rolled from her right side to her left, but the aggravation continued.

"I'm done for the night," she mumbled again.

Something pulled at her hair. She reached up and slapped at the cowboy's face. He snorted. She sat up with a jerk, then gasped and clapped a hand over her mouth to keep from screaming.

It was daylight, and as far as the eye could see in any direction, both the wagon and the mules they'd tied to it were surrounded by buffalo.

The heat from their bodies was visible in the form of rising steam from their great wooly humps in the cool morning air, and the smell was unlike anything she'd ever known — something dank and musky coupled with the overpowering scents of fresh urine and manure as they grazed their way past. Ever so often an intermittent bellow would sound from out beyond the wagon, at which time a small plume of dust would fill the air, along with the sound of heads butting and calves bawling.

Slowly, so as not to startle the vast sea of beasts, Letty crawled to her knees, then leaned over the side of the wagon. Even as she was leaning over, she was praying that Eulis was still there and not scattered in bits and pieces beneath a million hooves.

She thought she could see the corner of Eulis's blanket and leaned a little farther over, calling softly.

"Eulis, are you there?"

No sound. No answer.

Letty's throat tightened as fear spiked. She called a little louder.

"Eulis."

Nothing.

A buffalo cow shoved a young bull out of her way, and in the process knocked Letty's head against the wagon. The pain was quick and sharp and she quickly pulled herself up and crawled to the middle of the wagon bed, rubbing the ear that had been thumped. Her hands were shaking. She wanted to scream. Instead, she watched in horror as a large bull with a broken horn suddenly bumped the wagon with its head, shoving aside a young calf as if demanding smooth passage. For just a moment, Letty found herself staring into a pair of black, emotionless eyes and felt as if she was in the presence of the Devil himself.

Her stomach knotted. She started to pray.

"Oh Lord, please . . . I've never asked you for much and expected even less, but I'm begging you now, get us out of this mess . . . alive if you please."

At that point, she felt a loud thump on the bottom of the wagon bed and figured that Eulis was awake.

"Eulis, is that you?"

"Jesus God Almighty!"

Letty sighed. It was Eulis all right, and he was obviously awake.

"Don't move," she said.

"Too late," he mumbled, then started to curse.

"What's wrong?" she asked.

"Other than the fact that I peed my pants and we're probably gonna die, not a damned thing."

"Eulis —"

"What?"

"What are we going to do?"

"Hell if I know, Leticia! I can't see daylight farther than a foot on either side of this wagon. You tell me."

Letty looked about her and shuddered. "They're everywhere."

"What do you mean, everywhere?"

"They're as far as I can see in every direction."

"Lord have mercy," Eulis mumbled, then a few moments later, called out. "Don't panic, but I'm comin' up."

"No! No! What if they see you and start to stampede?"

Eulis sighed. "I know I'm not as pretty as you, but I ain't gonna make any sudden moves. Just stay still."

Before Letty could answer, she saw

Eulis's hands grip the back end of the wagon and then slowly, he pulled himself up and over, landing with a soft thump on top of Letty's legs. For once, she didn't have a thing to say, which in itself was frightening.

Finally, he got the guts to look and rose up on his hands and knees. If he hadn't already peed his pants, he might have done it again.

It was like looking at a dark and breathing flood of mass destruction, moving slowly upon the land and taking everything in its path.

He flinched, as if someone had just punched him in the belly, then looked at Letty.

"Eulis?"

He shook his head. "I reckon we're done for."

She started to cry.

Rescue the Perishing

The sun came up, illuminating even more the disastrous position in which Eulis and Letty had landed. Letty sat motionless with her head down on her knees, too overwhelmed to even look up or move for fear of setting off a stampede. The lack of water had even taken a back seat to the fact that they were most likely going to die and be trampled into bits and pieces. Letty wondered if it took longer to get to heaven if your body parts got scattered and you never got buried.

Eulis, on the other hand, had been so staggered by the situation in which they found themselves that he'd stretched out and gone to sleep.

To Letty's disgust and dismay, he continued to sleep, even as the sun slid slowly toward the western horizon. With every passing hour, the buffalo continued to move past them in a never-ending wave. Dust was so thick in the air that the horizon was blurred, and even though she couldn't see them, she knew a pack of wolves hovered somewhere in the distance. She heard them setting off an evening chorale of eerie howls and yips as they hung near the edge of the herd, hoping to pick off a straggler or a calf too young to keep up.

Suddenly, a massive bull went head first against the side of the wagon, as if pissed off that it was in his way.

The wagon rocked.

A mule brayed and then kicked.

Letty screamed.

And Eulis woke up, dismayed to find out that he wasn't back in Lizard Flats having himself a stiff drink after all.

"What's happenin'?" he mumbled.

"We're dying!" Letty screamed, and then covered her face with her hands and threw herself down into the wagon, unable to face anymore.

Eulis waited for the end, but nothing else happened. The pissed off bull moved on and the massive movement of wooly beasts continued to pass, politely parting to accommodate the wagon and mules in their paths. Finally, he reached down and shook Letty on the shoulder.

"Letty . . . Letty . . . I think it's all right."

Letty rolled up into a ball and pulled her bedroll over her head.

"It's never going to be all right again,"

she said, and then started to cry.

Eulis sighed. Considering the plight they were in, he was in no position to argue, and during the hours they'd been stranded, he had been doing some serious thinking. So serious, in fact, that he had come to the conclusion that God had meted out this punishment to them because of their deceit. When he'd agreed to Letty's original plan of impersonating the preacher, he hadn't given any thought to what God might think about the lie. He'd married and buried and christened and blessed in the name of God, but without any authority. It had seemed like a good idea at the time, but looking back, all he could think about was the fraud they'd committed upon innocent people.

As hard as he'd tried, he couldn't reconcile what they'd done as being just, and from the looks of their situation now, God wasn't in a forgiving mood, either. He'd put them square in the middle of hell on earth.

Eulis looked at Letty, who was little more than a lump beneath her covers. Even though he knew her lips were cracked and her face was burned bad from the sun, she was still one of the toughest women he'd ever known. If he had to be in this situation, he could not have picked a better partner to have at his back.

"Letty."

She pulled the covers off and sat up.

"What?" she whispered.

"Do you —"

"Sssh," she hissed, and slapped a hand over his mouth. "Not so loud."

He lowered his voice. "What's wrong?"

"The better question would be what's not wrong?"

"Why are we whisperin'?" Eulis asked.

A pair of cows suddenly butted heads, slamming one against the wagon bed while the other moved past, satisfied that she'd made her point.

"That's why," Letty said, pointing to the two massive cows. "Do you know what's gonna happen to us if they get spooked? There won't be enough left of us to bury. So I figure if we don't do anything stupid, we might have a chance."

"If they don't move on soon, we're gonna die anyway. We need water bad."

Letty wanted to argue, but she couldn't ignore the facts. He was right.

"You know what, Preacher Howe? I think you need to pray. I think we both need to pray."

Eulis shrugged. "I will if you will."

Letty frowned. "You're the preacher."

"Yeah, and the shit you're standin' in is as deep as mine."

Another buffalo bumped into the wagon. One of the mules on the other side brayed and kicked, connecting with a large cow who retaliated by knocking the mule completely down.

Letty gasped, and lunged over the side of the wagon. She grabbed hold of the rope with all her might and started pulling.

"Help me, Eulis, help me! We've got to get the mule up or they'll trample him."

Eulis threw himself forward, grabbed onto the rope and then lunged backward, putting all of his weight into the effort. Within seconds, the mule was up, wild-eyed and chomping at the makeshift halter that tethered him down.

Letty rocked back on her heels, and then started to shake.

"That was close," she said.

No sooner had their nerves started to calm, than a ripple of thunder came rolling down the valley. Stunned by the sound, they looked up at the quickly darkening sky, then flinched and ducked as a bolt of lightning suddenly ripped across the sky.

"Oh no," Letty muttered.

"What? We need the rain," Eulis said.

"Lightning. The lightning is going to

spook them. We've got to do something, and we've got to do it now."

No sooner had she said it, than the first drops of rain began to fall, splattering hard against the wide shoulders and wooly heads of the great beasts. In response, the movement of the herd perceptibly slowed and they began to draw closer and closer together. Eulis and Letty lifted their parched lips to the sky, reveling in the life-giving moisture falling onto them, as did their mules. As they sat with the rain falling on their faces and the herd gathering tighter and tighter together, Eulis lifted his gaze to the hills, and as he did, saw the chance for their only way out.

"I've got an idea," Eulis said. "Get the harness."

Soaked to the skin and with half sick from hunger and fear, Letty rolled over onto her hands and knees.

"The harness? Have you lost your mind?"

"Probably, but hand 'em here anyway."

Letty dragged the harnesses out from beneath the seat. Eulis took them from her while gauging the motion and mood of the herd against the oncoming storm. The mules' eyes were rolling wildly as they snorted and stomped. Even they seemed to sense the urgency of the moment.

"Here goes nothin'," he said, threw a leg over the side of the wagon and slid down until he was standing between the mules with the harness in his hands.

He began buckling the first mule into the gear as if nothing was different from any other day. He didn't look up. He wouldn't look around. He couldn't let himself acknowledge the danger he was in and still do what he had to do.

"Okay, Letty, now hand me the other one."

Letty handed over the rest of the harness as rain began to fall in earnest. Another bolt of lightning struck high on the hill above. The herd shifted en masse, moving slightly to the right, then slightly to the left, as if testing for the best track to run.

"Hurry," Letty said, and then went over the side after Eulis, knowing that, if they survived, it would take both of them to make this work.

Working side by side, they finished harnessing up, then Eulis took a deep breath and looked at Letty.

"You ready for this?"

"As ready as I'll ever be," she said.

Eulis nodded, but still he hesitated. He looked at her then, studying her in a way he'd never done before and saw past the hardened woman that life had repeatedly kicked in the teeth to the little twelve-year-old girl, hiding in an abandoned badger hole from the Indians who'd killed her father. He thought of the nights after she'd grown up when she'd gone out onto the balcony of the White Dove Saloon to listen for the call of the whippoorwill — keeping alive a ritual that her deceased mother had begun. She was a survivor who stood as tall as any man he knew.

"Uh . . . Letty?"

"What?"

"Just so you know, I ain't sorry about nothin'."

A lump of emotion swelled in Letty's throat.

"Swear?"

He nodded. "Swear."

"Then let's do this," Letty said.

Slowly, they took the mules by their harnesses and began moving through the herd to the front of the wagon. Both Letty and Eulis had been exposed to the herd for so long that they'd taken on their scent. Since the buffalo behind them sensed nothing foreign, and the ones in front had no way of knowing that the pressure to move forward was anything other than more of their own, the herd gave way. Soon, Eulis and

Letty had the mules in place. With shaking hands and muttered prayers, they hitched the team to the wagon.

"All done. Now let's see what happens," Eulis said. When Letty started to walk around one of the mules to get into the wagon, Eulis grabbed her. "Stay between the mules," he said.

"But the harness —"

"Step over or crawl under, but don't get out from between these mules."

She nodded, and slowly, they made their way back to the wagon, then up into the seat.

It wasn't until they were sitting high on the wagon that the herd saw them as something more than an object to walk around. They began pawing and snorting and more than one challenged their presence by going head on with the wagon or ramming a wheel. It was only a matter of time before the man-made wagon gave way to the bison's might. Added to that, the rain was falling harder now. With less than an hour before sundown, time was not on their side. Thinking matters could not be worse, they were soon proven wrong.

Eulis flipped the reins, signaling the mules with a series of clucks to move forward. Nothing happened. Exhausted, dehydrated, and stressed to the point of hysteria, the mules wouldn't budge.

Letty moaned as her shoulders slumped. "We're done for."

Eulis sat for a moment, studying the situation. Then suddenly, he grabbed Letty's shoulder and gave her a push.

"Get off the seat!"

"But —"

"Do it now!" he said, and shoved her backward into the wagon bed. Once she was down, he handed her the reins. "Hold on to these and no matter what happens to me, don't let go!"

Letty grabbed the reins, watching in horror as Eulis climbed down from the seat, then slipped between mules until he was standing with a hand on either head. He rubbed the spot on their foreheads between their ears, then leaned forward and whispered something in each mule's ear.

Eulis turned around once and looked straight into Letty's face.

"We can do this," he said.

"I'm right behind you," Letty said.

Eulis was surprised by what those few words meant to him as he slipped his fingers beneath the strapping and then curled them tight around the leather.

"Gee, Rosy . . . haw . . . Blackie . . . let's go. Come on, let's go."

He made a clucking sound with his tongue and leaned forward, using his weight as well as the sound of his voice to urge them on.

At first nothing happened, then slowly, slowly, Rosy, the lead mule took a step. Trained to follow, Blackie could do no less. The sound of the wagon's creaking wheels and Eulis's voice constantly urging the team forward were lost in the wind and the rain.

And so they went, with Letty crouched down behind the seat with the reins wrapped tight around both wrists and her feet braced against the back of the seat while Eulis led them forward.

The rain was blowing horizontally now, pushed by the gusting front of the on-coming storm. Ironically, the storm, which they feared would detonate a stampede, was also providing a distraction as it came upon them in full force.

Thunder rolled over them in a loud and long roar, deafening them to each other's voices. There was nothing to be heard but the rain hammering against the animals' backs and the wail of the wind.

Eulis could smell the fear and anxiety of

the herd, but the buffalo had gathered so tightly together that it was difficult to move any faster. His plan was to aim for the higher rim on the right — betting their lives on the fact that the herd would move with the rhythm and shape of the earth just as water seeks the lowest level. And so they went, moving through and with the herd while pressing constantly left and upward.

Letty rode with her feet braced beneath the wagon seat and a death grip on the reins. She could see the back of Eulis's head through the space between the seat and the wagon bed and she fixed upon that sight, knowing her life depended on his presence. She couldn't let herself think of what it would mean if he suddenly disappeared — of knowing that he would be trampled beneath the herd. She knew it could happen, yet she couldn't look away.

The downpour had flattened his hair to his face while the brim of his old black hat, weighed down by the rain, had unrolled. He looked as trail-worn as she felt, but his shoulders were broad and the last glimpse she'd had of his face had been one of determination. It occurred to Letty that Eulis Potter had changed in more ways than that of living under another man's identity. The extra weight that he'd carried for years was gone. Deprivation and hard work had toned his muscles and lengthened his stride. He no longer shuffled when he walked, but moved with his head up and his shoulders straight. His hair hung well below the collar of his shirt, and he was days in need of a shave. He looked rough and was in serious need of a bath, as was she. But now that his personality was no longer numbed by liquor, she'd come to appreciate his sense of humor, as well as his convictions.

Eulis Potter — once a childhood victim of outlaw Kiowa Bill — then the drunken gravedigger of Lizard Flats — had, through a series of unbelievable circumstances — become his own man.

Letty didn't know when she'd started depending on him — even trusting him — but it had happened. She knew, as surely as she knew her own name, that if they got out of this mess alive, it would be entirely due to him.

Then, when it seemed that nothing could get worse, she felt the first pebble of hail against her face.

"Thank you, Lord, for reminding us that you're still in charge," she muttered, and grabbed the reins even tighter.

As she did, the sky opened and hail spilled from the sky like marbles out of a can.

The mules bucked in harness. Caught unaware, Eulis lost hold and went down. One moment Letty was looking at the back of Eulis's head and then he was gone.

"No!" she screamed, and jumped to her feet, hauling back so hard on the reins that she felt a bone break in her wrist. The pain was sharp, but nothing compared to the fear of losing Eulis.

The mules stopped. Hail fell so thick and so hard that Letty knew they were in danger of being killed. Still, she couldn't let herself panic. Blocking out the pain in her injured wrist and the ice pellets peppering her, she tied off the reins, crawled over the seat, and slipped down between the rigging. The animals were bowed up with their backs to the force of the wind and their heads down, enduring what they couldn't escape. Hail hit repeatedly against the back of Letty's head and neck as she ducked between the mules in search of Eulis.

She saw him then, lying full length on his back between the mules' legs while hanging on to the double tree with every ounce of strength he had left. She went down on her hands and knees, crawling between the harness and the animals' legs without care for her own safety and then grabbed him by the ankles.

"Are you hurt? Talk to me, Eulis, can you move?"

He groaned. Hail was hitting him in the face so hard he didn't dare open his eyes. He wanted to turn loose and get up, but he was afraid if he let go that the mules would bolt and leave him behind to be trampled.

"Are we dead yet?"

Letty laughed to keep from crying. "No, you crazy man, not yet. But you need to get up. Are you hurt anywhere?"

"I'm goin' blind as we speak from this dadblamed hail. Other than that, I reckon I'll keep."

Letty crawled over him and grabbed the harness.

"I've got the mules, but hurry."

Eulis let go and pulled himself upright. For a moment, he and Letty were standing face to face. He saw her wincing as the hail pelted against her sunburned face and knew that if they lived, it would be bruised tomorrow.

"Leticia, pardon me for sayin' this, but you look like hell," then he jammed his hat on her head and shoved her toward the wagon. "Get in and hurry."

The hat was instant shelter and Letty knew he would suffer for his thoughtfulness.

"Eulis, I —"

"Get in, and grab hold of them reins. I got a feelin' we're in for a rough ride."

Letty scrambled past him, as she did, Blackie stepped sideways and came down on the top of Letty's foot.

"Oh . . . oh Lord, you stupid critter, get off! Get off!"

She slapped the mule hard on the rear and moments later as it stepped sideways again, she was free. She started to hobble across the hitch when suddenly she was airborne. She felt hands at her waist, lifting her over the harness and all but throwing her into the wagon seat. She came down hard on all fours, then screamed as a sharp pain went up her arm and out of top of her head. Suddenly, the wagon started to move. In a panic, she scrambled around, grabbed the reins and braced herself.

"Are you there?" she yelled.

"I'm here," Eulis said. "And I need you to hang on. We're gonna make a run for it."

She peered through the space between the wagon and the seat and saw that he'd mounted Rosy, the lead mule. She saw him kick her in the flanks and then lean forward.

A lightning bolt suddenly shattered what was left of the herd's control. One moment

286

they were moving slowly and the next few seconds, Eulis and Letty were caught up in the rush as the herd began to run.

"Have mercy, Jesus," Letty cried, and wrapped the reins so tight around her wrists that her fingers soon went numb.

Eulis gritted his teeth and hung on for dear life as they were bumped and buffeted by the motion of the moving mass. He wasn't certain if they were actually moving on their own power, or if they were being swept along by the stampede itself.

There was just enough light left for Eulis to see and with every ounce of strength he had in him, he angled the team against the tide of the stampede and began slowly moving them upward.

It seemed they ran forever and that the sound of the rain and hail and the thunder of the storm and the buffalo hooves would be forever etched in Letty's brain.

Then when she thought they could not run any more, she realized that the horizon was no longer dark with buffalo and that there was nothing in front of them but the storm and the distant mountains. And to double their relief, the hail had either stopped, or they'd outrun it. Either way, it was over.

She saw Eulis raise up on Rosy and start

hauling back on the reins. As he did, she planted her feet against the wagon, gritted her teeth against the oncoming pain and did the same.

They stopped, but Letty never knew it. She'd passed out. When Eulis finally crawled down off the mule and staggered back to the wagon, he found her flat on her back and unconscious. Shot through and through with new fear, he crawled up into the wagon bed and pulled Letty up into his arms.

"Letty! Letty! Talk to me, girl!"

She groaned. "Eulis?"

He rocked back on his heels and then started to shake. She was alive. Thank God she was alive.

"Leticia . . . talk to me. Where do you hurt?"

"My hands," she mumbled.

He looked down, then winced when he saw the reins wound around her wrists. Her fingers were swollen and bloodless and when he started unwinding the reins, she cried out in pain.

"My wrist . . . I think it's broken," Letty mumbled, then threw an arm over her face, trying to shelter herself from the rain.

Eulis tossed the reins aside, then pushed her beneath the overhang of the wagon seat. It was somewhat of a shelter, but not enough. He looked around, then grabbed the rain-soaked bedroll, shook it out then draped it over the seat. The bulk of it hung down into the wagon, forming a makeshift tent. It wasn't much, but it was the only protection he could offer her from the rain. Once he had it secured, he lifted a corner and peered in. She was lying curled up on her side and cradling her wrist against her chest. He felt like he needed to touch her, but couldn't bring himself to make the move. It seemed too personal, and personal was a bridge they had never managed to cross. Instead, he cleared his throat and muttered.

"You did real good, Sister Leticia. Real good."

Letty heard him talking, but she couldn't focus on what he said.

"Are we dead yet?" she asked, unintentionally mimicking what he'd asked earlier.

He looked up at the sky and the passing storm, then back down into the valley where the disappearing herd was barely visible. The mules were standing spraddle-legged with their heads down and their sides heaving. Everything Eulis and Letty owned was soaked through and through, but they were still alive and breathing.

"No, Letty, we ain't dead yet."

"Did you hear a whippoorwill? I've been listening and listening for the call."

He sighed. She was out of her head and it was no wonder. He felt a little crazy, himself.

"Yeah, I heard the whippoorwill. Listen close, honey. You'll hear it, too."

Then he dropped the cover back in place, picked up the reins and sat down on the seat. The mules felt the tug on the reins and actually turned their heads and looked back, as if to say, 'you've got to be kidding.'

"I know, I know," he said. "It's been an awful day, but if you could see your way to goin' just a little bit further, I can promise you won't be sorry."

This time when he flipped the reins on their rumps and clucked his tongue, then moved. Slowly. But they moved, and by the time true dark finally came, Eulis had found a good campsite with plenty of water and enough grass for the mules.

Letty woke up to the scent of wood smoke and cooking meat. She pushed aside the cover and rolled out from beneath the wagon seat. Her wrist was aching something awful, she smelled worse than she hurt, and she needed to pee. But when she started to push herself up, her wrist gave way.

"Ow," she cried.

Almost instantly, Eulis appeared, peering over the side of the wagon.

"You're awake."

"It appears so," she said. "Can you help me out? I need to go."

Eulis hauled her out without fuss and set her on her feet, then pointed toward the woods.

"There's a little clearing behind those bushes. When you're done, I saved you some rabbit."

Letty nodded, then stood and watched Eulis as he walked away. When he bent over and tossed another stick on the fire, she felt goose bumps popping out on the backs of her arms. She didn't know this man. She'd known the drunk and had been perfectly comfortable with him. But she didn't know her boundaries with this one.

Then he turned around and caught her staring.

"Letty? You all right?"

She flinched. "Yeah, sure," she said. "Be right back."

She stomped off into the woods, unaware that Eulis was now watching her.

Finally, he sighed and looked away. When she came back, he was cutting up what was left of the rabbit for her to eat.

"Here," he said. "Since you hurt your wrist, thought I better cut it up some for you."

Letty didn't bother to hide her surprise.

"How did you know it was hurt?" she asked.

"You told me," he said.

"I did?"

He nodded.

She frowned. "What else did I tell you?"

He stared at her a bit, then grinned. "Don't worry. I didn't believe a word of it."

She gasped.

He ignored that, too.

"Here. Sit down and eat. The rabbit needs salt, but what we had left dissolved in the storm."

He handed her a tin plate and then poured her a cup of water.

Letty took the plate with her good hand, backed up to a rock and sat. Then she balanced the plate in her lap and began eating. After the first couple of bites, Letty realized how hungry she was and soon finished off her share of the food.

"That was wonderful," she said, and leaned back with a sigh.

"Yeah, it was good," Eulis said, then pointed into the darkness. "Thanks to the storm, there's a pretty good run of water in that creek tonight. I reckon it's safe enough to take a bath in, if you're in a mind to take one."

Letty groaned. "I would love one," she said. "It will be wonderful to wash all over, again."

Eulis squinted, then looked away.

"I'll walk you down," he said. "When you're done, just holler and I'll come back and get you."

Letty set the plate aside and stood, still holding her wrist against her breast to keep from bumping it.

"Would you please get my blanket out of the wagon? I'm going to wash these stinking clothes, too."

Eulis did as she asked, then cupped her elbow and walked her down to the creek. The water was running fast and high and she could see foam on the current.

"It's right cold," he warned.

"After nearly dying of thirst, I will never complain about the temperature of water again."

"Need any help?" he asked, pointing to her clothes.

"Maybe you could help me off with my shoes."

"Lean on me," he said, and bent down.

Letty grabbed onto his back, steadying herself as he untied first one shoe, then the other, and took them off her feet.

"Anything else?" he asked.

She shook her head.

He nodded, started to say something more, then sighed and walked away.

"Call when you're ready to come back," he said.

"Yes, all right," Letty said, and began untying her rope belt, then taking off the rest of her clothes.

She kicked the clothes to the edge of the creek so that she could rinse them out, then stepped into the water.

Eulis had been right. It was, as her Daddy used to say, colder than a well-digger's ass, and her toes instantly went into cramps and curled downward in spasms. She flinched once, then walked into the knee-high flow, found a half-submerged rock and used it for a seat. With only one hand left to do her any good, she washed herself all over as best she could, then eased off the rock and all the way down into the water. It was almost up to her chin, but she didn't care. She undid the piece of leather holding her hair away from her face, put it between her teeth to keep from losing it, and then dropped her head forward. It was awkward having only one hand with which to scrub, but she managed.

Finally, she lifted her head, tossing her hair away from her face as she did and then dragged herself up. It wasn't until she was standing with the night air blowing against her skin that she realized how cold she really was, and she had yet to wash out her clothes. She took the strip of leather from her teeth and turned around. Eulis was standing on the creek bank with a blanket in his hands.

"Hurry on out," he said, as matter of fact as if he'd asked her to hand him a spoon.

She stumbled once, then caught herself and climbed out, only to find herself immediately engulfed in a warm and surprisingly dry blanket.

"Ooh, that feels good," she said.

Eulis grabbed her elbow.

"You need to get warm."

"My clothes," Letty said. "I've still got to wash out my clothes."

"I'm gonna take me a bath," Eulis said. "I'll do it when I wash mine out."

"Well, then . . . I thank you," Letty said.

"No problem," Eulis said, and hustled her back to the fire. "Get warm. I made up your bed in the wagon. When I come back, I'll help you up."

Letty didn't know what to say. Before, she'd been the one more or less in charge and Eulis had followed her suggestions and orders without much argument. Not only did she feel helpless, but with a broken wrist, also useless.

"I'm sorry about this," she said, and held up her wrist.

"Need to wrap it up some," he said briefly, then took some leather out of his pack and felt along both sides of her wrist to assure himself the break was clean and back in place. Once he was satisfied that all was as it should be, he wrapped it firmly and tied it off.

"Don't be tryin' to lift anything with that," he said.

"Okay."

"I'm gonna go take my bath now," he muttered.

Letty nodded, but there was a pain in her heart as he turned away. Suddenly, she couldn't stand the suspense any longer. She had to know.

"Eulis."

He stopped, but didn't turn around.

"What?"

"Are you mad at me?"

If her voice hadn't been so damned shaky, he would have been all right, but when he heard that tremble and knew she was feeling pain, he could no more ignore her than he could have quit breathing. He sighed, then turned around.

"Course not. We're partners now, aren't we?"

"I guess."

"All right then. Now get on back to that fire and get warm. I won't be long."

"Yes . . . okay," Letty said, and watched him walk away.

There was a funny pain in the pit of her stomach, which she chalked up to a saltless rabbit and a broken wrist and sat down by the fire. She didn't mean to, but exhaustion soon claimed her.

When Eulis came back from the creek, she was slumped over and sound asleep.

He stood over her for a few moments watching the way her nostrils flared slightly as she breathed in and breathed out, then picked her up and carried her to the wagon, taking great care not to bump her wrist.

She settled immediately, rolled over on

her other side and fell into an even deeper sleep.

Eulis pulled the covers closer to her then tucked them under before walking away. As soon as he'd strung their wet clothes on the surrounding tree limbs, he took off his own wet pants, hung them up, as well, and then wrapped up in his blanket.

He started to lay down beneath the wagon then thought to check on Letty one more time. She was curled up in the blanket and when he felt of her forehead, she moaned.

He frowned. He wasn't sure, but she might be getting a fever, and he wouldn't know it if he was under the wagon. Hesitating briefly, he got their rifle, crawled up into the wagon and then, wrapped up in his own blanket from toe to chin, lay down beside her and closed his eyes.

He fell asleep with his hand on the gun and dreamed of stampeding buffalo and hail and a woman who wouldn't quit.

Keeping the Promises

It had been five days since Letty and Eulis had survived the buffalo herd. During those five days, they'd gotten closer and closer to their destination, but farther and farther apart. There was an uneasiness between them that had never been there before. Letty found it difficult to look Eulis in the face when they were talking, and Eulis was having thoughts of Letty that were anything but proper. He couldn't help but wonder if Preacher Howe's weakness for women was rubbing off on him. He'd never had these problems before. It didn't occur to him that the reason he'd been uninterested in women before was because whiskey had captured his heart. But now that the whiskey was a thing of the past, his normal manly urges were resurrecting. And, added to that was his growing admiration for Letty. Except for when they'd been caught in the buffalo herd, she'd never wavered in her belief that they would endure.

Now, by Eulis's best guess, they should reach the location of the gold strike within the week. He'd been told back in Dripping Springs that it was at a place called Cherry Creek near the town of Denver, and while he'd never been there, he'd been given some landmarks to look for, one of which they'd passed just this morning.

He glanced over at Letty, who sat beside him in the wagon seat with the rifle across her lap. With her wrist still too painful to drive the team, she was riding shotgun and taking the job as seriously as she took everything else.

"How you doin'?" he asked.

"Fine," she said, without looking at him.

"Need to take a break?"

"No."

Eulis wanted to get a rise out of her. He didn't like getting the silent treatment, and because he missed the old Letty and her fiery temper, he pushed.

"You don't even need to pee?"

Letty flinched as if she'd been slapped. Before she could think to ignore him, she was already mad.

"No, I don't need to pee! Is that what you think of when you look at me? Poor stupid woman . . . tips an outhouse over on herself cause she had to go. Causes a terrible fuss on the stagecoach because she has to go pee again."

She hit him on the arm and then hunched her shoulders and looked away.

If someone had stuck a knife in Eulis's gut, he couldn't have felt any worse. He'd only wanted to tease a smile onto her face, not hurt her. He pulled the mules to a stop and tied off the reins onto the brake, then got down out of the wagon.

When he started to walk away without speaking, Letty looked up and yelled at him.

"Where are you going?"

He turned around and grinned.

"To pee. You wouldn't give me an excuse and I'm not tough enough to wait it out like you."

"Oh."

She sat and watched until he moved behind some bushes, then she got down and walked a short distance in the other direction. Trees were absent and undergrowth was sparse. The only thing she could hide behind was a large rock, so she headed for it.

She had her belt untied and was holding her pants up with one hand as she moved to the backside, and because she was looking over her shoulder to check on Eulis, she first missed the fact that she was no longer alone.

"Lord, have mercy, I am saved."

Expecting that she would be alone, Letty squealed and grabbed the gun with both hands. As she did, her pants fell the rest of the way to her ankles. It was then she saw the owner of the voice. Her mouth went slack in disbelief — her eyes bugged.

"Good God in heaven —"

"Emory James at your service, ma'am. Excuse me if I don't stand up, but as you can see, I am somewhat at a disadvantage."

"EEEuuullliiisss!"

The scream brought Eulis out of the bushes on the run. He thought of the rifle and groaned. Letty had their only weapon, and if she was in dire straits, then they were both for sure in trouble.

When he didn't see her at the wagon, his heart dropped. Then she screamed again. He turned abruptly and saw her up ahead and running out of the trees, holding her pants up with one hand and waving the rifle with the other.

He started running.

"Eulis! Eulis!"

He caught her on the run, yanked the rifle out of her hand and shoved her behind him.

"What is it? What's wrong?"

"There's a man behind that rock."

"Did he hurt you? Tell me, honey, did he hurt you?"

She was tying her belt as fast as she could while shaking her head.

"No, no, I'm all right, but he's . . . he's —" she shuddered, unable to finish what she'd been going to say and just grabbed Eulis's hand and started leading him back to the rock.

Eulis came with her, but he wasn't as sure of the urgency as he'd been before. As soon as they reached the rock, he stopped.

"Wait. I'm goin' in first," Eulis said.

"Okay . . . and, oh yeah . . . one other thing. He said his name was Emory James."

Eulis stared. "He introduced himself?"

"Sort of."

"Then what in blazes is the problem?"

She pointed. "You'll see."

Eulis circled the rock with the rifle at the ready then staggered to a stop.

"Oh God . . . oh man . . . Mister, Mister . . . how in blazes . . . what . . . who . . . ?"

"I'd be real happy to tell you the details, but could we talk after you get me out of this hole?"

Eulis pointed behind him. "The wagon. I got a shovel in the wagon. Wait here. I'll be right back."

Emory James would have grinned, but he was too miserable to make the effort. Instead, he chose sarcasm to cover the emotion of relief.

"Wait here? Yeah, sure. No problem."

Eulis blinked, then sucked his lower lip into his mouth and bolted for the wagon, thrusting the gun in Letty's hand as he went.

Letty circled the rock again, squatted down in front of the man and cradled the rifle across her lap.

"Mister —"

"Emory. Please call me Emory."

"Emory. So how did you get this way?"

Emory blew toward his nose then gave Letty a beseeching look.

"I know we've just met, but could I ask you to do me a favor and brush that ant off my face before it crawls up my nose?"

Letty hesitated a moment, then leaned forward and brushed the ant off the man's nose.

"Does it hurt?" she asked.

"Where's your man?" Emory asked. "I sure would like to get out of here."

Letty turned around to look. "He's coming."

"Reckon ya'll got yourselves a shovel?"

"We got one," she said, then eyed him closer. "How tall are you, anyway?"

"Less than six feet."

Letty nodded. "Who did this to you? Why would someone want to bury you like this, up to your neck and all? He had to know that you'd die. If he was that pissed, why didn't he just out and out kill you?"

The woman's curiosity struck Emory's funny bone, which somewhat surprised him, because if anyone had asked him, he would have said that Black Dog had broken the funny bone and everything else Emory had before he stuck him in this hole and buried him up to his neck.

He almost smiled, in spite of his bloodied and swollen lips.

"Considering the fact that it takes twice as long to die like this, I'd say that Black Dog was using his best options to make me suffer before I kicked."

"What happens if we dig you up and Black Dog finds out?"

"I'd advise you not to mention it around."

Letty shivered. She couldn't imagine running into someone who was capable of this kind of torture.

"What did you do to piss him off?" Letty asked.

"I was about to pork his woman."

That was something Letty understood. She stared long and hard at him and then rocked back on her heels.

"Then I reckon you're lucky he didn't cut off your dingus before he planted your ass."

Emory was still digesting that remark when Eulis came running around the rock. Letty stood up and then stepped back to give them more room. She eyed Emory James closely. She'd known a thousand men like him and not one of them had been worth saving. She couldn't help but wonder if they were doing Black Dog an injustice, but it was too late to question that now. If they walked away from this man after finding him like this, then they would be the ones killing him, and that wasn't something she took lightly.

Eulis chunked the shovel into the earth a distance away from where the man's shoulders should be and took out the first shovelful of dirt.

"He's not quite six feet tall," Letty offered.

Eulis looked up at her, surprised that she'd had the sense to ask and then smiled.

"Good thinkin', Sister Leticia."

Emory frowned as he looked at Letty, trying to figure out how an armed woman wearing men's pants and burned brown as the earth in which he was buried could have any religious connections.

"Sister? So is he your brother, or are you one of them nun women, one of them Catholics?"

"We're digging you out. That's all you need to know," Letty said.

Since Emory was in no position to argue, he didn't push the issue.

Time passed. Eulis dug with the shovel until he was forced to stop and dig with his hands to keep from injuring Emory James more. Finally, they managed to move enough dirt to get a rope beneath his arms and around his chest. The ground was looser from the waist down and Eulis figured they could hitch him to the mules and just pull him out.

Emory wasn't as convinced it would work and spoke up to the fact.

"You gonna do this all slow like, aren't you? I don't want to find myself pulled in half or anything."

"I'll go slow," Eulis promised.

"It probably wouldn't hurt to scare him some," Letty muttered, as she grabbed the other end of the rope and started toward the mules.

Emory's eyes rolled until all that was

visible were the whites of his eyes.

"She's not serious, is she?"

Eulis didn't answer.

Emory panicked. "Mister! Mister! She ain't serious is she?"

Eulis frowned. "Letty? Yeah, she's serious. She's always serious. I don't know what you said to her, but she's taken a dislike to you and nothin' I got to say is gonna change that. However, don't worry. I'm the one who'll be workin' the mules. Her wrist is broke."

Emory felt a warmth on the inside of his leg and knew that he'd just wet himself. But considering the day that he'd had, he considered himself lucky that he still had a dingus from which to pee.

"I'm sure grateful to you both," Emory said.

Eulis finished tying off the rope under Emory's armpits, then stood up.

"You're not out yet," Eulis said. "Better save your thanks for later."

At that moment, Emory felt a tug on the rope and knew that Letty was taking matters into her own hand.

"Wait!" he screamed. "Lady, wait!"

Eulis grabbed the rope, catching the slack as he ran toward the wagon.

"Letty! Wait!"

She was standing by the mules with a smile on her face.

"What's wrong?" she asked.

Eulis was breathing heavy by the time he got to her.

"What did you think you was doin'?"

"Giving him something to think about."

Eulis frowned. "What did he do, anyway?"

"Pissed off an Indian who calls himself Black Dog."

Eulis took a step backward, then grabbed onto the harness to steady himself.

"The hell you say."

"You know him?"

Eulis's face turned pale. "Of him. He's bad news."

"So what happens to us if Black Dog finds out we dug the man up?"

"We don't tell him," Eulis said.

"That what Emory James suggested, too."

"What did he do to Black Dog?" Eulis asked.

"His words were, he was about to pork Black Dog's woman and got caught in the act."

Eulis looked up at the surrounding hills and then turned a complete circle, searching the horizon for signs that they were being watched.

"What do you think we oughta do?" Eulis asked.

"If we leave him planted, then we're killing him, too," Letty said.

Eulis thought about it a minute and then nodded.

"I've got to move the wagon some so that we're pullin' the sucker straight. It would be a shame to drag him into that big rock, wouldn't it?"

"A crying shame," Letty said.

They smiled at each other, then just to give Emory James a second reminder of why he was still up to his ass in dirt, they each grabbed a mule and began moving them backward.

"Hey! Whoa! Goddamit, you people! You're killing me, here!"

"Did you hear somethin'?" Eulis asked.

"Might have," Letty said.

"Reckon we ought to go see who it was?"

She shrugged. "It's your call. If it was me, I don't think I would have stopped until the bastard was buried, head and all."

Eulis looked at Letty and then grinned.

"It's good to have you back," he said.

Letty frowned. "I don't know what you mean."

"Yes, you do," Eulis said. "We been tiptoein' around each other like two virgins facin' a troop of soldiers with permanent hard-ons."

Letty's frown turned to a glare.

"Well, it's all your fault."

"Mine? Why is it mine?"

"You started treating me nice, even taking care of me like I was something special. How else was I to act?"

Eulis glared back. "Dang it, Letty, you are somethin' special, whether you like it or not. Now are we gonna drag Emory James outta' his grave or leave him to it?"

"You move the wagon. I'll go tell the little bastard to stop yelling."

"All right then," Eulis said.

"All right then," Letty echoed.

She walked off while Eulis grabbed the reins and began leading the mules and wagon to get a better angle.

Emory James was hanging onto the rope for dear life when Letty rounded the rock.

"What the holy hell was you two tryin' to do to me?" he asked.

"There is not one damned thing about hell that is holy," Letty said, and then kicked a little dirt back in the hole to punctuate her statement. "Eulis is moving the wagon to get a better angle to pull you out. And, if I was you, I wouldn't be doing all that yelling. That Black Dog fella might have set himself up somewhere nearby just to watch you die."

Emory's stomach knotted as he looked around in panic.

"Why did you say that? Did you see him? Did you see sign of — ?"

"Shut up, Mister. You talk too much," Letty said.

Emory shut his mouth.

Eulis got the wagon in place.

"You ready?" he called.

"Let 'er rip," Letty called back.

Emory felt the first tug as the rope tightened around his chest.

"Easy . . . easy," he begged, as the pull tightened even more. His lower half was still planted where Black Dog had put him, and he couldn't feel any give. "Wait! Wait!" he begged.

"Ease up!" Letty called.

Eulis halted the mules.

Letty looked down at Emory.

"What's wrong?"

"I don't think this is gonna work," Emory said. "I don't feel any give below."

Letty picked up the shovel and dug a few more shovels full from around his waist, apologizing every time she nicked his hips and his butt with the shovel.

"Lord have mercy, woman," Emory finally begged. "You're gonna unman me with that shovel blade."

"I'm not trying to hurt you," Letty said. "However, if it happened, it would certainly take care of your weakness for other men's women, wouldn't it?"

Emory turned loose of the rope and started digging the dirt from around his waist, himself.

"Get back! Get back, damn it! You're a scary woman and that's a fact!"

"Are you ready?" Eulis called out.

Letty looked down at Emory, who was frantically digging dirt from around his waist.

"Yeah, he's ready!" she yelled.

Emory looked up in disbelief, then grabbed the rope just as the mules gave him another tug.

He screamed out in pain.

"More!" Letty yelled.

Emory's scream intensified and then suddenly he was out and flopping on the ground like a fish out of water. He was out and from the waist down, as naked as the day he was born.

"Whoa!" Letty called. "He's out!"

"Praise God," Eulis said. He untied the rope and then drove the team and wagon up to the rock.

"My pants! Where's my pants?" Emory groaned.

Letty looked at the man's dirty bare ass, then leaned over and peered into the hole.

"Would you look at this," she said. "They're still in the hole. We pulled you right out of your britches."

Eulis circled the rock and then stopped, taken aback by the man's nudity.

"What happened to your pants?" he asked.

Letty pointed to the hole.

"We pulled him right out of them."

Emory rolled over on his back then sat up, scrambling to get the rope from around his chest before this crazy pair decided to drag him behind the wagon just to see how much dust he could raise. Then he cupped his hands over his crotch.

"Would someone please hand me my pants?"

"You still got your legs," Letty said. "Get 'em yourself."

Emory cursed beneath his breath and tried to stand up, only to find his legs were still too numb to bear weight. He stumbled, then fell to his knees, baring his nude ass in an even more embarrassing pose. It occurred to him then that he was disliking this woman more and more with every passing minute.

"Here," Eulis said. "I'll get 'em for you."

"I would certainly appreciate it," Emory said, and glared at Letty.

Letty purposefully looked at what he could not hide and then grinned.

"You sure must have a high opinion of yourself," she said.

Emory frowned. "What makes you say that?"

She pointed to his dirty, shriveled dingus.

"You oughta know that you can't take a woman away from her man with something like that."

Eulis purposefully ignored them both, but Emory gasped. He'd never been insulted in such an intimate manner by anyone, let alone a woman. He stumbled to his feet just as Eulis pulled his pants from the hole, then yanked them out of Eulis's hands. He stumbled to the wagon, leaning against it to steady himself as he put on his pants. When he was completely covered, he eyed Eulis.

"You got yourself a real mean woman."

Eulis looked at Letty, who was rolling up the rope they'd used to pull him out of the hole, then grinned.

"Yeah, I know."

"How do you put up with her?" Emory asked.

"Mostly I just let her have her way," Eulis said.

Letty snorted beneath her breath and tossed the rope in the back of the wagon.

"If you two are through talking bad about me, it's time we got moving."

"You heard the woman," Eulis said. "If you want a ride to Cherry Creek, you better get in."

Emory grabbed onto the wagon and tried to climb in, but his arms and legs were still too weak.

"Oh, for Pete's sake," Letty said.

She bent down, grabbed him by the ankles with her good arm, then both lifted and pushed as he was pulling, which catapulted him into the wagon bed, head first.

He landed with a thud.

Letty heard him curse. She leaned over the wagon and looked in.

"I'm sorry. Were you talking to me?" she asked.

Emory rolled over on his back and ran his fingers over his nose and chin. He was missing some hide, but it was a small price to pay for being out of that hole.

"No, ma'am," he said. "And thanks for the help in getting in."

"No problem," Letty said, then felt Eulis's hand was on her back.

"Don't you think you've helped him enough?"

"I haven't decided," Letty said. "Where my rifle?"

"On the wagon seat," Eulis said. "Need some help gettin' up?"

"I can manage," Letty said, and started to climb up into the wagon, but only using one arm made it difficult.

"You sure you don't need some help?" Eulis asked.

Letty turned around and glared. "If I do, I'll ask for it."

"Fine then," Eulis said, and turned away just as Letty slipped. She landed butt first in the dirt and knocked the wind from her lungs.

Eulis sighed, then bent down and picked her up.

Letty batted at his hands, but was lacking the air to speak.

"Dang it, Leticia. Can't you for once just accept a little help without making a big fuss about it?"

He plopped her in the seat, then shoved at her leg.

"Scoot over," he said. "I'm still driving."

She took the rifle as she scooted, pointed the barrel so that it was straight in Emory's face as she turned around.

"So, Emory James, I'm trusting you're not the kind of man to try something when my back is turned."

"No, ma'am," Emory said, and scooted all the way back to the end of the wagon. "I'm just grateful. Real grateful for your help."

She nodded once, then turned and stared straight ahead.

"We're fine," she said.

"Good to know," Eulis said, and flipped the reins on Rosy and Blackie's back. "Gee, Rosy . . . Haw, Blackie . . . let's go."

He clucked his tongue sharply. The wheels started to turn, and they resumed their journey, drawing them just a little bit closer to Cherry Creek.

One More Mile to Go —
One Last Soul to Save

Black Dog was dead.

Millie Sees Crow had seen to that after he'd taken his knife to her face. She'd made up her mind to do it after he'd slashed her face for the second time. When he'd found her with the trapper, he'd been furious. He had cut her hair, her cheek and then cut off the end of her nose, claiming that he was going to make her too ugly for any other man to want. She still didn't understand what had made him so angry because he often sold her services to other men and kept the money for himself.

She'd killed Black Dog the night after he'd buried the trapper in the sand. She thought the trapper called himself James, but she wasn't sure. White men had strange names that meant nothing to her. After she'd killed Black Dog, she'd thought about going back and digging up the trapper, but she'd decided against it. For now, she was glad to be on her own. Her cheek was sore and her nose very painful. She touched them lightly, satisfied that there was still enough salve on the wounds to keep off flies.

Millie Sees Crow wasn't, by nature, a vicious woman, but Black Dog should not have marked her face. She'd told him so as she was cutting off his manhood. He'd screamed at her and cursed wildly in pain until she'd slit his throat. After that, he'd been quiet. She'd strung his penis on a long piece of rawhide, then tied it around her waist. Eventually, it would rot and fall off, which was fine with her. By then, she would have taken his power as her own.

She glanced toward the horizon, gauging the location of the sun to give her an idea of how much time before sunset. She'd never been this way before, but in the foothills of this vast mountain range were many small creeks and lots of forage for her two horses. When she was well, she was going back to her people, the Comanche, which meant backtracking over a lot of territory before she would be home. Even though her father had traded her to Black Dog for five horses and a dozen buffalo robes almost ten years ago, she thought he would welcome her home — especially after he saw what Black Dog had done to her. She had guns and knives and two horses. Maybe there would be a man among her people who would be willing to overlook her scars for the fine things she would bring to their lodge. She was still young enough to bear children, although all during the years she'd been with Black Dog and the men he sold her to, she had never become ripe with child. It occurred to her that she might be barren, but it was nothing she could control. All she needed to do now was heal, gather enough food to start her journey home, and hope to make it before the snow fell.

A rabbit bolted out from the underbrush along the path and ran in front of her horse. She pulled Black Dog's pistol out of her pocket and shot. The rabbit dropped in midleap. She grunted with satisfaction, pulled the horse to a halt and got off to retrieve her kill. It would fill her belly tonight and she would keep the fur to line moccasins she would wear when the winds grew cold.

She cut the rabbit's throat, bled it well and then skinned it with only a few swift strokes. Wrapping both meat and fur into pieces of rawhide then stowing it inside Black Dog's saddlebags, she remounted and resumed her journey. A couple of hours later, she stopped on a small rise above a creek, hobbled the horses and began to make camp. It was almost dark when she heard what sounded like a team and wagon. Millie Sees Crow didn't like surprises, so she picked up Black Dog's rifle and slipped into the trees.

Emory James's butt hurt from riding backside down in the back of the crazy couple's wagon. His ribs hurt because, when they'd pulled him out of the hole, they'd tried to pull his body in half. His head and face hurt because Black Dog had tried to rearrange his face before he'd planted him in the dirt. It had occurred to him more than once that he might be taller now than he had been before they'd pulled him out because every joint in his body below the waist had been stretched to the point of pain. He still couldn't stand up without wobbling and wondered if his knees would ever be the same.

He looked up at the couple in the wagon seat. The woman's name was Leticia, but the driver usually called her Letty. From the back, she looked ordinary — even pretty. She had nice curves and the long thick braid down her back was nut brown. But she was scary. She'd laughed at his pain and made fun of his dingus, which had totally pissed him off. Added to that, she hadn't said more than a dozen words since they'd begun their journey together and that had been hours ago.

Eulis, the driver, seemed all right, but he was definitely attached to the woman, although Emory was pretty sure that their relationship didn't have anything to do with sex. He couldn't put his finger on why they made him nervous, but he'd made up his mind that once they got to Cherry Creek, he would be going his own way.

"Hey!" he called out. "It's gonna be dark soon. Aren't you gonna make camp?"

"Been smellin' smoke for a while now," Eulis said. "Thought we'd make sure that whoever has made camp isn't a threat before we stop."

Emory's belly flopped.

"What if it's Black Dog? Damn it, man, why didn't you say somethin' sooner? If it's him, I'm a dead man. I want out! Let me out!"

Letty turned around. The gun turned with her and once again, Emory found himself staring down the barrel as Letty spoke.

"Mister, if we wanted you dead, we would have left you in the ground, right?"

Emory swallowed nervously, then nodded.

"So, wouldn't you think it would be in your best interests to be quiet until we find out a few things?"

He nodded.

"Good. Trust me. If that campfire belongs to the man who planted your ass, then we don't want to spend the night with him, either, do we?"

"No."

"So, if it was me, and I wasn't interested in meeting back up with this Black Dog, I'd be flat on my face in the wagon and hiding beneath that tarp."

Emory lurched toward the tarpaulin covering their goods and crawled under. Letty heard him moan once, then curse softly. Either he'd bumped something that hurt, or he'd wet himself. Either way, she didn't much care. She was still on the side of the woman who'd been caught in the middle of the mess, even if she was an Indian.

A few minutes later, they pulled into the campsite. The campfire was burning, but there was no one in sight.

"Hello the camp!" Eulis called.

No one appeared, although there was a rabbit on a spit slowly cooking over the open fire.

"Hello the camp!" he called again, then

thought about backing up and moving on down the road.

He didn't like the feel of this. Whoever this belonged to hadn't gone far. The rabbit was nearly done, and it was obvious they wouldn't go off and let it burn. He peered into the shadows beneath the trees, but saw no one.

At that point, Letty handed Eulis the rifle and started to get down. He grabbed her by the arm.

"Where are you goin'?"

"You have to ask?" she drawled.

"Lord, Leticia, your bladder sure does act up at the blamedest times. Can't you wait?"

"I been waiting for more than six hours."

"But this camp . . . it doesn't feel right."

"It can't feel any worse than my bladder," Letty said, and began to climb down.

At that moment, there was movement in the shadows. Eulis grabbed Letty's arm.

"Wait!"

She turned, watching as a small brown woman emerged from the trees with a gun aimed in their direction. Her face looked as if she'd been beaten and as they watched her come closer, realized that her hair had been chopped off, her cheek had been slashed and the end of her nose had been cut off, too.

"We saw your fire," Letty said. "We mean you no harm."

"You go now, I don't shoot you!" Millie Sees Crow said.

"Please," Letty said. "We need to water our mules."

"Don't forget to tell her that you also need to pee," Eulis drawled.

Letty glared.

Millie Sees Crow grinned. "You go make water there," she told Letty, pointing to the bushes behind the wagon.

"Thank you," Letty said, and was undoing the rope around her waist as she hurried away.

There was some noise in the wagon behind Eulis, and then suddenly Emory's head appeared over the side.

"That's Black Dog's woman. Watch out. He's still somewhere in the trees!"

Eulis spun, his fear for Letty uppermost.

"Letty! It's Black Dog's camp! Look out! Look out!"

Millie's eyes widened when she saw Emory's face. She pointed at him with her chin and then grinned.

"Aaiieee! It is the trapper, James. You don't die."

Emory ducked back down into the wagon.

Eulis didn't know what to do. For all he knew, Black Dog already had Letty in his clutches.

"Letty! Letty! Are you all right?"

Letty came out of the bushes tying the rope back around her waist.

"Yes, I'm fine. What's all the yelling about?"

"Emory said that's Black Dog's woman."

Letty's smile slipped sideways. Lord. Why was it that they always stepped into the shit instead of over it?

She scooted behind the wagon then peered over the side.

"Where's Black Dog?" she asked.

"Dead!" Millie said.

Emory came out from under the tarp within seconds.

"Dead? Where?"

Millie pointed with her chin. "Two days that way."

"Are you sure? How did it happen?"

"I sure. I stuck knife in him."

Everyone stared at the little brown woman. She didn't look like a killer, but they didn't have a reason to dispute her word.

Letty circled the wagon and moved toward the fire. She pointed at Millie's face.

"Did he do that to you?"

Millie nodded. "I cut off man part. See."

She held up a strip of rawhide that she'd tied around her waist. The trio stared in horror at the short piece of man meat hanging at the end of the strip.

"Good Lord," Letty muttered.

Eulis felt his testicles drawing up into his belly and cupped himself in reflex.

Emory climbed over the side of the wagon and then wobbled toward the fire.

"Sorry about what happened to your face, but it don't matter a bit to me" he said, then pointed to the rabbit. "Reckon I could have me a piece of that rabbit?"

Millie pointed her rifle in his face.

"Shoot your own," she said, and waved the gun in Emory's face.

Emory didn't take her seriously and saw this as his opportunity to get away from Letty and her gun.

"Come on, Millie, you're gonna need someone to take care of you. Black Dog hurt me, too. He took my horse, left me for dead. You and me, we'll be good together. I don't beat my women."

Letty didn't believe what she was hearing. Even if the woman was an Indian, she didn't deserve an asshole like Emory James.

"Millie? Your name is Millie?" Letty asked.

The little Indian woman frowned. "No. Black Dog call me that. I am Sees Crow of the Comanche. I need no one to take care of me. I take care of myself."

Letty eyed the piece of shriveled up prick dangling near the woman's knee and allowed as how the little woman sure could do that.

"We're gonna be moving on down the road now," Letty said.

Millie Sees Crow nodded. When Emory started toward her, she pointed the gun at his belly and frowned.

"You go now."

Emory flinched. "But what are you gonna do out here all alone? It's dangerous."

"I kill trouble like I kill Black Dog. You go."

Letty got in the wagon. Eulis started turning it around.

Emory didn't believe she was serious, and didn't move when she ordered him to go.

Then she pulled the hammer back on the rifle.

His eyes widened in disbelief.

"You wouldn't kill me? Not after all we've been through together?"

Eulis was pulling out of the campsite when he heard the rifle go off. He flipped the reins on the mules hard and fast. They bolted into an all-out run. He didn't look back.

But Letty did.

She saw Emory James jump and then turn around and run after them. But the mules were going too fast for him to catch up and she didn't bother to tell Eulis to slow down. She didn't like the man and from the way Millie Sees Crow had behaved, she didn't like him either.

"Is he dead?" Eulis asked, as they cleared the trees.

"Not yet," Letty said, which was the truth. Emory was still running and waving at them to stop.

"That was a close one, wasn't it?" he said.

She nodded, then settled the rifle back across her lap and turned her face toward the mountains.

"Eulis?"

"What?"

"Reckon it will be safe to make camp tonight?"

He thought about it, then frowned.

"We could go on until it's dark. I don't mind making cold camp if you don't."

"Works for me," she said, then added. "Let the mules run a bit, why don't you? The farther away I am from that mess, the better I'll sleep."

Eulis urged the mules on, letting them run for a bit longer before he slowed them down. That night, they made camp beneath an overhang of a rock. With the mountain at their backs and a clear view of the land in front of them, they felt confident that they were safely out of harm's way.

The next morning they resumed their journey and four days later, they found Cherry Creek.

It had rained on them last night as they'd slept beneath the wagon, using the bed as a shelter from the storm and this morning when they'd awakened, the air had been chilly, almost cold. Letty had put on two shirts instead of the usual one and put on two pair of socks to help warm her feet. Eulis had done the same, and then had to shed one shirt as the morning lengthened. But it was their first sign that the elevation was significantly higher, and the year was coming closer to an end.

They'd been on the road since daylight and knew that they were close to their final destination because they'd seen a pair of men on horseback late yesterday evening who were on their way back to Cherry Creek. It had been promising — even a little bit exciting — to know that they were on the verge of a new phase of their lives.

Last night as they'd made camp, Letty had wanted to talk and make plans about the future, but she had to keep reminding herself that her future was not necessarily Eulis's. There was bound to come a day when he wanted to move on — maybe even find a woman and marry. Now that he didn't drink any more, Letty was of the opinion that Eulis would make a good husband.

The thought of him leaving to marry another woman left her torn. On the one hand, she was happy that he'd changed his ways, and when she was feeling self-righteous, took most of the credit for his transformation. If it hadn't been for her, he would still be sweeping floors and digging graves for drinks. But then she also had to remember that a man had died before Eulis's chance for redemption had come. At that point, the image she had of herself being Eulis's redeemer became tarnished, since the man who had died, had died on top of her and in her bed.

She lived with the guilt on a daily basis, and even though she'd experienced a sense of salvation during Eulis's first revival preaching, she wasn't sure that her redemption was good enough for a happy-ever-after life for herself. So she stayed quiet about her dreams and never let on that she wanted more out of life than what she had.

"Eulis! Look! Oh my Lord . . . there's a house up ahead!"

It had been so long since they'd seen anything resembling civilization that Letty was ecstatic.

Eulis leaned forward, then smiled and nodded.

"By golly, Letty, you're right. It's a right nice lookin' house, too."

It wasn't until they got closer that they realized it wasn't just a house, it was an inn, and according to the sign, an inn called Four Mile Inn.

"Oh Eulis, can we stay here? Just for a night? I can't remember the last time I slept with a roof over my head."

"I reckon we oughta'," Eulis said. "To get the lay of the land, so to speak."

"I can't wait," Letty said. "I wonder if they've got a bath."

Eulis chuckled. "Shoulda' known you'd be wantin' a bath."

Letty grinned. "At least you won't be the one hauling the hot water up the stairs."

"And praise the Lord for that," Eulis said.

Mention of a higher power reminded Letty that they had yet to decide how they were going to introduce themselves back into society — even if it was going to be a rough and tumble gold field.

Letty glanced up at the towering trees bordering the narrow road and then took a slow, deep breath, inhaling the fresh, clean aroma of pine and rain washed air and thought about how far they'd come from Lizard Flats.

"Eulis?"

"What?"

"Are you gonna preach?"

"No. I told you before, it just ain't right."

She nodded. "Then that's that," she said.

He glanced at her and then clucked to the mules, urging them on as they traveled the last few hundred feet up the incline to the inn.

"Letty, are you mad at me?"

She frowned. "Of course not. Why would I be mad at you?"

"For not keepin' up the pretense."

Letty sighed. "Did you just hear what you said?"

"What do you mean?"

"Pretense. You said, pretense. That tells me that your heart was never in it — not in the way it ought to be."

He thought about it a moment, then nodded. "Yeah, I see what you mean."

"Don't get me wrong," Letty said. "You did good, and you made a whole lot of people happy. But unless you feel a real calling for the job, you don't need to be doing it."

"Yeah, okay. I just didn't want you to be mad at me."

Letty turned and looked at him then, gazing her fill at the lean, brown lines of his face and the hair in need of cutting and sighed.

"Eulis."

"Yeah?"

"I'm not the easiest person to be around and I know it. And I might get pissed off at you now and then, but not for anything real big. Truth is, I'm proud of you."

A big lump tied itself into a knot in the back of Eulis's throat.

"You are?"

"Yes."

He glanced at her briefly, then quickly

looked away, afraid that she might see what he was feeling in his eyes.

"I don't think anyone's ever said that to me before."

Letty saw a muscle jerking at the side of his jaw. She thought about hugging him and then decided he would get the wrong idea — or maybe the right one. Either way, it wouldn't do either one of them any good. He knew too much about her past to ever look at her as anything other than a whore.

"The past is the past," she said. "We got ourselves a second chance and, I don't know about you, but I'm gonna make the most of it."

Unaware of what was going through Letty's mind, and still overwhelmed by the fact that she'd praised him, Eulis just nodded in agreement.

"We're here," he said, as he pulled the wagon up to the inn.

"Yep, we sure are," Letty said, and quickly got down as Eulis set the brake and tied off the reins. It remained to be seen exactly where "here" was, but she was glad to be standing on solid ground.

Eulis shouldered the rifle and they walked into Four Mile Inn together.

It was a strange setup for a hotel. There

was a small saloon set up near the door with a bar barely as long as a man was tall. But the bottles on the shelf behind it and the stack of clean glasses were proof of its use. The room where travelers ate was one big space with an odd assortment of chairs and tables scattered about. Letty could smell food cooking, but the kitchen was somewhere out of sight. There was what appeared to be an even tinier general store in another part of the lobby. Before she could look further, a tall, middle-aged woman appeared in a doorway then moved toward them with a no-nonsense stride.

"Welcome, travelers. I'm Mrs. Cocker. You here just to eat or do you want a bed, too?"

Eulis glanced at Letty, who was unusually quiet.

"Two beds, please, and a meal. And do you, by any chance, have a bath house?" He pointed to Letty. "Letty, here, favors a tub bath real highly."

The woman nodded briskly while eyeing Letty's manly style of dress.

"Bath house out back. Got hot water on the stove. It'll cost extra."

"Lovely," Letty said, and then pointed to the small dry goods store. "Got any shoes for sale?"

"Women's shoes?" Mrs. Cocker asked.

"Actually, no. I need something sturdy. I've about walked the soles off these things. Besides which, it's coming on winter."

The woman peered down at Letty's feet then motioned for her to follow.

"Come with me. Maybe a small pair of men's shoes will fit. Since you're already wearing men's pants, I don't suppose you'll mind."

Letty heard the sarcasm. Once it would have hurt her feelings. Now it just pissed her off.

"Yeah, I'm wearing men's pants because my last dress burned up when I fell into the campfire. And the rest of my business is none of yours. Do you want to sell shoes and rent us a bed or do you want to criticize my fashion sense?"

"I'll sell you anything you need," she said. "Have a seat."

The moment passed. Letty found a pair of shoes that fit, but they didn't look new.

"These have been worn," she said.

"Oh, yeah, those belonged to a kid named Pete McKay. Young Scots. Red hair, freckles, big smile."

Letty stared down at the shoes on her feet.

"What happened to him?"

"Pneumonia. Died last spring. Broke his father's heart. He packed up the family and headed for California. Doubt if they made it past that damned desert, though."

Letty felt sick at standing in these shoes, as if she had transgressed on someone's grave.

"There's a desert between here and California?"

"That's what I hear," Mrs. Cocker said. "Never seen it myself. Don't plan to, neither." She pointed at Letty's feet. "You want the shoes or not?"

"Yes."

"That'll be four bits."

"I'll give you two and that's more than enough. They're used."

"Done," Mrs. Cocker said. "So you want the beds or not?"

"All of it," Letty said. "For one night, we want it all. Beds, bath and meals."

Mrs. Cocker nodded, then eyed Letty one more time. "That kid. Pete McKay."

"What about him?"

"I got some of his clothes, too. Throw in another two bits and you can have them, too."

Letty thought of their dwindling cash, but winter was coming and she couldn't exist on Eulis's castoffs through ice and snow.

"All right."

"I'll gather them up later, but for now, follow me. I'll show you to your beds and then get the hot water for your bath."

"I feel like I've died and gone to heaven," Letty murmured, more to herself than to Mrs. Cocker, but the woman heard her just the same.

"Honey, if you're not careful, you could die here at that. It's a hard place here, these gold fields. Men do bad things to good people for a little color, and you'd better beware. This place isn't heaven. It's closer to hell."

Letty glanced at Eulis, who was staring at the woman with a hard look on his face.

"Sorry to dispute your word, ma'am, but this ain't hell. We already been there and come out the other side. Maybe this is somewhere in between, in which case, I feel comfortable in tellin' you that me and Letty, here, are gonna be just fine."

Letty's heart swelled as she looked at Eulis with pride. If she hadn't already told him she was proud of him, she would have said it now. As it was, all she could do was follow him and the innkeeper to the dormitory-like room where the beds were to be had for nominal cost.

"Not much privacy here," Letty said, as she gave them two beds near a window.

Mrs. Cocker turned around and looked at Letty.

"If you don't mind my saying so, you might need to rethink your business here. In the gold fields, only the strong and the tough survive."

Eulis looked at Letty, wondering what she was going to say, but then she caught his eye and to his surprise, she started to grin.

He grinned back.

She chuckled, then looked away as she sat down on the bed, looked at him again and laughed out loud.

He was still grinning as he sat on his bed. He threw his hat on the floor and then chuckled as he watched her laughing. She was doubled over on the bed and trying to take off her new boots. But the harder she tried, the funnier everything became.

"Only the strong. Lord have mercy," and she rolled off the bed onto the floor. She pointed at Eulis and then slapped her hands over her face as she was struck with a fresh wave of hysteria. "Stop . . . stop . . . don't look at me," she begged.

The innkeeper frowned. "I don't know what I said that was so humorous. This is not Philadelphia."

Letty took a deep breath and bit her lower lip, but it was no use. She looked at Eulis and then rolled over on her belly, laid her forehead in the crook of one arm and started slapping the floor with the flat of her other hand as she laughed until she cried.

Eulis sighed. It was to be expected that the relief of reaching their destination would come out in some fashion, but he would never have expected this.

Mrs. Cocker stared at the woman as if she'd lost her mind and then turned to Eulis. "Is she all right? I mean, she's not touched in the head or anything, is she? I don't want no crazy woman sleeping under my roof."

Eulis grinned. "No ma'am, she's not crazy. She's also no sissy, and the fact that you looked at her and thought that might be the case is what has tickled her funny bone."

"I'm sorry. I don't get the joke," Mrs. Cocker said. "Stew's on the stove when you're ready to eat. Bathtubs are out back. I've got three, only one's got a hole in it. Pay up front."

"What'll we owe you?" Eulis asked.

"A dollar apiece," she said.

"A dollar?"

She put her hands on her hips and nodded again to accentuate her price.

"A dollar, and a cheap price at that. It's four miles to Denver and the gold fields from here. Things are a lot higher there."

Eulis counted out the money, then sat down on the bed and waited for Letty to regain her senses as the innkeeper left the room.

"You 'bout finished?" he finally asked.

Letty gave up one last laugh and then rolled over on her back and splayed her hands over her belly.

"Oh . . . oh . . . I hurt. I don't know when I've laughed so much. Can you believe she didn't think we were tough enough to be here?"

Eulis grinned. "Yeah, well, she doesn't know us, is all."

Letty sat up, then looked at Eulis, thinking as she did that he seemed really tall from down here.

"No. She doesn't know us."

Eulis reached down and pulled her up.

"Come on, Sister Leticia. You need to go wash that mean off you before you hurt someone."

She grinned. No matter what lay in wait for them, she was going to enjoy this night as it was meant to be enjoyed. No telling how long it would be again before she got to take a warm bath and sleep in a real bed — under a real roof.

Fever — Hot and Gold

In deference to her sex, Mrs. Cocker had offered Letty separate sleeping quarters behind a curtained alcove beyond the main sleeping room, but Letty had refused. After coming this far with Eulis at her side, she wasn't going to start separating herself from him now.

They had bathed, eaten a supper of stew and cornbread and some of the best dried apple pie that Letty had ever tasted, and after tending to their mules, had crawled wearily into bed.

There were at least two dozen beds in the room, and more than half of them were filled. Letty lay on her side with her face to the wall, listening to the sounds of the men settling down for the night. Except for Mrs. Cocker, Letty was the only female on the place, but she didn't feel threatened. The men who'd come to Cherry Creek had a fever all right, but not for women. They'd come for gold.

Eulis was unusually quiet. As Letty lay there, waiting for sleep to claim her, she realized that she was also listening to him. She heard the cot squeak as he settled himself into a comfortable spot, then felt the warmth of his breath against the back of her neck as he exhaled wearily. Somewhere off in the distance, she heard the faint echo of a gunshot and flinched. She'd heard of how wild a gold camp could be, but she'd been in rough places before. She consoled herself with the fact that at least this time, she wasn't at the mercy of men, depending on their favors for her living. Here, she was an equal. She had just as good a chance at striking it rich as any man here. All it was going to take was hard work, perseverance, and possibly more luck than anyone had a right to expect.

Another gunshot sounded, but she just smiled and closed her eyes and fell asleep, dreaming of a streambed lined with gold nuggets.

Eulis woke up once, raised up and leaned over to Letty's cot, pulled the cover back up over her shoulder and then looked around the room, making sure that all was as it should be. All but a half dozen beds were now full, and it appeared that everyone was asleep. However, he wasn't so green as to trust anyone except Letty in a place like this. So he rolled over on his other side with his back to Letty and his face to the room, felt again for the barrel of his rifle just beneath his bedroll and closed his eyes. Everything after tonight was going to be a new experience for him and for Letty. Still, he couldn't help but feel a sense of expectancy. In a place like this, anything was possible — then he amended the thought with another less comforting. Yes, anything was possible — but having gained it, knew that it could be taken away as quickly as it had come. So he, too, slept and dreamed, unaware that someone from their past was ten beds away on the other side of the room.

It was sometime after midnight when a commotion began in the hall outside the sleeping area. Eulis woke first and reached for his rifle as Letty rolled over and sat up on her cot.

"What's happening?" she said.

"I don't know. Sounds like a fight."

Several other sleepers in the room were roused as the noise became louder. They could distinguish Mrs. Cocker's voice, but the others were unrecognizable. Eulis took his rifle and started to get up when Letty grabbed him by the arm.

"Wait, you might get hurt."

"I think Mrs. Cocker is in trouble."

"Oh Lord . . . okay . . . but I'm coming with you."

"No," Eulis said. "Stay here."

He got up and started for the door, but he wasn't going alone. The other men in the room had also been awakened, and a couple of them appeared to have the same thought as Eulis. Letty watched as they got up with guns in hand and fell in behind Eulis.

Someone lit a lantern, and then someone else cursed and told him to blow it out before they became targets for whatever was happening beyond the door.

Letty grabbed her new boots and slipped them on, then quickly stuffed all of their belongings into their bags. If they had to run, she wanted to be ready, then she crawled into the corner of the bed, pulled her knees up beneath her chin and hoped for the best. When Eulis opened the door, he was momentarily silhouetted by the light from the next room, then the other men blocked Letty's view and she couldn't see any more. She held her breath, and like everyone else in the room, waited anxiously to learn what was happening.

"Get out of my inn and be quick about it!" Mrs. Cocker yelled, and then reached beneath the counter and pulled out a rifle. With one smooth movement, she had it cocked and aimed.

"You heard the lady," Eulis said, as he joined her with his rifle aimed.

The two other men who'd come out did the same, adding their presence and fire-power to the men who had challenged the innkeeper's demand. Unfortunately, the half-dozen men who'd come charging into Four Mile Inn had an agenda of their own, and they didn't appear to be in the mood to listen. One of them — a shaggy moun-tain of a man who appeared to be their leader — stepped forward.

"Now look here, Mrs. Cocker. We done told you why we come and we ain't goin' nowhere 'til we see if Art Masters is here."

"I don't know Art Masters," Cocker said, "but even if I did, I wouldn't tell you a thing. But I know you, Will Hodges, and I know that you're drunk. In fact, the whole lot of you are no better than a lynch mob."

"What's goin' on?" Eulis asked.

The big man's gaze swerved from the innkeeper's face to Eulis. He frowned.

"What's goin' on is none of your busi-ness. That's what's goin' on," Hodges said.

"When you come into the place where

I'm sleepin' and raise enough hell to wake the dead, then it becomes my business — it becomes all our business," he added, thereby reminding Will Hodges that there were now four guns aimed directly at their faces.

Hodges frowned, but acquiesced to the firepower.

"We don't aim to cause trouble for none of you," he said. "We're just lookin' for a back-stabbin' claim jumper by the name of Art Masters. He jumped a claim and shot the man it belonged to. That man was our friend and he lived long enough to tell us who shot him."

Mrs. Cocker frowned. There was no law in this part of the country and for the most part, there was also no justice. But claim jumping was serious business, and if that was the case, she had no desire to shelter a back-shooting thief such as that.

"You sure you know who you're looking for?" she asked.

Hodges nodded. "Ask any of these men. We was all present when our friend said the name, and we was all present when he died. So, is he here, or ain't he?"

"I told you the truth when I said I didn't know anyone by the name of Art Masters, but I also don't know the names of any of my guests. However, I won't be accused of sheltering a killer." She turned to the men who'd come to her aid. "Gentlemen, I thank you for coming to my assistance. However, I am going to let these men into the sleeping area. Please stand aside."

Eulis stepped back, but he didn't stand aside. Instead, he went back into the room and headed for Letty. If something happened, he intended to be between her and the shooting.

Mrs. Cocker followed him, carrying a lit lamp into the room.

"Gentlemen, I'm sorry for the inconvenience, but I must ask you to light the other lamps. There is a killer on the loose and these men are looking for him."

There was a loud grumbling until she mentioned the fact that the killer was also a claim jumper. At that point, a candle and two lamps were quickly lit. In the gold fields, a claim jumper was the worst sort of a criminal and one not to be tolerated.

"So, Mr. Hodges, do you see your man?"

The big man took the lamp from the woman's hand and began moving up and down the rows of beds, holding the lamp close to each face as he passed.

Eulis stood between Hodges and the lamp with his gun drawn. Thinking that

Eulis must have something to hide, Hodges headed that way first.

"The man you're lookin' for ain't over here, so back off," Eulis said.

"I reckon I'll see for myself," Hodges muttered, and started to shove Eulis aside.

Fearing Eulis would get himself hurt trying to protect her, she quickly crawled out of bed and stood beside him, meeting the big man's surprised gaze.

"Like he said, Mister. We aren't hiding anything. Look somewhere else for your killer."

There was noise on the other side of the room, as if someone was trying to make a run for it.

Everyone turned to look just as a young, stocky man made a run for the door.

"Grab him!" Hodges shouted.

Suddenly, the man was on the floor and begging for his life.

"Let me go! Let me go!" he begged, and then began to cry, bawling in earnest as he realized what his fate would be. "I didn't do anything. I swear, I didn't do anything. You've got the wrong man."

Hodges thrust the lamp near his face and then snarled.

"By God, it's you, Art Masters, it's you. You shot Henry Cummings in the back."

"I didn't. I swear, I didn't. You got the wrong man."

"He said your name before he died. He said you took his poke and then left him to die."

Subconsciously, the man's hand moved to his waist.

Hodges yanked it back, then ripped open his shirt. A small leather pouch fell out onto the floor. Hodges picked it up.

"Look here! All of you look! This leather pouch has Henry's initials. H.C. Why would a man named Art Masters be carryin' a pouch belongin' to a dead man unless he's the one who stole it off him?"

Realizing he was caught, Masters started to beg. "Take it! Here! Take it and be done with it. It was an accident anyway. Just let me go. I'll leave and never come back. You can have Cummings' claim. No one will know. No one will care."

"I'll know," Hodges said, then pointed to everyone who was staring at the man in disbelief. "And they'll know. All of them. You shot a man in the back, which makes you the dirtiest sort of a killer. You're a coward, man, and you're gonna die."

Masters started begging and pleading, but to no avail.

Letty watched, stunned into silence by

the violence of the moment. When they grabbed the man and dragged him out of the room, most of the others went back to their beds, while a few followed the vigilantes.

When Eulis saw that they were gone, he relaxed his stance and sat down on the side of the bed.

"What are they going to do with him?" Letty asked.

"Most likely hang him," Eulis said.

"Good Lord," Letty muttered, and dropped onto her cot with a thump. She stared down at her boots, uncertain whether to take them off or leave them on, just in case there was more trouble later.

"It's no more than he deserves," Eulis said. "People got to protect themselves the best way they know how in places like this. Claim jumpin' is as serious here as horse stealin'. You can't let a back shooter get away with murder." Then he turned around and looked at her. "Go back to sleep. I'll stay awake for a bit to make sure everything has settled down."

Letty nodded and stretched out on her cot, but she didn't close her eyes. Instead, she found herself looking at the back of Eulis's head and the hard set of his shoulders as he sat between her and the world, and it occurred to her that, not since her father, had anyone ever cared enough about her to look after her welfare. She didn't know whether Eulis was doing it out of duty, or because he cared, and right now she didn't much care. It felt good — real good — to know that he was there.

"Eulis."

"Huh?"

"Thank you."

"For what?"

Letty frowned. "I don't know, just thank you, okay?"

"Okay," he said, and then smiled to himself as he heard her hit the bed with a flop. A few minutes passed. The room and the men finally settled down, though a few, like Eulis, had decided that caution was needed, and they sat up on their cots with their guns at the ready.

Eulis was too busy watching the door to make sure there were no more surprises coming through it, that he missed seeing the man staring at them from the other side of the room. But if he had, he would have been none too happy to know that Boston Jones, the gambler who'd been one of the passengers on the stagecoach on which they'd been riding earlier was once again, back in their lives.

Boston was surprised to see them here and more than curious as to what had happened to them. If it hadn't been for the woman speaking up, he wouldn't have recognized either one of them, but her voice had been unmistakable. Only there were noticeable differences about them from the first time they'd met.

The preacher was leaner and there was a hard expression on his face that hadn't been there before. The woman was thinner, too, and wearing men's clothing. But the thing he noticed most was that they seemed to have switched power. Before, Sister Leticia had been bossy, constantly ordering the preacher around, but now it was just the reverse. Right now, the preacher was on guard with his rifle across his lap and the woman had gone back to bed, obviously trusting him to take care of them both.

Boston stretched his legs out on the cot, locked his hands behind his head and leaned back until he was resting against the wall. He sat that way for a while, listening to a couple of men talking quietly in the back while the man next to him snored. Soon, he began to grow sleepy again. He stood up, straightened his bedclothes and then lay back down. One more time, he glanced across the room to where the preacher and his woman were sleeping and realized the preacher was lying down and already asleep.

Boston frowned. Ordinarily, he wasn't so unobservant. He swiped a hand over his face then felt beneath his bedroll, making sure his handgun was handy and closed his eyes. When he opened them next, it was morning.

Someone yelled, "breakfast". Within moments, all of the sleepers were rousing, anxious not to miss the meal that came with the cost of the room. Letty got up quickly and made a quick run to the out-house, leaving Eulis to see to their belongings. He rolled up their bedrolls and stacked them on top of their bags, then carried his rifle with him as he took a quick trip outside, himself. By the time he came back, diners were gathering at the table, only Letty was noticeably missing. He felt a brief moment of panic and then backtracked.

Although it was still early, barely day-break, the air was warm and still. The sky was a dirty color of gray and held a promise of rain. Eulis paused on the back stoop, listening for anything that seemed out of place, but heard nothing alarming. He was just about to go in search of Letty when she came around the corner of the inn.

She looked startled when she saw him.

"What's wrong?" she asked.

"I was about to ask you the same question," Eulis said.

Letty frowned. "I told you where I was going."

"I know."

"There was a line."

"Oh! Well, I was just coming to check, that's all."

"I'm fine. Let's eat."

Eulis followed her back into the inn, pausing only once to look behind him, then firmly closed the door.

Mrs. Cocker was carrying in a huge platter of hot biscuits when Letty took a seat at the table. "Good morning, Missus," the innkeeper said.

"It's Miss," Letty said, and scooted over slightly so that Eulis had room to sit down.

The innkeeper arched her eyebrows, but said nothing more.

Letty glanced up only long enough to see if anyone had been paying attention, then breathed a sigh of relief when she realized that the men were too intent on eating to pay attention to what the two women had been saying.

Eulis leaned over and spoke quietly in Letty's ear.

"Food looks good, don't it, Letty?"

"Smells even better," Letty said. "Sure beats what we've been calling food."

"Now that we're here, we'll do better."

"Not unless you do the cooking," she said.

The only eating utensils were large spoons, but Letty could have cared less. She was starved for real food and would have gladly eaten it with her fingers, if necessary. She picked up her spoon and was about to take her first bite, when she heard a familiar voice.

"Since there's a preacher here at the table, don't you reckon we oughta' have him bless the food? Especially after the set-to we had last night."

Letty felt Eulis flinch as she looked up. Boston Jones was staring at them from the other end of the table.

"Preacher? Who's a preacher?" Mrs. Cocker asked.

Boston pointed at Eulis. "That man there is Reverend Howe. Right, preacher?" Then he tipped his hat at Letty and smirked. "Good morning, Sister Leticia. I trust you slept well after the trouble last night."

"I slept fine," Letty said, and then saw Mrs. Cocker smiling congenially, far more friendly than she'd been when they had arrived yesterday evening.

She glanced at Eulis, who was grim-faced and pale. She grabbed his hand beneath the table and gave it a squeeze, then picked up her spoon as if nothing was amiss and stared pointedly at Boston Jones.

"The preacher has suffered a setback in his calling since we last saw you. He no longer wishes to be referred to as preacher and in fact no longer wishes to be called by his given name. He has taken the name of his maternal grandfather, Eulis Potter. And in the same vein, I would appreciate just being called by my name, Leticia Murphy, or Letty. I'm sure you'll understand."

Mrs. Cocker looked disappointed, but didn't comment. Instead, she shoved a platter of hot cakes toward Eulis, offering him first serving.

"Help yourself," she said. "No ceremony around here."

Eulis slid a couple of hot cakes onto his plate then passed the plate to Letty, who took a helping and passed it on. Conversation quickly resumed among the men. They were more than familiar with bad turns in life. For most of them it was the reason they were here hoping to strike it rich — hoping for a miracle. No one cared if some preacher had lost his religion. They cared even less that the ex-preacher had a female companion who was not his wife. But Boston Jones wasn't as easily sidetracked.

"So you're saying that we shouldn't be expecting any rousing sermons intended to save our souls?"

"That's right," Eulis said, then smiled at Mrs. Cocker. "Real fine biscuits, ma'am."

She beamed.

"That's a shame," Boston said.

Letty was tired of his needling. She'd never liked the man anyway, but he was really starting to get on her nerves. She licked the gravy off her spoon, then pointed it at Boston Jones.

"Not half as big a shame as all the gold dust you'll probably steal from the miners in your crooked card games."

Boston flinched. He'd underestimated the woman. The men gathered around the table were all looking at him with new interest and most of it didn't look good. He

361

glared back at Letty, blaming her for the wave of mistrust. This didn't bode well for the success that he'd expected.

"I do not run a crooked game and I take exception to the accusation. Are you insinuating that I'm a crook?" he asked.

Eulis was starting to get nervous. Letty had accused the man of that very thing without any proof.

"Letty, maybe you should —"

Letty pointed down the table at the platter of fried eggs.

"Would someone please pass the eggs?"

Eulis sighed. He recognized the jut of Letty's chin and went back to his food.

The gambler didn't have Eulis's knowledge of the woman or his experience of her persistence. He would have been better off if he'd concentrated on his food instead of pissing off the former Sister Leticia. But since he didn't know, he pushed when he should have shut his mouth.

The egg platter came down the table, hand to hand, but when it got to Boston Jones, he didn't pass it on. Instead, he held it.

"Lady, I asked you a question. You called me a crook, but you had nothing to back that up other than the fact that we spent a miserable trip together in the same coach."

Letty had no qualms about revealing this man's true colors because he'd thrown the first rock. He'd belittled both her and Eulis and insinuated that there was something criminal about them using another name. As far as she was concerned, he'd asked for what he was about to get.

"Actually, it was during that same trip that I saw what you can do. That deck of cards that you fiddled with all the way from Dodge City to Fort Mays was marked."

He slammed the platter of eggs on the table and stood abruptly.

"You lie! You're just trying to ruin my reputation to further that damned religion you claimed to preach. You're nothing but some pious, mealy-mouthed female with a hate against men."

"I don't lie and I don't give a horse's ass for your reputation. You threw the first stone here, mister, when you started this conversation, and just for the record, I am anything but pious."

Eulis grabbed her arm.

"Don't, Letty. Don't speak ill of yourself just to prove he's a bastard."

"What is he talking about?" Boston asked.

Letty lifted her chin and stared him straight in the face.

"Oh, that's just Eulis trying to protect me from myself, which he's been trying to do, and without success, for some years. I know you're crooked because I saw your marked deck, and if anyone should recognize a marked deck, that would be me. My last place of residence, before my friend and I started on the "Amen Trail", was at the White Dove Saloon in Lizard Flats. So don't tell me I don't know a marked deck when I see one, or a bastard when I meet one. I'm an expert at men. I used to sleep with them for money."

There was a gasp behind her, which Letty knew came from Mrs. Cocker, followed by a stunned silence from the men at the table. Then Eulis cleared his throat.

"Gentlemen, Letty here asked someone to pass the eggs."

The man next to Boston snagged the platter and passed it down, then nodded cordially at Letty.

"Name's Riley Whitmore. Right nice to meet you, ma'am," he said, and then nodded at Eulis, too. "Ever been to a gold camp?"

"Nope," Eulis said.

"Me neither," he said. "I reckon I'm about half scared and the rest of the way excited. Had a farm back in Pennsylvania.

Got flooded out three years in a row then hailed out the next year. Decided to try my hand at something a little easier."

"Ain't nothin' easy about pannin' for gold," another man said.

Whitmore grinned. "Obviously, you ain't never tried your hand at farming."

The men laughed and the tension disappeared. But Boston Jones didn't laugh. He quickly finished his food, then got his pack and rode away, anxious to set himself up in Denver City. He told himself these few men didn't matter. There were hundreds, maybe even thousands of men in the gold fields. He had no reason to assume he'd ever come in contact with any of these people again.

But that didn't include Letty Murphy and he promised himself that if the situation ever occurred, he would get his revenge against that woman or know the reason why.

The Tower of Babel

With Four Mile Inn behind them, Letty and Eulis set off for Denver City. Whether they would admit it to themselves or not, they each had dreams of striking it rich. Funny thing was, their dreams never went beyond the strike. Eulis couldn't see his future past today and Letty was afraid to think of a future for fear of jinxing it.

But their excitement was obvious as they chattered amiably while hitching up the team. It continued through the early morning until they rounded a bend in the road about a quarter of a mile from their destination. There, hanging from the limb of a very large oak tree, was the claim jumper the men had hauled out of the Inn last night. Whatever personal goals Art Masters had entertained were over. And by leaving his body hanging in plain sight on the road into town, the message was plain. Claim jumpers and back-shooters were not tolerated.

Eulis looked away, then grew silent. But Letty kept looking, staring at the man's darkened face and soiled clothes and as she did, noticed that he was wearing only one shoe. It wasn't until they drew even with the dangling body that she saw the other one near an old wooden bucket that had been abandoned by the road. She'd seen men hanged before and was familiar with what some called the dance of death — the kicking and jerking that a hanging man does as the life and breath are strangled out of him.

"Looks like he kicked the bucket," she said, and pointed.

Eulis's eyes widened as he saw what she was pointing at, then he looked at Letty, unable to believe that she'd just made a joke about a dead man.

"Dang it, Letty. You hadn't oughta make fun of a man like that."

"A man like what?" Letty asked.

Eulis frowned. "You know what I meant. The man's dead."

"So's the fellow he back-shot."

Eulis was silent for a moment, then he looked back at Letty and nodded.

"You know what? You're right. The fellow don't deserve a second thought."

Letty smiled smugly. "Of course I'm right. I'm always right." Then she laughed out loud and elbowed Eulis. "And don't you forget it."

Eulis grinned and the moment passed.

Within the half hour, they came upon Denver City. Eulis pulled up at the top of the hill to look down into the valley below.

"Holy Moses," he muttered, then whistled between his teeth.

"What in hell is that?" Letty asked.

"You cursed," Eulis said. "They're callin' it Denver City.

"I sure did," Letty said. "And I misspoke. What I meant to say was, is that hell?"

The sight below was like nothing either one of them had ever seen. It was like looking at the inside of a very busy, but very violent anthill. There were people everywhere — in the creek, in the dirt-packed streets, going into tents, coming out of tents, loading wagons, unloading wagons — and fighting. What seemed most at odds with the sight was the Arapaho encampment on one side of the creek.

The land at Cherry Creek and the surrounding areas had been given to the Arapaho under the 1851 Fort Laramie Treaty, but once gold had been discovered, the treaty was as good as gone. The Arapaho were a small tribe with light skin and a predilection for chest tattoos, and they had learned long ago that to get along, they went along — often despite misgivings. Their chief, Little Raven, had welcomed the white men, whom the Arapaho referred to as the "spider people", which was an oblique reference to the white man's constant habit of leaving roads, survey stakes and fences behind them as they went. The Arapaho even went so far as sharing their women with the miners, as was the custom of the tribe, in hopes that they could learn to live together. But it seemed evident that Indians and whites were never going to live side by side in harmony when the whites couldn't even accomplish that alone.

On the other side of the creek were men and tents and horses and noise — noise at such a level that it seemed impossible any one word could be distinguished from the other. A few rough-cut buildings had been erected. Letty could read the signs from here.

One was an eating house. The only sign above the doorway said MEALS. Another was a saloon called ARLIE'S BAR. The third was a dry goods store, with a sign stating the obvious. They could see another two other buildings in different stages of completion. The rest were tents. There was a sign outside one of the larger ones that read BATHS, which made Letty smile.

"Look, Eulis. They got a bath house."

Eulis resisted the urge to roll his eyes.

"Baths down there ain't gonna come free."

"I know," she said.

"Things are gonna cost a whole bunch more than they're worth."

"I know. I heard Mrs. Cocker at breakfast this morning, too, you know."

"That means we're gonna have to watch the little bit of money we got left. We gonna need to outfit ourselves for huntin' gold."

"How so?" Letty asked.

"I don't know," Eulis said. "I ain't never went huntin' for gold before, but there's bound to be things we need."

"I guess, only I don't think hunting is the right word. We can't exactly go out there and track it and shoot it down like we did those squirrels we ate."

Eulis rolled his eyes and refused to answer.

Letty sniffed politely, convinced that she'd had the last word, which she took to mean she was right.

Then a gunshot rang out and they looked back into the valley, watching as one man staggered out of the water, threw down what looked like a big flat pan, then punched the guy standing on the bank. That man fell backward onto his butt, then shook his head, yanked off his hat, got up with a roar and started swinging.

"Mercy," Letty said. "Wonder what set them off?"

"The Tower of Babel," Eulis said, unaware that he'd spoken out loud.

"What? Where?" Letty asked. "I don't see any tower."

Eulis shook his head. "Not here. In the Bible."

"I don't get it," Letty said.

"I don't remember all the details cause I only read about it once, but there's this story in the Bible about some people all being forced to build this big stone tower. It was to honor some king or somethin' and I think he swore he was gonna build it all the way to heaven. So God put some kind of spell on all the workers and all of a sudden they began speakin' in different languages. They could no longer understand each other and the work came to a halt because orders couldn't be followed. They called it the Tower of Babel. I reckon that's where we got the word, babble. You know, doin' a lot of talkin' without really sayin' anything."

"Oh." She looked down at the chaos below and then nodded. "I get it." Then she added. "Way to go, Preacher Howe."

Eulis frowned. "Not anymore — and don't make a mistake and call me that again. We done run into one fella from our past out here. We don't want to come across someone from back home who knew the preacher from Lizard Flats, cause they will likely have known of me, too. I know I don't look like I used to, but I reckon there's not two Eulis Potters who would be runnin' with a woman from the White Dove Saloon."

Instantly, Letty regretted her words.

"I'm sorry, Eulis. Sometimes I talk before I think."

"Wouldn't be a very smart thing to do out here."

She thought back to the hanging man and shivered.

"I'm sorry. Real sorry."

Eulis patted her knee. "It's all right, girl. Just wanted you to think a bit, you know?"

She nodded.

He flipped the reins across Rosy's and Blackie's backs and the wagon began to roll down the hill into their future.

Little Bird was sad. She'd been sad for many moons now — ever since the spider people had come to Cherry Creek. Before, it had been a joyous place to be. Game had been plentiful and the chokecherry bushes for which Cherry Creek had been named were always heavily laden with the bittersweet cherries. Now everything was wrong. The chokecherries had been sparse and the ones that had ripened were small with a tendency to rot on the bush. The deer that had survived the white men's indiscriminate hunting practices had gone up to a higher elevation and the pure water of Cherry Creek that had sustained The People for so long was fouled by the spider people and their thirst for gold.

But what bothered Little Bird even more than all of the other put together was that she no longer felt safe in her own tipi.

White men came into their camp almost every night wanting a woman to lie with. Because it was the custom of The People to share their women from time to time, the warriors obliged. But Little Bird hated the white men and their ways. They were brutal and hairy, and smelled foul, as if their bodies were rotting, although they had yet to die.

And today was no different. The morning had dawned cold and gray. Her man was still sleeping beneath his blankets and her cooking fire had gone out. When she got up and went out to relieve herself, she'd been accosted by a white man walking into the camp. He staggered as he walked and smelled of the white man's drink. Before she knew it, she was flat on her back with her legs spread and he was fumbling with his breeches.

Little Bird pushed at the man, trying to get him off of her, but he wouldn't budge, so she reached for the nearest weapon, which happened to be a large rock, and swung it at him as hard as she could. There was a sound, not unlike that of a clay pot breaking, and then he was still.

Little Bird pushed him off her then crawled to her feet. To her surprise, she was still alone. Afraid of the backlash that might occur between the spider people and the Arapaho, she grabbed the man by the arms and began dragging him into the trees.

Letty had been awake for hours, waiting for daylight. It was sometime after midnight when she'd heard moisture dropping from the leaves onto their tent. She'd

rolled over with a muffled curse and reminded herself that she and Eulis had to
make different sleeping arrangements soon
because there was no way they could spend
the winter in this tent and survive.

Already the population of Denver City
was half of what it had been when they'd
arrived two weeks ago. Almost overnight,
the leaves on the trees had turned and
once in a while, there was a thin crust of
ice on the creek at first light.

When they'd picked a place to camp and
pan, it hadn't been based on any scientific
reasoning. They'd just gone to the land office and registered their claim. Picking it
had been a simple case of availability with
as much privacy as possible, and that had
meant going up creek to a somewhat
higher elevation. Letty hadn't minded, although it meant hitching up the wagon
and mules every time they needed supplies.

The first time they'd found color, Letty
had been absent. She'd taken a break and
gone into the bushes to pee, leaving Eulis
ankle deep in water. He scooped a fresh
pan of sediment from the bottom of the
creek, then began circling the grit and
water, letting the silt and rocks sluice out
with the assumption that the gold, which
was heavier, would stay on the bottom. But

it called for a sharp eye and the knowledge of how to tell floss from dross. More than one man had made a fool of himself over iron pyrite, often called "fool's gold", by running into Denver City waving a poke of the stuff. By the time the assayer's office had verified the 'strike' as worthless, the miner's face was red, and he was sneaking out of town a lot quieter than the way he'd come in.

Eulis's hands were cold, but his feet were colder. The water was getting colder and colder by the day. Panning was soon going to be impossible once the water froze, but they had yet to find even a nugget. If something didn't happen soon, they would have to leave. They'd never make it through the winter without food and shelter, and at the present time, they had no money for either.

With her bladder protesting, Letty tossed her pan onto the creek bank and stomped out of the water.

"Headin' for the bushes. Be right back."

Eulis nodded without comment. Letty's frequent trips to nature's outhouse were a common occurrence and no longer a source of amusement for either. He was too busy watching the bottom of his pan and the circling water as it washed out the dirt and pebbles when it suddenly dawned on him that this time, there was something in the bottom that hadn't been there before.

He straightened abruptly and almost ran out of the creek, afraid that he was mistaken, then afraid if he'd really found gold, that he would spill it back into the water from which it had come.

"Oh man," he muttered, as he dug through the tiny grit and sand, then pulled out the small nugget. It was a bright spot of color and appeared as if it had once been liquefied then hardened somewhat flat.

He pinched it between his thumb and forefinger, then laid it in the palm of his hand and tilted it toward the sun. It didn't exactly sparkle, but there was what Eulis considered a glimmer, and that was good enough for him. He curled his fingers around the rock as he called Letty's name.

"Letty!"

"Just a minute!" she yelled. "I'm busy."

"Letty! You gotta come here!"

"For pity's sake, Eulis! I said, I'm busy!"

"Leticia!"

She stood up from behind some bushes, holding up her pants with one hand as she parted the bushes with her other.

"What?"

He held out his hand. "I think I found gold!"

Letty gasped and ran from the bushes, forgetting that her pants were not fastened. Two steps later, she was flat on her face with her pants around her ankles.

Eulis ran to her.

"Dang, Letty! Are you all right?"

Ignoring the fact that Eulis had a more than ample view of her bare butt, Letty rolled over and got up, pulling her pants up as she went.

"Let me see! Let me see!" she begged.

Eulis grinned. "Soon as you button your britches."

"Eulis!" she begged, and then began fumbling with the buttons.

He laughed again, filled with joy and a hope that he'd thought himself too far gone to ever know again, and opened the palm of his hand.

"Give me your hand," he said.

Letty extended her hand. Moments later, Eulis laid the nugget in her palm.

"Oh Lord," Letty whispered. "Just look! Oh, Eulis, just look!"

"I'm lookin'," Eulis said, but he was no longer looking at the nugget. He was looking at Letty.

She was bone thin, with a scrape on her

nose where she'd just taken a fall, and her hands were callused and rough, even cracked and bleeding in places from the water and the cold. There was a bit of red leaf stuck on the braid down her back and she was about the prettiest woman he thought he'd ever seen.

Letty turned the nugget over and over, mentally marking and weighing it in her mind.

"Reckon it's some of that fool's gold?" Eulis asked.

"No. I looked at that stuff real close in the assayer's office. This is the real stuff, Eulis! The real stuff!"

Then she threw her arms around his neck and started jumping up and down.

Eulis grabbed the back of her britches to keep them from falling down around her knees again, then grinned.

"Here!" he said, and handed her a small leather pouch. "I been savin' this for our first find. I reckon this is it."

Letty opened the bag and dropped in the gold, then handed it back to Eulis. Her eyes were shining and there was a look in her eyes he'd never seen before.

A funny feeling came in the pit of his stomach — sort of a knotting, drawing pain that made him want to cry and laugh all at the same time. A feeling that swelled his heart and caused him to choke on whatever he'd been going to say next.

"You did good," she said softly. "You did real good."

He shrugged, swallowed nervously and turned loose of her pants. She grabbed them before they fell again, and by the time she was buttoned back up, he'd put the pouch in his pocket and buttoned the flap and the moment had passed.

That had been then, and this was now. Weeks later, their tiny pouch was only about half full. Enough to know that they would be able to afford food for the winter, but not enough to buy them a decent place to stay.

And it was with that thought in mind that Letty watched the first gray fingers of light pulling aside the curtain of night. As soon as she could distinguish shape and substance, she put on her boots and crawled out of the tent, leaving Eulis still asleep in his blankets.

After a quick trip to the bushes, she began gathering some dry wood for the fire, although the chore took longer and longer each morning, due to the fact that they were quickly using up all the deadfall. The next time they went into Denver City, they were going to have to buy something larger than their hatchet to cut wood.

Letty didn't realize how far she'd gone from camp until she heard a twig snap in the bushes. She looked up and then spun around, only to come face to face with a young Arapaho woman.

The woman gasped.

Letty took a step backward and dropped the wood in her arms just as the woman dropped the man she'd been dragging.

Letty eyed the man, taking in the fact that there was a lot of blood on the side of his head, that his pants were undone and that he reeked of liquor. Also, that the young woman looked scared out of her mind. Almost immediately, Letty flashed on the Reverend Randall Ward Howe, who'd died unceremoniously on top of her in her bed on the second floor of the White Dove Saloon.

She knew the Arapaho shared their women and before this, had given no thought to whether the women had been in on the decision. But she thought about it now and recognized the panic in the Indian woman's eyes. She remembered how scared she'd been when Howe had died of a heart attack, and had it not been for Eulis, she would have probably been hanged. Despite her fear of Indians, she felt a greater bond — that of woman to woman, and so she pointed to the man at their feet.

"Did he hurt you?" Letty asked.

Little Bird's eyes widened. She knew enough of the white man's words to get by, and unconsciously put a hand to her breast, feeling the tenderness where the man had grabbed her as he'd shoved her to the ground.

Letty's eyes narrowed in anger as she looked down at the man again. Then she looked up.

"My name is Letty."

Little Bird touched her chest. "Little Bird."

Letty pointed at the man.

"Is he dead?"

Little Bird nodded soulfully.

Letty brushed off the palms of her hands.

"Then I reckon we'd better get rid of him. Need some help?"

Little Bird couldn't have been more surprised by the offer, but she was too desperate to say no. She nodded once.

"All right then," Letty said. "You take one arm. I'll take the other. Got a place in mind to put him?"

Little Bird pointed up the path.

"Cave. Bear sleeps in winter."

Letty flinched. "Reckon the bear is in there yet?"

"Soon," Little Bird said.

"Then we'd better get at it," Letty said, and together, they began dragging the man up the path.

By Letty's best guess, it had taken the better part of thirty minutes to reach the cave, but she had to admit that once there, it was the perfect hiding place — almost as good as the grave where they'd buried the real Randall Howe.

When they started inside, she had a moment of hesitation, fearing that a bear would already be occupying the spot, but to her relief, it was empty. They dragged him as far back into the cave as they could see to go, then dropped him like a hot potato and made a run for the light.

Once outside, they were almost giddy with relief, and Letty found herself grinning at her co-conspirator.

"It is done," Little Bird said, and then sat down at the side of the path, covered her face with her hands, and began to weep.

Letty knew the feeling all too well. She knelt beside her, then tentatively touched her shoulder.

"Hey, Little Bird, it's over. No need to cry now."

"Afraid," Little Bird said.

"Yeah, I understand. But I won't tell."

Little Bird looked up. Tears were hanging on her lashes like dew on the grass.

"It's our secret," Letty said. "You know secrets?"

Little Bird shook her head and frowned.

Letty sighed. "It's something that two people know, but do not tell." Then she pointed to the cave, then to herself. "I know." Then she pointed at Little Bird. "And you know." Then she closed her fists, as if holding something tight. "But no one else knows. Ever."

Little Bird's eyes widened as she thought about what the woman had said and pointed to the cave.

"No talk more ever."

"Right," Letty said, and then held out her hand. "Come on. Let's head back down. I need to find wood for a fire."

Little Bird almost smiled. "I, too, make fire."

"Well, then," Letty said, somewhat surprised to realize how similar their lives probably were. "Let's go."

Little Bird got up, tore a limb from a

small bush and began brushing out any signs of their passing as they retraced their steps. It wasn't until they were back where they'd first met up, that they stopped and spoke.

"There's my wood," Letty said, and began gathering it back up in her arms.

"I go," Little Bird said.

Letty nodded. "Goodbye Little Bird."

She eyed Letty thoughtfully, then finally smiled.

"Secret," she said.

Letty smiled back.

"Secret."

Little Bird lifted her hand in a gesture of goodbye and then disappeared before Letty's eyes. She gathered up the rest of the firewood that she'd dropped and headed for camp. By the time she returned, Eulis was up and had managed to revive the embers of the dead fire with the last of their kindling. When he saw Letty coming back into camp with the firewood, he grinned.

"Wondered where you were. Thought you might have gone fishin'."

"Nope. Just getting wood for the fire," Letty said. "I reckon it's too cold for fish to be moving this early."

Eulis nodded. "Probably. Have we got any flour left?"

"A little," Letty said.

"Then I'll make us some flapjacks. Soon as we eat, I reckon we'd better hitch up the team and make a trip down for supplies."

"And maybe see about wintering in town."

"Yeah. Maybe, although I reckon we might have left that a little too late."

Letty frowned. That was the story of her life. Too late and a dollar short.

"And maybe not," she said. "Won't know until we try."

No Room at the Inn

Letty and Eulis began the trip into Denver City just as the first flakes of snow were starting to fall. They looked nervously at the sky, then at each other before Eulis clucked to Rosy and Blackie to hurry them along.

"Don't worry, Letty. This don't mean winter has set in. It's just a few flakes of snow. I doubt it will last long."

"Right."

"We'll go ahead and get a good bait of winter supplies, just in case, but I don't think this is gonna amount to much."

She didn't doubt his prediction, but she *was* concerned about the future.

"Eulis, exactly where are we gonna spend the winter?"

"Oh, we'll get us some rooms in town. Lay out pannin' for the winter and get fat and sassy."

She tried to laugh, but fear of the unknown didn't let it get past a smile. She didn't want to put a damper on the plan by suggesting that there might not be rooms to be had. She decided to wait until misfortune fell before she started to bemoan the fact that, if that happened, they might not live to see another spring. Yet as frightening and uncertain as their future was, for the first time in her life, Letty felt like she was truly alive.

Suddenly, Eulis pointed up in the trees to their right.

"Look at that! Ain't he a fine one!"

A twelve-point buck was looking down at them from a rock promontory. The majesty of the animal in its natural habitat was stunning, but Letty was too practical to ignore the opportunity that had just been presented. Reality raised its ugly head as she reached for the rifle. As if sensing imminent danger, the buck leaped from the rock and into the trees. Seconds later, it was gone.

"Dang," Letty said. "That buck would have been good eating."

Eulis nodded. "Still, it was a beaut. Sorta glad it got away, you know?"

Letty shrugged. "It didn't really get away. As long as it stays around here, it's only a matter of time before someone shoots it. Might as well have been me."

Eulis eyed Letty critically.

Letty saw the look and frowned. "What?"

"I don't know — just thinkin'."

"About what?" Letty asked.

" 'Bout how much you've changed."

Suddenly, Letty felt threatened, which was an odd emotion to be feeling around Eulis.

"What do you mean?"

He shrugged. "You know, before when we were at Lizard Flats, your emotions and all — well, they were hard — you were hard."

"And now?" she asked. "What about now?"

"Well, we got things tougher now than we ever had 'em before, and I reckon that would make anyone, man or woman, tough and hard. Only you ain't that way anymore."

Letty turned around and stared, not believing what she was hearing.

"Are you calling me a sissy?"

Eulis's eyes widened, then he started to grin. Wisps of Letty's hair had come undone from her braid and the hat she was wearing had one of the widest brims he'd ever seen. There was a scrape on her chin and her fingernails were broken and dirty and she thought he'd just called her a sissy. He laughed.

"Not hardly, Missy."

Letty frowned. "You're laughing at me."

"Well, Lordy, Leticia, you are the touchiest woman I ever knew. I wasn't callin' you no sissy, and I wasn't talkin' mean about you. I was tryin' to pay you a compliment."

"Then you better keep talking, 'cause I haven't heard one yet."

"What I was tryin' to say was that no matter how tough we've had it, you just keep gettin' stronger. You ain't hardhearted anymore, Sister Leticia. You're strong, and one might even say you got tough, but tough is good. It means life can't beat you down anymore."

Letty didn't know what to think. She'd been too busy trying to stay alive to think about the past. She sat there for a few moments, then looked at him and grinned.

"That was the compliment, wasn't it?"

Eulis nodded. "That was it."

"It was almost a good one."

"Thank you," he said.

"No, thank you."

Eulis smiled. He hadn't felt this good in a long time.

Letty rubbed her hands together and then put them in her pockets. The snow was coming down a little harder now.

"Good thing we're almost there," she said. "It's snowing heavier."

"Looks like goose feathers," Eulis said.

"But not nearly as comforting to sleep on," Letty countered.

The wagon continued to roll. Once, Letty shivered, then quickly looked behind them, as if expecting to see danger on their heels, but saw nothing except snow. Shrugging off the feeling, she turned back around and pulled the collar of her coat up around her ears.

"Still wish I'd gotten a shot off at that buck."

Eulis threw his head back and laughed, but the sound was smothered by the snow as they started down the hill into Denver City.

Because of Leticia Murphy's revelation months ago at Four Mile Inn regarding Boston Jones' gambling habits, he had been forced to clean up his act. Word had spread quickly that he'd been accused of using a marked deck, so he'd had to rely solely on his wits and skill to skin the miners out of their pokes. As a result, he didn't have nearly as much socked away as he'd planned. Now winter was upon them and he was stuck in Denver City until spring, which was also not what he'd planned. It galled him greatly to know that a woman's inability to keep her mouth shut had hampered his business, and often day-dreamed about the various ways he might get back at her, although nothing ever came to fruition.

Today, as it was his habit to do so every morning, he was in his room, sitting at the window overlooking the road that led in and out of Denver City. He was contemplating the fact that it was beginning to snow when he saw Letty and Eulis coming into town in their wagon. He recognized the mules first, then the wide-brimmed hat that Letty had taken to wearing.

The streets were jammed with miners who'd come into the city to winter. He grinned to himself as Letty and Eulis passed beneath his window, because he knew there were no more rooms to be had — hadn't been for more than a week. Even the stable and the bathhouse had been turned into rough sleeping quarters. For the men who'd been sleeping in tents strung along Cherry Creek and the South Platte, the cold nights had been warning enough for them. Denver City was teeming with more miners than rooms, so much so that a good number of them were buying available horses and wagons, intent on heading down out of the mountains before it was too late.

Boston struck a sulphur match and lit the thin, dark cigar he'd been holding, drawing one, then two, then three good puffs from the tightly rolled tobacco leaves before it flared properly. The scent of a good cigar and a warm room made him smile. Add a soft, feminine woman who knew when to keep her mouth shut and he'd be set for the winter.

He leaned forward, watching until the used-to-be preacher's wagon rolled out of sight and wondered how soft Sister Leticia's body might be, then shrugged off the thought as he remembered how she'd grabbed his dingus and given it a yank. Trying to cuddle up to her would be like cuddling a rattlesnake.

He kicked back in his chair, propped the heels of his boots on the windowsill and enjoyed his smoke, knowing full well that whatever goods were still for sale in this city had gone sky-high, and hoping they didn't have enough gold dust to buy a can of beans. It would serve them right.

About halfway through his cigar, someone knocked on the door. He got up to answer and found a small Chinese man holding a stack of freshly washed and ironed shirts.

"Gottchee wash. You give two bits."

"Put it on the bed," Boston said, as he dug the money out of his vest.

The Chinese man put down the stack of clean clothes and pocketed the money Boston gave him on his way out the door. Boston watched the little man scurrying down the hotel hallway, his long black braid swaying like the pendulum of a clock; then he shrugged and closed the door. Odd people, those Chinese, he thought. They would work like dogs for next to nothing and seem all the more happy for it. Boston would have been shocked to know that the man who'd brought him his laundry was worth more than the hotel owner three times over.

His belly growled as he was putting the shirts inside the wardrobe. As soon as he was done, he reached for his hat and coat. It was time for breakfast.

Letty was brushing snow from her coat as she entered the general store. The warmth from the potbelly stove put a smile on her face, but the smile quickly disappeared when she realized that the shelves inside the general store were close to empty and there was a line of people at the counter. The nervousness of the men standing in line was contagious. There wouldn't be enough food to go around, let alone enough to get them through the winter. She thought of all the hard work she and Eulis had put in just to garner the small pouch of nuggets they had now. But dust and nuggets were of no use if there was nothing to buy. She turned quickly and headed back out the door, meeting Eulis as he was tying the team off at a hitching post.

"Eulis."

"What? Whatcha' doin' out here?"

"There's nothing left," she said.

Eulis's smile faded.

"What do you mean, there's nothing left?"

"The shelves are almost empty and there's a line of customers halfway to the door. What are we gonna do?"

Eulis hid his panic. They'd left it too late. Finding gold had seemed the most important thing to do, and now that they had some, there was nothing left to buy. He looked up, blinking rapidly to deflect the snow, then turned to Letty and jammed his hat down on his head.

"Wait here. I'm gonna go see about getting us a room."

Letty grabbed his arm as he was walking away.

"What?"

"If there's no food to be had, we'll just be paying for a room to starve in. I'd rather take my chances on the mountain. Remember that buck? At least there's game to be had."

He nodded. She was most likely right about that. However, they couldn't winter in a tent. They needed a saw and an axe, and whatever goods they could buy. He wasn't willing to leave without giving it a try, and standing in line was easier than standing knee-deep in ice water trying to find gold.

"Most likely they'll be gettin' in some more goods any day now. I'm gonna go in and see. I reckon you just scared yourself needlessly."

"Do you think so?"

Eulis smiled and patted her on the shoulder.

"Yeah, I think so. Wait here and I'll see what I can find out."

Letty crawled up into the wagon seat, hunched her shoulders against the cold and waited for Eulis to come back. Minutes passed, and it wasn't until one of the mules suddenly brayed that she realized she'd been listening to what sounded like a runaway team. She reached for the reins, then realized that Eulis had tied them off at the hitching post. Panicked, she stared intently into what was fast becoming a blizzard.

Now she could hear the thunder of the horses' hooves and the squeak of a wooden wheel badly in need of grease. She looked nervously toward the store, and started to get down when, suddenly she saw a wagon and horses coming out of the snow, racing wildly toward her without any indication of slowing down. Even more frightening was the fact that no one was at the reins.

"Eeuulliiss!"

She didn't even realize that she'd screamed his name until he came running out of the store. He dropped the axe and saw he was carrying, tossed a sack full of goods into the wagon, and jumped off the steps and out into the street.

"Eulis! No!" Letty screamed, then one second she could see him running in front of their team and the next moment he was gone, swallowed up by the sound and the storm.

Once, she heard him shouting, and thought she could see him waving his arms, intent on turning the runaway team from hitting their own, then everything turned upside down. Before she could brace herself, the mules reared up and

Letty went down — head over heels into the back of the wagon. She felt the team lurch forward, then stop just as suddenly. It wasn't until she managed to crawl to her knees to peer over the wagon bed that she realized everyone who'd been in the store was now out in the street. Someone was holding the mules' harness, while another man was reaching over into the wagon to help her to her feet.

"Lady . . . Lady . . . you all right?"

"Yes, I think so," Letty said, and then jumped out and circled the wagon, desperately searching for Eulis. She couldn't bear to think of him lying broken and bloody beneath that runaway team.

"Eulis! Eulis!" she shouted, then realized someone had her by the arm and was pulling her back. "Let me go!" she screamed.

"I suggest you stay out of the way and for once let real men tend to the business of the day."

Letty flinched, then turned to find herself face to face with Boston Jones. The derisive tone in his voice was like a slap in the face.

"I'd be happy to, but I don't see any yet," she countered, and pulled away from his grasp.

Not even the snowfall could hide the fury on his face as she ran past him, but she didn't see and wouldn't have cared.

"Eulis! Eulis!"

"Here! I'm here," he yelled.

She heard his voice coming from somewhere above her and looked up. At that point, she saw Eulis standing in the back of the runaway wagon and holding the limp body of a woman in his arms.

"She's burning up with fever!" Eulis said, as he staggered to the side of the wagon and handed her off to a pair of men who quickly carried her inside the general store.

"Someone go get the doctor!" another man cried.

They passed within inches of where Letty was standing, and as they did, the woman's head lolled loosely against Letty's shoulder. She looked down, then gasped.

"Lord, Lord," she muttered, and reached for Eulis's arm. "Get out of there! Get out of there now!" she cried, and yanked hard.

Eulis staggered, then jumped, steadying himself just before he went face down in the snow.

"Dang it, Leticia! What's wrong with you?" he shouted, but Letty wasn't talking, she just kept grabbing at his arm and pulling him through the crowd to their wagon. He picked up the axe and saw that he'd dropped and tossed it into the wagon, when Letty pushed at his back.

"Get in!" she yelled.

"I ain't had time to check on the rooms at —"

She grabbed him by the arms and yanked him around until they were standing so close they could feel the heat of each other's breath.

"We got to get out of here! Now get in the wagon and don't argue! Please!"

It was the, please, that did it — that and the panic he saw on her face. He didn't understand, but they'd come too far together to start doubting each other now.

Letty bolted for the wagon as Eulis yanked the reins from a miner and crawled up beside her.

"Look out!" he yelled, and slapped the reins across the mules' rump. "Hi-yah! Hi-yah!"

Miners scattered in every direction like the snow that kept falling as their wagon began to roll. Boston Jones watched from inside the store, frowning as he watched them leaving the city, then shrugged. Crazy. Both of them just crazy. He glanced over his shoulder at the woman lying on the counter. Everyone around her was pointing and talking but he couldn't be bothered. He took another puff of his cigar and walked out of the store as Letty and Eulis disappeared.

It wasn't until they had reached the top of the hill above the city before Eulis pulled the team to a halt.

"Now talk to me," Eulis said. "What was that all about?"

Letty's face was as white as the snow swirling around their heads. She put her hand on the arm of Eulis's coat, then on his collar, then splayed her cold and numbing fingers across the front of his chest.

"You held her here, and here," then she started to cry.

Eulis's heart started to pound. He didn't understand, but she was scaring him just the same.

"Letty. For God's sake, please. Tell me what's wrong."

Tears were freezing on her cheeks, but nothing was as cold as the place around her heart. Each breath that she took came slower than the last, as if everything inside of her was dying. She stared into Eulis's face, watching the way the snowflakes settled on his eyelashes and the two frown lines that formed between his eyebrows when he was on the verge of angry. Never had she cared for him as much or been as scared.

"Letty, damn it!"

She bit her lip, then opened her mouth. Even though she knew she was talking, she couldn't hear herself saying the words.

"Smallpox. That woman had smallpox."

Eulis grunted as if he'd been sucker-punched. He looked down at his hands and then back up at Letty.

"Are you sure?"

She nodded.

"Then don't touch me," he said.

"It's too late," Letty said. "Besides, I've had it."

Eulis went weak with relief. "Thank God," he said, and before he thought, he hugged her.

Eulis's arms were around Letty for only a few moments, but it felt like forever. She could smell the scent of tobacco on his coat and the wood smoke from their morning fire, as well as the cold. She'd never noticed that cold had its own particular scent until now, and inhaled it deeply, intent on remembering this moment for as long as she lived. It was ironic that the most horrifying moment of her life might also be the moment she knew that she'd fallen in love.

Seconds later, Eulis turned loose of her, looking as uncomfortable as she felt.

"Well, then," he said shortly. "Maybe it'll be all right. I didn't hold her long and it's really cold."

"Yeah," Letty said. "That's right. It wasn't for long. But we'd better get back to camp. I'm going hunting for that buck while you start chopping down some trees. It won't take long to fix us up some kind of lean-to. We'll make it just fine. You'll see."

"Yeah, that's right. We can do anything if we stick together, can't we?"

Letty's chin trembled, but she wouldn't let go of her terror.

"Let's get moving," she said.

He clucked to the team and the wagon wheels began to roll. Less than five minutes later, they came upon some Arapaho walking toward the city. Letty recognized the woman she'd helped in the woods. The woman who called herself Little Bird.

"Eulis, wait!" she said, and jumped out of the wagon before he could stop her.

She ran toward the group and then stopped a few feet away.

"Go back!" she cried, and motioned for them to retrace their steps.

They stopped, startled by her aggressive behavior while one of the warriors with the women reached for his knife.

"No, no. I'm not trying to harm you," Letty said, and then slapped her legs in frustration.

Eulis started to get down and come to her aid, but she held up her hand.

"No! Don't!" she said. "If you're contagious —"

He looked as if she'd slapped him across the face, then sat back down.

Letty turned back to the Arapaho, fixing her attention solely on Little Bird.

"You speak English, yes?"

Little Bird glanced at the warrior who was holding the knife, then nodded at Letty.

"There is sickness in the city. White man's sickness."

Little Bird gasped, and then spoke to the others in her native tongue.

"Smallpox," Letty said. "Tell them it's smallpox. Tell them to pack up their tents and leave now. Don't talk to or touch anyone who's been down in Denver City."

Little Bird's eyes widened with horror as she translated what Letty just said.

Immediately, the group turned around and began running back through the trees. It wasn't the first time that the white man's sickness had come into their world. Back then, they'd buried hundreds of their own and the knowledge that it had returned struck fear in their hearts. But Little Bird stayed. She saw the empty wagon, the cold on their faces, and the fear in their eyes and knew they faced worse problems than a sickness.

"You have no home," Little Bird said.

Letty's shoulders sagged.

"That's the understatement of the week," Letty muttered.

Little Bird frowned. "I not know your words."

Letty sighed. "You are right. We have no home."

"I know place," Little Bird said. "You pack up. I come to you."

Within seconds she was gone, leaving Letty standing in the ever-deepening snow.

"Letty!"

She jerked, then turned and ran for the wagon.

"Head for camp," she said. "We've got to pack."

"Pack? And go where? It's too late to get out of the mountains, and without supplies, we'd never make it back to Fort Dodge."

"Little Bird says she knows where we can winter."

"Little Bird? How do you know her name?"

"It's a long story," Letty said. "Just hurry. We don't have much time."

Within the hour, they were at their camp loading up their meager belongings. Eulis was folding up the tent when Rosy lifted her head and brayed.

He turned around just as an Arapaho man and woman rode into camp.

"Letty!"

She looked up, then waved.

"You come now," Little Bird said.

They tossed the last of their things into the back of the wagon, and then crawled up into the seat. Within the hour, the snow had covered up every trace of their presence. It was as if they'd never been there.

Less than an hour later, the snow stopped falling, but not before every trace of a road had been covered with a good six inches of powder. By late afternoon, the mules were exhausted and had faltered twice, as if too weary to go on. The third time it happened, Eulis got down from the wagon, walked to the front of the team and began leading them, trying desperately to stay up with the Arapahos on horseback in front of them.

More than once it occurred to Eulis that they might be following the Arapaho to their death. He had no reason to trust them and no earthly idea of where they were going, and he certainly didn't understand the bond that seemed to exist between Letty and the woman she called Little Bird. But Letty seemed certain that she could be trusted and so they went, farther up the mountain, trusting their lives to savages.

It was nearing sundown when Little Bird suddenly stopped her pony and then motioned for Letty to come. Letty got down from the wagon and slogged her way through the snow while wondering if she'd ever be warm again.

"What?" she asked.

Little Bird pointed.

"There. You go there."

Letty moved past their horses and found herself looking down into a small, sheltered valley. In the distance, she could see a cabin that had been built up against the back wall of the mountain, and less than a hundred yards away, a small waterfall shot out of a crevice in the rocks about halfway down from the top.

"Oh. Oh, my," she whispered, then looked up at Little Bird.

"Man die — two, maybe three winters ago. Plenty grass, plenty game. Good water. You go."

Letty knew that their lives had just been saved.

"Little Bird. Thank you. Thank you."

The little Indian woman shrugged. "You help me. I help you. We go now."

Letty stepped aside.

The Arapaho warrior who was with Little Bird eyed Letty curiously. She wondered if Little Bird had told him what they'd done, then knew that it didn't matter. The tribe was safe from the smallpox and she and Eulis had found sanctuary. Now if God was vigilant on their behalf and Eulis was saved from the disease, their lives would be perfect.

Refusing to accept that Eulis had been exposed, she ran back to the wagon and climbed in.

"What did she say?" Eulis asked.

Letty pointed to the break in the trees.

"That way," she said. "You'll see."

And they did.

The valley below was blanketed by both

a layer of snow and natural grasses that would provide all the winter fodder their animals would need. As Eulis remarked upon the cabin and the water, Letty watched a herd of elk moving slowly across the valley.

"Unbelievable," Eulis said. "But what about the owner of that cabin?"

"Little Bird said he's dead. Let's go, Eulis. The cabin is bound to need cleaning and it's getting late."

"As long as it's got a roof and four walls, it's gonna satisfy me," Eulis said, and clucked to the mules.

He wouldn't let himself think about getting sick, or dying down here in this valley and leaving Letty all alone to try and find her way out come spring. For now, their dilemma had been solved, and he was too cold and weary to worry about tomorrow.

Raising Lazarus

Letty named the place Eden. Eulis thought it was a bit too fancy for a one room cabin that smelled faintly of polecat and dust, but after they had unpacked their belongings and started a fire, he could almost believe she'd been right. The relief of knowing they had shelter for the winter did seem like a gift from above.

The fireplace smoked some, and Eulis figured some birds had probably built a nest up in the flue, but if it didn't burn itself clean by morning, he was going to climb up on the roof and dig out the clog.

To Letty's delight, she found two tin plates, a couple of spoons and one large cooking pot in a box beneath the bed. Added to the few pots and pans they'd brought with them, she could now lay claim to a good assortment of cookware. The oversized bed near the fireplace was a surprise and a blessing, although the leather strapping that been strung between the bedposts to serve as a mattress was stiff and dry, while a couple of the strips had come undone. One of the braces holding the footboard together had come loose, leaving the bed angled slightly toward the floor, but to Letty, who hadn't slept in a bed since their night at Four Mile Inn, it looked magnificent. While Eulis gathered firewood from the deadfall around the cabin, Letty pounded a loose wooden peg back into the bed and rethreaded the leather strapping on the bed. By the time Eulis had built the fire, Letty had made up their bedrolls onto the bed and was trying to wipe away the worst of the dust from the floor. When Eulis found a hand-made broom in the corner behind the fireplace, Letty clapped her hands and laughed.

Eulis grinned.

"Dang, Letty, it don't take much to make you happy."

Surprised by the pure truth of Eulis's words, she paused to look down at her hands. They were red and numb from the cold as they curled around the broom handle, but she hadn't given them much thought. She looked up at Eulis. Snow had frozen in his hair and on his partially bearded face, and there were red patches on his skin, which she knew probably mirrored her own. They'd come close to frostbite more than once, and yet the simplicity of finding a much-needed broom had brought her joy.

"You know something, Eulis, you're right."

His grin widened.

"Course I'm right."

This time when she laughed, she swung at him with the broom. He ducked and sidestepped, then pointed at her playfully.

"Woman, you watch out now. You don't want to put me out of commission when we ain't got a damn thing to eat except some jerky and beans."

"You've got a point," Letty said, and resumed sweeping, cleaning the floor of everything from dirt, leaves and mouse turds to the bones of some small animal — most likely rabbit.

Within the space of a couple of hours, the cabin had taken on a homely feel. The warmth from the fire had taken the chill out of the air and Eulis had fastened their tent over the cabin door, blocking out the cold air that kept blowing through a large crack.

"I'll fix that crack in the door tomorrow," Letty said, as she dished up the re-heated beans they'd carried from the low camp.

"And I'll go for an elk at first light."

Having stated an immediate plan for the future, they settled down to their beans and jerky and took comfort in the shelter from the cold and the dark.

And when it came time to lie down and rest, they lay down side by side on the bed without thought for propriety or sex. For now, they were two people who, despite the odds against them, had not only survived, but thrived.

Still, long after Eulis had fallen asleep and begun to snore, Letty watched the silhouette of his face highlighted against the glowing embers from the fire and prayed to God that he would not succumb to disease. She knew all too well how few survived and living without Eulis seemed obscene.

Within the week, there were two elks hanging in the shed and enough firewood to last through most of the winter. The crack in the door had been fixed with a mixture of mud, grass and some clay Letty had found near the waterfall, which had hardened like brick. She had used the rest of it to patch the chinking between the logs, then let the fire in the chimney die back so that she could run a long branch up the flue. Her digging quickly knocked down a half-dozen charred and smoking bird nests from the chimney. She rebuilt the fire, taking great satisfaction that smoke no longer backed up into the room.

Rosy and Blackie had plenty of grazing and water. All they had to do was dig down past the snow to the dry grass beneath. Each night, Eulis brought them in from the meadow and put them in a small lean-to on the south side of the cabin. It wasn't much in the way of shelter, but their proximity to the cabin deterred the occasional bear or cougar from attacking, although every night Letty heard wolves howling out in the valley. Even more daunting was the trail of footprints circling the cabin that the pack left behind each night.

Each day, Eulis taught Letty one thing new. He'd showed her the best way to fell trees, using the mules to drag them to the cabin, and then showed her how to split them for firewood. Yesterday it had been setting snares for rabbits. Today he'd showed her how to clean green skins for tanning. There was water to be had and food to be cooked. She knew enough to take care of herself until spring, and she knew the way out of the valley. For Eulis, who figured he was living each day on borrowed time, it was all he thought about. He'd gotten her into this mess by dragging her to the gold fields, and if it was the last thing he did, he was going to make sure she got out alive.

Letty stayed so busy and there was so much to learn, that she put the smallpox scare into the back of her mind. She'd laughed more since coming to this valley than she ever had in her life, and she slept sounder lying beside Eulis than she'd ever slept before. They'd earned their right to happiness. Surely, God wouldn't let any more tragedies befall them.

On the eighth day, morning dawned on a clear sky. The sun was so bright on the snow that looking upon the valley was painful to the eyes. By midmorning, Letty had an elk roast simmering over the fireplace for their supper and was out by the lean-to, scraping the same elk's skin that Eulis had stretched for her. She'd never made anything from the skin of an animal, but figured there was a first time for everything.

Despite the sun, the air was cold, leaving a bite to the skin. Blackie was grazing nearby while Eulis had taken Rosy with him to fell trees. Already, they'd dragged two large dead pines to the cabin to be cut up later for firewood.

Letty glanced toward the trees periodically as she worked, taking note of the time that Eulis and Rosy had been gone. She was just beginning to be concerned when she saw them coming out of the trees again. Only this time Eulis wasn't leading Rosy as he'd done both times before. He was riding her bareback. She watched for a moment, then flinched when Eulis swayed. She put down her knife then bent down and grabbed a handful of snow to clean her hands without looking away.

Rosy kept walking.

Eulis was still astraddle the black mule.

Everything was fine. She told herself that he was just tired. After all, it was their third trip. Taking a ride didn't have to mean anything was wrong.

She walked a few steps away from the house, kicking snow as she went. Her shoes were wet. Her feet were numb. She ignored both.

Blackie stopped grazing and looked up, braying when he saw Rosy coming.

Letty waved.

Eulis slumped forward, then as if in slow motion, slid off the mule into the snow.

"No," Letty moaned, and started running.

Blackie shied and then brayed and

kicked as Letty dashed past. The snow was halfway to her knees and wet. For Letty, who was scared half out of her mind, it felt as if she was trying to run through a lake of mud. The weight of the snow sucked at her shoes, more than once threatening to pull them clean off her feet, and yet she kept moving, afraid that if she stopped, then so would her heart.

Finally, she was there, pulling at Eulis's coat in a desperate attempt to get his face out of the snow before he suffocated. She rolled him over and began digging snow from his mouth and nose, then slapping at his cheek in an effort to wake him. The first thing she felt was the heat of his skin beneath her palms, and when she did, she rocked back on her heels and wailed.

Once at fate for dealing them one more blow.

Once at God for letting it happen.

And once for herself, knowing full well what still lay ahead.

Then she dragged herself up, slid her hands beneath Eulis's arms, and started yelling at him as she pulled.

"Get up!" she screamed. "Open your eyes and get up!"

Eulis could hear Letty's voice and although he couldn't quite focus on the words, recognized the panic in her voice.

"I'm sick," he mumbled.

Letty moaned, then tugged even harder.

"I know you're sick, but you've got to help me or you're damn sure gonna die. Stand up, Eulis. Stand up long enough for me to get you back on Rosy."

He tried to get up, but his legs wouldn't work, and there was something wrong with the sky. It was spinning around his head like a top.

"Letty?"

"I'm here," Letty said. "I need you to get up."

"Can't," Eulis said. "Gonna die."

"Not if I can help it," she muttered, then saw the rope dragging behind the mule and grabbed it.

When she tried to put it around Eulis's chest, he began struggling against her intent.

"Don't," Letty begged, pushing at his hands as he pulled at the rope. "Quit it, Eulis. You can't get up and I've got to get you to the cabin."

But he kept batting at her hands, undoing everything she tried to do.

"Don't wanna hang. They hang deserters. Don't wanna hang."

Letty shuddered. He was already out of

his head. Fear made her angry and she took it out on him.

"Damn it, Eulis Potter! You're not gonna hang, but you're gonna freeze to death unless you let me help."

"Cold," he muttered.

She laid her hand against his face. The fire beneath his skin was frightening.

"I know honey," she said softly. "I know you're cold. Let's go inside the cabin, okay?"

"Okay," he said, and passed out.

She took advantage of the moment by quickly wrapping the rope around his chest and tying it off. She pulled the rope as taut as she dared without getting him too close to Rosy's hooves, then grabbed Rosy's halter. She began leading her toward the cabin as fast as she dared, dragging Eulis behind. Twice she had to stop and brush snow from his face, but they finally made it to the cabin. She dragged him all the way to the doorsill, then untied the rope and somehow pulled him inside the cabin. Quickly, she unhitched Rosy and left her free to graze as she ran back inside.

Eulis was lying where she'd left him. Snow was melting from his pants and coat, leaving him lying in a swiftly spreading puddle.

Letty shut the door, removed her coat, then knelt at Eulis's side.

"Got to get these wet things off you," she said, and started pulling at his boots.

He moaned once, but didn't move. His silence was more frightening than when he'd fought her before.

She shoved the wet boots near the fire to dry and then began tugging off his pants. It took longer to get off his coat and shirt, because she had to keep rolling him from side to side.

Finally, he was naked, and Letty started to shake. Already the first signs of the pox were visible on his skin.

"God give me strength," she prayed softly, and then squatted behind him, slid her hands beneath his arms and started to pull.

"Help me, Eulis. Please God, help him to help me."

She pulled again, this time pulling up in an effort to get him to his feet and into bed. Somehow he moved. The success of her effort gave her strength, so she pulled again, and he moved, and she pulled again and again until finally he was on the bed. He rolled over onto his side, then moaned. When she tried to cover him up, he kicked off the covers.

"Hot . . . too hot."

Letty grabbed the bucket and ran out the door, coming back moments later with it packed full of snow. She scooped some of it into a pan and then set the bucket by the fire to melt. With shaking fingers, she began bathing his skin with the snow, hoping to lower his temperature.

It wasn't until sundown that she remembered the mules and ran out into the night, carrying the rifle to bring them home. To her relief, they'd come to the lean-to on their own and she quickly shut the gate. Then she set the rifle against the porch and carried in as much firewood as she thought they might need before getting a fresh bucket of snow.

The last thing she brought in was the rifle. Once inside, she let the door swing shut. The sound echoed and Letty flinched. She turned and stared at the door, then down at the man on the bed. Before, when she'd shut them in each night, it had been to keep them safe from danger. Only tonight, the danger was within and there was little she could do to keep it out.

By morning, he was covered in pox and out of his head. Letty had spent the night by his side, bathing his body with the melted snow and when she could, getting water down his throat. She was so tired she was shaking and nearly blind from exhaustion, yet sleep was impossible. If she closed her eyes, Eulis might die, and she couldn't let that happen.

After a quick trip outside to relieve herself and to let out the mules, she came back carrying a chunk of bone with a little meat and fat that they'd butchered from the elk. She started it to simmer, adding a little salt and a pinch of dried sage. Maybe today Eulis would feel better, and if he did, he would need sustenance. Nothing heavy, just a little broth of elk soup.

Once she'd put the soup bone on to cook, she felt better, as if by planning ahead, she'd given Eulis a future she'd been uncertain he would have.

A familiar stench rose from the bed and Letty turned abruptly.

"Poor baby," she said softly, then took a pan of warm water from the hearth and carried it to the bed. Eulis would hate what was happening to him, but in a way, it was just as well that he didn't know. He would rather have died than know he was soiling himself and that Letty was cleaning him up as if he were a baby.

Once the job was finished, she carried the wastewater outside and dumped it on the other side of the lean-to. When she turned around to go back into the cabin, she found herself face to face with a wolf.

"God in heaven," she gasped, and took a step backward.

The wolf snarled, then lowered its head. It was then Letty saw the blood spreading around its foot and staining the snow.

It appeared as if some toes were missing, probably from being caught in a trap. Back in Lizard Flats, she'd heard trappers talking about catching wolves in traps only to have them chew off their own foot rather than stay caught.

The wolf's sides were gaunt. It was obvious he'd been unable to hunt, and she was standing between him and the scent of elk meat. The wolf curled its lip, showing its teeth as it snarled. Hunger had overcome every fear it might have had regarding man, and it was willing to do what it took to feed.

A growl rumbled low in its throat as it took another step forward.

Letty thought of the rifle inside the cabin and groaned.

"Get!" she shouted, and waved the pan in the air.

The wolf flinched and dodged, but didn't go far. When she moved toward the cabin, instinctively, the wolf shifted, too. Again, she was pinned. Then, to her horror, the wolf started toward her, this time with no intent of stopping.

Letty moved backward, too, backing all the way up to the firewood. When she hit the stack with her heel, she suddenly realized she had all the weapons she would need at her back. Her fingers curled around a large branch only seconds before the wolf leaped.

Letty screamed as she swung. The branch hit the wolf in midair, landing solid up the side of its head. Blood splattered again, only this time on her. The wolf dropped at her feet then twitched, probably in the throes of death, but Letty wasn't taking any chances. She hit it again and then again, until blood and brains were spilled all over the snow, and she was staggering from the shock of what she'd done.

She dropped the branch into the snow and looked around for her pan. It was right where she'd dropped it, but when she bent down to pick it up, she swayed, then went to her knees. She took what she meant to be a deep, calming breath, and then started to sob. She cried until her head hurt and her feet and legs were numb from the cold.

When she tried to stand up, she stumbled and fell, only to find herself lying face to face with what was left of the wolf. She stared long and hard at the flattened skull and sightless eyes, then she gritted her teeth. It was dead. She was not. This time when she stood, she was steady on her feet.

She toed the carcass with the end of her boot.

"You shouldn't have gotten in my way," she said softly, then walked into the cabin.

Eulis was right where she'd left him, clean and warm beneath the covers. She felt his forehead, which was still hot to the touch, then slipped her hand beneath his head and raised it just enough that he might drink from the cup she held to his lips.

"Drink, honey," she begged. "Open your mouth and take a drink."

He moaned, then began muttering the same thing over and over.

"Don't drink . . . not anymore . . . not anymore . . . not anymore."

Letty pried his lips apart and gently poured the liquid in.

"Swallow it, Eulis. It's just water. I swear."

The water dribbled down both sides of his lips but enough went into his mouth to satisfy her intent. Carefully, she lowered his head, then checked on the soup. It was bubbling.

She looked down at her pants, frowning at the blood on the legs, then looked at her hands and shuddered.

She'd killed a man once when she'd taken him to bed, but that had been in the throes of sex and he'd paid her to die. She'd never killed anything with her hands before, and had often wondered if she had it in her to do the deed. So now she knew.

She took the skinning knife from the mantle and started for the door, pausing but a moment by Eulis's bed.

"I'll be right back," she said. "Don't bother getting up. I'll see myself out the door."

She laughed aloud at the absurdity of what she'd just said, and then choked back another sob. There were things to be done and she was burning daylight. She put another stick of wood on the fire and then headed for the door, taking care to carry the rifle this time when she left.

She'd lost track of the days that had come and gone. All she knew was that she was so weary from lack of sleep that she'd begun hallucinating. It had taken everything she had to make it to the falls, and now she staggered back into the cabin with a bucket of fresh water. She looked toward the fireplace and then froze. For a second, all she could see was the wolf that she'd killed, only it wasn't dead anymore. It was standing near the fireplace, snarling at her all over again.

She screamed, then stumbled, and fell over the doorsill, going face first onto the floor. The water spilled as she busted her lip. When she rolled over and looked up, she realized that it wasn't the wolf, but the skin. She'd stretched it like Eulis had shown her, and spent hours scraping the hide before the fire. It galled her that, even in death, its spirit was still strong enough to scare her.

But she reminded herself that it was dead and she wasn't, so for a few moments, she lay where she'd fallen, too exhausted to care that she was lying in water. She inhaled slowly, then exhaled on a sigh as she stared up at the raftered ceiling. After a few moments, she closed her eyes.

The scent of sickness filled the room. The pox on Eulis's body had begun to break and run and the stench was not unlike that of something rotten. She'd tried so hard to keep him alive, but she didn't think it was going to happen. She'd quit praying to God right after she'd skinned the wolf and tossed the carcass out into the meadow for scavengers to devour. The way she figured it, she'd done too many sins in her life for God to hear her now, and Eulis was going to pay for her mistakes. She knew she was helpless to save him, and since God wasn't answering any of her prayers, Eulis was bound to be doomed.

"You're gettin' wet."

"Like I don't know it," Letty muttered, then opened her eyes and screamed. "Eulis! You're awake!"

"You're still wet," he mumbled, then closed his eyes.

She jumped to her feet and ran to him, feeling his forehead and then his cheeks. His skin felt damp and clammy, but he wasn't as hot as he'd been. Could it be? Was it possible? Was the fever breaking? Was Eulis going to live after all?

"Eulis! Eulis! Can you talk to me?"

"Water."

Letty grabbed his cup and then lifted his head enough that he could swallow without choking. To her overwhelming relief, the water actually went down. It was only one small swallow, but for a man who hadn't done anything more than breathe in and breathe out for days, it was a miracle.

As soon as she lowered his head, he passed out. But this time she didn't care. She stripped off her wet coat, took the broom to the floor and used it like a mop until the water she'd spilled had worked its way between the floorboards into the dirt below. Then she ladled a bowl of elk broth into a cup to let it cool. When he woke up again, she was going to get some of it down him or die trying.

A few minutes later, he opened his eyes. The first thing he saw was a spoon coming toward him. He opened his mouth in reflex. The warm broth slid between his lips onto his tongue. He choked, then swallowed to keep from choking again.

"What's that smell?" he murmured.

"Yourself," Letty said. "Pox stinks."

"God. I am rotting."

Letty spooned another bit of broth into his mouth. This time he only choked once.

"Up. Raise me up."

She wadded up her coat and used it to pillow his head.

Immediately, Eulis moaned, and quickly closed his eyes. The bed was spinning one way, the room the other. It was too much motion too soon.

"Down. Down," he begged.

She moved the coat and then gently lowered his head back to the bed.

"I'm sorry," she said. "Did that make you sick?"

He blinked once for yes, and then closed his eyes.

"Want to eat any more soup?"

Unable to stand the sound of his own voice, he just mouthed the word, no.

Letty set the cup aside and then went to get a pan of water and the washrag. She pulled aside the covers and began to bathe his body, gently washing away the rotting skin and pus. And for the first time since she'd laid him in the bed, Eulis began to object.

"Pants . . . nekked butt. . . ." he muttered, and tried to push away her hands.

Too weary to be delicate, Letty shoved them aside and continued her task.

"Be quiet, fool. I have been looking at your naked butt for more than a week and I haven't passed out yet, so hush."

He hushed, and while he was considering the indignity he was enduring, quietly passed out again.

As soon as Letty had him cleaned, she covered him back up and then tossed the water outside. She added another stick of wood to the fire, blotted his peeled and drying lips with a clean wet cloth, and then wrapped herself in a blanket and lay down on the floor beside his bed. Confident that the worst had passed, and knowing that if she didn't get some rest, she would pass with it, she closed her eyes. Within seconds, she was asleep.

The Time of Revelations

It was snowing the day Eulis stood up on his own. The wind was a constant wail, not unlike the howls of the wolf pack that visited them every night. The storm was a whiteout of thick snow blowing horizontally from north to south. The wall beside the fireplace was stacked high with firewood while a large hunk of elk roasted on a spit over the fire. Letty sat on a stool near the hearth, stitching the soles to the tops on a pair of moccasins she was making for Eulis. She'd measured his feet while he'd been sleeping and was hoping to finish them up before he woke. Since Eulis had gotten sick, she'd lost track of time and wasn't even sure what day of the week it was, but she figured Christmas wasn't far away. The holiday had never meant a lot to her before, but considering their metamorphosis from drunk and whore, she thought it seemly to honor the day. She had yet to tell him about her encounter with the wolf and thought it great fun to surprise him with shoes made from the hide of their uninvited marauder.

She was almost through pulling the leather lacing through the hide when Eulis started to stir. Quickly, she gathered up the pieces and stuffed them in a box underneath the bed just as Eulis opened his eyes.

He hadn't expected to see her watching him from the foot of the bed and was still sensitive to the way he looked with the pox in the very last stages of healing as well as the scars they were leaving behind. He rose up on his elbows and frowned.

"If you were plannin' on givin' me another bath, you better think again. I wash my own butt from here on in."

Letty was so happy that he was alive to complain, that she didn't let his smart mouth get to her as she might have. So instead of arguing, she changed the subject.

"You hungry? I got a roast on the spit and some soup left over from yesterday."

His indignation was replaced with shame. She'd just spent the past weeks keeping his sorry ass alive and now here she was offering him some food and all he could do was complain. He rolled over and then swung his feet off the side of the bed.

"I reckon I could eat a bite."

Letty hurried to the fireplace, happy to be doing something productive. Before he'd gotten sick, she'd been in the habit of working outside for at least a part of the day because being cooped up in the cabin was more than a little confining. She grabbed a plate, sliced off an outside piece of the roast that was already done, then ladled a cup full of soup and carried them to the table. But when she turned around to help him to the table, she was surprised to see that he'd started on his own.

He had wrapped himself in one of the blankets and was more than a little unsteady on his legs, but he was walking alone, and for Letty, it was the final proof that he was almost healed.

"Oh Eulis," she said, and then burst into tears.

"Well, here now, what are you cryin' about?"

She quickly swiped at the tears on her cheeks as she took his elbow and steadied his steps until he could sit down.

"There were days when I didn't think I'd ever see you do this again. I'm just happy, that's all."

He sighed, then gave her a quick hug as she settled him into the chair.

"There were days when I didn't think I would do this again, either." His voice shook. "I owe you my life."

Letty tried to laugh it off, but the moment was too precious to jest. She looked down into his dear, familiar face and ached for the pain that he'd suffered.

"Yeah, well, you helped me hide that preacher's body and kept me from hanging, so I reckon now we're even."

He grinned slowly, then shook his head as she moved to the other side of the table.

"You know somethin'?"

"I know lots of somethings," she said.

He laughed and then took a sip of the soup.

"You don't know my somethin'," he countered.

"So, I'm listening."

"The people we were in Lizard Flats —"

She hated to be reminded of that life. It always left her feeling worthless and dirty.

"What about them?"

"They don't exist anymore. They died as surely as if we buried 'em in the grave with the real Randall Howe and that trapper."

Letty was too moved to speak. All she could manage was a nod of agreement.

"In fact, they're so dead that I think we oughta bury 'em right and proper."

"Bury them? Have you lost your mind?"

He took a bite of meat and then chewed slowly, contemplating what she'd suggested.

"You know, I might have — just a bit. But that don't change the fact that we're not the same people we once was and I'm sayin' that the best way to forget the past is to bury it. What do you think?"

Letty knew she was gawking because her mouth was agape, but for the life of her, she couldn't find the words to answer.

Eulis took another drink of soup and then reached across the table and took her by the hand. She hesitated for just a moment, then slowly opened her fingers and threaded them through his.

"What's happening to us?" Letty asked.

"I don't know 'bout you, but I been fallin' in love with you for some time now."

It was the last thing she'd expected to hear, and yet the best thing that he could have told her. She figured she ought to be giggling, or at the least try to simper and flirt, but it was beyond her. It was all she could do not to shout, hallelujah. She felt his thumb rubbing across the outside of her hand and shivered.

"You sure? I mean, I'm nobody's perfect little woman. I can't be all prissy and pretend to be helpless and innocent."

"Well that's a relief," Eulis drawled. "I'm a deserter and a used-to-be drunk. Why would you think I'd be wantin' some use-less, prissy-fied female?"

"I don't know."

"Well, all right then," Eulis said, and popped a bite of roast into his mouth and started to chew.

"You sure you know what you're talking about?" Letty asked. "I'm all bossy and opinionated and I'm always talking when I oughta be listening."

"I know," Eulis said. "You've also got a real mean streak."

Letty's lips went slack.

"Well, I never!" she muttered.

"Yeah, you did," he said. "Remember back in Lizard Flats how you used to yell at me on my bad days?"

"Dang it, Eulis, I never could tell the difference between your good days and bad. Besides, if you hadn't been so plowed, I wouldn't have had to raise my voice."

He shrugged. "It don't matter now. I let that man die. Reckon when it stops snowing, I'm gonna bury him deep."

"You're serious, aren't you?" she asked.

"Yep."

"All right then," Letty said.

Eulis frowned. "All right about what? Havin' a funeral for our old selves, or all right you ain't mad at me for fallin' in love with you?"

"Both."

"All right then," Eulis said again, and then smiled.

"Are you laughing at me?" Letty asked.

"Nope."

"Then why the grin?"

"It's simple, Sister Leticia. I'm happy, that's why."

"I'm happy, too."

Eulis nodded, and returned to his meal, although he couldn't manage it all. By the time he'd finished the soup and eaten a few more bites of the roast, he'd broken out into a cold sweat.

"I reckon I'd better lie down for a bit," he said. "Still a mite weak."

Letty helped him to the bed, then covered him up as soon as he stretched out.

The wind rattled the door on its hinges, but the patches she'd made in the cabin held strong.

"Sure glad we're not in that tent," he said.

"Me, too," Letty said, and then went back to the table to clean up.

Eulis eyed her as she worked, studying

the curve of her face and the stubborn thrust of her chin.

"Letty —"

"Yeah?"

"You never did tell me how you come to know that Indian woman. That Little Bird."

She stopped, and for a moment, stood without moving, her back to the bed. When she turned around, there was a strange expression on her face.

"Letty?"

"I helped her hide a dead man."

He sat straight up in bed.

"The hell you say! What made you do somethin' like that?"

"You helped me do the same thing once, remember?"

He sat there for a moment, then finally shook his head.

"If I live to be a hundred, and the way things are goin' I sincerely doubt that will ever happen, I don't think you'll ever fail to surprise me."

Letty bit her lower lip then lifted her chin.

"Is that bad or good?"

"Good — damn good," he said softly.

"You cursed," she reminded him.

"Yeah, and I expect you'll drive me to it

again before we get out of this valley."

"Close your eyes and go to sleep," Letty said.

"Lay down beside me," Eulis asked.

It was the last thing she expected, and all of a sudden, the thing she wanted most to do.

"You'll be safe. I'm still a sick man," Eulis said. "Besides, it's cold. You can help keep me warm."

Letty snorted beneath her breath, but put a couple of logs on the fire anyway, then stirred the coals. The logs caught and the added warmth was soon felt within the small room. When she turned around, he was still watching her.

"You're making me nervous. Close your eyes."

He closed his eyes, but he was still smiling. She had the strongest urge to see what the smile tasted like, but wouldn't follow the thought. Instead, she picked up the broom and began sweeping the floor. When she next looked at the bed, Eulis had truly fallen asleep. It was only then that she put up the broom, stirred the fire one more time, then slid into the bed, wrapped her arms around him as he slept and closed her eyes.

Sometime during the night, the wind

stopped blowing. Letty woke, felt the chill in the room and got up to add wood to the fire. When she turned to go back to bed, Eulis was sitting up in bed. He was little more than a silhouette, but she could hear him breathing. It was slow and even, a blessing after his near brush with death.

"Are you all right?" Letty asked. "Do you need a drink of water? Do you need to pee? I can —"

"All I need is you. Come lay with me, Letty."

Letty sighed. The tenderness in his voice was her undoing. Still, she knew that once they crossed this particular bridge in their relationship, nothing would ever be the same. She shook her head and frowned.

"You're too sick to fool around."

"There ain't nothin' foolish about what I'm feelin'."

"There's something you need to know," Letty said.

"No there ain't," he said softly.

"So you don't care to know if I love you back?"

There was a long moment of silence, then he cleared his throat.

"I care."

"All right then. I felt it was only fair that we start even in this matter."

Glad that it was too dark for her to see his face, he let himself smile. God how he loved this woman. She might drive him mad, but he was gonna love her all the way to his grave.

"So, you have feelings for me, too?"

Letty had never been so scared in her life. To admit this was to show weakness, and everything that she'd survived had taught her never to let them see her cry. Still, he'd been sick and she didn't have it in her to lie — not to Eulis — never to Eulis.

"Yes, I have feelings, strong feelings."

"Then come to bed with me, darlin'."

Letty sighed. The inevitability of this moment had been lingering between them ever since her day of desperation when she'd promised him free pokes for life if he'd just help her get rid of the body of Reverend Randall Ward Howe.

"Only if you let me do all the work," Letty said.

Eulis chuckled. "I reckon that'll be all right . . . for now."

Letty unbuttoned her shirt and then stepped out of her pants. Immediately, goose bumps rose on her skin.

"I hope we don't regret this tomorrow," she said, as she slid beneath the covers.

He wrapped her up in his arms and then pulled her close.

"I won't if you won't," he offered.

Letty laughed and then laid her head upon his chest.

"This is crazy," she mumbled.

"Then lock me up later," Eulis begged.

She raised up on her elbows. The smile on his face was somewhere between hopeful and scared to death that she'd back out.

"You sure you want to do this?" she asked.

"Yes, Lord, yes. Have mercy, love. Have mercy on me."

She touched his face with her hand, then lowered her head and for the first time in all the years that she'd known him, kissed him squarely on the lips.

Much later, and after the passion of the moment had passed, Letty lay within the shelter of Eulis's arms and slept. And as she slept, she dreamed of a little brown bird that kept calling to its mate. She'd dreamed the same dream her entire life, but tonight the dream was different. Tonight, she heard the whippoorwill's call, as well as the answer from its mate.

A week later, Eulis was cursing the taste of elk and swearing that if they ever got out of this valley, he would never eat elk meat again. Letty let him gripe without comment because it did her good to see him up and moving around.

It hadn't snowed in days, and what snow there was wore a two-inch crust of ice. Herds of elk were visible from the doorway, as were small herds of buffalo. The mules had suffered the most, having little to no shelter, and Eulis feared that one of Blackie's ears had frozen so badly that he was going to lose the top half. Still, the animals had been able to stomp down the snow enough to graze and they'd made a path to the waterfall and back.

Eulis came in the doorway with an armload of firewood and set it against the wall.

"That oughta' be enough for today. I'll bring more in before dark," he said, and then took the rifle down from the mantle.

Letty tried not to let her uneasiness show, as she realized he was determined to go hunting.

"You sure you're ready for this?" she asked.

"I'm fine," Eulis said. "I'm sick of elk. I'm goin' rabbit huntin', and that's that."

"All right," Letty said. "Just watch out for wolves."

"There's plenty of game in the valley. They ain't gonna bother me."

She thought of the wolf she'd encountered just outside their door and frowned. She had yet to tell him, only now she felt obligated to do so, so that he would be vigilant.

"I was bothered by one when you were sick," she said.

Eulis was all the way out the door, but something about the way she said that turned him around. He walked back into the cabin and shut the door.

"What do you mean, bothered?"

"Um . . . it uh . . . I —"

"Damn it, Letty."

"You cursed."

He sighed. "I told you that you were bound to drive me to it again, and you have, so you should be happy. Now talk to me. What happened to you while I was sick, and why am I just hearin' about it now?"

She threw up her hands and then pulled the box with the moccasins that she'd made out from under the bed.

"I wanted to surprise you. I was saving them for Christmas, but for all I know, it's already come and gone. So — Merry Christmas."

Eulis stared at the moccasins in disbelief. "Where did you get these?"

"I made them."

"From what?"

Letty rolled her eyes. "From the wolf."

"You shot a wolf."

"No. The rifle was in the cabin."

"So, what did you do, talk it to death? For God's sake, Leticia. Quit beatin' around the bush and tell me what happened."

The tone of his voice pissed her off. He wanted to know what happened. Fine. She'd be happy to tell him.

"Well, it was like this. I'd just finished washing the poop off your butt and went outside to dump the water. When I turned around, the wolf was standing between me and the door."

Eulis's face paled. She didn't know whether it was from the fact that she'd washed poop off his ass or been attacked by the wolf, and right now she didn't care.

"I waved the poop pan at him, but it didn't seem to faze him. His foot was bleeding and he was missing some toes. Looked real hungry. It seemed obvious that he wasn't about to get picky about what to chew on. He was willing to settle for me or the elk hanging in the lean-to."

"God All Mighty," Eulis whispered, and

sat down on the bed. "Did it hurt you?"

"No."

"What happened?"

"I brained it with a stick of firewood and skinned it out. I cured it like you showed me then measured your foot while you were sleeping and made these for you. If you don't want them, I do."

Eulis clutched the moccasins against his chest, then looked away. To his utter embarrassment, he started to cry.

It was the last thing Letty would have expected him to do and attributed it to his recently weakened state.

"Look, it won't hurt my feelings if you —"

"You could have been killed. You could have laid out there in the snow and died and I wouldn't have known a thing."

"But I wasn't hurt," Letty said, then sat down beside him.

He stared at her, unashamed of his tears and then shook his head.

"You killed it with a stick."

She nodded and wiped the tears from his face.

"It was a big stick," she added.

He looked at her for a minute, then started to grin.

"What?" she asked.

"Just like in the Bible."

"What's like in the Bible?"

"You know, David the shepherd boy who kills that giant Goliath with a rock and sling? That's you, Letty, only you used a stick, not a rock."

A little pleased with his analogy, she couldn't help but grin.

"The critter wasn't hardly a giant."

Eulis ran his hands inside the moccasin, then kicked off his boots.

"I thought you were going hunting," Letty said.

"I changed my mind," he said. "Elk meat is fine with me. I'm gonna sit here in our home with these fine shoes on my feet and think how blessed we've been."

"Blessed? You got smallpox and I got attacked by a wolf and you call that blessed?"

"But we didn't die. We could have, but we didn't. I call that blessed."

Letty stared at the man she'd come to love and then finally shook her head.

"You know what? Despite the fact that you've given up preaching, I'm thinking you're still a preacher at heart."

He pulled on the moccasins, then wiggled the toes against the fur lining.

"Feels real good," he said. "I reckon I'm gonna wear 'em when we have the funeral."

"We can't have a funeral for the wolf. I dumped its carcass out in the meadow weeks ago."

"Not the wolf. Us. Remember the night of the blizzard?"

She arched an eyebrow. It was their first night to make love.

"Of course I remember that night. I remember it very well, thank you."

"I think my superb lovemakin' has driven the rest of the night from your mind."

Letty rolled her eyes.

Eulis ignored her as he continued.

"I told you that when I got better, we were goin' to have a funeral and bury our old selves, remember?"

"You were serious?"

"Yes, ma'am."

"But what in the world are we going to bury?"

Eulis frowned. "It's got to be somethin' we still have from before. Somethin' that don't belong here anymore."

Letty shook her head. "I think I left all that behind."

"I got a flask of whiskey in my bag."

Letty gasped.

"Not to drink, you understand. Just to prove to myself I didn't want it no more."

Letty rested her head against his shoulder, just for a moment, but long enough to let him know she understood. Then she got her bag from the corner of the room and set it on the bed.

Eulis stood up and moved away, figuring she might need some privacy to find the part of her that was already dead. He watched her unfasten the bag and, one by one, remove the articles from inside.

There was a tortoise-shell comb that he'd never seen her wear.

"My mother's," she said, and set it aside.

Next came stockings and her old pair of shoes — part of her life as Sister Leticia, but nothing to do with the White Dove Saloon.

She took out a handful of books, then a small wooden box with a tintype inside.

Eulis peered over her shoulder.

"Who's the kid?" he asked, staring intently at the little girl with a large bow in her hair who was missing her front teeth.

"Me."

A lump came to his throat, thinking of the years of hardship that little girl had endured before she'd come to this place. He put his hand on the back of her head and then left it there, as if cushioning her from some unseen blow.

"Here," she said, suddenly, and handed him a small bag.

"What's in it?" he asked.

"See for yourself," she said, and dumped the contents onto the bed. "Rouge for my cheeks, kohl for my eyes, and color for my lips. War paint from the White Dove."

Eulis gathered up the makeup and dropped it back into the bag.

"War's over," he said gently. "Time to bury the past."

"I'll get the shovel," she said. "Only I don't know where we'll dig, seeing as how the ground is frozen and all."

"Not where the mules shelter," Eulis said. "And I'll get the shovel. You carry this." He handed her what was left of their past.

Letty put on her coat and then clutched the items close to her chest as she followed him out the door.

The air was so cold that snot froze on Eulis's upper lip, and he was thankful for the fur-lined shoes he was wearing. He swiped at his lip with the back of his hand as he slogged through the snow to the lean-to.

The ground was pitted and rough from the mules' hooves. Manure in various forms of decomposition lay scattered all around. He kicked at a frozen clump near the gate and then walked inside. The immediate shelter was a welcome relief from the wind.

Eulis thrust the shovel into the ground, grunting slightly when it didn't give. He moved to a different location and tried again, this time meeting with some success. Finally, he had the hole dug — small, but deep. He turned to Letty.

"The bodies, please."

She placed the whiskey and the makeup bag down in the hole, then stepped back, watching solemnly as Eulis covered them with dirt. Then he set the shovel aside and took off his hat.

"Dearly beloved, we are gathered here today to —"

Letty hissed, then rolled her eyes.

"That's for weddings," she muttered.

"I know," he said softly, and took her by the hand. "As I was sayin', we are gathered here today for two reasons. Buryin' what was left of the old Letty Murphy and Eulis Potter, and joinin' together in holy matrimony, the new man and woman who have come to take their place."

Letty gawked. Leave it up to Eulis to do something weird, but sweet.

"You never asked me to marry you," she mumbled.

"Will you?" he asked.

"Yes," she answered.

"Then hush up and let me finish what I been tryin' to say."

Letty bit her lip to keep from spouting off, then tried not to grin. This was certainly nothing like the romantic wedding she'd dreamed of as a girl. Hellsfire, it wasn't even a wedding. It was supposed to be a funeral of sorts. Eulis, being the frugal kind, had tossed the vows in for free.

Eulis took her by the hand.

"Do you, Leticia Murphy, take this man as your lawful wedded husband?"

"Yes, only I —"

"Now, you ask me," Eulis countered.

Letty sighed. "But I'm not the preacher."

He grinned. "And neither am I, so that makes it even."

She frowned. There was a mistake in that logic somewhere; she just couldn't put her finger on the spot.

"All right. Do you, Eulis Potter, take me as your lawful wedded wife?"

"I sure do," he said, and then took her by the hands. "By the power I have taken upon myself, I now pronounce us as husband and wife. And God help any fool who tries to put you under."

"Asunder," Letty mumbled. "The word is asunder."

"Whatever," Eulis said, and kissed her soundly.

Letty found herself kissing him back.

A blanket of snow slid off the roof of the lean-to and landed with a shower of ice crystals at their feet.

"Where are we going for our honeymoon?" Letty asked.

"To bed," Eulis said.

"Fine with me."

A quiet descended upon the meadow as the cabin door swung shut. Smoke from the chimney thickened as extra wood was added to the fire, but one needed warmth in a room when one was not wearing any clothes.

Hidden Riches

Almost a month had passed since the marrying and the burying. By Eulis's best guess, January should be almost gone. Within a couple of months, the first signs of spring should be evident, which meant they would be leaving Letty's Eden.

Each night as Eulis undressed for bed, he inspected the skin on his body, and each time he did, the scars from his smallpox seemed a little bit smaller and a bit less pink. With time, they would fade even more, although vanity was not something he dwelled upon. His thoughts were all mixed up with the newness of his and Letty's personal relationship, and his responsibility to her as a husband. Here, in this hidden-away valley, it was easy to get by. Money was unnecessary if you were willing to live on nothing but meat, and dress like an Indian. But the clothes on their backs were wearing out and come spring, there was a strong possibility that they would be forced to wear buckskin back into Denver City. Although he kept his beard cut short, he'd let his hair grow long. It hung down his back. Still, it was nowhere near as long as Letty's, although the only time she wore it down was when she intended to wash it, and only until it was dry. After that, she would gather it all over one shoulder, brush it until it was as dark and shiny as the pelt of a mink, then braid it back up. He would watch her do that at night as she sat on the stool by the hearth. It often occurred to him that a man could die happy from that sight alone. But he didn't want to spend the rest of his life isolating himself and Letty from the rest of the world. Decisions would have to be made soon, and they would do it together, just as they'd done all along.

What concerned him most was where they would go from there. He wasn't of a mind to go back to panning for bits and pieces of gold and living in a tent, and it wasn't fair to subject Letty to that hardship again. They still had most of the small poke of gold nuggets that they'd panned from Cherry Creek last fall, but it was hardly enough money to set them up for life. What he needed was a plan.

Before he'd been a drunk he'd been a soldier, and before that and only briefly, his father had tried to farm. But being orphaned at such an early age had shortened any apprenticeship he might have experienced. Like Letty, all he knew how to do was survive.

Unaware of Eulis's concerns, Letty went from day to day without thinking too far ahead. It was how she'd kept from going insane while sleeping with men for money, and habit was a hard thing to break.

What had changed most for her was her self-esteem. It didn't make sense and it shouldn't have mattered, but symbolically burying herself had made a marked changed in Letty's attitude. She held her head up higher when she walked, and she moved with a confidence and pride that she'd never had before. But she wasn't the only one who'd changed. If Eulis could grow wings, he would be flying.

He woke up smiling, and went through the hard winter days with gusto. Cutting wood was a blessing, and bringing in a brace of rabbits now and then as a change to their diet gave him joy. Once in a while, they talked about the future and where they might go, but not often. Until the spring thaw, they were just marking time.

On this particular day, the sun had come up to reveal a clear sky. For the time being, the sunshine was melting some of the snow from the roof. In some places it splattered, in others it ran in rivulets onto the snow and ice at the base of the cabin. Eulis had taken the mules out of the valley and up into the tree line to haul back some wood, while Letty decided to make good use of his absence by giving the cabin a thorough cleaning. After wiping ash from all the flat surfaces inside the cabin, she set a bucket of snow by the hearth to melt for mop water. While it was melting, she took the broom to the far corner of the room where they'd been stacking the firewood, and began sweeping up the leaves and wood chips with a passion.

Soon, the air in the room was swirling with dry ash and dust motes. When the dust began to make her cough, she decided a little air on the subject wouldn't be amiss and opened the door just a crack.

The air was cold, but it smelled fresh and clean, and as she leaned outside, she took a deep cleansing breath before returning to her task. It wasn't until she went back to the dirt she was sweeping that she saw something odd. The addition of light into the room was highlighting the tiny bits of dust still floating in the air. Only the bits were no longer floating. Something was pulling them toward the back wall.

If it had been toward the chimney, it would have made sense. After all, there would be a natural draft from the doorway to the flue, but there was no reason this should be happening — at least not from the door to the corner of the room.

Curious, she moved toward the wall, then pressed her hands against the rough-hewn wood, tracing the path of the chinking between the logs. To her surprise, she felt a rush of cold air, which didn't make sense. The cabin had been built flush up against the mountain. There shouldn't be anything back there to make a draft and yet it was there.

She stood for a moment, studying the darkened corner, then got the poker from the fireplace and began tapping it along the wall. Within seconds, she heard a difference in the sound and tapped the poker again, thumping on the logs until she settled on a section that sounded different — almost hollow.

Frustrated by lack of light, she hurried back to the door and opened it back as far as it would go. Cold air immediately filled the room, but it couldn't be helped. She had a mystery to solve.

The addition of light was more than revealing. Almost immediately, she could see a faint, but distinct cut in the logs from about three feet below the ceiling, then all the way to the floor. Still uncertain of what it was that she'd found, she began pushing against the logs in an effort to see if anything moved.

The only thing that happened was that the room kept getting colder. Irked with herself for letting out so much heat, she decided to give up the search and ran to close the door.

Even though the fire was burning hot, the room was now freezing. She stirred the fire then added another log. Her hands were like ice and her feet weren't much better. The way she figured it, she would get warmer faster if she continued to work. The mop water had melted, so she sloshed it across the floor, then took the broom and began sweeping it down. She was working her way toward the corner when she stepped on a piece of bark that she'd missed while sweeping. Before she knew it, her ankle gave way and she was falling backward against the wall. A second later, the wall swung inward. The unexpected motion caught her off guard and she fell hard, hitting her head on the floor with a thump.

★ ★ ★

Eulis was thinking of the warm cabin and spit-roasted rabbit as he came down from the trees, pulling a felled tree behind each mule. As he neared the cabin, the smoke coming out of the chimney was as good as any welcome sign he'd ever seen.

"Gee, Rosy . . . Haw, Blackie . . . let's go home."

The mules dug in a little deeper and the trees they were pulling slid a little faster against the snow. They were as anxious to get unhitched as Eulis was to see Letty. Within minutes, they were back at the cabin.

Eulis unhooked the trees near the wood-pile, then unhitched the mules. Rosy tossed her head and gave a quick kick before running out into the meadow. Blackie wasn't far behind. Eulis laughed at their antics and then stomped the snow from his boots as he got to the door. But when he walked inside, the chill in the air made him frown. It shouldn't be cold.

"Letty?"

She didn't answer. He saw the water on the floor, and seconds later, saw her. She was flat on her back and lying halfway into some kind of opening. Shot through with panic, he picked her up into his arms and

461

carried her to the bed. When he put her down, his hand came away bloody. Sick to his stomach and so scared he could barely think, he found a cut on the back of her head.

"Letty . . . Letty . . . what have you done?" he muttered, then ran for some clean rags to put a compress against the wound. As he eased her head up, she moaned, and then blinked.

"Eulis?"

"I'm here, darlin'. Lie still."

"What happened?" Letty murmured, and reached for her head.

"I'm not sure, but it appears you've gone and knocked a hole in the wall."

She frowned. "I think you went and hit your head, too. You're talkin' crazy."

Ignoring the obvious opening in the back of the room, he began running his hands up and down her arms and legs to check for further injuries.

Letty swatted at his hands.

"Not now, Eulis. I'm not exactly in the mood."

He had to laugh. It was that, or curse, and she was highly opposed to that happening.

"You ain't the only one with lust in the dust. You might near scared the life outta' me. I'm tryin' to see if you're still all in one piece, okay?"

She sighed, then moaned. "I know, I'm sorry. I'm a bit out of my head."

"No wonder," he said. "You've got a goose egg of a knot and you're bleedin' some."

"Oh, Lord, I don't want to get blood on the bed," Letty said, and tried to sit up.

"It don't matter," Eulis said. "Just lie still."

Letty groaned again, then relaxed.

Eulis patted her cheek, then glanced over his shoulder to the opening in the wall.

"What did you go and find, girl?"

"Find? What are you talking about?"

He pointed toward the corner of the room.

When she saw what had happened, she gasped, then started to get up, but the motion made her dizzy, and she sat back down with a thump.

"Easy, darlin'," Eulis said. "You stay here. I'm gonna take a closer look."

He peered inside, but it was so dark he couldn't see beyond the doorway.

"Where's that piece of candle?" he asked.

"On the shelf above the cooking pans," she said.

He got it, lit it with an ember from the

fireplace, and then carried it to the darkened opening.

"Lord have mercy," he whispered, and took a couple of steps inside. Almost immediately, he could tell that it was some kind of a shaft and that it ran straight back into the mountain.

Letty held the compress to her head as she got up, staggering a bit until she got her balance, then followed Eulis. She ducked underneath his arm and then stopped.

"Is it a mine? Did we find a mine?"

"Well . . . I don't know about that, but it's definitely a tunnel."

"It's a mine," she repeated, then took him by the hand and pulled him forward.

"Careful," he said. "The floor feels a little uneven." Then he lowered the candle for a better view.

There were no holes in the floor of the tunnel, but there were a lot of rocks. He kicked them aside and then started forward when the faint light from the candle caught and held in something bright.

Letty had seen it too.

"What was that?" she asked, then took the candle from his hand and knelt down.

The floor of the shaft appeared to be littered with rocks, but rocks like she'd never seen before. Her heart started to pound as beads of sweat appeared on her upper lip. Since it was anything but hot inside the tunnel, and she was still chilled from lying on the cold floor, she figured she was about to pass out. And since she already had one knot on her head, she figured the best thing she could do was stay down. At least this time she wouldn't have far to fall.

She handed Eulis the candle, then sat.

"Honey . . . are you all right?" Eulis asked.

"No. I got an extra hole in my head. Hurts something fierce, but that's beside the point. Do you see what I see?"

He squatted down beside her, holding the candle even closer to the rocks, unable to believe what he was seeing. But it was there just the same. Thick veins of gold ran through everything he picked up. Then he stood and lifted the candle up high, shedding a faint but persistent light on the walls of the shaft. The veins there were as wide as his arm. He thrust his knife into the wall to see how deep it ran. When it went all the way to the hilt without stopping, he thought he was dreaming.

"Letty, are you seein' what I'm seein'?"

"If you're seeing gold, then yes. I reckon we've found us a gold mine, and if this stuff is as good as it looks, we're most likely rich."

"Wait here," he said, and moved a few yards forward, curious as to how far back the shaft went.

He hadn't gone more than twenty or thirty yards when he saw a bundle of rags lying against the wall. Upon closer inspection, he realized there was a skeleton within them. He took a deep breath, and then called back.

"Letty."

"Yes?"

"There's a dead man back here."

Letty yelped, then scrambled to her feet. Using the wall to steady herself, she moved toward the candlelight. Seconds later, she, too, saw the skeleton.

"Oh Lord. Wonder what happened to him?"

"Most likely, he just died of natural causes."

Letty leaned down, staring at the slack jaw of the skull and the empty eye sockets and whispered.

"How can you tell?"

"Well, if someone had done him in, they would have most likely gone and laid claim to the gold. But since that Indian woman told you the man who lived here was dead, most likely when he didn't show up any-more, they assumed the obvious, and the mine became his tomb."

"That doesn't make sense," Letty said. "If he had just up and disappeared, then why would she say he died? Assumption would lead anyone to believe that he'd just left for greener pastures, so to speak."

Eulis frowned. "You're right."

"Of course, I'm right," Letty said, then leaned a bit closer and moved aside the rotting fabric of the shirt. Suddenly she gasped and pointed. "Eulis! Look down there, on the ground between his ribs."

Eulis held the candle closer. Then he saw it, too.

"That's an arrowhead."

"Part of the shaft is broken off," Letty said.

"I'll be danged," Eulis muttered. "He was gut-shot. Broke the arrow off at the belly. But why did he crawl off in here?"

The hair on the back of Letty's neck suddenly stood on end. In her mind, she was twelve years old again, and hiding in that hollowed-out badger hole, listening to the shrill war cries of the Indians as they'd attacked her father and burned their home to the ground. She knew why he'd come in here.

"He was hiding," she said.

Eulis knew enough about her past to know what she was remembering. He squatted down beside her, then slid an arm around her shoulders.

"But it's safe now," he said. "The Arapahos are right friendly to the white man."

"Not to all," she said, pointing to the arrowhead and remembering the dead white man she'd helped Little Bird hide.

"I reckon they had their reasons," Eulis said.

When she looked down, the floor started to move. She flattened her hands against the dirt, but it kept on swaying.

"Do you feel that?" she asked.

"Feel what?" Eulis said.

"The floor's moving."

He remembered the knot on her head and cursed himself for being so dense.

"Here, honey. Hold this," he said, and handed her the candle, then bent down and picked her up.

"I think I can walk."

"I don't think you can even stand, and since I'll be carryin' you to the bed, you might as well just hush."

Then he kissed her once on the cheek to soften his words before taking her out of the tunnel.

When he gently laid her on the bed, Letty pointed back at the wall.

"Close that doorway. We haven't had any visitors, but I wouldn't want to bet that gold on the fact that we won't. Besides, it's not going anywhere, and we've got the rest of the winter to figure out what we're going to do."

Eulis studied the opening for a bit before pulling it shut, then tried opening it over and over until he figured out how the hidden door worked. Satisfied that their discovery was safe, he hurried back to Letty.

She was dabbing a wet cloth on her head, trying to wash off the blood. When he offered to help, she shooed him away, so he stood at the foot of the bed, marveling at the intensity with which she was working. After a bit, he started grinning.

At that point, Letty looked up.

"What's so funny?" she asked.

"You did it, honey. You found a mother lode."

"No. All I did was find someone else's mine. It's not ours until we register this claim and even then we gotta keep this secret. If those miners in Denver City find out what we've got and where it's at, we'll be dead before dark."

He frowned. She was right.

"How do you reckon we'd best go about this?"

"I don't know for sure," she said. "But we got a few months to think on it before we have to make a decision."

He brightened up. "That's so," he said. "Now lay back and rest your poor little head."

She sighed and did as he suggested, but she couldn't be still. There was something still bothering her.

"Eulis."

"What, honey?"

"When the ground thaws, we need to give that man a Christian burial."

Eulis nodded, then glanced back at the wall.

"Kinda' gives me the creeps, knowin' he's just layin' back there like that."

"A dead man doesn't scare me," Letty said. "Except for you, that's the only kind of man that I trust."

Except for the day Letty had admitted to loving him, it was the first real compliment she'd ever given him. Even though it was a bit backhanded, Eulis took it to heart.

"Well, all right, then," he said gently, and despite her fuss, took the wet rag out of her hand and cleaned up her wound. After putting a dry compress on it, he made her lie down. "I'm goin' outside to cut up that wood. You rest. If you need something, call me."

He cupped her cheek with his hand, then leaned over and kissed her.

"I'm sorry you hurt."

She caught his hand as he started to pull away.

"There's something I want to tell you, something I should have said months ago."

"What?"

"I'm so sorry for all those years I treated you bad, for yelling at you when you were bringing up my bath water and calling you names because I wanted someone to be more miserable than I was. I was terrible mean to you."

Eulis laughed. It was the last thing she expected him to do.

"That makes you laugh?" she asked.

"No, no, you don't understand. It's right dear of you to be sorry like that, but you gotta know somethin'. Despite what I've said, I don't remember even one time when you yelled at me. I was too drunk. Even when I wasn't drunk, I was so hung over, I couldn't focus on anything but my own misery."

Letty sighed. "Still, I did it, and I'm sorry."

He shook his head. "Don't be. I haven't been sorry for one day of my life since we left Lizard Flats together."

Letty smiled as she fought back tears, then held the words close to her heart long after he'd gone outside.

Weeks passed.

Snow came again, then melted back some.

Days were getting longer, which meant their time left in the valley was becoming shorter.

The End of the Trail

The wind came up in the night as Eulis and Letty slept. The sound alone wasn't enough to awaken them to what was happening outside, although it blew and it blew in nerve-wracking gusts that never stopped, blasting from peak to peak and down into the valley, blowing all night long, rattling the door, and sucking air up the chimney so fast that the fire went completely out.

Eulis woke just before morning and needing to pee, but when his bare feet hit the cold floor, shock almost drove the notion from his mind. He looked toward the fireplace, surprised to see that not only had the fire gone out, but there were no live coals left either.

"What in blazes?"

Letty roused, then rolled over, realizing Eulis was up.

"What's wrong?" she asked.

"Something's wrong. Fire's out," he said shortly. Then he turned toward the door. "And the wind's stopped blowing."

She sat up, then pulled the covers up to her chin.

"Oooh, it's freezing in here," she said.

"Like I said, fire's out. Even the coals."

Letty frowned, then threw back the covers.

"I'll help," she said. "There's some kindling in the corner."

"We don't have any more matches," he said.

Letty panicked, but only for a moment. "We've got flint."

Eulis turned and looked at her. "Why do we have flint, and why didn't I know it?"

"I found it by the fireplace on our first day. My daddy used flint to make fire all the time, so I knew what it was. I just put it up."

"Where is it?" he asked.

"On the shelf behind the pan you used to make coffee, when we still had some to drink."

He shoved aside the pan, grabbed the flint, then hurried back to the fireplace. Within a few minutes, they had a small fire going. Letty sat on the stool by the fire, wrapped in a blanket from the bed and slowly added wood as needed, while Eulis went to get dressed.

The sun was just a wink away when he

opened the door to go let the mules out of the shed.

"Letty! Look! Lord have mercy, would you look at that!"

She ran to the door, then started to laugh.

"It's gone! It's gone! The snow is gone. What happened? How could it all melt this fast?"

"Chinook," Eulis said. "I heard of 'em. Never saw what one could do, though."

"What's a Chinook?" Letty asked.

"It's a warm wind that comes outta the south and melts the snow right down. I reckon this is our first sign of spring comin'."

"Will it snow more?"

"Might, but probably nothin' like it has before."

"What do you think?" Letty asked.

Eulis knew what she meant. "I think we oughta make plans to leave."

All of a sudden, the thought of the unknown was unsettling. Here, she knew what to do. Out there, every day was uncertain. Then she thought of the gold. Whatever they did they would be doing it in style.

"How are we gonna pack out the gold?" Letty asked.

Eulis looked toward the wagon. Melted snow was still dripping through the cracks in the wagon bed. The wheels were okay, but the hubs would be needing grease, especially with a heavy load. There was some still in what they'd packed from Fort Dodge, although when he thought about that time, it seemed like a lifetime ago.

"We'll figure somethin' out, but we will have to wait a couple of days until the ground freezes back or we'll bog down in the wagon before we get across the meadow."

"I'm scared," Letty said, and then couldn't believe she'd admitted to being weak.

Eulis put his arm around her.

"Yeah, so am I."

The silence after their confessions was short. Letty was the first to laugh, and it came out in a snort.

"I shouldn't have said I was scared. I think that's the wrong word. Scared was when I saw you fall off of Rosy into the snow and I didn't think I was gonna get you back to the cabin. Scared was watching you burning up with fever and not being able to do anything but pray you wouldn't die. Scared was when that wolf wanted me for breakfast. I don't know why I said I was scared."

But Eulis just patted her shoulder. "We

ain't never been rich before. Maybe that's what's wrong."

Letty frowned. "That's right enough, but we're not leaving that gold behind, so whatever it is that's gotten in my craw, I intend to get over it."

Eulis grinned. "I guess you're right."

"No guess about it," Letty said. "I'm going to get dressed. After you let the mules out, bring me some meat from the shed to cook up for breakfast. After we eat, I think we need to dig that grave."

The mention of the miner's skeleton drove all the silliness from the moment. Weeks ago and before they'd ever started mining the ore, they'd put the man's remains in a box and set it in the shed where their meat was hanging.

They had no idea how much ore they'd dug out of the mine, but it was in piles all along the shaft, just waiting to be carried out. Now that the time was here, a whole new set of worries evolved. Leaving the valley meant coming in contact with people again — people who would be willing to kill for what they'd found.

"I take all that back," Letty said. "I am scared, after all."

Eulis pulled her close and gave her shoulder a squeeze.

"Tell me what scares you, darlin'."

"Anyone with gold fever. We're gonna have to watch our backs."

"Naw, we're gonna be fine. When they find out that you cured me of smallpox and killed a wolf with your bare hands, there ain't gonna be a man for miles who'll be willin' to mess with you."

"You think so?"

He grinned.

"Yeah, warrior woman, I think so."

About five days later when the ground had frozen back as hard as ice, they made the decision to leave. When all was said and done about how to get the ore to Denver City, they wound up just dumping it loose in the back of the wagon, then throwing their belongings on top of it. After that, they covered everything with six of the elk hides Letty had tanned. Eulis tied it all down, and for the first time in months, harnessed the mules to the wagon.

Letty went into the cabin one last time to make sure that they weren't leaving something important behind. Without their things scattered about, the room seemed larger. She stood motionless in the doorway, remembering the work they'd put in to make the old cabin weatherproof, then the long, frightening days and nights as Eulis lay near death. The cabin had been their sanctuary when they'd needed it most, as well as a tomb for the man who'd come before them. She eyed the wood stacked against the door to the mine, knowing that its presence would keep their secret safe, then closed the door behind her.

Eulis was sitting in the wagon with the reins in his hands.

"Ready?" he asked.

She climbed up into the seat, then picked up the rifle down in the boot and put it across her lap.

"I'm ready," she said.

"Wonder how Denver City survived the pox," Eulis said.

"We'll soon find out," Letty said. "Let's go."

Eulis flipped the reins across the backs of the mules.

"Gee, Rosy, haw, Blackie."

The mules put their heads down and started to pull, but the wheels barely moved. Eulis held his breath, wondering if they had loaded too much ore.

"Come on, you two fat backs. You had it too easy. Now it's time to get back to work."

He clucked at the mules and flipped the reins across their backs. To his relief, they dug in and pulled, and the wagon started to roll. The farther they went, the easier they rode. By the time they reached the crest of the hill above the valley, he stopped them to give them a little rest.

"It's all downhill from here," he said.

"Just don't wreck us," Letty said.

He frowned. "Well, hell, woman, I wasn't plannin' on it."

"You cursed."

"And if I hear anything that stupid again I might be forced to repeat myself."

"Are you callin' me stupid?" Letty asked.

Eulis rolled his eyes. "No, ma'am, I'm not."

"Okay then," she muttered, and shifted the rifle across her lap.

Eulis saw tears in her eyes and suddenly realized that she was emotionally torn about leaving. He knew just how she felt. Back there had been simple compared to what lay ahead. He reached out and patted her knee.

"Just save all that piss and vinegar for them gold-fevered miners you keep worryin' about."

She sighed, then nodded.

"You okay, darlin'?"

She nodded again.

"Good enough," he said. "Denver City, here we come."

It was the absence of the Arapahos and the size of the cemetery that Eulis and Letty noticed first.

"Oh Lord, Eulis, from the number of crosses, it appears that not everyone was as blessed as you."

"Sure glad I didn't have to dig all them graves," he said, and then looked away, unwilling to think about how close he'd come to being under one of those markers.

As they passed, she scanned the crosses, silently marking the names that she recognized.

Yung Chi. A little Chinese man who had done laundry.

Marvin Handleman. A lawyer from Philadelphia who'd been disbarred and come west to seek his fortune.

Corliss Sheffield. A woman who'd plied her trade at one of the saloons.

Emory James. He'd outrun Millie Sees Crow's bullets, but had been unable to outrun the pox.

Boston Jones.

As soon as the last name registered, Letty flinched. She thought of the gambler and the times they'd crossed paths, but she would not have wished the hell of that death on anyone.

Looking away from the cemetery, Letty clutched the rifle a little firmer and sat up a bit straighter in the seat as she focused on the city before them. Despite the smallpox epidemic that had gone through it, Denver City had grown. There were people everywhere. A good number of the tents had been replaced by wooden buildings, and someone had even had the foresight to lay sidewalk. Now, most of the businesses were connected by a maze of narrow wooden planks, and considering the size of the frozen ruts in the streets, it was a good thing.

"It's a good thing that the ground is still froze, or we'd bog sure as shootin'," Eulis said, as they pulled into the city.

"Where do we go first?" Letty asked.

"I reckon to the assayer's office to make sure what we got is the real thing, then straight to the land office to register the claim."

Letty thought about it a minute and then shook her head.

"Let's go to the land office first."

"But what if we got ourselves a wagonload of fool's gold?" Eulis asked.

"I've seen fool's gold. It doesn't look like

this," Letty said. "We do the land office first."

"Okay. Land office it is."

Letty felt a little easier, but didn't relax.

They rolled into town amidst a good dozen of other wagons coming and going. A very new saloon had sprung up on the first corner in town. As they passed, the wood they'd used to build it was so green that they could see droplets of frozen sap on the outer walls. A pair of saloon girls were standing in the doorway, trying to lure customers inside with a mixture of lewd gestures and remarks.

Letty flinched.

"Rest easy, wife," Eulis said softly.

Wife. That one word settled her quicker than anything else he could have said.

"There's the land office," she said, pointing down the street.

A few moments later, Eulis stopped the wagon directly in front so that he would have a clear view of Letty, who was going to stand guard outside.

"You gonna be all right?" he asked.

Letty lifted her chin.

"I'll be fine."

He nodded, and then jumped down from the wagon and walked inside.

Letty saw him through the window as he

walked up to the counter and watched until he and the land agent began to converse. After that, she turned her attention to the job at hand.

The rarity of a decent woman in the gold camps was still unusual enough to warrant curiosity from the men on the streets. A good number of them stared and a few tipped their hats, but it was the ones who stopped and came closer that made her nervous. One in particular set Letty's nerves on edge.

He came out of a cafe picking his teeth with the point of his knife, which was enough in itself to make her gag. He was huge — well over six feet tall, and walked spraddle-legged to accommodate the size of his belly. His hair was carrot orange and curly and stuck out in all directions from beneath the hat he'd jammed on his head. His pants had been patched a number of times and his coat was obviously handmade from beaver pelts that were still bearing the heads of some of the beavers to whom the pelts had first belonged. He looked like something out of a bad dream, and she knew it the first moment he spied her. At that point, she glanced nervously toward the land office. Eulis was still at the counter.

"I killed a wolf. I can handle one ugly fat man," she muttered, but clutched the rifle a little tighter just the same.

Sean Clancy had been at Cherry Creek almost from the beginning of the strike. Like all the others who'd come to Denver City, he'd dreamed of gold just lying around waiting to be gathered up, somewhat like when he'd been small and his mother had made him gather in the hen eggs. It had taken him exactly one week to learn that he'd been sorely mistaken. He'd lost his grubstake in a poker game, then crippled the gambler. If it had been anyone other than a card shark, they would have hung him on the spot. As it was, he convinced enough of them that he'd been swindled, and so they turned him out on the street and the gambler over to the doctor, who patched him up and advised him to get the hell out of Denver City while the getting was good.

But Clancy hadn't been as smart as the gambler. He'd stayed on, trying to beg a grubstake from anyone who looked willing to share, and sleeping with Arapaho women every chance he got. Ironically, it was his lust for the Indian women that probably saved his life. He was in the

Arapaho camp when word spread that there was smallpox in Denver City. The Arapaho had sent him packing as they gathered up and moved out. Afraid of the pox, he hid out along the creek, watching the various claims to see if any became abandoned. By the end of the second week, he'd taken the belongings of four miners who succumbed to the pox and then holed up in a cave above the city.

It had been a long, lonely winter and there were days when he'd thought he would go mad. But the Chinook thawed him out just as it had Eulis and Letty, and he'd come to town with a winter's worth of stored-up frustration, looking to hump a few women and fight the good fight.

When he saw the raggedy woman perched on the wagon seat, his instinct for trouble led him straight to her. He rubbed the front of his pants in a suggestive manner, then pointed at her.

"I been waitin' for you all winter," he said, and stepped off the curb.

Letty swung the rifle straight at his belly. "You in a hurry to die?"

When she cocked the hammer back on the rifle, he stumbled. In an effort to steady himself, he reached for the mules. The unexpected slam of his body weight made Rosy and Blackie step sideways, and in doing so, moved the last obstacle from Sean Clancy's path. He went face first onto the frozen ground and came up with a busted lip, a sore nose, and a handful of fresh mule manure on the front of his coat.

"Son-of-a-holy-bitch!" Clancy roared, and reached for the barrel of Letty's rifle.

Tempted to aim for the mule shit he was wearing, Letty changed her mind at the last second, swung the rifle up and fired it off in the air instead.

The gunshot stopped Clancy dead in his tracks and brought Eulis running out of the land office with the agent not far behind him.

"What's going on out here?" Eulis yelled, then saw the determination on Letty's face. "Are you all right?"

"So far," she said. "Fat-ass here, seemed to think I'd been waiting out the winter just for his arrival."

Eulis eyed the mountain of a man with a calm that came out of nowhere. He doubled up his fists, ready to wade into the man while completely aware that he would most likely take a whipping.

"That's my wife, you insulted," Eulis said. "Apologize to her now, or I'm gonna have to whip you where you stand."

Sean Clancy started to laugh, then he remembered the rifle aimed straight at his chest.

"Hell, mister, ease up. I didn't know she was yore wife."

"You do now," Eulis said. "Apologize to her."

Clancy gritted his teeth as he turned around. Once again, he was face to face with the woman, only she didn't appear as raggedy as she had a few minutes ago. There was a fire in her eyes and a jut to her chin that should have warned him she wasn't one to mess with.

"Look, Missus, if I offended you —"

Letty didn't blink.

"You did."

His face turned as ruddy as his hair, but the bore of that rifle she kept aimed at his face spoke loudly.

"Then I'm sorry," he muttered.

"Time to move on," Eulis said shortly.

Clancy kept his head down as he quickly moved past.

"Are you done in there?" Letty asked, as the land agent went back inside.

"Yeah, we're done," Eulis said, then winked and grinned as he got up in the seat. "For better or for worse, that claim is ours."

Letty turned around to make sure that the redheaded man was still walking away. She watched until he disappeared around the corner of the street.

"Now the assayer's office," Letty said.

Eulis clucked to the mules and the wagon rolled on, taking them and their future a little farther down the street.

"Assayer's office," Eulis said.

"I'll wait here," Letty said.

"No, darlin', this time it's your turn."

Her eyes widened. "What are you saying?"

"You found it. It's only fair that you get to be the one to see what it's worth."

Letty smiled, then handed Eulis the rifle and hugged him something fierce before jumping down from the wagon. Eulis tossed her the small bag of ore they'd kept back.

"I'll be here when you're done."

Letty clutched the bag against her chest, then turned abruptly and headed into the office.

The bell over the door jingled as Letty walked in, but the assayer didn't bother to look up.

"Be with you in a minute."

"Take your time," Letty said, and plopped the sack of ore on the counter.

It was the female voice that changed the assayer's focus. Immediately, he set aside a set of scales and jumped to his feet.

"I'm sorry, ma'am. How can I help you?"

She shoved the bag of ore toward him.

"Kinda curious as to what this might be worth."

He hefted the bag and then grinned.

"Well, little lady, let's see what you've got here."

He was still smiling as he dumped the contents out onto the counter. It lasted just until he picked up the first chunk of ore, then his smile changed to respect.

"This looks promising," he said. "Give me a few minutes and we'll see what we have here."

Letty nodded, then watched as he placed some of the ore on a large piece of leather. He took a small hammer and began hacking at the dirt and rock, separating it from the color while muttering to himself as he worked. Letty couldn't tell if that was good or bad, but when he dragged out some chemicals and a set of scales, Letty caught herself holding her breath.

Not once during the entire process did she take her eyes off him, although he could have been making bear stew and she wouldn't have known the difference. Once, she glanced out the window, making sure Eulis was still there and wondering if he should be here instead of her. If the assayer decided to lie to her, she wouldn't know the difference.

Then the man turned around, and the look on his face made her heart skip a beat. His hands were shaking as he began sacking up the ore that he'd dumped.

"Ma'am?"

Letty braced herself for disappointment.

"What?"

"Is there any more of this?"

She thought of what was in the wagon bed as well as what they'd left behind.

"Yes."

He started to grin.

"This is without doubt the purest color I've seen since I came here. Have you filed a claim?"

"Yes, but what do we do now?"

"We? You mean your partner?"

"My husband," she said, and as she pointed out the window, realized that was the first time she'd had occasion to lay claim to him in this way.

"Well, ma'am, let me be the first to tell you that, if what you say is true, then you are a very rich woman."

Letty heard the words, but couldn't believe what he'd said.

"Say it again," she said.

The assayer grinned. "Lady, you and your man have just struck it rich."

"So, what do we do now?" Letty asked.

"Ore like this has to be taken to a smelter."

"Is there one in town?" she asked.

"Actually, there are a couple," he said.

"Are they honest?" she asked.

The little man hesitated, then handed her the bag.

"I didn't tell you this, but if this was mine, I'd be doing business with Brian Moody."

"Where's his business located?" Letty asked.

"Follow the road to the end of town, then look to your right. You'll see it there."

"How much do we owe you?" Letty asked.

He pointed to the bit that he'd used for testing.

"That will do me just fine," he said.

Letty nodded, then headed for the door. She reached for the doorknob, then stopped and turned around.

"You're sure? About this being good, I mean?"

"As sure as my name is Edward White."

"Then, Mr. White, I thank you."

He followed her to the door. "Tell your man to be careful when he brings the ore into town. There's people here who'd kill you without a second thought for what you got in that bag."

"Then they'd have themselves a real heart attack if they knew what was in our wagon, wouldn't they?"

Edward White frowned. "What do you mean?"

"The wagon is full of ore."

He looked past her, saw Eulis sitting in the seat with a rifle across his lap, and then stared at her in disbelief.

"You brought it with you? In that wagon? Loose?"

"Yes."

"Lord have mercy."

"Oh, He already has," Letty said. "Thank you for your help. I'm sure we'll be seeing you around."

Eulis saw her coming, and he knew before she said it, that the ore was good.

"Are we rich yet?" he asked.

"Yep," Letty said. "Only we got to take this to a smelter."

Eulis nodded. "I know."

Letty sniffed. "Well, I didn't. Edward says that Brian Moody is an honest man."

Eulis frowned. "Who's Edward?"

"Edward White. He's the assayer."

"And who is this Brian Moody?"

"The owner of the smelter."

Eulis tried not to feel jealous, but he was beginning to think he should have been the one to take the ore into the assayer after all.

"Do we know where this smelter is?"

"Follow the road through town then look to the right."

"All right, then," he said, and handed her the rifle. "I reckon we'd better get on down there before someone figures out what we're hauling."

She laughed.

"What's so funny?" he asked.

"Us. We look like the tail end of hard times, and we're hauling enough gold to set the whole city into a riot."

He clucked his tongue as he flipped the reins across Rosy and Blackie's backs.

"Just a little bit farther and then it's oats and water for the both of you."

Rosy's ears twitched as the wagon rolled on through town. Lots of people saw the bedraggled looking pair, but paid them little attention. It would be the last anonymous day of their lives.

Brian Moody was working on a cigar when he saw a team and wagon pulling up to the smelter. He took a last puff, then dropped the cigar in the ashtray before brushing the ashes off his vest. Being one of two smelters in a town when only one would have served, he didn't want to miss any business. He smoothed his hands over his head, straightened his suit coat, then hurried outside.

"Hello to you, sir," he called, and then hurried down the steps. "I'm Brian Moody. How can I help you?"

Eulis nodded to the man.

"I'm Eulis Potter, this is my wife, Letty. We got some ore for you."

Moody glanced toward the wagon and saw elk skins and bedrolls, as well as cook pans, and imagined a sack or so of ore to be had. It probably wouldn't amount to much, but it was why he was here.

"All right then," he said. "Glad to be of service."

Eulis got down and began untying the ropes. Letty followed, with the rifle at the ready.

Moody nodded politely to Letty.

"Ma'am, there's a chair in my office if

you'd care to wait there while we carry in your ore."

"Thank you just the same, but I think I'll stand guard," Letty said. Brian stifled a grin and tried not to stare at their ragged appearance.

"I doubt that's necessary, ma'am."

"Sir. I assure you, it is," she said, and pointed to the wagon just as Eulis was tossing the elk hides and the last of their belongings to the ground.

Moody grinned as he peered into the bed, and then he actually grunted out loud.

"Good God, man! What have you done?"

Eulis pointed. "My wife hit pay dirt. I reckon we're rich."

Moody looked up, struggling to find the words to speak.

"Is this all of it?" he asked.

"Shoot no," Eulis said.

Brian Moody stared at the both of them as if they'd suddenly grown horns, then he started to grin. He slapped his leg, whooped and hollered out loud, then shook Eulis's hand and tipped his hat to Letty.

"Ma'am, Sir, it's gonna be a pleasure to do business with you."

Eulis nodded. "What do we do first?"

"Come with me to the office. We'll handle the paperwork while I get the men to come unload the wagon."

"I reckon I'll just stay with the wagon," Letty said.

"Ma'am, it behooves me to be honest with you if I want to continue to do business with you, right?"

She frowned, then nodded.

"Having said that, I can promise you that both you and your gold will be safe with me."

And when she saw the size of the men who came for the wagon, she thought he was most likely right. Except for that big redheaded man who'd accosted her on the street, they were three of the biggest, woolliest men she'd ever seen.

Moody pointed at Eulis and Letty as he addressed his workers.

"Men, this here is Mr. and Mrs. Eulis Potter. Mark their faces, because we're going to be in business together for a long, long time."

It was to their credit that the men took the wagon away without much comment, but Letty saw them talking among themselves and gesturing wildly as they drove away.

She turned just as Eulis was going into

the office with Brian Moody, but instead of immediately following, she looked toward the mountains.

The air was sharp, but the warmth of the sun felt good on her face. She lifted her chin as she stood, remembering where they'd been and how far they'd come, and knew that from this day forward, their lives would never be the same. With a heartfelt sigh, she shifted the rifle to her other hand and followed her husband into the office.

By the time they came down from the smelter, it was obvious that the word was out. People came out of their businesses, waving and shouting, while others ran alongside the wagon, begging for money, or to be put to work.

Eulis was oddly noncommittal, but Letty felt threatened and let it be known by setting the stock of the rifle against her leg with the barrel pointing skyward as a reminder that they were armed. When a man grabbed at Rosy's harness, Letty flinched.

"Eulis —"

"It's all right, darlin'," he said quietly. "They're just excited, is all."

But Letty saw more than excitement in their faces. She saw the fever burned as bright in their eyes as it had burned in

Eulis's body — only this fever was a fever without cure or end. All around her, she felt danger and death.

As they drew nearer to the livery stable, she saw the redheaded stranger who'd accosted her at the land office. He was staring at them without waving, as most everyone else had been doing, and she felt an odd shiver of foreboding, as if they weren't finished with each other, yet.

Still, she couldn't let a loser like him ruin the joy of this day. She drew her gaze away from Sean Clancy and looked to Eulis.

"What are we going to do?"

"For starters, I reckon we'll need to stable the mules, get us a room, and something to eat."

"And after that?"

"Mr. Moody said to open an account at the bank."

"Yeah, right," Letty said, then grinned. "I never did that before."

"Me, either," Eulis said. "But there can't be all that much to it. They get the gold outta the ore, sell it at market price, and put the money in our account at the bank."

"What about all the rest of the gold up in the mine?"

"Brian suggested we buy some wagons,

hire some men, pay them fair wages, and dig for all we're worth."

She wanted to giggle. Instead, she kept her eye on the crowd that was following along behind.

"Then we can spend it?"

He grinned.

"Yeah, then we spend it. What do you want to buy first?"

Letty looked past the people running alongside their wagon, to the city itself. It was rough and raw, but the possibilities were endless. Law was still hit and miss, and society had yet to set up a hierarchy of social status. There was a doctor in residence, and a barber who'd gone from a tent in the street to his own building, complete with a red and white barber pole hanging out front. There were too many men and not enough women, but Letty knew that would change. One day there would be schools and churches and places where women met for tea to discuss works of literary merit, and Letty wanted to be a part of that metamorphosis like she'd never wanted anything before.

Eulis stopped at the livery, then looked at his wife.

"What's wrong, girl? Cat got your tongue?"

"No."

"Then tell me. What do you want to buy first?"

"Propriety, and a good name."

It was the last thing he would have expected her to say, and yet he understood immediately where it had come from.

"How you reckon to do that?"

Her eyes narrowed as she looked up at the hill overlooking the main part of town. It was covered in trees without a path in sight, and yet that was where she knew she should be.

"We're gonna lay claim to that hill up there," she said. "And we're gonna build a fine house with a large veranda so that we can sit out in the cool of the evening and watch the city grow. And we're going to wear nice clothes and have someone clean our house and someone else cook our food, and when the first preacher comes to town and sets up shop, we're going to sit in church every Sunday and listen to him preach."

When she added, "Even if he's not as good as you," he grinned.

Letty was wound up now and began ticking off the plans on her fingers.

"And when the bankers bring out their wives, and decency comes to this place, we're going to be ahead of the game. That's how we're going to do that."

"Hey Mister! Mister! Did you really strike it rich? I need a job. Do you need someone to work in your mine?"

Letty looked down at the middle-aged man who was clinging to the side of the wagon, then back up at Eulis.

"Well, Mr. Potter? Do you need someone to work in your mine?"

He looked down at the man, then past the worn out clothes to the healing pockmarks on his face and felt a moment of empathy for what they'd both survived.

"Not right now," he said. "But most likely, I will in the future. When I do, you'll be the first man I hire."

The man looked as if he was going to cry.

"Thank you, Mr. Potter. Thank you, Sir. My name is Winston Bailey. Everyone knows my name. When you're ready, just ask for me on the street."

"And me!" someone else yelled. "Hire me!"

"And me!"

"I need a job!"

"Hire me!"

Surrounded by the echoes of desperation, Eulis waved everyone away with a promise to post a notice when they needed to hire. Once the mules and wagon were stabled, they started down the street to the restaurant.

It took forever to walk three blocks. Letty clung to the rifle with cold-eyed intent and had little to say to the crowd that persisted in following them. But Eulis seemed in his element, and once again Letty was reminded of how he'd taken to preaching as if he'd been born to the task.

A slight smile crossed her face as she let her fancy wander, thinking into the future, to the day when this place would be as fancy and proper as any city back east. But it would take time for that to happen. Right now, Denver City was as rough and raw as the people who were building it, and like her and Eulis, it would take years to polish up a shine. By the time that happened, maybe they would be up to the task, but until then, she was satisfied knowing that they fit in here real well.

And as if that wasn't enough, Eulis had made it plain to all who asked that it was his wife, Letty, who'd made the strike.

"Lady! Lady! Blow me a kiss for luck!" someone shouted.

Letty didn't know whether to laugh or to cry. Being called lady was enough in itself to bring tears to her eyes, but thinking of herself and luck in the same breath just didn't make sense.

"Come on, lady, just one kiss," he begged.

Eulis winked at her and then grinned.

"Long as you're only blowin' 'em, I reckon I don't mind."

Letty looked up at him then, into the dark eyes and gentle smile and knew her cup runneth over.

She handed Eulis the rifle, then winked back at him before turning to the surrounding crowd. Before she changed her mind, she pressed both hands to her lips, then flung them outward, as if scattering the kisses into the air.

Men whooped and hollered, then began rubbing each other's faces, as if trying to wipe off her kisses onto their own cheeks, desperate for what they all called luck.

It was madness.

It was hysteria.

For Eulis and Letty, it was just the end of the trail, but the beginning of the rest of their lives.